THE HIDING PLACE

ALSO BY PAULA MUNIER

BLIND SEARCH

A BORROWING OF BONES

THE HIDING PLACE

A MERCY CARR MYSTERY

PAULA MUNIER

MINOTAUR BOOKS

NEW YORK

First published in the United States by Minotaur Books, an imprint of St. Martin's Publishing Group.

THE HIDING PLACE. Copyright © 2021 by Paula Munier. All rights reserved.
Printed in the United States of America. For information, address
St. Martin's Publishing Group, 120 Broadway, New York, NY 10271.

www.minotaurbooks.com

The Library of Congress Cataloging-in-Publication Data is available upon request.

ISBN 978-1-250-15307-4 (hardcover)
ISBN 978-1-250-15308-1 (ebook)

Our books may be purchased in bulk for promotional, educational, or business use.
Please contact your local bookseller or the Macmillan Corporate and Premium Sales Department at
1-800-221-7945, extension 5442, or by email at MacmillanSpecialMarkets@macmillan.com.

First Edition: 2021

10 9 8 7 6 5 4 3 2 1

For Michael

To those who keep their hearts their own
The winter is the spring.

—JOHN CLARE

THE HIDING
PLACE

SUMMER 2000

*B*eautiful women kept you waiting with a clear conscience because they really believed that the party didn't start until they got there. Ruby was one of those women, Beth thought, as she waited for her friend in the ornate if faded lobby of the Two Rivers Theater. Ruby was in the ladies' room, freshening up her face, as she called it. Ruby was always freshening up her face.

Beth only used makeup to hide the bruises. She glanced at her watch. It was getting late. If she didn't get home before Thomas, she might have more black-and-blue to cover.

Ruby sauntered into the lobby as if she owned the place. Beth envied that confidence. She wondered what it would be like to go through the world believing it was your oyster.

"I've got to get back."

"No, you don't." Ruby smiled the Las Vegas smile that had seduced half the men in Lamoille County. "You've got to get out. You and me both."

"Where would we go?"

"Anywhere but Vermont. If we don't get out of here, I'm going to die of boredom and you're going to die, period."

THOMAS KILGORE WATCHED the two women from behind the popcorn stand on the other side of the lobby, where they couldn't see him. They were about the same size, but his wife seemed much smaller. Bethie was a mouse of a girl, afraid of her own shadow. Even more afraid of his.

Her friend didn't look afraid of anything. She was the kind of woman who was bound to get a guy in trouble sooner or later. The kind of woman his wife had no business hanging out with. She was waving her arms around as she talked to Bethie—and Bethie was listening closely to her, her dark eyes peeping out from under her long bangs. The bangs she'd grown to cover that jagged little scar over her left brow.

Bethie's friend was up to no good. He was right to have followed them. And he'd keep on following them, until he knew what was going on—and what needed to be done.

CHAPTER ONE

S OME PEOPLE TAKE THEIR SECRETS WITH THEM TO THE GRAVE.
Others leave them behind on their deathbeds, riddles for the sur-
vivors to solve. Mercy Carr suspected that August Pitts was one of
the latter. She stood in the neat living room of his farmhouse, at the
foot of the portable hospital bed on which he lay dying. She knew he
was dying by the way her Belgian shepherd, Elvis, the smartest dog in
the world, huddled with the old man's golden retriever, Sunny. Both
of their noses pointed through the metal bars onto Pitts' bony hip.
One dark muzzle and one yellow muzzle, side by side, shiny black
noses stark against the white cotton sheets.

Pitts raised a mottled hand to pet them. The effort was great, and his
arm fell limply back toward the bed, catching on the dogs' ears. Elvis
and Sunny licked his knobbled fingers.

He smiled. But even that small gesture seemed too much for him.
His weary face tightened against the pain, and the lines crisscrossing his
face deepened. He closed his eyes.

She hoped to hell that was a morphine drip in his arm.

"He does that a lot." Pitts' sister Eveline stepped up to join Mercy.
The heavy-limbed woman wore too-tight yoga clothes and a smile
to match. "The painkillers, you know."

"Will he wake up again soon?"

"Hard to tell. Not usually." Eveline lowered her voice to a stage
whisper. "He's not long for this world. Every breath could be his last."

Pitts was in the late stages of cancer; Eveline had told her as much when she called to ask her to come up to Lamoille County to see him. "It's his dying wish," she'd said.

Pitts was her Grandpa Red's last partner. Her grandfather was the sheriff, and Pitts his deputy, when he'd died in an arrest gone wrong when Mercy was nine years old. She still missed him.

"We'll wait awhile," she told Eveline.

"Suit yourself." Eveline pointed to a worn brown vinyl recliner in the corner. "Make yourself at home." She stomped off to the kitchen nook at the far side of the great room and busied herself at the sink.

Mercy settled into the old recliner and tried not to sweat. The farmhouse was as warm as a hothouse, its noisy old furnace obviously working overtime to keep the cold gales of early March at bay. Elvis and Sunny panted as they continued their watch at the old man's bedside. Both dogs would need water before long.

Her grandmother Patience had warned her against this trip.

"Nothing good ever came of your grandfather's association with that man and nothing good will come of yours, either." Pitts was late to work the day her husband died, and Patience believed the deputy's absence contributed to his death. She had never forgiven him, and her dislike of the man only intensified over the years.

"He says he needs to see me. For Grandpa Red's sake."

"He's unreliable and untrustworthy. You can't believe a word he says."

"I'll hear him out. It may be nothing."

"You just want to get out of Dodge. To avoid running into a certain game warden."

It was true that she'd had a falling out with Troy Warner a few months ago, but that had nothing to do with this. This she had to do for her grandfather.

"Out of the frying pan into the fire," her grandmother said when she realized there was no talking Mercy out of heading north to Lamoille County.

But as she sat there watching August Pitts, his breath shallow and his lips moving in his fitful sleep, she could see no fire. No fire at all.

Only the cool specter of death, hovering over the old man as he slept. *His death's upon him,* as Shakespeare would say.

"He left those for you." Eveline was back, a kitchen towel tossed over her shoulder. She pointed to a stack of dilapidated cardboard file boxes stacked in the corner next to an old brown crock filled with fishing poles and hockey sticks. "Something to do with Sheriff O'Sullivan. He wanted you to have them."

Deputy Pitts opened his eyes, staring at Mercy. He grabbed the bed rails and pulled himself up, his watery blue eyes still on her.

Eveline rushed forward, grabbing the remote and pressing the button to raise the head of the bed. "You know you're supposed to use the control, August."

Pitts ignored his sister. He leaned forward, and started to speak, his voice weak with pain. Mercy left the recliner, squeezing between Elvis and Sunny at the edge of the bed.

"Find the girl," he whispered.

"What girl?"

He fell back against the pillows, wheezing.

"That's enough," said Eveline, pushing Mercy aside and stepping on Sunny's paw in the process. The retriever yelped.

"Sorry, dog," Eveline said.

You don't sound sorry, thought Mercy. As if to confirm her suspicion, Elvis growled.

Eveline ignored the shepherd. "He's upset. Talking about that girl always upsets him." She put down the remote and picked up a glass of water from the table next to the bed and placed the rim up against her brother's lips. "Drink, August."

"I don't know anything about any girl," said Mercy.

The old man jerked his head away from the glass, spitting water at his sister.

"Great," said Eveline crossly. She used the kitchen towel to wipe the spittle from her face and then her brother's. He whined a bit under her rough ministrations. "That's enough out of you." She turned to Mercy. "You need to go now. Take those boxes with you."

"Sure." She told Elvis to stay and spent the next several minutes loading the boxes—all labeled BETH KILGORE—into the back of her Jeep. Pitts watched her from his bed, but he didn't say anything, maybe because his sister was standing guard, her arms crossed and her lips pursed.

"I think that's all of them," said Mercy. "Do you think we could come back and visit again?" She knew she'd have questions about what was in those boxes.

Eveline shrugged. "If he's still alive."

Mercy glanced over at the old man, and was relieved to see he appeared to have nodded off again. She pulled a card from a pocket of her cargo pants and handed it to Eveline. "Please keep me informed of his condition."

"Hold on a minute." Eveline disappeared down the hallway. As soon as she was out of sight, Pitts spoke, startling Mercy.

"Save my dog," he said, his eyes still shut.

"What?" She wasn't sure that she'd heard the old man right.

"Find Beth for Red," he wheezed. "Save Sunny for me."

At the sound of his sister's footsteps he fell silent again, appearing even closer to death than he had before.

Eveline handed Mercy a sheet of paper with a photo of a much younger August Pitts with a full head of strawberry-blond hair, and a headline that read "Obituary." At her dismayed look, Eveline frowned. "The paper said to have it ready. The information about the memorial service is all there. All I have to do is add the date when the time comes."

"Right." Eveline was certainly ready for her brother to pass, thought Mercy. She must stand to inherit. "What will happen to the farmhouse?"

"I'm his only kin."

"He never married?"

"Not the marrying kind, my brother."

"I see." Mercy paused to scratch the golden retriever's head. "And Sunny?"

"I'm allergic."

Not, thought Mercy. She feared for this lovely golden. "What will happen to her?"

"She'll be fine."

"But if you're allergic . . ." Mercy let her voice trail off, the better to let Eveline finish the sentence.

"After I sell the house, I'll take her home with me. Find her a forever family there."

"Home?"

"North Carolina."

"Uh huh." She suspected that Eveline would get home and drop Sunny off at the nearest kill shelter. There were plenty down there. She'd found Elvis in North Carolina, crowded into a cramped "kennel" with several other military working dogs, deserted by the defense contractor responsible for them. She took Elvis home to Vermont, but not before emailing the kennel's GPS coordinates along with video of his neglected pals to the local newspaper and several animal rights organizations so they'd be rescued, too.

Elvis growled again. He didn't trust Eveline any more than she did. Patience had warned her against August Pitts, but at least he was good to his dog.

A phone rang somewhere deeper in the farmhouse.

"I'd better get that. You can let yourself out." Eveline tramped down the hallway toward what Mercy assumed were the bedrooms in the back.

Now that the coast was clear, she hesitated. Sunny was not hers to take, and she doubted the golden retriever would willingly leave her dying master's side. She wasn't even sure that taking Sunny was what the old man meant when he told her to save the dog. She looked at Elvis. "What to do?" The shepherd nuzzled Sunny, but the golden retriever did not react. She seemed resolved to stay put for the foreseeable future.

Mercy didn't know what was worse, forcing the golden to abandon her post or leaving her to an uncertain fate with the unpredictable Eveline. "Come on, Elvis."

The Malinois snorted his displeasure, but he heeded her call and headed for the door. When Sunny didn't follow, Elvis returned to the hospital bed, leaning against the golden retriever. She pushed back. A zero sum game.

"Good girl." Deputy Pitts patted his devoted dog's head with a limp hand. "Now go."

Sunny whined, licking his curled fingers.

He pulled his hand away. "Go," he said again, more harshly this time.

"Sir," Mercy began, not sure what to say. In the background, she heard Eveline on the phone, her voice growing louder, coming closer.

"Take her now." The old man stared at her, faded blue eyes wet with tears. "Before it's too late."

"Sir." Mercy slipped her hand around Sunny's collar and guided her out of the farmhouse into the wind, Elvis on her heels. She opened the passenger door to the Jeep with one hand and held the dog with the other. Elvis leapt in without hesitation. Mercy picked up the reluctant retriever, who had to weigh around seventy pounds, grunting as she placed her on the seat next to the shepherd, and shut the door.

Spotting Eveline on the porch, Mercy hustled around the vehicle, scrambled into her seat, and started the engine. Squealing down the drive and onto the county road as Eveline shouted after them, she headed south.

Sunny barked all the way to Northshire.

CHAPTER TWO

Vermont Game Warden Troy Warner and his park ranger pal Gil Guerrette trudged along in companionable silence, the click of their snowshoes echoing through the forest. They were hiking through one of the most remote areas of the Green Mountain National Forest, and one of the most beautiful. Troy's Newfoundland retriever mix Susie Bear scampered ahead, circling back to them from time to time whenever they zigged when she zagged. Troy and Gil were both in good shape, but they couldn't keep up with the energetic Susie Bear, who loved the snow almost as much as she loved the hunt. The hulk of shiny black fluff was arguably the best search-and-rescue dog in Vermont, and she seemed to know they were on a mission, even though she had yet to hear the magic word *Search*.

Spring may have been only a few weeks off according to the calendar, but it was still winter here in the forest. March was typically the state's snowiest month, and the deep drifts were more than proof of that. Not to mention the wind, which howled through the woods, tossing bare branches and pine boughs alike.

All of which made their task more difficult. Troy and Gil were on the lookout for Joey Colby, a young wildlife biologist and filmmaker from the University of Vermont. Colby was spending the winter tracking moose deep in the forest. He'd missed his daily check-in with his department head two days running. His professor called Gil, and Gil called Troy. They both knew how to read the woods, but Susie Bear was their secret weapon.

Colby had been following a young moose calf navigating his first winter on his own. He was documenting his work on film, for all the world to see. The truth was, moose were in trouble in Vermont. After nearly going extinct in the mid-1800s, the moose population rebounded in the 1970s as abandoned farmlands went wild again and forest management practices changed. But now the moose were under the gun again, not so much from hunters but from loss of habitat, the scourge of winter ticks, and the insidious brainworm disease.

"Colby knows what he is doing," Gil told Troy. "He was here last year, too. Tracking another calf. She did not make it. Died in April, emaciated by ticks. The coyotes got what was left of her."

Troy shook his head. Warmer winters meant more ticks and more ticks meant more dead calves. The death rate for young moose was up as high as 70 percent these days.

"And this year?"

"He is tracking a new calf. The good news is, winter started early this year."

"Less time for the little bloodsuckers to find hosts for the winter."

"Exactly. All we can do now is pray for a wicked long cold season."

The earlier winter sets in and the longer it lasts and the snowier it gets, the less harm the moose ticks could do. And the better the chances for New England's favorite mammal to survive and thrive.

"Colby's no neophyte. What do you think happened to him?"

"I do not know. Nothing good." Gil pointed to a thinning of the trees ahead. "His last known campsite is in that clearing up there. With any luck, that will shed some light."

Susie Bear bound ahead of them, heading straight toward the little glen, squeezing between the snow-covered red spruces and disappearing from sight. Troy and Gil hurried after her, crunching along in their snowshoes at a faster clip now that their initial target was in sight.

The wildlife biologist had set up a nice camp with a state-of-the-art cold-weather tent. There was a sled parked nearby.

"Doesn't seem to be anyone around." Troy and Gil both examined the ground, looking for prints.

"With this wind, we may not find any tracks," said Gil.

"That's why we've got Susie Bear."

"I will check inside." Gil stepped out of his snowshoes. He unzipped the tent and scooted in. Susie Bear bounced up to the opening, eager to follow the ranger, but Troy waved Susie Bear into a sit. There was only so much room in the tent, and she was a very big dog.

"Good girl," he said, and scratched between her ears while they waited for Gil to reappear.

It wasn't long before the ranger popped his head outside the tent. "Not much in here."

"No bedding, no gear?"

"Nada. Just a few articles of random clothing at the bottom of his duffel."

"Weird."

Gil frowned. "Looks like someone raided his camp."

"Then where's Colby?"

Gil shrugged.

"I guess it's up to Susie Bear. Anything in there we can use as a scent article? A shirt or a pair of socks would be good."

The ranger disappeared back into the tent, re-emerging momentarily, waving a gray wool beanie. "How about a hat?"

"That'll do." Troy reached for the cap. Susie Bear swatted her tail hard against the snow as he held it out for her to smell. She knew the game was afoot.

"Show time." Gil laughed.

The big black dog buried her snout in the fine merino wool, sniffing and snuffling and snorting. There was nothing subtle about Susie Bear. She snorted again, looking up from the beanie to Troy. Waiting for him to say the magic word.

"Search," he said.

The Newfie dog jigged, acknowledging her love of her job, and then jogged away through the trees, nose down.

"*Allons-y!*" said Gil with another laugh.

And they were off.

AN HOUR LATER, Susie Bear found him. Or what was left of the dead body they assumed was Colby. Troy wasn't sure if she'd followed the scent of the live Colby to the crime scene or whether she'd been drawn by the smell of the cadaver. Or both.

Either way, Colby was dead. And practically naked, except for his socks. Scavengers had been feasting on his corpse for a while. But enough of the man remained to tell that his death had not been an accident.

Gil pointed to the caved-in side of his head. "Looks like blunt force trauma."

"Yeah." Troy looked around the small glen where Colby had set up his camera. The camera was gone, but the tripod had been knocked to the ground in what looked like a scuffle by the faint confusion of marks in the snow. "Whoever killed him took the camera."

"And his clothes." Gil shook his head. "I mean, why leave his socks?"

"He must not have needed them."

"Is that what your Mercy would say?" He pronounced Mercy as if it were the French word *merci*. He always did this, and it always bothered Troy.

He looked away from the ranger. He did not want to talk about Mercy Carr.

"I get it. She is still not speaking to you. You need to do something about that, man."

Troy checked his cell. No signal. The state couldn't afford sat phones, not that they always worked so deep in the forest anyway. They were way off grid up here. "You go on down and call it in. I'll wait here with Susie Bear. Keep the critters at bay."

"Leaving me to deal with Harrington."

Detective Kai Harrington was the head of the Major Crime Unit. He was not a big fan of either Troy or Susie Bear.

"We're in a national forest. Your jurisdiction, not mine."

"Yeah, like Harrington will honor that."

"I'm just a fish cop." Troy grinned. "Not my problem."

"In your dreams." Gil grinned back, tapping his brow in a quick salute. "While I am gone, you can tape up the crime scene. And think about what you can do to get Mercy back. Grand gesture, *mon ami*. Women love a grand gesture."

The ranger stomped away, snowshoes clicking. Troy and Susie Bear watched him disappear into the gloom, swallowed up by snow and trees.

"Grand gesture," he repeated to the Newfie. "Whatever that means."

She thumped her tail and tilted her big pumpkin head up at him. As if to say that she knew exactly what that meant.

And that he should, too.

CHAPTER THREE

"WHO'S THIS?" PATIENCE GREETED MERCY AND THE DOGS at the door of the big Victorian on Route 7, which served double duty as her home and veterinary clinic. She regarded the golden retriever with a compassionate vet's eye. Mercy knew she cared for a lot of goldens in her practice, and that she was very fond of the breed.

"This is Sunny, Pitts' dog."

"Seriously? You stole his dog?" Her grandmother hustled Mercy and the dogs into the house as if she were concealing stolen property.

"I didn't steal her."

They followed Patience into the entry and past the living room with its window seat crowded with sleeping rescue cats of every color and size. On into the kitchen, one of Mercy's very favorite places. Her grandmother was a dedicated amateur chef who'd modeled her warm and welcoming kitchen after those in Provence where she studied the art of cooking for a week every summer. With its large windows and deep yellow walls, gleaming copper pots and pans and colorful pottery, the space made Mercy feel like she was in one of Van Gogh's sunflower paintings.

The best part was the big white marble-topped island, where there was always a freshly baked cake under glass perched on an antique cobalt-blue stand. She pulled a stool up to the island, happy to see that today's cake was a cinnamon buttermilk coffee cake, known to everyone who'd ever tasted it as The Best Coffee Cake in the World.

"We'll have tea and cake, and you can tell me how you ended up with that man's dog." Patience filled two cerulean bowls with water and placed them on the floor in the corner. She treated both Elvis and Sunny to a pat and a peanut butter doggie biscuit from her ever-present fanny pack full of treats before flipping on the electric teapot.

Mercy grabbed a blue-and-white dessert plate from the open shelves gracing the yellow walls and helped herself to a generous piece of coffee cake. She watched her grandmother as she steeped the tea, the winter sun shining through the windows illuminating her neat silver-blond head. Elvis and Sunny sprawled in their corner, their eyes on Patience, too. Hoping for another cookie. They'd probably get it.

Patience handed her a bright orange mug full of steaming spicy chai. "Let's hear it."

"Pitts asked me to take her."

"Why would he do that? He doesn't know you."

"He's dying, and he doesn't trust his sister to take care of her. I guess he saw Elvis and decided Sunny was better off with me." Mercy pinched off another bit of coffee cake and popped into her mouth. Heaven.

"What did the sister say?"

"Said she was allergic to dogs. And would be taking her back to North Carolina to find her a 'forever home.'" Mercy used her fingers to indicate the quote marks.

"More like 'forever dead.'" Patience was vehemently opposed to kill shelters, volunteering her services for any animals rescued from them.

"He practically begged me."

"I'm surprised she came so quietly." She glanced over at the golden retriever, who'd given up on more treats and curled up for a nap.

"She didn't." Mercy told her about the long, noisy ride home with the unhappy dog.

"You did the right thing. I'll do a quick check on her before you go home." Her grandmother gave her an amused look. "Getting kind of crowded at your cabin."

Mercy had taken in a teenage mother and her baby girl last summer when it became clear they had nowhere else to go. There was also the kitten they'd rescued from a crime scene at Elvis's insistence earlier that year. And now this retriever. "Let's hope she likes cats."

"Goldens are usually good with cats," said Patience. "If she's not, or if you just think it's too much to take on, I can ask around. There's always someone looking to adopt a sweet girl like Sunny."

"Thanks. But let's see how it goes first." Mercy believed that she was somehow meant to have Sunny. Just like she was somehow meant to have her grandfather's case files.

"Okay. But you know you don't owe that man a thing." Patience's voice took on a sharp edge. "What did he want, anyway?"

"He didn't say much. He couldn't say much." She told her grandmother about the boxes labeled BETH KILGORE, and the dying deputy's plea that she "find the girl."

"I should have known. That case haunted him."

"You remember it?"

"Of course." Patience sighed, pointing to the coffee cake on the blue stand. "Long story. You might as well have another piece."

Mercy grinned and cut a thick slice. The only thing better than one piece of Patience's cake was two pieces.

"Beth was a very unlucky young woman. Raised—if you could call it that—by her father, mostly, a miserable man named Clem Verdette. He married her off when she was just a teenager to Thomas Kilgore, a loser if there ever was one."

"She didn't have to marry him. Why would she agree to do that?"

"Her mother ran off when she was a child, no doubt to save herself. Why she didn't take Beth along with her is something I'll never understand. She was a pretty little thing, with dark hair and warm brown eyes. Smart, too." Patience paused. "Why her own mother would sentence that poor girl to life with the man she herself couldn't bear to live with anymore ... Well, there's just no understanding some people."

"No." Mercy knew that from the war, where understanding was often in short supply on all sides. Patience took another sip of tea. "Clem was a drunkard given to rages. Marriage probably seemed like an escape."

"Only it wasn't."

"Not at all. Kilgore had a temper even worse than her father's. Your grandfather saved her more than once from being beaten to death."

"Why didn't she leave, get a divorce?"

"She was too frightened. And so young. Just seventeen when she married him. She always refused to press charges. Not much your grandfather could do. Times were different back then—and not in a good way."

"But then she disappeared?"

"They both did. People said they moved to California. Her husband was always talking about moving to San Diego. But your grandfather was convinced that he killed her and then took off."

"No body?"

"No body."

Proving murder without a body was very difficult. But her grandfather must have had something to go on. Maybe she'd find it in those files. "What happened?"

"Clem came to visit your grandfather. Said his daughter never showed up to make him supper. Apparently, the old goat still bullied her into doing his housework and cooking for him even after she got married and moved out. So, your grandfather went up to their double-wide in Marvin. Tiny village up near Belvidere Mountain."

"Where the old asbestos mine is."

"Yes, that's right." Patience tossed each dog another biscuit. Sunny was calm now, as happy to be at Patience's feet as Elvis and every other canine who'd had the pleasure of her company. "They finally shut it down in 1993, but it remains a toxic waste nightmare. We're still fighting to get it cleaned up properly."

Mercy knew that her grandmother's efforts to protect the flora and fauna of the beautiful state of Vermont were tireless and never-ending.

"A desolate place, then as now."

"What did Grandpa Red find up there?"

"Nothing. No sign of foul play at all. No sign of anything but despair."

"But he kept on investigating."

"Yes. Her father filed a missing persons report on Beth."

"What about her husband?"

"His family—if you could call it a family—believed that they'd moved to California for good. Supposedly he owed them money—them and everyone else in the county. Good riddance seemed to be their attitude."

"But Grandpa Red didn't believe that."

"No. Clem agreed with him. Once his daughter disappeared, he became the world's most attentive father. He pestered Red about the investigation all the time. And then Clem died. Lung cancer." Patience looked past Mercy into a memory only she could see. "I think that's why your grandfather was so obsessed with finding Beth. Her own father, such as he was, was gone. Beth was an orphan. Red would have been father to all the orphans of the world if he could have."

Mercy gave her grandmother a moment. When Patience focused those bright blue eyes back on her, marking her return to the present, she asked another question. "Beth had no other family?"

"No." Patience retrieved her Brown Betty teapot from the kitchen counter and topped off Mercy's cup of tea, and then her own. "Beth was a good kid. Did well at school until she dropped out to marry Kilgore. Stayed out of trouble. Spent whatever free time she had reading books from the library." She looked at Mercy. "That's where she was last seen. At the library."

CHAPTER FOUR

MERCY SAT AT THE OLD FARM TABLE THAT SEPARATED HER kitchen from the great room of her cabin, sorting through the first box of the Beth Kilgore cold case files. She'd been at it for about an hour, but she hadn't found anything remarkable yet. Just the usual reports and statements, interviews and records.

Amy and her boyfriend, Brodie, had gone off to Boston for a steampunk convention, baby Helena in tow. It was just Mercy and Elvis and Sunny and Muse. The little cat was curled up on one of the dining room chairs, while the dogs kept watch at Mercy's feet, ever vigilant.

Elvis sat up suddenly and barked, just once. His signal bark, alerting Mercy to someone coming up the drive. The golden Sunny raised her silky head, but she didn't move or bark, letting the shepherd take the lead in his own home.

Mercy looked out the window, but she didn't recognize the red Toyota truck pulling alongside the cabin. Or the wiry guy in jeans and brown barn coat loping up the gravel path to the house. She figured from the erect way he carried himself that he was military, and when he paused to salute the American flag that fluttered from a tall pole in the middle of the garden, she knew she was right.

The flag flew in honor of Sergeant Juan Miguel Pedro Martinez. Her fiancé, and Elvis's handler. He was killed in action in Afghanistan, in the same battle that left Mercy wounded and Elvis traumatized. They missed him still. They always would.

The guy in the brown barn coat did a neat quarter turn and continued up the walkway to the porch. Elvis did not bark again. Friend, not foe. Weird, because Mercy did not know this guy. He was no friend of hers.

She moved toward the entryway, and Elvis trotted beside her. Sunny followed them at a discreet distance, hanging back as they approached the door.

Mercy looked down at the shepherd. "Who is he?"

Elvis cocked his handsome head, perked his triangular ears, and wagged his curlicue tail. The stranger on the other side of her front door knocked. Three quick raps. Like the S in SOS in Morse code. Mercy stood perfectly still, apprehension holding her in place. Three more raps, more slowly this time, or maybe that was just her imagination.

Elvis was still wagging his tail. This proud dog was not an indiscriminate wagger.

It was not Mercy's imagination. He knew this stranger and he liked him.

She could just wait until the guy gave up and went away. The shepherd nudged the back of her knee with his nose. His way of telling her to get on with it.

"Okay, but I'd better not regret this," she told him, even though her gut told her that for once she was right and Elvis was wrong.

She took a deep breath. Held it for a moment. Blew it out.

Flung open the door.

Elvis leapt forward to greet the man in the brown barn coat. The man fell back, laughing. He steadied himself, then bent forward to hug the shepherd.

Mercy stepped out onto the porch, Sunny at her heels.

Elvis leaned into the man, licking his cheeks, which Mercy could see were wet with tears. She wasn't sure which surprised her most, the licking—Elvis was *not* a licker—or the tears. This man did not strike her as the kind of guy who cried easily. Few soldiers were.

"Who are you?" she asked, more to herself than to the stranger.

"Sorry." He straightened up and slapped his hip with his palm. Elvis dropped into a sit at his side.

Whoa, thought Mercy. It wasn't like Elvis to obey just anyone. Her sixth sense was in overdrive now. She fought the urge to throw this guy off her porch.

"Wesley Hallett." He held out his hand for her to shake.

Up close he was very good-looking in that soldier-next-door kind of way. Sandy hair, hazel eyes, cleft in his chin. Not as tall as Troy Warner, but he was cut from the same cloth. Another reason not to trust him.

"Mercy Carr." She shook his hand perfunctorily.

"Pleasure to meet you."

Mercy was not so sure. She was not feeling very friendly towards him in return, no matter how friendly he seemed or how much Elvis seemed to like him. She was feeling very wary. She did not ask him inside, even though it was a cold and windy, if bright and sunny afternoon and she was only wearing a light sweatshirt over her usual Henley and cargo pants. She shut the door behind her, as if to fend off evil spirits from her home. "How do you know Elvis?"

Hallett laughed. "He's my dog."

"I don't think so."

The severe tone of her voice seemed to catch him up short.

"Look, I know you don't know me from Adam. But Elvis and I have history." He opened his arms wide. "It's a long story." He glanced at the rocking chairs on the porch, the ones her grandmother had bequeathed to her when she bought the cabin. "Maybe we could sit down for a minute?"

The wind picked up, sweeping across the porch in successive blasts of frigid air. She shivered. No point in catching pneumonia, as her mother would say. And whatever this guy's story, he was obviously fellow military personnel, one of her own. "Come on in."

She opened the door and led the interloper and the dogs into the great room, waving a hand at the sofa by the fireplace. "Have a seat."

"Thank you." He settled onto her butter-colored leather sofa as if he'd been dropping by her place for years. Her side of her sofa.

Elvis jumped up on his side at the other end, alert as ever, dark eyes moving back and forth from Hallett to Mercy as if he were watching a tennis match. Maybe he was. She wondered if the shepherd knew that he was the ball.

Sunny curled up on the dog bed at the other side of the room, the one Elvis never used. Away from the drama unfolding in her living room. Smart dog. The kitty, Muse, slept on, not stirring, on the dining room chair.

Hallett sat with his knees wide apart, his elbows balanced on his thighs, strong hands folded, in a stillness that spoke of patience. Like all good soldiers, he was good at waiting.

He was also extremely comfortable in his own skin, she thought. And that's when she saw it—the transtibial prosthetic where his left foot should have been. The prosthesis ran from his sneaker up the leg of his jeans to about mid-shin, Mercy guessed.

"Would you like something to drink? Coffee? Something stronger?" She could use something stronger.

"Water would be fine, thank you."

Mercy went over to the sink and poured the man a glass of water. She placed it on the coffee table before him, and retreated to Elvis, perching on the arm of the sofa next to him, her hand resting lightly on the shepherd's sleek tawny-coated spine. She watched Hallett as he drank, draining the glass in one long and steady sip. She was good at waiting, too.

He placed the glass gently onto the table. He looked up at her, his hazel eyes softer now. "I was sorry to hear about Martinez."

At the sound of his name, Elvis's ears perked, and Mercy's heart dropped.

"You knew him?"

"Yes. At Lackland." Hallett smiled. "We were both training to be handlers. Elvis was assigned to me. His litter mate, Garth, was assigned to Martinez. The dogs were inseparable, so we were, too."

"He never told me about you." They'd told each other everything. At least she thought they had.

"Not a pretty story."

She glared at him. "Two tours in Afghanistan." She hadn't lost a foot, but she had scars of her own. She didn't need pretty stories. She needed the truth. If she had to drop her pants and show him the jagged slashes across her ass, she would.

"Of course." As if he could read her mind, he flushed; to his credit, he was embarrassed. "We shipped over there with our dogs. Elvis and I went north, Martinez and Garth went west."

He paused.

She knew that her fiancé had been stationed at another post there before she met him. "And then what happened?"

"Bad times for us both. Humvee rolled over and crushed my foot. Sniper took down Garth." Hallett looked down at his hands, still folded, fingers tightening, white blotches against his lightly tanned skin.

"They sent me home," he said. "Elvis got transferred to Martinez."

"And Garth?"

"They cremated him. Scattered his ashes across the poppy fields."

Martinez had never told her about Garth. His first sniffer dog. Maybe losing him was just too painful to talk about.

"He died nearly two years ago. Why are you here now?"

"I didn't know what happened." Hallett leaned his head back against the back of the couch. He closed his eyes, inhaled deeply, and then exhaled.

Sunny slipped out of Elvis's dog bed and across the room, squeezing between the man's knees, placing her head gently on his lap. He opened his eyes and smiled at the golden retriever, scratching the sweet spot between her silky ears. Looking away from Mercy. "When I got back to the world, I was depressed and angry and more than a little crazy. I got lost for a while. By the time I came to my senses, Martinez was gone. Nobody could tell me where Elvis was."

"His last words to me were, 'Take care of my dog.'" Mercy stroked the shepherd's back. "And I did. I found him and I took care of him."

"Yes, you did." He paused. "But technically you stole him."

"He would have died in that place." She told him about the so-called kennel where Elvis and the other defense contractor dogs had been abandoned to an uncertain fate. "I saved him. I saved them all."

"I understand."

No, you don't, she thought. *You don't understand. I saved Elvis and Elvis saved me.* "I'm not sure you do understand," she said aloud.

"It's common practice for military dogs to be repatriated with their handlers."

"Elvis is not an Army dog. He's one of those dogs procured from a defense contractor. If I stole him from anyone, I stole him from them. But it wasn't stealing, because they dumped him. They dumped all of those hero dogs. Once they finished their deployments. Once the checks stopped coming." It was not a fine argument, and Mercy knew it. She'd always worried that this moment would come. Ever since she'd rescued Elvis from that abominable place down South. But she'd thought it would be the defense contractor coming to retrieve him. Not a dog handler. Not a fellow soldier. Not a veteran missing a limb.

"You did good. You found him, which was more than I could do."

"You found me."

"Yeah. I subscribe to a clipping service that notifies me whenever a Malinois or a military dog or a working dog named Elvis is in the news. I read about your exploits."

Mercy shunned the press as much as possible. But she couldn't stop them from running stories about the cases she and Elvis had helped local law enforcement solve over the past several months. She should have tried harder.

"I decided to come see for myself if this was the same Elvis."

"And here you are."

"Yes."

"You have no formal claim over Elvis."

"No, I don't. No legal claim, either." He gave her an appraising look. "Neither do you."

Possession is nine-tenths of the law, she thought.

Hallett patted Sunny's silky head, still in his lap. "You already have a dog. And a cat. You don't need Elvis."

"Sunny is not my dog. I'm just watching her for a friend. The cat belongs to Elvis. He rescued her."

"Elvis isn't your dog, either."

Elvis was all she had left of Martinez. She couldn't let him go. Besides, he was her dog now. Or was he? She looked at the handsome Belgian shepherd who sat perfectly still while they discussed who and what he was. She could feel the tears gathering in the corners of her eyes. Her turn to cry. Soldiers crying everywhere.

Elvis was his own dog. He didn't belong to her or Hallett or anyone else. No matter what the law or the Army or Hallett said.

As if to validate that assertion, Elvis leapt gracefully from the sofa and disappeared down the entry hallway. Sunny scrambled after him. Muse slept on.

Seconds later the doorbell rang, as Mercy suspected it would. Now what, she thought.

"Excuse me," she said to Hallett, rising to her feet with a poise she did not feel. Surely, she'd had enough visitors for one day. She hoped this one brought better news.

CHAPTER FIVE

MERCY LET CAPTAIN FLOYD THRASHER OF THE VERMONT Fish and Wildlife Department stride right past her and down the hall into the great room, the dogs on his heels. She watched as he stooped over briefly to give Elvis and Sunny a pat, then straightened up, scanning the premises as he did so. The captain was an extraordinarily handsome man, which Mercy knew he considered a threat to his authority. He made up for it by cutting such a commanding figure that no one would dare acknowledge his movie-star good looks. He stood tall in his uniform, as unyielding as a silo, his brown hands clasped behind his back, regarding Hallett with an imperious glare. He then turned his sharp blue-green eyes back on Mercy. "We need to talk."

She introduced the two men briefly.

"Hallett was just leaving," she said, expecting her unwanted guest to take the hint.

But he didn't move. Neither did Thrasher. For a long moment neither said anything as the two men stared each other down. Thrasher won.

"I'd better be going," said Hallett. "But I'll be back." He gave Elvis a good scratch between the ears. "See you later, buddy." He headed for the door, then pivoted to give Mercy a pointed look. "Take care of my dog." And then he was gone.

"His dog?" Thrasher folded his arms across his chest. The dogs settled at the captain's feet. Elvis understood that the man was always good for a treat, and Sunny would learn that for herself soon enough.

"What did he mean by that?"

"It's nothing," said Mercy. "What's wrong?"

Thrasher was not the kind of guy who just dropped by for a cup of tea and a chat, unless he knew that her grandmother would be by soon to serve up dinner and dessert. He—like every other man in the county—was particularly fond of Patience's famous Yankee pot roast.

"It's just a precaution," said Thrasher. "But I thought you should know."

"Okay." Mercy knew that the captain was a careful and strategic thinker not given to rash or reckless decision-making. "You're scaring me. What should I know?"

"George Rucker," said Thrasher.

"The man who killed my grandfather."

"Yes. He's disappeared."

"What? I thought he was still in prison. In Mississippi."

Short on space for convicted criminals, the Vermont Department of Corrections contracted with privately run prisons outside the state. Last she heard, Rucker had been transferred from a facility in rural Pennsylvania to one located in a small town in Mississippi.

"Apparently he was taken to a nearby hospital after a suicide attempt. He overpowered the hospital guard, stole his gun, and ran."

"He can't get very far on foot. Surely they'll catch him."

Thrasher shrugged. "Maybe. He's a resourceful guy, and local authorities believe he had help. Rocky Simko, one of his fellow prisoners, was released a couple of weeks ago. They think he helped plan Rucker's escape. They may be on the run together."

"I thought Rucker was crazy."

"Not crazy, exactly. Depressed. After his wife left him, he started drinking again. One night he got drunk, started waving a shotgun around, threatening to kill himself and anyone else who got in his way. The neighbors called for assistance."

"I know the story. Grandpa Red tried to talk him out it. And Rucker shot him."

"It was a difficult situation. Unpredictable." Thrasher looked at her, his blue-green eyes shining with a rare gentleness. "They say he should have called for backup."

"He did call for backup. But Deputy Pitts was late. By the time he got there it was all over. My grandmother still blames him." She told Thrasher about her trip up to Lamoille County to see August Pitts, and the Kilgore case. "Sunny is his dog."

"She's a good girl." He stroked the golden's soft ears. "I'm sorry to hear about Pitts. From what I understand, he stepped up after Red passed. He may not have been quite the man that your grandfather was, but he was a good sheriff."

"Not good enough to find Beth Kilgore."

"So he's left it to you." Thrasher shook his head. "Forget about Pitts and that cold case. You have bigger things to worry about."

"Rucker?"

Thrasher nodded.

"But he must be halfway to Mexico by now."

"Maybe. But we have reason to believe that he may be heading this way."

"Why would he do that? There's nothing for him here."

Thrasher leaned toward her. "Your grandmother is here."

Mercy stared at him. "What's Patience got to do with it?"

"We believe she might be in danger." Thrasher wore the impassive face of a good cop attempting to deliver bad news without panicking the recipient. But she could see his square jaw tighten ever-so-slightly.

Not a good sign. "Why would Rucker want to hurt her?"

"I'm not sure. But he told his cellmate she was going to pay for what she did."

In her mind, Mercy ran through all she knew about the case, which was only so much as she'd been so young at the time. Even so she was flummoxed. Something didn't add up. "That doesn't make any sense. What aren't you telling me?"

"You're going to have to ask your grandmother that."

"Seriously?" Mercy stepped toward the captain, and he raised his palm to stop her. She stepped back again. "I don't understand why you're withholding information."

"I'm not withholding anything." The captain lowered his hand,

and Sunny nuzzled his fingers. He gave her a good scratch. And one for Elvis, too. "You know what I know. When I tried to talk to her about it, she practically threw me out of her house. Maybe you'll have better luck."

"She hasn't said a word to me about any of this."

"I'm not surprised. That's why I'm here. I thought that maybe you could talk some sense into her."

"Thank you." Mercy smiled.

"You're welcome." Thrasher smiled back. "If you need anything, call me any time. Or Troy Warner."

"I'm sure that won't be necessary." She and Elvis would take care of Patience. She didn't need Troy Warner's help.

"You have to forgive him sometime," Thrasher said.

She chose to ignore that. "Thanks again, Captain. If there's nothing else, I think it's time I paid my grandmother a visit."

"Understood."

He smiled at her one more time, pulled a couple of dog treats from his pocket, and tossed them to Elvis and Sunny before heading for the door.

Mercy accompanied him. "Thanks again."

He waved her off without a word. But he turned just as he stepped onto the porch.

"Elvis is a one-woman dog," he said, and continued on his way.

He didn't look back.

CHAPTER SIX

MERCY STARED AT THE BRONZE WOODPECKER KNOCKER on her grandmother's front door. The knocker had been a Christmas present to Patience from Mercy's mother, Grace. Every time she saw it, Mercy was reminded of her mother's talent for choosing the perfect gift for everyone except her own only daughter. Grace gave other people what she believed they would love most, but she gave Mercy what she believed she would need most. That's why Mercy had a closet full of "necessary" clothes she'd never worn.

Elvis and Sunny flanked her, still as stone but tense with the desire to bolt inside, where the treats and the treater were. She knew they were waiting for her to move already. Usually she would just barrel on in, as was her right as the favorite granddaughter. But this was a call that would invade Patience's privacy, a call she did not want to make, and so she hung back. She was not bearing gifts her grandmother would love most, the kind Grace would give her. She was bearing unwelcome memories her grandmother might think best left in the past, where she felt they belonged. That was the way her family dealt with pain. They put it behind them and marched on. Until it came back to bite them in the butt.

Like now.

Elvis barked. He knew she was stalling. Finally, she settled on slapping the bronze tail feathers of the woodpecker against the branch strike. *Rat a tat tat. Rat a tat tat. Rat a tat tat.*

It took a long time for Patience to answer the door. When she did, she raised her eyebrows at Mercy. "You rang?"

"I need to talk to you."

"I'm not sure I like the sound of that." Patience smiled at her.

Mercy didn't know what to say, so she said nothing.

"Well, come on in." Her grandmother ushered them all down into the parlor right off the entry, the most formal room in the old Victorian, done in elegant shades of lavender and blue. She waved Mercy into one of the slate-colored velvet love seats and sat down in the other, facing her. Sunny curled up at her grandmother's feet. *Traitor*, thought Mercy.

Elvis sank into his trademark Sphinx pose by the glass and brass coffee table between the love seats, the middleman poised to monitor the delicate operation underway. Soldier, sniffer dog, diplomat. The dog who could do it all. Mercy nearly smiled.

Patience folded her hands in her lap and regarded her with an air of noblesse oblige worthy of her aristocratic forebears. Mercy suddenly felt as if she were trapped in an Edith Wharton novel.

"What's this all about?" asked her grandmother.

There was no easy way to say it. *So just say it,* Mercy thought. "George Rucker has escaped from prison."

"Old news. Captain Thrasher told me all about it."

"And you're not concerned?"

"Not in the least." Patience raised her chin, giving Mercy that cool blue-eyed reproof usually reserved for people who did not care well enough for their animals.

"Thrasher is concerned."

Patience did not deign to acknowledge that remark.

Mercy leaned forward and tried another tack. "Is it true you threw the captain out of the house?"

"He was barking up the wrong tree. I don't have time for old gossip."

"So you dismissed him."

Her grandmother unfolded her hands, palms facing one another, thumb to thumb. She tapped the tips of her fingers together, as if she were deciding how to dispatch with her granddaughter next. "I suppose he sent you here in the hope of succeeding where he has failed."

"Thrasher is no alarmist. If he's worried, I'm worried. And you should be, too."

"Nonsense."

This was a side of her grandmother she'd never seen before. A side that reminded her of her mother, Grace. Maybe Grace had come by her hauteur honestly. The dark side of Patience. Mercy would just have to forge onward, like she did with her mother. "What aren't you telling me?"

"There is nothing to tell. George Rucker was not a well man. When his wife left him, he fell apart. Your grandfather died trying to help him. End of story."

"Thrasher says there was more to it. That George Rucker bears a grudge against Grandpa Red. And that you know why."

"Again, he was not a well man. Who knows what he believed or why he believed it? It doesn't bear thinking about."

Patience never talked about Red much. When she did, it was either a happy memory about their life together courting and marrying and raising kids—The Love Story of the 20th Century—or a cautionary tale. *Don't be a hero like your grandfather.* Like that time when he went on surveillance in a blizzard, slid off the road into a ditch, and damn near died. Or when he dropped by the convenience store in Rutland County and stopped an armed robbery in progress using himself as a shield. Or when he tried to keep George Rucker from hurting himself or anyone else and ended up dead. Those were the stories she repeated to Mercy when she joined the Army and became an MP. *Don't go off half-cocked. Don't go off alone. Wait for backup. Red didn't wait for backup, and it killed him. Don't let that happen to you.*

"You're lying." Mercy knew she was right about her grandmother's lying, and right to call out the lie, but being right didn't feel good. Being right rankled, as it often did. It was like finding out the sun was just a little star like all the billion trillion others in the sky. Or at least the observable universe.

"I don't have the time for this." Mercy watched as her grandmother bolted upright, her spine straight and her cheeks flushed.

"I don't think you've ever lied to me before," she said quietly.

Her grandmother blanched. She sank back down into the love seat and was silent for a moment. "I'm sorry," she said finally.

Mercy waited for her to tell the truth.

She hoped that whatever that truth was, it wasn't too bad. She'd always assumed that Patience and Red had a happy marriage, which is what she supposed all kids and grandkids assumed, unless presented with clear evidence to the contrary. Her parents had a good marriage, too. At least she thought they did. She thought good marriages ran in the family, that she was destined to meet The One. Just as her mother had met her father, and her grandmother had met Red.

Mercy believed that Martinez was The One, and that they were destined to enjoy the same sort of happy marriage she imagined her parents and grandparents had. That they'd earned their chance at happiness by fighting the good fight in Afghanistan. And that they would make the most of it, and not fall victim to the demons that destroyed other veterans' lives when they got back home. They would beat the odds, on the battlefields of life and love and loss, because she'd inherited the ability to form a happy lifelong partnership in the same way she'd inherited her red hair and straight shooting from her grandfather and her long legs and love of the natural world from her grandmother. Or her father's penchant for the Elizabethan poets or her mother's tendency to overthink everything. It was in her very genes, this capacity to form a lasting pair bond. Like bald eagles and wolves and macaroni penguins.

Or so she'd thought.

"Let's continue this conversation in the kitchen," said Patience, with a hint of surrender in her voice. "I've got a cake to bake."

Now that was the woman she knew and loved, Mercy thought. She waited until her grandmother had left the room to smile.

Patience called baking her zen. She baked the way other people did yoga or sat meditation or practiced tai chi. The fact that she was escaping to her kitchen now gave her away; she was more upset about this George Rucker business than she would let on.

The dogs looked up at Mercy, waiting for the signal that they could follow Patience into her kitchen, one of their favorite places on earth. "Oh, go on, I'm right behind you."

They scampered off and she trailed them. She was in no hurry to force her grandmother's hand. Even though that was her aim in coming here and she seemed to be on the edge of victory.

Patience was already at work at the marble island, her Provençal apron on and her fingers dusted with flour. The smell of vanilla and sugar and chocolate filled the air. The soothing scents of Mercy's childhood.

She made herself at home on one of the stools on the other side of the island, and Elvis sat at her side. Sunny trotted around to Patience's side of the island and curled up at her grandmother's feet. Mercy was beginning to believe that the golden retriever was always drawn to the most stressed-out person in the room, whether that stress was due to anxiety or fear or just plain ordinary unhappiness. She was the mood ring of dogs.

"You're baking," she said to her grandmother, her voice heavy with meaning.

"I'm always baking." Patience shrugged. "No big deal."

Mercy surveyed the island before her. The gleaming marble surface was cluttered with mixing bowls and whisks and measuring cups, cake pans, and a stainless-steel layer cake slicer. That slicer could only mean one thing. "You're making a *doberge* cake? It's not my birthday."

"Not yet." Patience grinned at her, obviously pleased to change the conversation from one about her to one about Mercy.

"Not yet is right." Her thirtieth birthday was coming up in a couple of weeks, and she was not happy about it. Just thinking about it made her feel old and inexperienced at the same time.

"You need a reason to bake a *doberge* cake."

Chocolate *doberge* cake was Mercy's favorite. The New Orleans specialty was a multilayered confection made of six thinly sliced layers of buttermilk cake stacked high, a delicious custard filling sweetening each layer, topped with a buttercream and fondant icing. A Big Easy makeover of the Hungarian *Dobos* torte. A labor of love her grandmother made only on very special occasions, namely Mercy's birthday, and times of deep stress. The more upset Patience was, the more complicated the recipe.

Her grandmother ignored her and began assembling her ingredients—

flour, baking powder, salt. Patience focused on the battered recipe card in front of her. She pulled a carton of eggs from the refrigerator and placed it in front of Mercy. "Make yourself useful. Separate five eggs for me, please."

"Sure." Mercy leaned over the counter and grabbed three little glass bowls, one for whites, one for yolks, and a spare. The spare was the net over which she would separate the egg, just in case yolk inadvertently spilled into the white. She cracked the first egg over the spare bowl, did the delicate dance between white and yolk, allowing the white to fall into the whites bowl, and then emptying the yolk into the yolks bowl. Time for egg two.

"Did I ever tell you about James?"

Mercy looked up at her grandmother. "James."

"My first sweetheart."

"No." As far as she knew, Red had been her first and only true love. Patience met and wed him young, and when he died, she did not remarry. Instead, she went to veterinary school and set up her animal hospital. She'd been dating Claude Renault, an animal surgeon from Quebec, for many years now, but she refused to marry him. And Mercy knew he'd proposed more than once. He was a nice guy, and sometimes she felt sorry for him.

"We met in the seventh grade." Patience measured out two cups of flour and tossed it into a large orange mixing bowl. "We were the smartest kids in the class—the brainiacs—and the kids teased us. I suppose we were destined to find one another."

"Destined? What were you, twelve?"

"Destiny can strike at any age." Patience looked at her with those bright blue eyes. "He was the first boy to ever hold my hand. The night of my thirteenth birthday party." She smiled at the memory. "I held my own hand under my pillow for weeks afterward."

Mercy laughed, careful not to disturb the eggshell halves in her hands. "You did not."

"I did." Patience measured out another two cups of flour. "We were inseparable. Kindred spirits. We took long walks in the woods, shared our favorite books, read each other poetry. We even checked each other's homework."

"How romantic."

"I know it seems silly. But James was the first boy to see me as I really was and love me anyway."

"But not the last," said Mercy, thinking of her grandfather.

Patience didn't answer, and that gave Mercy pause. "What happened?"

"His father got transferred. They moved out West."

"And you lost touch?"

"We wrote letters back and forth for years. He invited me to his senior prom, but my parents refused to let me go. He went to the Naval Academy, and I promised to visit him there. But then I met your grandfather." Patience poured two cups of sugar into a stainless steel bowl and added three sticks of softened unsalted butter.

"Do you ever regret it?"

"What?"

"Not going to that prom."

Patience wiped her hands on her apron. "No. I loved your grandfather, and we had a good life together. Three beautiful children. And even more beautiful grandchildren." She smiled at Mercy. "But I sometimes wonder how my life would have been different had I gone to that prom."

"Different how?"

"I think I would have become a veterinarian much sooner."

"Really? Grandpa Red kept you from being a vet?"

"No, not really. But he was a strong personality, and I was very young. It took me a long time to come into my own."

"And you could have done that sooner with James."

"Perhaps. Who knows. I do know that I wouldn't trade those years with Red for anything." She watched as Mercy separated the last of the eggs. "The point is, I thought James was the one for me. But it just so happened that your grandfather was the one for me."

This was her grandmother's not-so-subtle way of telling her that maybe Martinez was not the one for her. Maybe Troy was.

Mercy needed to get this conversation back on track, back to her grandfather and George Rucker. "And then Grandpa Red died."

Patience hooked the bowl into her cranberry-colored KitchenAid mixer and switched it on. The whirring effectively ended their little talk.

Mercy frowned. Elvis's ears perked. He leapt to his feet and sprinted from the room just as the woodpecker knocker sounded. Sunny followed suit.

Rat a tat tat. Rat a tat tat. Rat a tat.

Patience waved a hand toward the front of the house.

"Got it." Mercy hustled to the foyer, where she found Elvis sniffing at the slim streak of light at the bottom of her grandmother's front door. Tail wagging.

She peered through the peephole and saw no one. Nothing. She opened the door to find a cardboard box covered with a threadbare pink blanket on the welcome mat. The blanket was moving and meowing.

She knelt down to take a closer look just as Elvis pushed the blanket aside with his nose. Six kittens—three inky black and three gray—squirmed and squealed inside. Mercy snatched up the box and pulled the blanket back over the top before any could escape. She looked around the yard, but she saw no one.

Which wasn't unusual. Vermonters were very good about spaying and neutering their pets, so most of the rescues people adopted came from kill shelters farther south. This was especially true for the dogs. But there were always feral cats around, as well as abandoned pit bulls. Locals knew that Patience—known as the Doctor Dolittle of Northshire—would always find a place for them. It was understood that if they dropped them off on her front doorstep—as opposed to the entrance of her vet office around back—they could do it anonymously, no questions asked. Good Samaritans also dropped off donations of food, kitty litter, and other pet supplies.

Mercy started back to the kitchen, box of mewling kittens in hand, Sunny the golden retriever on her heels.

"Come on, Elvis," she yelled over her shoulder.

She planted the box of kittens on the kitchen table. "Special delivery."

Patience looked up from her mixer. "Grab a playpen from the pantry and set it up here. I'll check them out as soon as I get these cakes in the oven."

Mercy did as she was told, setting up the colorful play yard in the corner, and scooping the kittens one by one from the box and depositing them into the pen. "They're so cute! What will you do with them all?"

"I'm sure the Cat Ladies will help." The Cat Ladies ran a rescue organization out of an eighteenth-century farmhouse they'd inherited from a rich aunt. They found forever homes for hundreds of cats every year—and those too feral to adopt had the run of the place.

"Mr. Horgan could use some company." Mr. Horgan was an elderly widower still grieving for his late wife, the town's longtime librarian. Two of Mercy's favorite people.

Patience smiled. "An excellent idea."

"Maybe this little guy." Mercy held up an adorable black kitty, the largest and noisiest of the litter.

"Even better. The black cats are the hardest to place in forever homes. A lot of people still let those silly old superstitions get the better of them, and they won't have one in the house. But I doubt Walter will mind."

Sunny leaned her pretty golden muzzle on the edge of the playpen, the better to guard the little feline newcomers. The kittens fell over themselves as they explored their new home.

"They're probably hungry. Why don't you—"

Another, louder *rat a tat tat* interrupted Patience, and she stopped mid-sentence. She raised an eyebrow at Mercy. "More kittens?"

"I'll go."

"No, you stay here with your new charges. Find a litter box for that pen."

Patience left the room and Mercy started for the pantry again. She heard Elvis bark and stopped short. Elvis had not returned to the kitchen when she'd called him. He'd stayed at the door. Maybe knowing there were more kittens to come.

But if it were just more kittens, he would not be barking.

Something was wrong.

Mercy sprinted through the kitchen and down the entry. Elvis had dropped down on his haunches by the front door. Still, tense, ears perked.

This was his alert position, the posture he assumed when he sniffed out weapons or explosives. IEDs had been his specialty in Afghanistan.

Patience stood at the door, her back to Mercy. Her hand on the knob.

She twisted it. Pulling at the door.

"Wait!" yelled Mercy. Just seconds too late.

Her grandmother turned toward Mercy.

Elvis leapt to his feet. He rose up on his back legs and lunged at her grandmother. Pushing her away from the door. She stumbled, cursing as she fell to the floor.

Mercy threw herself on top of her grandmother just as a deafening roar filled her ears and a blinding light seared her eyes.

The last thing she felt before she felt nothing at all was the soft brush of fur against her cheek.

CHAPTER SEVEN

S HE DREAMED OF MEWLING KITTENS ABANDONED ON DOORSTEPS and barking dogs abandoned in kennels, and she struggled to rescue them all but they kept on slipping away. Out of their boxes and off their leads and into the cold, dark night after the *rat a tat tat* of the Pied Piper.

Beyond her reach. She called and called and called for them to return to her. The sounds of their howling retreating into the midnight gloom on the heels of the man with the staccato song. She caught a last glimpse of Elvis—Elvis!—as he disappeared into the shadows after the Pied Piper, his black-tipped tail dissolving to black.

She opened her eyes and there he was. Wesley Hallett. He was sitting in an orange plastic chair at the side of her bed. Her hospital bed. For a moment she thought she must still be dreaming. But Hallett was real. "What happened?"

"From what I understand you were in an explosion yesterday. Don't you remember?"

She remembered a great flare and a great noise and a great fall. But that was all she remembered. There must be more.

Elvis. She jolted upright, and her brain drubbed inside her skull. Her body throbbed from the exertion. She closed her eyes and fell back, teeth clenched against the pain. No way was she tearing up in front of this guy again.

Hallett held his right hand out, palm up. "Hey, take it easy."

She turned her head slowly, carefully, deliberately until the man came into full view. "What are you doing here?"

"I heard what happened and I wanted to make sure you were all right."

She reached for the remote and raised the bed so she could sit up and look him in the eye. "You wanted to make sure Elvis was all right."

He shrugged. "I wanted to make sure you were both all right."

She knew if Elvis were hurt, Hallett would be with him, not her. So he was okay. Relief flooded her. "Where is Elvis?"

"At home with your family."

A flash of Patience hitting the floor pierced the banging that beat against her bones from the inside out. She willed away the pain. "Is my grandmother all right?"

"Apparently she broke her arm in the fall. But she's okay otherwise."

If that were true, my family wouldn't be here, Mercy thought. If by *family* Hallett meant her parents. She'd find out the truth, but first she needed to get rid of this guy. She couldn't deal with him and her mother at the same time.

"What about Sunny?"

He looked at her blankly.

"The golden retriever. My friend's dog."

"That I don't know." Hallett started to rise from his chair. "But I can find out for you."

"That won't be necessary. My mother will know. I'm sure she has everything in hand."

He sat back down. Not what Mercy had in mind.

"Look, Patience is fine. Elvis is fine. I'm fine." She wanted him out of her sight and out of her life right now. Forever. But she knew he wouldn't give up on Elvis that easily. Because she wouldn't. "You can leave now." She didn't know how she could say it plainer than that.

He gave her an appraising look, the kind her mother gave her whenever she saw her only daughter after any length of time. A look that said, *Really? You still haven't done anything with your hair? Your career? Your life?*

"Really. We're all fine."

"I know that Elvis has PTSD."

She wondered who told him that. "All of us have PTSD. Some worse than others. You know that."

Hallett grabbed the bed's metal sidearm that separated them and leaned forward. "An explosion like this is bound to provoke reactions in both of you."

It was true that when she first brought Elvis home, he would sometimes behave erratically, especially in the face of triggers like slamming doors and thunderstorms and fireworks. She didn't like that kind of noise much, either. But together she and the shepherd had overcome their fears and when they found themselves on the wrong end of gunfire last summer, they had both performed like the capable and experienced soldiers they were. She was proud of Elvis, and proud of herself.

"I don't know why you keep putting yourself in these situations." Hallett's face softened. "But you do. And you keep dragging Elvis into them, too."

"I didn't drag Elvis into anything. And we're not even sure what this is about yet."

"You know what I mean. You've gotten involved in these murder investigations. Putting yourself and Elvis in harm's way."

"Coming home doesn't keep you out of harm's way." Mercy stared him down. "Surely you've figured that out by now."

He backed off, sinking down into the orange plastic chair, his arms at his side. "That's a very pessimistic attitude."

"That's the reality. And you know it." She paused a moment. "Besides, Elvis loves to work."

"You love to work."

Mercy sighed. "Elvis needs to work."

"He's earned his retirement."

"Of course he has. We all have. But some of us are not ready to retire. I'm not, and neither is Elvis. We still have work to do." That was the truth, whether he recognized it or not. And she was ready to fight for that truth.

"There are all kinds of work. You're just replacing one mission with another."

"And what's wrong with that? We all need a mission, even after we leave the service. Maybe even more after we leave." She gave him the same appraising look he'd given her. One worthy of her mother. "How's retirement going for you?"

Hallett flushed. "I told you I had a rough time for a while. But I got through it."

"Because you found a new mission."

He stood there, his face creased with emotion now. "I work with vets at the veterans hospital in Springfield."

"Vermont?"

"Missouri."

Missouri, she thought. What would Elvis do in Missouri? What did anyone do in Missouri?

"I could give him a good life. A safe life."

"Safety is an illusion." Every soldier knew that. But she figured that Hallett was one of those soldiers who was not ready to admit that. He wanted to believe that now that he was home, everything would be all right. That was his prerogative, but she wasn't going to let his delusions dictate Elvis's future. She'd just have to play along with them. She wondered if he knew she came from a family of brilliant and uncompromising attorneys. Not that asking her mother for help was ever an appealing option. Maybe Troy's divorce lawyer handled dog custody battles.

"Elvis is safe with me." She wasn't letting Elvis move to Missouri. Martinez would never forgive her and she would never forgive herself. What's more, Elvis would never forgive her. "What happened today is an anomaly. Elvis is fine."

"This time." He stood up and leaned over her. "He got lucky. You got lucky."

"Does Elvis seem unhappy to you?"

"No. But he's never known anything else. He's never had the opportunity to know anything else. Elvis would live with me. Keep the other vets company. They would love him."

"You want to turn Elvis into a lap dog. No way."

"You're always going to get into trouble. You can't help yourself."

Mercy laughed. "You don't know me."

"We have other dogs, too. He'd have friends."

"Elvis has friends."

Hallett frowned. "I thought you had a falling out with that game warden and his search-and-rescue dog."

"Time for you to leave." Troy Warner appeared at the door of the hospital room. He was in uniform, and Susie Bear was with him.

Hallett seemed surprised to see him and his dog. He didn't know that Susie Bear had special privileges, even here at the hospital, thought Mercy. She had a feeling Troy would see to it that he learned the hard way.

"Speak of the devil." Mercy laughed.

Hallett just looked confused.

"How did he even get in here?" Troy asked Mercy, ignoring Hallett.

"I don't know. He must be hanging out at Crossroads." Crossroads was a place on the outskirts of town where locals showed up to drink coffee and chat. Part gas station, part general store, part pizza parlor, part deli—a whole far greater than its parts in terms of gossip.

Susie Bear bounded in ahead of Troy, knocking Hallett back into the orange plastic chair as she clamored to Mercy's side. He plopped down heavily, catching the sides of the chair to steady himself.

"Sorry," said Troy, without a trace of remorse. "She gets a little excited when she sees Mercy."

The big dog planted her pumpkin head on the bed at Mercy's feet. She leaned down to give the Newfie mutt a good scratch between the ears. When she sat back up, she caught Troy smiling at her. It was the first time she'd seen him since that awful evening at the Wild Game Supper last autumn, where she'd had an unexpected and unpleasant encounter with his estranged wife. She and Troy were dancing, and Madeline cut right in. Mercy winced at the memory, or maybe it was the pain in her head. She wasn't sure.

Madeline had run off to Florida with an orthopedist a couple of years before—but she'd come back to reclaim her husband before it was too late. Mercy had assumed Troy was divorced. And the discovery that he was not—right there on the dance floor in front of the whole town—surprised and unsettled her.

Troy had lied to her, by omission if nothing else. He was not the man she thought he was. She was done with dancing. Done with men. Done with Troy Warner. Period.

She'd gone out of her way to avoid him ever since. But she was wildly glad to see him now. And Susie Bear, too. For once, she really felt like she needed the backup.

Hallett rose to his feet and introduced himself. Troy shook his hand, and then pointed to the door. "You shouldn't be here. Family only, you know."

"And you're family?"

"Family *and* law enforcement." He tapped the badge secured above his left breast pocket.

"Understood." Hallett bowed at Mercy. "I'm very glad you and Elvis are all right. Please think about what I said. I'm sure you want to do what's best for Elvis."

Susie Bear lifted her head at the sound of Elvis's name. Mercy nodded at Hallett and watched as he walked past Troy, each man eyeing the other. Two soldiers sizing each other up.

When he was gone, Troy shut the door. "That's the guy who's after Elvis." A statement, not a question.

"Yes." The captain must have told Troy about meeting him at her cabin. She wondered what else he told him. "Have a seat."

He took Hallett's place in the orange plastic chair, which was a little small for him. He stretched out his long legs in front of him, his boots under the bed. "Thrasher had me run his plates."

Mercy smiled. Of course he did.

"His name is Wesley John Hallett. Thirty-two years old. Born and raised in Springfield, Missouri. Served two tours in Afghanistan. Infantryman, then dog handler. Wounded when his Humvee hit an IED. Lost his left foot."

"He told me that." Mercy looked at Troy, and from the way he squared his jaw she could tell he was holding something back. "What didn't he tell me?"

Troy frowned. "Awarded the Purple Heart." He paused. "And the Silver Star, for pulling two fellow soldiers from the wreckage. Saved their lives."

"With only one foot." Mercy sighed, and blinked back tears. Her head ached again, and this time she knew it wasn't from the explosion. "I won't hand Elvis over to him no matter how many medals he's won. I suppose that makes me a terrible person."

"No, it doesn't." Troy took her hand in his.

She wanted to pull away, but instead she found herself wrapping her fingers around his. *Any port in a storm,* she thought. But that was unfair. If anyone could understand how she felt about this extraordinary Belgian shepherd, Troy could.

"You have to do what's best for Elvis," he said. "And what's best for Elvis is *you*."

"Hallett will never believe that."

"Then we'll just have to prove it to him."

"We?"

"You, me, Susie Bear, Elvis, Patience, the captain. Between us we'll think of something."

"Excuse me." A perfectly coiffed blond head popped up around the door.

"Mom." Mercy didn't know whether to be glad or mad. The effect her mother inevitably had on her.

Troy stood up. "Ma'am."

"Warden Warner." Grace nodded at Troy and strode to the other side of Mercy's hospital bed. She snapped her fingers at Susie Bear, and the dog shambled away over to Troy. For the daughter of a veterinarian, her mother was not very fond of animals. Or game wardens sworn to protect wildlife. Grace—Mercy called her *Mom* at her insistence but somehow always thought of her as Grace—wanted her to go to law school, join the family firm, marry a nice up-and-coming lawyer, and have two lovely children destined to become lawyers themselves. A Carr–O'Sullivan dynasty of attorneys.

Mercy would rather eat dirt.

Outside of her mother's view, Troy waggled his eyebrows at her, and she bit back a laugh. She had to admit, if only to herself, that one of the things she liked best about him was how unsuitable her mother believed the game warden to be for her one and only daughter. And how unperturbed he was by that disapproval.

"Warden Warner, if you don't mind . . ." Grace spoke with the cultured Yankee cadence of Katharine Hepburn, but her intent was clear.

"Ma'am." Troy stepped forward toward Mercy and leaned in, whispering in her ear. "Let me know when you can talk. Something's come up that you should know about."

"Warden Warner." Grace's tone was downright icy now.

"We were just leaving." He smiled at Mercy, then addressed her mother. "Take good care of her."

Grace just glared at him.

"Thanks for coming." Mercy gave the Newfie one last pat.

"No problem. Come on, Susie Bear."

She and her mother watched them go.

"That young man has some nerve showing up here after that unforgivable scene at the Wild Game Supper."

"He didn't know Madeline would be there." At least she hoped he hadn't known.

"Everyone in Northshire knew she'd be there."

Mercy flushed. "I didn't know."

Grace sat on the edge of the bed, smoothing her skirt. She was dressed in her usual Ralph Lauren ensemble: black wool crêpe pencil skirt, cream silk blouse, and fitted black wool crêpe jacket. Tasteful gold jewelry. Artfully applied makeup. Italian leather equestrian-style boots, her mother's only concession to the wintry mix that was New England weather in early March.

In other words, the picture of Newbury Street elegance. Mercy sighed in anticipation of the carefully worded attorney's argument to come. Her head pounded again. Having a lawyer for a mother was a headache waiting to happen even when you didn't feel like you'd just gotten hit by a truck.

"Of course you didn't. You never were one for gossip." Her mother brushed a perfectly manicured hand across Mercy's brow, pushing away the wayward curls she'd spent her daughter's entire childhood trying to tame.

As soon as Mercy left home, she'd abandoned all hair products and let her tangle of red hair revert to its wild state. It drove her mother crazy.

"Even as a teenager," Grace went on, "you were oblivious to the machinations of the mean girls at school."

Not oblivious, thought Mercy, just indifferent. She'd stayed above the fray, saving her strength for battles that mattered: Defying her parents and joining the Army. Fighting in Afghanistan. Finding Elvis.

And now keeping him. If Troy could help her do that, then Madeline didn't matter.

"You're not listening to me."

"Sorry." She changed the subject. "How's Patience?"

Her mother shook her head, her chicly cut blond hair sliding to and fro across her cheeks before falling perfectly back into place. "You know how she is. Says she's fine, even when she's not." Her tone made it clear that Mercy was just like her grandmother, and that Grace did not appreciate it. "She broke her scaphoid bone. One of the carpal bones of the wrist, apparently the one that takes the longest to heal."

"Poor Patience."

"She's in a long arm cast. At least it was her left wrist."

"She's going to hate that."

"She needs to take it easy. It was a clean break, but she is not getting any younger. Neither are you."

Mercy ignored the reference to her upcoming birthday. "Does she remember what happened?"

"Not a thing. At the risk of repeating myself, she's not getting any younger."

"My recollection is a little hazy, too."

"Of course it is. You were in an explosion."

"And I'm not getting any younger, either," she said, beating her mother to the punch. She smiled in spite of herself. "Where's Elvis?"

"He's at your cabin with Patience."

"How is he?"

"From what I understand he's fine."

"What does that mean?"

"Physically he's fine, according to your grandmother. A little shell-shocked, which is to be expected."

More ammunition for Wesley Hallett, Mercy thought. "And Sunny?"

"Sunny?"

"The golden retriever I've, uh, inherited."

"You don't need another dog."

"Sunny was with me at Patience's house when the pipe bomb blew. How is she?"

"I don't know. I assume the dog is fine, or we would have heard something."

"That's only so reassuring."

"I'll see what I can find out for you."

"Thanks. You're sure Patience and Elvis are okay?"

"Yes," her mother said briskly. "Your father is with them. They'll stay there until the police are finished processing the crime scene at her house. Then Ed will drop by and do what he can to secure the place before she goes home."

Ed was her cousin, a master carpenter who could fix anything. He'd built the floor-to-ceiling bookshelves in her great room. Complete with a rolling ladder. He loved Patience, who kept him in truck dogs. He had a lab mix now, a friendly brindle rescue named Joiner.

"Sounds good." Mercy paused. "Did Thrasher tell you anything?" Her parents were friendly with the captain; they were friendly with everyone worth knowing in New England, from Boston to Vermont and back again.

Grace's forehead wrinkled prettily. "They're still working on the forensics. But he told your father it was probably a homemade device. The kind of pipe bomb anyone can build with nails and matches and a detonating cord. The instructions can be found all over the internet."

"No sign of the perpetrator?"

"No."

"Was it the same guy who left the kittens?"

"What kittens?"

Mercy tried to think. Beyond the beating in her brain was a persistent niggling that told her she was forgetting something. Something significant. "I can't remember."

"Let it go." Grace took Mercy's clammy freckled hands into her pale, cool ones. "There's a reason they kept you here overnight. And that they're keeping you here today for observation."

"I'm fine. Just a little sore."

"Nonsense. You've been sleeping for nearly twenty-four hours. You obviously need your rest."

"I'm missing something. I have to figure out what's going on before something worse happens."

"Leave it to law enforcement. That's their job."

"I can't do that." She squeezed her mother's hands, then shook free of them.

"Why do you always feel that it's up to you? You're just one person."

"Have they captured George Rucker?"

"George Rucker?" Grace hesitated. "What does he have to do with this?"

"I don't know. But he's escaped from prison and he's on the run." Interesting that the captain failed to tell her mother that. Maybe he didn't want to worry her. Maybe he told her father instead, and that's why he was with her grandmother right now. On guard duty. Her father may be a citified attorney, but he was also a very good shot.

"I need to talk to Patience." Mercy pulled the drip out of her arm and swung her legs over the bed, ignoring the drubbing under her skin.

"What are you doing?" Grace stood up, facing Mercy, fists on her narrow hips. "You aren't going anywhere, young lady."

"Thrasher says George Rucker bears a grudge against Grandpa Red. And with Red long dead and gone, he might be going after Patience instead. When I asked her about it, she got very cagey."

Grace dropped back down on the bed. "What did she say?"

"Basically that he was not in his right mind and didn't know what he was doing when he shot Red. But I know she was lying."

Grace looked down at her lap and picked an invisible piece of lint from her skirt. Buying time, Mercy knew, to compose herself.

"She was making a *doberge* cake."

Grace looked up at Mercy, fully composed now. Or so she thought.

No one reads a mother's body language better than her child. Mercy searched Grace's inscrutable face for confirmation—and found it in her slightly flared nostrils. Her mother's only tell.

"You'd better tell me, Mom, before someone else gets hurt."

CHAPTER EIGHT

G RACE LEFT HER SEAT ON THE HOSPITAL BED AND WENT around to the other side of the bed. She pulled the orange plastic chair closer to Mercy and sat down, crossing her long legs. She looked like she needed a cigarette. She'd given up smoking when she'd had kids, but Mercy and her brother Nick would sometimes find her on the balcony of their brownstone in Boston late at night, her blond hair hidden by a silk scarf and her eyes covered in dark sunglasses, sucking on a Marlboro Light as if her sanity depended on it. Maybe it did.

"Your grandmother told us not to pay any attention to the talk around town," she began, staring at the wall behind Mercy as if she were watching a film. "Just small-minded people repeating small-minded prattle."

"But you knew better. Because you're good at gossip."

Grace gave her a sharp look. "All hearsay."

Always the lawyer, thought Mercy. "Go on."

"The rumor was that your grandfather was having an affair with George's wife."

"Wow."

"Wow indeed."

"No wonder Patience didn't want to talk about it."

"She'd rather believe he was faithful to the end." Grace sighed. "What wife wouldn't?"

"So it was true."

Grace shrugged her thin shoulders. "Who knows. George's wife was a very attractive and very adventurous young woman. She had lots of affairs with local men, if the grapevine is to be believed."

"That doesn't explain why she left town."

"She left because she wanted more than George Rucker and Lamoille County could give her. She left because she was dying a slow death in Vermont."

Mercy knew her mother had felt the same way when she was young. Which is why she'd left Vermont for law school in Boston and never looked back. "Then why blame Grandpa Red?"

"George Rucker believed that when your grandfather broke up with her, that was the last straw for her. So she took off."

"That doesn't make a lot of sense."

"Well, he was crazy." Grace frowned. "I guess he still is. It doesn't really matter if it's true or not, if he believes it's true."

"It matters to Patience." Mercy slipped out of the hospital bed, looking around for her clothes and her shoes.

"What are you doing?"

"Don't change the subject." She stepped to the foot of the bed, facing off with her mother. "What do you believe? Was Red having an affair or not?"

"I don't know. I loved my father. But I'm ashamed to say that I liked him a little less when the rumors started." Grace stood up, then sat down again. "A lot less, really. And then he died."

"Before you could find out the truth."

"Before I could get past it, whatever it was. I didn't want to know the truth then. I'm not sure I want to know it now."

That did not surprise Mercy. Her mother was a genius in the courtroom, ferreting out the worst sort of truths from anyone unfortunate enough to inhabit the witness stand. But she ignored any truths that might complicate her life on the home front.

Mercy left the bed and crossed the room, opening the narrow closet that stood on the far wall next to the TV. "Where are my things?"

"Nothing salvageable, I'm afraid, thanks to the explosion." Grace pointed to a small Coach case in the corner. "I packed you a bag of essentials."

"Uh-huh." Mercy could only imagine what her mother considered essentials. Certainly not the long-sleeved T-shirts and fleece-lined cargo pants she favored this time of year. She unzipped the bag and pulled out an oversized ivory cashmere sweater and slouchy wool trousers in a slightly deeper shade of taupe. Matching wool socks and light brown leather ankle boots. At least they were pants, she thought, and not another little black dress she'd never wear. "Thanks, Mom."

Grace beamed. "You're welcome."

I really should let her do this more often, Mercy thought. *It makes her so happy.*

"There's a headband in there, too," said Grace.

And this is why I don't, she thought. "I'm going to get dressed now."

"You really should stay here at the hospital until the doctor says you're well enough to leave." Grace rose gracefully out of the orange plastic chair and stood between Mercy and the exit.

"I need to get home to Patience and Elvis."

"I suppose there's no talking you out of it."

"No."

"I could just stand here blocking the door."

"You could." Mercy laughed, which pained her more than she'd ever admit to her mother. She slipped on the pants and pulled the sweater over her messy hair, tucked her feet into the socks and boots. She left the headband in the bag where it belonged. "But you won't."

"I won't." Grace stepped aside.

"Because?" Mercy waited for the answer she'd heard a thousand times before.

Grace smiled. "Because there's just no stopping you."

MERCY WAS DOWN in the reception area before she realized she had no phone, no money, and no ride. Her Jeep was still parked at her grandmother's house. And she had no idea where her keys were. She looked across the room at the elevators, where she expected her mother to emerge triumphant any moment, that Coach bag stuffed with doctor's instructions and meds, ready to take her stubborn daughter home with her.

Or not. Mercy could feel her cheeks redden just thinking of the humiliation to come.

"Is everything all right?" Troy appeared behind her, Susie Bear on his heels.

"You're still here?"

"We thought we'd just hang around and catch you on your way out."

"You could have been in for a long wait."

He shook his head. "*Nah*. We knew they couldn't keep you in that hospital bed for much longer."

Since when am I so transparent? she thought. The elevator doors opened and she caught sight of her mother.

"I need a ride," she told him, and strode quickly toward the hospital exit.

CHAPTER NINE

S URE." TROY AND SUSIE BEAR CAUGHT UP WITH HER AND escorted her to his Ford F-150. He swept his citation book off the passenger seat and placed it in a back cab crowded with supplies and paperwork and weaponry, all neatly secured on one side to make room for Susie Bear on the other.

Mercy climbed into the truck and immediately regretted her impulsive request for a ride home. Tight quarters here, with nothing but the game warden's radio system between them, and Susie Bear leaning her heavy head on the top of the seat and panting into her ear.

Troy grinned at her from behind the wheel. "Where are we going?"

"Home," she said, keeping her eyes on the road ahead of her. "But I'd like to stop at Patience's house on the way." It was already late afternoon and she needed to see the blast site before it grew too dark.

"Not much left to see. The staties have been all over the place. Firefighters and state hazmat crews. The bomb squad, too."

Susie Bear pushed her large cold nose under Mercy's arm and forced it onto her pumpkin head, which now dominated the center console between her and Troy. The radio system teetered dangerously toward the gearshift. She reached for it just as Troy did the same, and their fingers briefly touched.

Mercy remembered how she'd clung to him earlier in the hospital when Hallett had been in the room. She hoped he didn't remember.

"Got it," he said, so softly that she knew he remembered, after all.

He propped the radio system back up, while she gently moved the Newfie's head back to accommodate it. Then she changed the subject. "How's Harrington?"

"He's in his glory. Between this and the Colby murder he's getting more press than he can handle. He's even made the national news."

"What Colby murder?"

Troy filled in her on the untimely death of the wildlife biologist.

"That's terrible." Mercy wondered who would kill a guy whose mission in life was to save moose calves. She wondered who would save the moose calves now. There were always more missions than there were men and women to take them on. Or maybe it just seemed that way on her bad days. This was one of her bad days. "Do you think there's any connection between Patience's pipe bomb and what happened to Colby?"

"Hard to say. We don't know who killed Colby, or why."

A moose hater, thought Mercy. "The killer stole his gear and his clothes and his boots. Left him with only his socks." A moose hater and a petty thief.

"That's right. His camera is missing, too."

A moose hater and a petty thief and an amateur cinematographer. Mercy's head ached. She obviously wasn't thinking clearly.

"Are you okay?" Troy looked at her with those warm brown eyes.

"I'm fine." She tried focusing on Colby. "Maybe Colby surprised the murderer when he raided his camp. He panicked and killed him."

"It's a good theory, but he wasn't killed at the campsite. At least he didn't appear to be. He was found about a hundred yards due north."

"What was on the camera?"

"As far as we know, moose calves. At least that's what Colby was shooting."

"Moose as a motive for murder." Mercy paused. "Poachers?"

"It's possible. So few moose can be hunted legally these days that most harvested moose are taken by poachers."

Mercy knew that only hunters who won the moose lottery could harvest moose legally in Vermont. And then only in October during the hunting season. Given the shrinking population, fewer and fewer lottery winners were awarded hunting licenses for moose.

"Besides," Troy went on, "most moose poachers are trophy-game hunters, looking for the adult males with the biggest racks. Wrong time of year for that."

"Because they lose their antlers every winter." Mercy grinned.

"Yep." Troy nodded. "By now all but the youngest have shed their paddles."

"When I was a little girl, maybe six or seven, my Grandpa Red took me hiking in the woods like he always did on Thanksgiving morning. We caught sight of a big bull shaking his enormous head. I'd never seen a moose that close up before. His left antler fell right off, and I was terrified for him. My grandfather clapped his hand across my mouth before I could scream." She laughed. "I was so worried about the moose, but Grandpa Red explained that he'd lose the other one, too. I really, really, really wanted to take that antler home to show my brother Nick, but Red told me we should leave it there, for the squirrels and mice and porcupines to eat."

Troy smiled. "Your grandfather sounds like a good guy."

"Yeah. I thought so." Mercy told him about the rumors that he'd had an affair with George Rucker's wife. "I don't know what to think."

"I'm sure you'll figure it out."

"For better or worse." Mercy changed the subject. "What about food? Could Colby have caught someone poaching moose for food on his camera?"

"Maybe if they're hungry enough. One moose can feed a family for a year."

"Even if Colby did catch someone in the act, murder seems like an extreme reaction."

"Hunters can be a little crazy."

Mercy nodded. That's what made Troy's job so dangerous: He was always going after guys with guns in the forest. And most of them were good shots. "You said he was hit in the head and left naked except for his socks."

"Right."

"Wouldn't a hunter just shoot him and hide his body?"

"Exactly." Troy shook his head. "It doesn't make any sense. We're hoping forensics will tell us more."

"Who knows what he actually caught on camera."

"We need to find that camera."

"And George Rucker?"

"Still at large. As is his former fellow prisoner Rocky Simko, who was seen in the area where Rucker escaped. Simko was released a couple of weeks ago after serving time for auto theft and carjacking."

"Nice."

"Too many variables. Too many unknowns. All we have so far are some strange coincidences."

Mercy counted them off on her fingers. "One, George Rucker escapes from prison in Mississippi. Two, a wildlife biologist is found with his head bashed in deep in the Vermont woods. Three, someone plants a pipe bomb on my grandmother's porch."

"Rucker is connected to Patience," said Troy. "But there's no connection between Colby and Patience, or Colby and Rucker."

"That we know of."

"That we know of," Troy conceded. "We need to know more."

"I forgot one."

"One what?"

"One coincidence." Mercy told Troy about Deputy Pitts and the cold case files he'd given her.

"What does this cold case have to do with what's happening now?"

"Maybe nothing. Nothing at all. But Pitts is connected to Patience and Rucker."

Mercy found herself smiling. This was one of the things she missed most about not seeing Troy these past couple of months. Talking through the aspects of a case, analyzing the facts, debating theories, finding and fitting pieces of the puzzle. Together.

She stole a glance at Troy as he steered into the drive that led up to her grandmother's house. He was smiling, too.

His smile faded as he pulled the truck up to the side of the house. From here they could see the front of the Victorian. Where a front porch once stood welcoming guests to the front door—an antique made of solid mahogany adorned by a peephole and that bronze woodpecker knocker—now there was only a gaping hole. The porch and the lovely old door were gone.

A narrow temporary ramp made of plywood led up to the former entryway, where her cousin Ed was pounding nails into more plywood in an attempt to close up the empty space fronting the house.

"Hyah, Mercy." Ed put down his hammer and came down the ramp to greet her, powerful arms out, ready to wrap her in one of his signature bear hugs.

She stepped back. "Not really up to a hug, Ed."

He dropped his arms to his sides. "Are you all right?"

"I'm fine. Just a little sore all over."

Ed took a good long look at her. "You look tired. And your hair is a mess." He grinned at her.

"My hair is always a mess."

"And we like it that way." He reached out and gently brushed a wayward curl from her forehead with a large calloused hand. "Except for Aunt Grace."

"Ed." Troy grinned at him.

Her cousin clapped Troy on the shoulder, then squatted down to give Susie Bear a hug. "You know I love Elvis, but this, *this* is a dog." He looked up at Mercy. "You know what I mean?"

"I know what you mean. She's the friendliest dog in the world." If Ed were a dog, Mercy thought, he'd be this happy Newfie mutt. They were kindred spirits. "Where's Joiner?"

"I left him at home. There's enough animal-related excitement around here right now." Ed rose to his feet. "What can I do you for?"

"I don't remember much. I feel like I'm missing something."

"Something important."

"Yeah. I thought maybe if I came back here, it would help jog my memory."

Ed retrieved his hammer. "You can go ahead and look around if you want. The bomb squad photographed everything, sorted through all the evidence, labeled it, packed it up, and took it away. They're sending it to the FBI for analysis."

"And you know this because?"

"I've been hanging around keeping the place safe for the animals. And telling the reporters to get lost. As you'll see, the explosion impacted the porch the most. Thanks to that great old mahogany door, there's less wreckage inside than you'd expect. There's some damage to the hallway, but the rest of the house is in pretty good shape."

"And the veterinary wing?"

"Solid. But the patients went a little nuts. Claude and the Cat Ladies are still there trying to calm them down. Go on in and see for yourself." Ed started pounding away at the plywood again.

Mercy led Troy and Susie Bear around to the back of the house, to the official entry of the Sterling Animal Hospital, named in honor of her grandfather, Sterling "Red" O'Sullivan, himself named after the Sterling Mountain of his native Lamoille County. Walking into the cheerful yellow-and-orange reception area, you'd never know that the front of the building had been ripped apart by an explosive device. The lines were clean and bright and modern, the walls and floors and furniture coordinated in a palette Patience described as zen. Her grandmother believed in the healing power of color: passing through the warm and welcoming reception area to the calming blues and greens of the surgery and treatment rooms and into the soothing violets and purples of the recovery and post-op rooms was like taking a ride through a rainbow.

In the huge Rufus Ruckus Room—a riot of dog toys and tunnels and cones in primary colors—they found Patience's longtime boyfriend, Claude Renault, sitting on a box jump surrounded by dogs of all shapes and sizes. One harlequin Great Dane, two black labs, three border collies, a basset hound, and a miniature dachshund ran circles around the silver-haired animal surgeon, while a clutch of chihuahuas in a play yard clamored for his attention. Mercy was thrilled to see Sunny sitting calmly at his side, her head on his knee. But when the golden noticed the three of them coming into the room, she darted over to greet them, exchanging sniffs with the Newfie mutt and offering her forehead up to Mercy for a quick scratch between her ears.

"I'm so glad you're okay," Mercy told the deputy's dog. She would never forgive herself if anything happened to her.

"Who do we have here?" Troy held out his fist to let Sunny have a sniff.

Mercy told him about Deputy Pitts begging her to take the golden retriever.

"So of course you took her, no questions asked." Troy grinned. "You're always saving somebody."

"Not true," she said, even as she was thinking he might be right. But she wasn't going to admit that to him.

Claude didn't notice them arrive; he'd swapped out Patience's preferred playlist of kirtan and reggae for Québécois folk songs, and he was humming along as he played with the dogs.

"Claude!" Mercy raised her voice to be heard over the cacophony of barks and bellows and yips and yaps and accordions and fiddles and Ginette Reno and Raoul Roy.

"Le silence commence!" roared Claude, and all the dogs stopped dead in their tracks. He waved a long arm toward the floor and they all dropped to their haunches. Even the chihuahuas. And Sunny and Susie Bear. The only sound was the last soaring note of "l'Alouette."

Claude rose to his feet. *"Reste,"* he told the dogs, as he joined Mercy and Troy. "Everything is okay. I treated the animals who needed immediate care. The Cat Ladies are calling all the owners, and most of them are coming to collect their animals today if they haven't already. We'll keep the ones who require additional care or whose people are out of town or otherwise unavailable."

"What about your own practice?"

"My partner can cover me for a while. But Patience is going to need more help now that she's in that cast. I'll stay until she can hire a veterinary assistant."

"I can help, too." Mercy worked at the animal clinic off and on, whenever her grandmother needed her.

Claude smiled. "Your grandmother has needed a full-time veterinary assistant for years. It's time she got one."

"We agree completely," said the Cat Ladies in unison as they scurried into the room, followed by an elegant woman who looked vaguely familiar. Doris and Maureen were the silver-haired sisters who ran the estate known as the Cat House, which their very wealthy great-aunt Clara had left in trust for "cats in need." As her devoted trustees, they were so in sync that they tended to speak in the "royal we" and finish one another's sentences.

"Claude is right," said Doris, the older and more outgoing sister, shaking her head. "What has happened here."

"A bomb," said Maureen, her eyes bright with excitement.

"Intended for *Patience,*" said Doris, with a hard look at her younger sister.

"Our *wonderful* Patience." Maureen cast her eyes down as if in apology.

"Unthinkable."

"But it happened," said Maureen, looking around the clinic as if she'd never seen it before.

"Right here." Doris cut her off. "We're so relieved."

"That she's all right." Maureen nodded vigorously.

"But a broken arm," Doris went on.

"Will slow her down," said Maureen.

"A bit," said Doris. "We know that."

"Are you okay?" Maureen leaned in toward Mercy and patted her arm.

"You must have been hurt, too." Doris leaned in, and patted her other arm.

Mercy half expected them to examine her right then and there. She straightened her spine. "I'm fine, really. It's Patience I'm worried about."

"You must be careful," said Maureen as if she hadn't heard. "That brute."

"Is still running about," said Doris, looking at Troy as if that were all his fault. "We all need to be careful."

"We're doing everything we can to bring the perpetrator to justice," said Troy.

Maureen dismissed him with a wave of a tiny hand and addressed Mercy. "*You'll* find the culprit."

"That's your métier now," said Doris.

"Solving mysteries," said Maureen.

"Our own little Jessica Fletcher!" Doris and Maureen looked at Mercy, eyebrows raised, waiting for a reply.

Troy looked away, studying Claude and his daycare of obedient dogs, and Mercy knew that he was struggling not to laugh. She ignored him and took advantage of the pause to acknowledge the woman who'd come in with the sisters and had been waiting patiently as the sisters chattered. She was petite and pretty, with shoulder-length dark hair brightened by a thick bolt of white that began at her widow's peak and ran the length of her sleek bob, giving her a look of sophistication reinforced by the stylish red knit tunic she wore over velveteen black leggings with black suede wedge boots. A look Mercy's mother, Grace, would no doubt applaud.

She stepped forward, hand outstretched. "I'm Mercy."

"Bea Garcia." She shook her hand with a friendly and firm grip. "I don't think we've ever been formally introduced, but I feel like we've run into each other somewhere." She smiled. "I know your grandmother. And Lillian Jenkins."

Lillian Jenkins was Patience's oldest and dearest friend. Between the two of them they knew everyone in southern Vermont, if not the entire state.

"Thank you for coming."

"I'm happy to help Patience and the animals in any way I can." Bea shook her head. "Such a terrible thing."

Mercy introduced Troy and the dogs.

"Of course." Bea looked from Mercy to Troy and back again. "The Wild Game Supper."

CHAPTER TEN

M ERCY WAS NOT GOING TO TALK ABOUT THE WILD GAME Supper with this woman or anyone else. She could feel her pale freckled skin start to boil with embarrassment. The ruddy curse of the redhead. She didn't dare look at Troy, but she knew he was looking at her.

"I'm so sorry." Bea had obviously realized her faux pas and was now as red-faced as Mercy. "I didn't mean to . . ."

"Bea is a very talented amateur photographer," said Doris, interrupting her.

"She takes lovely portraits," said her sister breathlessly.

"Of the cats."

"Even the wild ones," said Maureen.

"Will sit for her." Doris pulled her cell phone from her jeans pocket and started swiping through the photos on her phone, holding them up for them all to admire. "See?"

The pictures were remarkable, thought Mercy, all beautifully lit and shot against a black matte background. There was a pale ginger kitten in pearls, a close-up of a majestic Maine coon with golden eyes, an adorable trio of sleeping calicos, twin tabbies peeking out of a basket, and a one-eyed Siamese in a ruff worthy of Queen Victoria.

Bea *was* talented. Mercy could see how these appealing pictures could help the Cat Ladies find even the most hard-to-place cats forever homes.

"These are great," said Troy.

Mercy could hear the relief in his voice. And she could feel her coloring returning to normal.

Saved by the Cat Ladies.

She smiled at Claude. "You all seem to have everything under control."

"We'll be fine as soon as we get that assistant. I'll hire one myself if I have to."

"And we'll do whatever needs to be done," said Doris.

"We need to get back," said her sister.

"To the phones," said Doris.

"There are still some animals that need picking up," said Bea.

"Thank you," said Mercy. "I know my grandmother appreciates it. We all appreciate it."

She gave the Cat Ladies each a hug and nodded at Bea. She watched the three of them go, grateful that her grandmother's patients were in such good hands. That was one less worry off her mind. But another popped up in its place right away.

"What about Patience's cats?"

"Don't know," said Claude. "No one has seen them. They must have scattered when the explosion hit."

"So we don't know if any of them were hurt." Patience had so many rescue cats, and it would break her heart if any had suffered. She'd blame herself, even though it wasn't her fault.

"We don't think so." Claude shook his head. "We haven't found any evidence of that. We think they're hiding in the main house."

"Let's hope so. It's freezing outside. What about the kittens left on the doorstep?"

"I don't know anything about any kittens," said Claude.

"Maybe they're hiding, too," said Troy.

"They were in a play yard in the kitchen."

"Susie Bear and I will help you find them."

Mercy kissed Claude on the cheek. "Thank you for all your help."

"*De rien.*" He snapped his fingers and the room zoomed back to life. The dogs scampered over to Claude, tails wagging. The chihuahuas chittered like angry birds as they careened around their little pen.

"Come on, Susie Bear," said Troy when the Newfie mutt balked at leaving her newfound canine friends behind in the Rufus Ruckus Room. "We're going to find some cats."

"You, too, Sunny," said Mercy.

That promise prompted the big dog to shamble along with the golden after Mercy and Troy. They left the hospital wing and entered Patience's kitchen. The room was much as it was before the explosion—no evidence of foul play here. She saw her Jeep keys on the island, next to the layer slicer. The Cat Ladies must have cleaned up the rest of the cake-making mess. Poor Patience. With her forearm in a cast, she wouldn't be doing much baking for a while. Her grandmother would have to find another way to deal with stress. Maybe yoga, Mercy thought. She and Elvis could share their practice with her.

Mercy pocketed her keys and looked around.

No kittens anywhere.

The play yard was askew, having fallen on its side.

"Let's search the rest of the house," said Troy.

At the sound of the word "search," Susie Bear was off. She ignored the hallway, which was cordoned off with crime scene tape, and headed straight upstairs. Sunny looked at Mercy.

"Go on," said Mercy, and the golden raced up the steps after the Newfie.

"What about me?"

"You, too. I want to stay down here. See if I can remember anything."

She watched as Troy charged up the stairs, two steps at a time. When he disappeared around the stairwell, she swiveled to face the blast site. There wasn't much to see. The parts of the walls, floor, and ceiling affected by the detonation of the pipe bomb had been removed by the investigators. Right down to the studs.

"I told you they took everything." Ed appeared at her side.

"They have to," said Mercy. "This is a crime scene at its most three-dimensional. Fragments of glass, bits of electronics, chemical residue—any and all evidence must be found and analyzed, no matter where it ends up." She waved her arms around the forlorn space. "And it can end up anywhere."

"Quite a job."

"Yeah, and it can take a while. Meanwhile, we have to keep Patience safe."

Ed frowned. "That won't be easy. You know how she is."

"That's why we need to nail this guy, the sooner the better." Mercy closed her eyes and tried to remember. *Nothing.* Her mind was protecting her from the memory, and she was probably asking for trouble by trying to retrieve it. Once she remembered, she might not be able to forget. The way she could never forget the day Martinez died and she got shot and Elvis got PTSD.

"What are you doing?"

She opened her eyes. "I'm trying to re-create the moments before the blast."

"Gotcha. I'll be right here if you need me."

Mercy smiled at that. Ed was good shelter. *He's the rock, the oak not to be wind-shaken.* She closed her eyes again and breathed deeply. In and out. In and out. In and out.

She pictured her grandmother at the kitchen island. She pictured herself, separating the eggs. The *rat a tat tat* of the door knocker, the black and gray kittens in the cardboard box on the porch, wrapped in the pale pink blanket. She saw herself bring in the kittens, put them in the play yard. She heard Elvis bark, her grandmother head toward the hallway as the knocker sounded again. She saw herself run for the door. There was Elvis in his alert position. Patience's hand on the knob. Her own voice, screaming. Elvis leaping. Patience tumbling. Light blinding. Darkness.

Her own voice, screaming.

Her eyes, wide open.

Her body, falling.

"It's okay."

She felt her cousin's strong arms steadying her as she teetered on the balls of her feet.

"I got you."

She closed her eyes again and leaned against Ed the Oak. Grateful that he was not Troy. And disappointed at the same time.

"Everything all right?" Troy stood at the edge of the crime scene tape, his arms full of squirming kittens.

"You found them." Mercy wriggled free of Ed and reached for the wayward inky black kitten crawling down Troy's shirtsleeve.

"Four here. Two more upstairs. Susie Bear and Sunny are standing guard."

"Six altogether. As it should be."

"Plus seven full-grown rescue cats," added Troy.

"That sounds about right," said Mercy. "We can call Patience and make sure."

"The Cat Ladies will take the kittens," said Ed. "Claude and I can handle Patience's cats."

"You can just put the kittens back in the box they came in." Mercy stopped short. "The box."

"What box?"

Mercy handed the black kitty to Ed. "Hold this. I'll be right back." She ran into Patience's kitchen, where she spotted the cardboard box in a corner by the recycling bin. The worn pink blanket was inside.

She took the box back to Troy. "Right before the pipe bomb was delivered, the kittens were delivered in this, covered with this blanket."

"By the same person? The bomber?"

"I don't know. But I know how we can find out."

CHAPTER ELEVEN

PATIENCE HAD ONE OF THOSE MOTION CAMERAS ON THE porch. So that she could see the people who left animals on her doorstep."

"I thought it was anonymous," said Troy. "I thought that was the whole point of the rescue drop-off station."

"It was," said Mercy. "It *is*. But in case anything goes wrong, she needs to be able to contact them. Like if the animals turn out to have rabies or some other communicable disease."

"Does that ever happen?" asked Ed.

"I don't know. But that's not the point. The point is, we should have film of whoever left those kittens on the porch."

"And whoever left the bomb." Troy grinned at her as he struggled to keep the kittens in his arms.

"Exactly," said Mercy, taking the little gray one from him, and stroking her.

"I'm confused," said Ed. "There's nothing left of the porch. The camera is long gone. Destroyed."

"I don't think that matters," said Mercy. "I think that it's one of those cameras that doesn't store images."

"It sends the images to the cloud." Troy grinned at her again. "Brilliant."

"I hope so."

"How long does the cloud store them?" asked Ed.

"I think it varies from camera to camera," said Troy. "Twenty-four hours? Forty-eight hours? Longer?"

"I don't know. If you're right, we may not have much time. So we need to find Patience's laptop and take it to her right now. See if those images are still there. And who is on them."

Troy frowned. "If you're right, then technically that laptop is evidence. As are any images on it. The same goes for the box and the blanket. We might be able to pull prints, DNA, and other forensics off them."

"You'll find my prints all over them," Mercy said.

"Harrington will love that."

"That's not good," said Ed, who'd had his own run-ins with Harrington at town meetings over budgets and building codes.

"You can turn it all over to Harrington as soon as we see what's on that film," Mercy said. "Promise."

She could see Troy weighing the options and considering the consequences of giving the evidence to Harrington later rather than sooner. "There may be nothing on it at all."

"The camera may not have been working," added Ed. "You know how fragile technology is."

Mercy smiled. She knew that Ed preferred his old-school tools over tech toys any day.

"Or the images may be so blurry we can't recognize anyone," Ed went on, warming to his subject. "Or maybe they wore a disguise."

"Okay, okay." Troy laughed. "We're getting a little ahead of ourselves here."

"Troy's right. Let's set these kittens up in the play yard in the kitchen and then we can figure this out."

Together they all marched back to Patience's kitchen, armed with kittens. Mercy righted the play yard with one hand and placed her little gray kitten inside with the other. Ed and Troy deposited their kittens in the pen, too. For a moment they all watched the feline cuties scamper all over each other.

"I'll get the last two," she said, and trudged up the stairs. She could hear Troy on her heels, his boots heavy on the treads. At the top of the landing, a long antique church pew with a burgundy velvet cushion sat in front of a tall window. Mercy counted seven cats curled up there, nose to nose and tail to tail, snoring lightly.

Patience's rescue cats. But no kittens. She turned to look at Troy.

"First room on the right," he said.

Patience's bedroom. A lovely long room that ran the length of the house, with high ceilings, light sage-colored walls, and a pale pink marble fireplace. When Mercy was a girl, she'd sneak into the big four-poster cherry bed on stormy nights and sleep with her grandmother, safe and snug under down comforters covered in pink raw silk. Patience would rub her back and sing James Taylor songs in her sweet mezzo-soprano voice until Mercy fell asleep. She could understand why the kittens had found refuge here in this room, just as she had when she was small.

Susie Bear lay on the parquet floor at the foot of the bed, her colossal head out of view, plumed tail thudding away. Sunny stretched out beside the Newfie, head also under the bed, tail still.

"I guess they're under the bed," said Mercy.

Troy grinned. "Good guess."

Mercy lowered her sore body slowly to the floor, lying on her belly, and looked under the high bedframe. There she spotted one gray kitten and one black kitten knitted together like yin and yang, asleep, up near the head of the bed, their tails tucked against the tall stacked white baseboard. She scooted toward them, wrapping her arms together in a large circle and catching the kittens in its center. She pulled the dozing babies toward her, and carefully moved back out from under the bed.

"Success," she said, as Susie Bear and Sunny sniffed at the kittens to make sure they were all right. "That's good," she told the dogs, gathering the little felines in her arms and allowing Troy to help her to her feet.

"Nice room," Troy said, as he closed the door behind them and they started down the stairs.

"Yes." Mercy thought of those summer storms and "Sweet Baby James."

WITH THE KITTENS romping in the play yard, and Ed watching over them until the Cat Ladies arrived to find them forever homes, Mercy resumed her search for Patience's laptop. She found it on her desk in her office under a stack of billings, right where she always kept it. She promised Claude she'd bring it right back, since it was the computer her grandmother used for the veterinary office as well.

Although Patience would need a new one now, a desktop version that the new assistant could access, too. Like it or not, she was going to have to make some changes. Allow other people into her world, permanently. It occurred to Mercy that she and her grandmother were very much alike—and not always in the best ways. Why was it that the advice she was so tempted to give to others was always the advice she loathed to hear herself?

"Remember to tell the Cat Ladies to save the big black one for me to give to Mr. Horgan," she told Claude as they prepared to leave. He'd left the dogs in the Rufus Ruckus Room and stood by the back entrance, personally escorting Mercy and Troy out of the clinic.

"Will do," Claude said. "And you be sure to tell me what you find out."

"I'm sure Patience will tell you herself."

"Don't be so sure." Claude sounded tired, and Mercy wondered if all this drama was wearing him out. He seemed suddenly sadder and older.

"She doesn't like to tell me anything that might encourage me to worry about her," he said. "Or God forbid, to help her."

"You're helping her now," said Troy quietly.

"And the Cat Ladies and Bea Garcia."

"It took a broken bone for that to happen." Claude sighed, and in that sigh, Mercy heard more than fatigue and frustration, she heard resignation.

She wished her grandmother would just marry the guy already. "She's very independent."

"There's a difference between independence and isolation," Claude said.

Mercy had never thought of her grandmother as isolated. "But she has lots of friends and family. She has you."

"She doesn't have me, not really. She won't have me. She won't have anyone. That would mean letting us do for her the way she does for us."

"I never thought of it that way."

"No, you wouldn't."

Troy smiled.

"What's so funny?"

"Nothing."

Claude took her gently by the shoulders. "Think about it. You don't want to make the same mistake."

Mercy flushed. "I'd better get this laptop over to Patience." The sooner she got away from the well-meaning Claude, the better. She fished her keys out of her pocket.

Troy stepped forward and she avoided his concerned glance. "We'll give you a ride."

"No need."

"You shouldn't be driving," said Claude.

"I'm fine."

"Don't make me call your grandmother," said Claude. "Or your mother."

She knew he was only half kidding. And she was barely holding the weariness that threatened to overtake her at bay. She may as well surrender graciously. "Okay, but no fair bringing my mother into it."

Claude laughed. He was still laughing when she and Troy followed Susie Bear and Sunny out to the truck.

THE RIDE TO her cabin was mercifully quiet. Troy seemed to understand that she wasn't in the mood to talk. He kept his eyes on the road and she stared out of the window. It was tough driving this time of year; frost heaves and salt and sand battered the roadways and you had to watch out for the patches of black ice hiding in the mix of gray mushy snow and mud that splattered the ground. The early evening sky was gray-white, too, that full-of-snow color that meant a winter storm was on the way.

The truck bounced along and they sat in silence, the only sound the thumping of Susie Bear's tail and the huffing and puffing of her breath on Mercy's neck. She tried not to think about Troy and Madeline and his divorce, and her bereavement, and Wesley Hallett and Elvis, and the fact that someone had tried to kill her grandmother, one of the best people she knew and the one human on earth besides Martinez who really loved her for who she really was.

She tried not to think at all. Just waited for the snow to fall—and when it began, slowly at first, in big fat flakes that shone in the head-lights, she realized that she was caught in this snow globe of a pickup truck with a good-looking game warden and his friendly dog, a Hall-mark happily-ever-after movie waiting to begin—if she believed in happily-ever-afters. Which she didn't.

It was a long ride, if only in her mind, and she was relieved when Troy finally pulled into the long driveway that led up the hill to her cabin. Elvis was waiting for her. She could see his handsome profile in the window, a dark shadow with triangular ears that disappeared the moment he recognized the sound of Troy's Ford F-150 and aban-doned the window seat for the front door. She didn't know what she'd do if he weren't there waiting for her.

"Elvis isn't going anywhere," said Troy.

Startling her out of her thoughts. And unsettling her as it always did when she caught him reading her mind. "I hope you're right."

She grabbed the laptop and scrambled out of his truck as soon as he switched off the engine, stumbling through the newly fallen snow in her mother's fancy ankle boots. The temperature was dropping as the sun slipped behind the mountains and the snow intensified. She threw open the door, stepped inside, unzipped the boots, kicked them off and under the window seat. Then she fell to her knees and hugged Elvis, who favored her with a rare lick of a kiss and then placed his muzzle on her shoulder. She inspected him from head to tail, and he seemed no worse for the wear by his brush with death. He licked her cheek again, and then wiggled out of her arms to greet Susie Bear and Sunny, knowing they were just outside.

"Come on in," she yelled.

Troy, the Newfie, and the golden blasted into the cabin on a burst of cold air and wet flurries.

"Go on through." She came to her feet and followed them into the great room, where she found her grandmother seated next to her mother on the couch by the fireplace. Her father was stoking the fire. Elvis, Susie Bear, and Sunny made the rounds, getting good belly rubs from everyone but her mother, who ignored them.

Mercy kissed each of her loved ones on the cheek in turn, while Troy said his hellos. Her mother greeted the game warden stiffly, but her father was gracious as always.

Everyone loved him; Duncan Carr had the gift of making you feel like you were the only person in the room. Even Mercy felt this glow, although as his daughter she knew that her mother was the only person in the room for him, as he was in return for her. They were one of those couples who created their own orbit; it was their own little world and everybody else was just, well, everybody else.

Mercy sat on the floor by the sofa close to her grandmother. "Are you okay?"

"I'm fine." Patience knocked on her neon-pink cast with her other hand. "You'll have to sign this thing. Draw a flower or something."

"Sure."

"You, too," Patience said to Troy, and then addressed Mercy. "How about you? Are you okay?"

"I'm fine."

"You're both delusional," said Grace. "Duncan, say something."

"Fine is in the eye of the beholder." Her father winked at Mercy when he thought her mother wasn't looking.

"You're as bad as they are," said Grace.

Mercy ignored the exchange to focus on her grandmother. "You still have that camera on the porch, right?"

Patience shrugged. "Well, I did until that pipe bomb went off."

"So you can go online and check the footage from yesterday." She handed her the laptop.

Patience stared at her for a moment. Her eyes brightened when she realized what Mercy meant. She took Mercy's face in her free hand. "You are a genius."

"Let's see if it works first," she said.

No one spoke as her grandmother balanced the computer on her knees, punched on her computer, went online, and signed onto the website—all with one hand.

"It's here," she said.

Everyone gathered around Patience as she fast-forwarded through the footage to that recording yesterday afternoon. She hit PLAY and up popped Patience's porch and lawn, as seen from the high corner of the porch ceiling to the left of the front door. There were Mercy and Elvis, Patience letting them into the house. Then nothing until a slender figure in jeans and a hoodie approached the porch, holding a cardboard box in gloved hands. Sitting the box down and knocking quickly, then bolting down the hill.

"The kittens," said Mercy.

"Looks like a young man," said her father.

"Unremarkable clothing," added her mother. "Not helpful."

"And he's wearing gloves," Patience pointed out. "Maybe to avoid fingerprints."

"Or maybe he's just cold," said Mercy.

"He must have parked down the hill on the side of the road," said her father. "Route 7 is always busy that time of day. Maybe someone saw him. Or the vehicle."

"Harrington should have officers canvassing the neighborhood," said Troy. "This could help."

They continued to watch. Another figure came into view from the other side of the frame, this one shorter and stockier than the last, wearing dark ski clothes and gloves. Face hidden by a balaclava. Carrying another cardboard box, similar to the first. The figure bent over the box, blocking the view from the camera. Rising up and sprinting to the right and out of sight. A flash of light and then nothing.

"That's it," said Patience.

"Did you recognize him?" asked Troy.

"I don't know," said Patience.

"Do you think it could be George Rucker?"

"I haven't seen the man in twenty years," said Patience. "I thought he was taller. It was a very long time ago."

"How tall is Rocky Simko?" Mercy asked Troy.

Troy checked his phone. "Simko is the ex-con we believe helped Rucker escape. Says here he's five-seven, one sixty-five pounds." He held up his phone to show Simko's mugshot, an unflattering picture of a man in his early thirties with a tattoo of the word *Skins* high on his forehead.

"George Rucker was around six feet, I'd say," said Patience triumphantly.

"This could still be Simko."

"Impossible to imagine George Rucker with friends like that. I just can't believe that he could be behind this. Such a mild-mannered man."

"He's a murderer, Mother," said Grace.

Patience frowned. Whether at Grace calling Rucker a murderer or calling her "Mother" was anyone's guess. But Mercy suspected both annoyed her. She knew that her grandmother preferred to be called Patience by everyone, and that included her own children and grandchildren. She'd always honored that preference, but her mother honored it only when she cared to—and she hardly ever cared to when she was unhappy with Patience. Like now.

Mercy looked over Troy's shoulder as he pulled out his phone and tapped, bringing up the mug shot of Rucker on the All Points Bulletin issued when he escaped from prison. The middle-aged man in the photo looked tired and tough. He had a square face with a short salt-and-pepper buzz cut, deep circles under his dark eyes, and what looked like a Celtic tattoo on his neck.

Troy passed the cell phone around so everyone could see Rucker's photo. "Good memory, Patience. According to this, Rucker is five-eleven, one eighty-five pounds."

"He certainly looks like a murderer," said Grace. "Then as now."

"More now," said her father. "Prison life has not been kind to him."

"Of course it hasn't," said Patience. "He doesn't belong there."

"Well, he's not there now," said Grace dryly.

"He belongs in an institution. He's not a well man."

"I'll say." Grace rolled her eyes. "He killed your husband and maybe just blew up your house."

"That was not George Rucker. And he did not plan to kill Red. He just snapped. Up until the day he killed your father, he had never committed a violent act in his life."

"Even if that's true, people change in prison," said her father.

"Mild-mannered men do not survive incarceration for very long. He's survived two decades. He's not the same man you knew."

Troy had borrowed the laptop and was watching the footage from Patience's porch again. "Definitely two different people. The one dropping off the kittens seems too young to be Rucker."

"And the one with the bomb is too short."

"But it could be Simko."

"If they were male," said her father.

"Looks like males to me," said her mother. "The way they walk, the way they run, the way they carry themselves."

"Maybe the techs can tell us more," said Troy.

"Either way, it's clear that the bomber used the distraction of the kittens and the rescue drop-off to his advantage," said her father.

"Agreed," said Troy. "He was definitely watching."

"Which begs the question," said her father, "was Patience the intended target?"

"What do you mean?" Grace's voice was unnaturally high. "It was her house."

"But Mercy answered the first knock," said Troy. "She got the kittens."

"If he were watching—and we think he was—then he would have known it was Mercy answering the door the first time, and so he might assume that she'd answer it the second time."

"If it's Rucker," said Troy, "and if he wants revenge, he may not care who gets hurt, as long as it's someone related to Red."

"What George Rucker wanted was his wife back," said Patience. "It's all he's ever wanted."

"Did he ever look for her?" asked Mercy.

"She sent him a postcard from Las Vegas," said Patience. "All it said was something like, 'I'm not coming back. Get over it. XOXO Ruby.'"

"That's brutal," said Mercy. She avoided looking at Troy, whose own wife, Madeline, had done something similar to him when she'd run off with the orthopedist from Florida. But Madeline had come back, after all.

"It was a poor match from the start," said Grace. "That woman was never going to be happy with George Rucker. Or with life in Lamoille County."

"What ever happened to her?" asked Mercy.

"That's what Harrington is trying to find out." Troy gave the laptop back to her grandmother. "They think she could lead them to Rucker."

"If he's still obsessed with Ruby," said Mercy.

"His cellmate in Mississippi believed he was," said Troy. "He told the authorities that he never stopped talking about her."

"Then why come after you?" Mercy asked her grandmother.

"George believed that your grandfather was having an affair with Ruby," said Patience. "It was ridiculous."

Grace rolled her eyes again and Patience slapped at her hand. "It *was* ridiculous. Red was no angel, but he was no cheater, either. And even if he were, he would never have cheated on me with a woman like that."

"Why did she marry George?" asked Mercy.

"They met in Las Vegas," said Patience. "That's where she was from. George was kind of cute in a baby-faced poor little rich boy kind of way. He worshiped her, and he had money. I think she figured once she married him, she could talk him into moving back home to Las Vegas, or New York or L.A. Anywhere more glamorous than upstate Vermont."

"But George wouldn't leave," said Grace. "His family was in real estate; they were tied to Vermont."

"Look, it was clear she was unhappy," said Patience. "She wanted out of her marriage and she wanted out of Lamoille County."

"And so she took off," said Mercy.

"Yes. It had nothing to do with your grandfather."

"How can you be so sure?" asked Grace. "The rumors were fierce. And where there's smoke . . ." She let her voice trail off.

"Your father was good at keeping secrets," Patience told Grace. "He could have had another family in New Hampshire or Maine or Quebec and I would never have known about it. But he never would have fooled around in his own jurisdiction. Too risky."

"Don't poop where you eat," said Mercy.

"Exactly."

"That was one of Grandpa Red's favorite expressions," Mercy told Troy.

"Only he preferred the more colorful version," said her father. He cleared his throat. Mercy knew that meant he was about to change the subject. For her mother's sake, because he understood that all this talk with Patience about her grandfather's possible infidelity was making his wife uncomfortable. Her father hated seeing Grace uncomfortable. "The bomber took pains to disguise himself. Maybe he knew about the camera."

"Or maybe he just didn't want to take the chance of being recognized," said Troy.

"If it were Rucker, Patience may have recognized him," said her father. "Even all these years later."

This was a conversation going nowhere, Mercy thought. Or maybe she was just tired. The explosion catching up with her. She closed her eyes for a minute, and felt her mother's cool fingers on her forehead.

"You feel warm," Grace said. "You should have something to eat and drink and go to bed."

"I'm fine, really."

"I don't think so." Grace rose to her feet. "Let me make you something." She fixed a stern prosecutor's gaze on the others. "She needs her rest. And you do, too, Mother."

"Absolutely right," said her father. "Troy, maybe you could drop Patience off at Lillian Jenkins's house. She and Claude are staying there."

"Sure."

"Thank you, Troy. We'll hang out here with Mercy."

"That's not necessary, Dad." The last thing she needed was her mother hovering over her. "Are you staying at the Athena?" The Athena was a five-star historic hotel and spa complex, the most luxurious in Northshire, where her parents invariably stayed when they were in town.

Her father nodded, but it was her mother who spoke. "We insist."

"Amy and Brodie and Helena should be back soon," said Mercy. "I won't be alone."

"They won't be much help, if any." Her mother set a glass of milk and a plate holding a peanut butter and jelly sandwich in front of her.

Mercy smiled. Her mother wasn't much of a cook—she couldn't be bothered with domestic tasks—but she made a very good peanut butter and jelly sandwich. And all of a sudden, Mercy was starving.

Elvis and Susie Bear and Sunny hurried over to sit at her feet in the hope of a bite. But she wasn't sharing. She finished off the sandwich quickly and washed it down with the milk while they all watched her. Even the dogs. Especially the dogs.

"Okay, I ate my dinner. You can go home now."

"We'll stay until your roommates come home," said Grace firmly.

Her mother insisted on calling Amy and Helena her roommates, even though they were more like family. But her mother would never understand that. Family was blood, and that was that.

"The rest of you go on," said Grace.

"*Everyone* go on," Mercy said. "I've got my Elvis and my Beretta. That's all I need."

CHAPTER TWELVE

IN THE END THEY ALL LEFT, IF UNDER CONSIDERABLE PROTEST.
As she listened to the last rumble of their vehicles fade away,
Mercy slipped her firearm under a pillow and cuddled up on her side
at her end of the couch. Elvis took his usual place at the other end,
his head on her feet. The little kitten Muse jumped up onto the sofa
and curled up in the curve of Mercy's legs. Sunny curled up on Elvis's
unused dog bed on the other side of the room. Her bed now.

Mercy closed her eyes. The only sounds now were the crackle of
the fire, the rattle of sleet hitting the windows, and the faint purring
of the cat.

Peace and quiet, she thought. At least for now.

Amy, Brodie, and Helena were due back sometime this evening.
She wanted to stay awake long enough to greet them when they
returned home—and to fill them in. She hadn't yet told them about
the incidents of the past forty-eight hours, but they were bound to
hear sooner or later. She wanted them to hear it from her.

The local news had gotten wind of the explosion, and pestered
Patience for an interview she was unlikely ever to give. But no reporters had shown up at Mercy's cabin, and as it was the weekend the
news hadn't been picked up by the Boston media yet. Amy and Brodie might not have heard anything. She hoped not. She didn't want
them worrying any more than necessary.

But it was getting late and she was tired and despite the fact that she'd apparently spent much of the past twenty-four hours asleep, she felt herself dozing off. "Goodnight, Elvis," she said. "Goodnight, Muse. Goodnight, Sunny."

And she allowed herself to drift off to sleep. George Rucker and August Pitts be damned.

SHE WASN'T SURE what woke her. The abrupt departure of Elvis from the couch. The screech of the kitten and the knit of her tiny claws on Mercy's blanketed knees. The whimpering of Sunny across the room. The creak of the front door opening and the deep growl of a guard dog ready to pounce.

She grabbed the Beretta from under her pillow and ran to the front of the cabin, colliding with a figure clothed in black, wearing a bala-clava mask. The force of the blow rocked her and she staggered, her legs slipping out from under her. She fell backwards, her head spin-ning. She heard Sunny barking like a hellhound on fire. She watched the guy grab a box of the deputy's files from the old farm table as if through a kaleidoscope.

Mercy tried to catch herself, grabbing at the wall with her free hand to steady herself. Too late. She went down, banging the back of her skull. Her arms slammed to her sides.

The gun skittered from her fingers and across the wide pine planks toward the intruder.

He caught sight of it, swiveled the box to his left hip, and bent down. He reached for the gun with one hand, steadying the box with the other. Elvis leapt at his outstretched arm, and slammed his strong jaws shut around it. Crunching the guy's wrist.

The intruder cursed, dropping the box. Files scattered like marbles. He swung at the shepherd with his free arm, punching his dark muz-zle with his fist and kicking his belly with his steel-toed boots. The dog did not let go.

"Hold on, Elvis," Mercy shouted over Sunny's incessant yowling. She struggled to her knees, crawling toward the gun, which lay at the edge of the wall about a yard away.

Elvis yanked harder, pulling the man toward the floor. The intruder was losing the fight and he knew it. On his way down he grabbed at the nearest chair and thrust it down at Elvis, smashing the shepherd's nose.

Mercy was within inches of the gun now. She jerked forward and curled her fingers around the grip of the gun.

Elvis yelped, losing his grip on the guy's wrist.

The man bolted for the front door. Mercy heaved herself up and yelled, "Stop!"

He kept on running. Elvis bounded after him. Sunny sprinted after them both.

"Down!" she shouted at the dogs.

The shepherd dropped to the floor, his growl now a low and angry whimper. Sunny came to a dead stop, too, crawling toward Elvis. Mercy took her first shot just as the guy tore out of the house, slamming the door behind him. Slowing the bullet down long enough for him to get away.

Mercy rushed forward, throwing open the door and tripping the porch light. She ran out into the dark through the yard to the lighted flagpole. She stared out into the night under the pool of light illuminating the Stars and Stripes. Ahead of her, nothing but the murky glow of the icy snow-covered hill curving down to the road hidden below. Behind her, nothing but the hulking shadows of the forest beyond the small patch of light that was her cabin. Above her, nothing but Martinez's flag framed by countless stars and the silver sliver of a waning moon.

The intruder was gone.

Somewhere in the distance she heard the rumble of an engine. *I should run down the driveway, try to catch him,* she thought, but her body was slow to react. She started down the hill, skidding on the snow. She felt her knees buckle, and she sank onto the ground.

I'm ruining my mother's pants, she thought, as she rolled onto her back, sprawling in the snow. She lay there, looking up at the midnight sky, as the stars slowly faded away to nothing.

"WHAT ARE YOU doing out here? It's freezing."

Mercy felt the sting of a sharp slap across her cheek. She opened her eyes to see Amy crouched beside her. Brodie stood above her, a sleeping baby Helena in his arms. Elvis flanked her, his head on her left shoulder. Sunny was curled up on her right side, tucked in by Mercy's knees.

"Take the baby in, Brodie," ordered Amy. "Put her in her crib and then come back out and we'll carry Mercy in together."

The thought of two teenagers lugging her along through the snow as their deadweight motivated Mercy to sit up. Elvis licked her cheek, Sunny licked her frozen fingers, and Amy hugged her. "You're alive!"

"Yes, I'm alive." She wondered how long she'd been out here. Her feet felt like frozen boats. Her right hand, too. Her left hand seemed fine, maybe because her left arm was tucked under Elvis's torso. He'd been keeping her warm, she realized. Saving her once again.

And Sunny, following suit.

"Do you know this dog?"

"That's Sunny."

"Tell me later. Can you get up? Let me help." Amy grabbed her by the elbows and guided her to a standing position.

Mercy stamped her clodhopper feet, grateful for her Darn Tough wool socks, which were probably all that stood between her and frostbite.

Brodie came out of the house. "What happened in there?"

"Long story," said Mercy.

"First things first. Brodie, we need to get her inside."

"Right."

The two teenagers flanked her, holding her under her arms and supporting her as she hobbled onto the porch and into the cabin. She collapsed onto her lovely couch. Amy helped her out of her clothes and into her warmest cashmere pajamas, another gift from her mother, one of the few she actually wore. Amy slipped a snug pair of Darn Tough socks over her cold feet and a pair of brightly colored wool mittens Patience had knitted for her last Christmas over her frigid fingers. Then Amy wrapped her in every quilt she could find, and Elvis settled at her feet, his handsome head warming her toes. Sunny was back in the dog bed, snoring lightly.

"Brodie is making you a cup of Earl Grey tea."

"Thank you," she said simply, thinking of Claude's admonition earlier that day. She'd sent her parents and Troy and her grandmother away and look what had happened. She should let Amy and Brodie take care of her.

"How long were you out there?" Amy perched on the coffee table, observing her carefully.

"I don't know. Not very long, I don't think, or I'd be suffering from hypothermia."

"Or frostbite."

"Or frostbite." She'd been very lucky that Amy and Brodie had shown up when they did. "What time is it?"

"It's nearly nine o'clock."

"I believe it was around eight-thirty when the intruder broke in."

"That explains the mess." Brodie handed her the tea. He'd poured it into the biggest mug she owned, the one with the bear and Exit, Pursued by a Bear emblazoned on it. She could feel the heat even through the thick woolen mittens. It felt amazingly good.

She told them about the break-in, which only prompted more questions on their part. "Sorry, I forgot you've missed all of the excitement. But before I fill you in on everything, we need to check Elvis's nose. The bastard hit him with a chair."

"Keep your hands in those mittens. Drink your tea. I'll do it." Amy was only eighteen but she'd taken to mothering like a loon to diving—and had mastered the bossy-because-I-love-you maternal voice like a pro.

Amy examined the patient shepherd's muzzle, checking it thoroughly under the bright cell phone light that Brodie provided without her prompting. He was learning to be a good caregiver, too. Elvis, for his part, sat there calmly and allowed Amy's examination without complaint. Mercy was proud of them all. And relieved that Elvis appeared to be all right.

"No blood. No broken skin. His nose seems fine. His teeth look okay, too." Amy petted Elvis one last time. "Rest, boy."

"We'll have Claude check him over tomorrow," said Mercy.

"Claude?" Amy looked at Mercy. "You'd better start at the beginning, if you're up to it."

"I'm up to it." Mercy nodded. "We're going to need more tea." She reached over to scratch the sweet spot between Elvis's ears. He closed his eyes and she kept on stroking the fur on his neck until he started snoring lightly. The bass to Sunny's contralto.

Brodie carried an old silver tray holding her grandmother's Old English Rose bone-china teapot, some napkins, and a plate of ham sandwiches he'd made for everyone—ham sandwiches being the one thing he could make well, thanks to her larder full of Harrington's ham and Vermont cheddar and Gérard sourdough—and placed the tray on the coffee table in front of the sofa.

He and Amy curled up together across from her and Elvis, in the butter-colored leather love seat she'd bought to match her couch when it became obvious that she'd need more seating now that Brodie would be hanging around for the foreseeable future.

"Eat." Amy pointed to the sandwiches. "You really need to eat something."

"Okay." She knew Amy was right. It seemed a lifetime ago that her mother had made her that peanut butter and jelly sandwich. She took three napkins and three sandwiches, keeping one on a napkin for herself and placing the other on a napkin near Elvis. Mid-snore, the shepherd opened his eyes and nudged the sandwich with his nose, grabbing it and gobbling it down in two big bites. Licking his chops, he closed his eyes again and went back to sleep. She wrapped the third sandwich in the last napkin and asked Brodie to take it to Sunny. He left it lying on the napkin on the dog bed by her muzzle. Sooner or later Sunny would awaken to a treat.

Mercy nibbled at her sandwich as she told Amy and Brodie about Pitts and the cold case, Patience, and the pipe bomb.

"You should have called us," said Amy. "We would have come right back."

"There was nothing you could have done."

"But we're like, like *family*." Amy flushed and looked away.

"I didn't want to ruin your weekend." Mercy realized that she'd hurt Amy's feelings. She looked at Brodie, who shook his head. "And it could have been dangerous. It might still be."

"Family sticks together," said Amy. "Your parents are here. Claude is here." She crossed her arms across her chest. "We're here. And we're not going anywhere."

Maybe Claude was right, and she was too much like her grandmother. Maybe she needed to let people help her. For their sake as well as for hers.

"We *are* like family," she told Amy. "You're the little sister I always wanted."

Amy beamed and Mercy smiled back. "Thank you for being here."

"You're welcome. That's what family is for." Amy cuddled with Brodie. "Right, Brodie?"

"Right." Brodie kissed her on the forehead.

They were sweet together, Amy and Brodie. He drove Mercy a little crazy with his unerring knack for stating the obvious, but he genuinely adored Amy and Helena and treated them both with kindness and affection. Amy could count on him, and that was a good thing.

"You need to tell Troy about the break-in," said Amy.

"I will." Mercy knew Amy was right, but she hesitated.

"When?"

"First thing tomorrow."

Amy gave her the same look she gave little Helena when she wouldn't settle down for a nap.

"Promise."

"Why do you always push him away? You know he likes you."

"And you like him," added Brodie.

Mercy ignored that. "If I tell him now, he'll insist on coming over, calling the captain, getting forensics over here, the works." She gathered the quilts more closely around her. "It's been quite a night. I just want to go to bed."

"He'll be very upset if you don't tell him right away." Amy sat up abruptly, leaning forward. "It's the right thing to do."

"He should know," agreed Brodie. "He's like family, too."

CHAPTER THIRTEEN

B RODIE INSISTED ON STAYING THE NIGHT. TO PROTECT HIS girls, he said, and Mercy bit back a smile. He was a good kid, but how good he'd be in an actual fight was yet to be determined. Mercy hoped they'd never have to find out.

Amy and Brodie refused to go to bed until she contacted Troy. They watched from the love seat as she sat cross-legged on the couch and texted Troy, telling him what happened and asking him to check on her grandmother and her parents. She wasn't up to talking to her mother right now.

He called immediately.

"Are you sure you're all right?"

"I'm fine. We're all fine. But the guy is hurting." She told him how Elvis took the guy down. "He's got an injured hand, if not a broken wrist."

"Good for Elvis. I'll talk to Thrasher. Get a forensics team over there."

"Nothing to find. He wore gloves and a mask."

"Let us be the judge of that."

There was no arguing with him.

"Please wait until morning. We're all exhausted here."

"Understood. But meanwhile we'll get a uniform to watch your place."

"Not necessary. I've got Elvis and my Beretta. And Sunny." She told him how good the golden was at raising the alarm about intruders with her frenzied barking, even if she didn't go after them the way Elvis did. That was, after all, the fierce Malinois's job, and he was very good at it.

Troy didn't say anything, and she knew he was not convinced. "It couldn't hurt to have a uniform drive by if they're in the neighborhood," she conceded. Not that her cabin was even in a neighborhood per se. Unless you counted the woods.

"I'll talk to Thrasher."

"Thanks. I would feel a lot better if I knew Patience was safe."

"Roger that."

She slipped the phone into the pocket of her pajamas and looked over at Amy and Brodie. "We may as well all go to bed."

"What about the mess?" asked Amy.

"We'll leave it for forensics."

"You promise you'll go to bed, too." Amy squared her fists on her hips.

"I am not leaving this couch."

"Okay." Amy frowned as if she were not convinced. She hovered over Mercy, plumping the pillows and tucking the quilts more tightly around her before kissing the top of her head as if she were a child. "Try to get some sleep."

"Yes, Mom," said Mercy.

The teenager rolled her eyes and tugged at Brodie's shirt.

"Goodnight," he said, and together the young couple disappeared down the hall to the room Amy shared with little Helena.

Mercy and Elvis stayed right there on the sofa as promised. She was nice and warm now. The shepherd was comfortable, too, dropping off to dreamland as soon as he knew she was serious about getting some shut-eye. Sunny was already asleep across the room in Elvis's abandoned doggie bed.

Poor Sunny, thought Mercy. The golden retriever had led a much quieter life with August Pitts. She might not be cut out for life with her and Elvis. Their life was much more adventurous. If not downright dangerous, as Wesley Hallett would no doubt say.

She tried to go to sleep herself, but she found herself wide awake. Maybe it was all that tea.

Or maybe it was those files on the old farm table. She replayed the scene with the intruder in her mind. Initially, she thought he was just using the box of files as a shield to get away from Elvis, but she might be wrong. Maybe the files were what he was after all along. He could have thought the cabin was empty if the last time he'd seen her had been at Patience's house, and her Jeep was still there. There were no cars parked at the cabin when he'd broken in; maybe he thought no one was home. Maybe he didn't want anyone to be home. He hadn't been armed, so he wasn't expecting a confrontation. And he wasn't setting off another pipe bomb.

There must be a reason he was after those files. Mercy untangled herself from the tumult of quilts and went to the kitchen, stepping around the files scattered all over the floor and pulling a pair of plastic gloves from the stash she kept in a bottom drawer. She put them on, and then sat down on the floor, carefully going through each folder before putting it back where it had fallen. She knew wearing gloves would only mollify the crime scene techs so much, but she wanted to get a good look at the files before they showed up.

There were the usual documents: the original missing persons report filed by Beth Kilgore's father, photographs, witness statements, including the ones from Kilgore's drinking buddies and family members from both sides confirming when and where they'd last seen her and her husband, and a couple of sightings that went nowhere. Since there was no body and no crime scene, there was only so much data. Still, overall, her grandfather had put together as thorough and comprehensive a case file as possible given the paucity of information.

Seeing her Grandpa Red's notes in his bold handwriting took her back to her childhood. Her grandfather was your classic Vermont outdoorsman; he'd taught her to swim and ski and snowshoe, shoot with rifle and bow, identify local flora and fauna, track two-legged and four-legged creatures through the forest. They'd gone ice fishing in the winter and fly fishing in the summer, jet skiing in warm weather and snowmobiling in cold weather, hiking through the Green Mountains in every season. She owed much of who she grew up to be to those early years of her childhood. The years with Grandpa Red.

She thought he would have approved of her life as a soldier and military police officer. He would have loved Elvis; he loved a good dog and trained his own hunting dogs. Pointers, mostly, but she remembered a sweet Weimaraner named Baron and a rambunctious vizsla named Copper, too. She wished he were here to help her decide what to do about Hallett. About Troy. About her life.

No time to think about that now. There were still more boxes to sort through, the ones left undisturbed during her scuffle with the intruder. It was getting cold on the floor, so she dragged the remaining boxes over to the sofa and settled back into the quilts. The Malinois slept on.

She started to read.

The files in the next box were mostly background on Beth and her father, Clem, Thomas Kilgore, and his family. News clippings and court documents outlining Clem's many drunk-and-disorderly arrests, along with two DUIs, one resisting-arrest charge, and three counts of poaching. Only the poaching charges stuck. Thomas Kilgore's record was not much better; he was by all these accounts a drinker and a gambler who spent most of his time drunk and broke and looking for an easy score. Seemed like Clem had simply chosen a younger and meaner version of himself to be his only child's husband.

There wasn't much about Beth Kilgore herself. There were a few photos: Beth at seventeen as the smiling president of the French Hill High School Book Club, Beth as a shy bride in a simple white empire-style dress with a scoop neckline and lace cap sleeves holding a bouquet of wildflowers, Beth standing awkwardly with her hulk of a husband, Thomas, in front of the double-wide up in Marvin, squinting into the sun. Mercy wondered who had taken this photograph, which substantiated what Patience had told her about the place. It was a dump. She tried to imagine what it would be like living in that trailer married to that man. She bet she'd had more fun in Afghanistan.

She looked again, this time studying Beth's face. From the time she'd gotten married to the time this Marvin photo was taken, she'd had her nose broken. Her devoted husband showing his deep affection for her, no doubt.

Beth Kilgore had led a very small life. And a very short one, if her grandfather had been right about her fate.

She'd found nothing that supported Red's claim, at least not so far. But she still had a couple of boxes to go. She pulled the empty box toward her, the better to repack the files. She lifted the first stack of files and straightened them. Leaning forward to replace them, she spotted something tucked in the corner, one edge sticking to the side. She'd nearly missed it. She set the files down on the floor under the coffee table and retrieved the card from the box.

It was a postcard of the Las Vegas Strip in Nevada. The brightly colored illustration captured the long line of casinos from the Luxor and the Hacienda at one end of Las Vegas Boulevard, to the Stratosphere at the other end. Mercy had only been to Las Vegas once, with her parents years ago when she was a teenager. They'd stayed at Caesars Palace, where her parents were attending a lawyers' conference. Mercy was left on her own most of the time. She was too young to gamble, not that she would have found playing the slots much fun anyway, and it was 110 degrees, too hot for anything but swimming. She'd spent most of the time cooling off at the casino's biggest pool, watching her fellow tourists take pictures and wishing she were back home in the mountains of Vermont.

She flipped the card over, to the address side. There she found a note written in metallic gold ink that read: *Hello from Sin City. Glad to be home. Don't look for me. It's over. XOXO Ruby.* Under the signature someone had planted a kiss in what was once bright red lipstick. The lips were just a faded smooch now.

The postmark was dated Las Vegas, Nevada, August 5, 2000. The card was addressed to George Rucker, care of Rucker Realty on Main Street in Peace Junction, Vermont.

Nice, thought Mercy. Ruby didn't send her *Dear George* letter in an envelope to her husband's home address, she dumped him on a postcard for the world to see, and mailed it to his family's business, where all his relatives would witness his humiliation up close and personal.

Mercy stared at Ruby's girly handwriting, with its loops and whirls and hearts dotting the i's. This was the demeaning missive that drove George Rucker to drink, to madness, to thoughts of suicide—and, ultimately, to murder. She felt bad for George, but she felt worse for her grandfather.

She placed the postcard on the coffee table in front of her. *One of these things is not like the others,* she thought. This last recorded communication between Ruby and George did not belong in Beth Kilgore's missing persons case file.

So why was it here? Her grandfather must have put it in here for a reason. Her grandfather may not have been quite the man she thought he was, if the rumors of his affair with Ruby were true, but he was a first-rate sheriff. He was not a sloppy cop, he was a thorough and dogged investigator. He was a professional, and his case files were consummate models of good police work.

So why was the postcard here in the Beth Kilgore files? What did one case have to do with the other? She had to go through the rest of the files, to see what else she might find that would shed light on both the Beth Kilgore cold case and Ruby's decamping for Vegas.

She made herself another cup of tea and got to work. She went through the last two boxes, examining each and every file. She did find a copy of the domestic violence report filed by a doctor who treated Beth at the free clinic for her broken nose. Her husband was the prime suspect in the assault but Beth refused to press charges. She had just turned eighteen—there was a note from her grandfather that this punch in the face had been a kind of sick birthday present—and so there was nothing the police could do about it.

Mercy found nothing else related to Ruby and George Rucker. These files just held more of the same records documenting her grandfather's fruitless search for Beth Kilgore and Thomas Kilgore. Maybe Red was wrong and she hadn't disappeared, after all. Maybe the postcard had been misfiled by a clerk or even Deputy Pitts.

But she didn't believe that. She still believed in her grandfather, even if her mother, Grace, did not. If he believed that Beth Kilgore had met with foul play, and given her abusive husband that was not much of a stretch, then she would proceed on that assumption. If he believed that her disappearance was somehow linked to this postcard from Ruby, then she would proceed on that assumption as well. No matter how tenuous the link may be.

She was not ready to give up on Red.

She yawned. She was getting sleepy, and she really should get some rest. It had been a very long day. And tomorrow would be another long day.

She was going back to Lamoille County.

CHAPTER FOURTEEN

Troy and Susie Bear spent the night in the truck, parked just far enough down the long driveway from Mercy's cabin that she and the dogs wouldn't notice. Susie Bear loved surveillance, sitting up front and placing her big pumpkin head on the dash, watching for trouble while Troy dozed off and on.

Not long before dawn he got a text from the captain telling him to meet him at Eggs Over Easy at 7:00 A.M.

"Red flag," he told Susie Bear as they left the cabin and headed for Main Street to the best breakfast joint in town. Normally Troy would just call in their favorite order—triple servings of venison blueberry sausage, wild turkey hash, cornbread, and coffee—and pick it up on his way into work before the place was even technically open. The better to avoid the hungry customers who lined up in the cold outside the tiny restaurant hoping for a table as soon as the doors opened, and the flirty hostess, Monique, who, like most of the women in town, had a crush on the captain. The fact that his boss was willing to breach that queue and brave that woman to eat inside was troubling.

Troy pulled the Ford F-150 into a parking spot on a side street a block away. Susie Bear barked, acknowledging their proximity to one of her favorite eateries. He hooked her lead onto the thick red leather collar buried in her dense double coat and let her out of the truck. She shuffled alongside him, enormous head held high, already sniffing the sweet scents of a meat-lover's breakfast that always wafted down from the restaurant, which was located on the second floor of a revitalized nineteenth-century mill building once famous for its textiles. The friendly Newfie greeted everyone lining the steps up to the entrance of Eggs Over Easy, licking the fingers of those who reached out to pet her. She made dealing with the public easy for Troy, smoothing the way as breezily as a drum major leading a marching band.

"Let the game warden and the mutt through," yelled Monique from the top of the stairs. "Come on up, Susie Bear!"

The big dog barked a hello and scrambled up the remaining steps, her gaze focused on Monique. Restaurant people were Susie Bear's favorite people, and that was saying something, because she liked practically all people.

"We open to the rest of you in five," the hostess shouted as she let Troy and Susie Bear into the café and shut the door behind her.

Monique led them toward a table tucked in a corner at the very back of the otherwise empty dining area, where Troy spotted Captain Thrasher and Detective Kai Harrington.

"Told you," he said to the Newfie, who held back at the sight and smell of the arrogant head of the Major Crime Unit. The one person she did *not* like very much. "It's okay, girl."

Thrasher waved them over. His expression was neutral, but Troy thought he could read a warning in his eyes.

Harrington smiled at Troy in welcome. That was a first. Usually the detective greeted him with a scowl and an order to remove Susie Bear from the premises. This 180-degree turnaround only made Troy more uneasy.

The detective was wearing his usual bespoke slim gray suit with a bright white button-down shirt and black-and-white polka-dotted silk tie, and black Chelsea boots. His expensive black woolen over-coat was neatly folded over the back of his chair. He reminded Troy of a rooster, although Mercy, who tended to classify humans accord-ing to dog breeds, once told him that the detective reminded her of a Doberman—sleek and handsome and liable to attack when you least expected it. "Have a seat, Warner. Monique, please get this fine canine a bowl of water."

"Sure."

Harrington kept his eyes on the attractive brunette until she disappeared around a screen that separated the front desk from the rest of the restaurant. Troy exchanged a glance with Thrasher. Harrington was always just a woman away from a sexual harassment charge.

"We've gone ahead and ordered," said Thrasher. "The usual for you."

"And Susie Bear." Harrington smiled again.

Troy felt actual alarm. "What's going on?"

"That's just it," said the detective. "There is so much going on." He tapped his fork on the blond wood table. "The Colby murder, the pipe bomb at Patience O'Sullivan's, George Rucker's prison escape."

Monique appeared with a pot of coffee and a bowl of water for Susie Bear. As the hostess, her main duty was running the front desk and seating the customers, not playing waitress, but for the captain she made an exception. She put the water down on the floor for the dog, poured a new cup of coffee for Troy, and topped Harrington's and Thrasher's cups, making sure to brush the captain's shoulder when she poured his. He did not react, his face still unreadable. "I'll be back with your order right away," she said, her eyes on the captain.

He nodded, and she strutted away like the cat with the canary. Harrington frowned. Troy smiled. The detective always expected to be the center of attention. And when Thrasher was around, he wasn't. Troy took advantage of the distraction to ask a question of his own. "Any word on Rucker?"

"Not yet," said Thrasher. "They had a possible sighting in Tennessee the day after his escape, but nothing since."

"Any forensics in from the blast site?"

Harrington leaned in toward Troy. "You know how the feds are. They keep us at arm's length until they need us." He straightened up as Monique returned with a tray holding four plates heaped with sausage, hash, and cornbread. She served Troy and the others and then placed Susie Bear's plate next to the water bowl on the floor. She balanced the empty tray on her left hip, tilting her right one against the captain's chair. "If you need anything else, gentlemen, you just whistle." With a flounce of her skirt she went back to the front desk.

"How is Mercy Carr?" Harrington slathered butter on his corn-bread. "I understand she surprised an intruder at her cabin."

"Yes," he said. This sudden interest in Mercy's welfare set off more alarms. Harrington didn't like Mercy any more than he liked Troy.

"She should never have checked herself out of the hospital," said Harrington. "Why would she do that?"

"My guess is that she wanted to get back to Patience," said Troy.

"Of course." The detective finished off the cornbread and started in on the sausage and hash. He ate nearly as quickly as Susie Bear, though admittedly more neatly. "Her devotion to her grandmother is admirable." He wiped his mouth with his napkin. "She'll want to protect Patience from any further danger. She'll believe that the only way to do that is to get to the bottom of this nasty business."

Troy sensed a trap. He looked at Thrasher, but the captain didn't say anything. So he didn't, either.

"She has a history of interfering with our investigations," said the detective.

"She has a history of solving our investigations," said Troy.

Harrington gave him a sharp look. "She is clever, I'll give you that. But we have a murderer running around on the loose, a bomber run-ning around on the loose, and an escaped prisoner running around on the loose. We can't have Mercy Carr running around on the loose, too."

"I'm not sure how we can stop her, short of arresting her," said the captain dryly.

Troy stared at Thrasher. Whose side was he on? The captain smiled at him enigmatically.

"Obviously we can't arrest her," said Harrington, as if there were nothing that he wanted to do more. "The press is calling her a hero—along with that damn dog of hers. Again."

"They did save Patience O'Sullivan's life," said Troy.

"Whatever." Harrington carefully placed his knife and fork in the middle of his plate, signaling that the meal was over. "But you know that won't be enough for her. She'll want to do more. She's probably doing more as we speak. So you'd better get moving."

"I'm not sure what you mean."

"I mean, get over there. Pay your interfering friend a visit."

"Forensics will be by to check out the crime scene soon," said Thrasher. "It would be good for you to get there first."

"You can't be serious." Troy tried to keep the furor out of his voice, but he failed. If the detective was saying what he thought he was saying, well, that was simply unacceptable.

Harrington ignored his angry tone. "I want to know what she knows. I want to know where she goes, what she does, who she talks to."

"You want me to spy on her." Troy couldn't believe it. He looked to the captain for assistance, but he remained conspicuously silent.

The detective sipped the last of his coffee and rose to his feet. "And her dog."

Troy rose to his feet, too, his arms at his side, hands clenched into fists.

"Steady, man," said the captain quietly.

"I'll expect a full report by the end of the day." Harrington retrieved his coat and sauntered out of the restaurant.

Troy watched him go, and then turned back to glare at Thrasher. "You know I can't do this."

"You spent the entire night surveilling her house."

"That's different."

"Not by much." The captain smiled. "Think of it as a way to spend time with her and pursue the investigation at the same time. You make a good team."

"She already hates me for not telling her about still being married. I can't not tell her about this."

"So tell her."

Troy stared at Thrasher. "What do you mean?"

"Do what you have to do to keep her and her family safe and solve the crimes." The captain pulled out his wallet. "Ask for her help with the case. Tell her you know Harrington will screw it up. Women can never resist a call for help." He put a fifty-dollar bill on the table. "Tell Monique to keep the change."

"Sir."

"Think outside the box," said the captain. "If you want to keep up with Mercy Carr—and I know you do—you're going to have to get creative."

CHAPTER FIFTEEN

MERCY MEANT TO GET UP EARLY SO SHE AND ELVIS COULD get out of the house before anyone could object. But it was nearly eight o'clock when she awoke, still sore all over. She took a quick shower, washing her matted red hair carefully. She stood there under the rain showerhead, soothed by the water streaming over her weary bones, grateful for the simple gifts of hot water and lavender soap on a cold day. For the first time in forty-eight hours, she felt fully human again.

She applied moisturizer and a pale pink lip gloss and blow-dried her hair. Normally she'd just let it dry naturally, and let her unruly curls fall where they may, but it was nippy outside and she wanted to get on the road as soon as possible. She slipped on a pair of black winter-weight running tights and a striped heather-and-white thermal-knit Henley, pulled on clean socks and her prized furry Eddie Bauer snow boots. This was her idea of dressing up when snow was in the forecast.

She was glad to be back in her own clothes and her own boots. In her own house. Living life her own way.

Like going to Lamoille County this morning before anyone could try to stop her.

But she wasn't quite quick enough. By the time she finished her *toilette,* as her mother called it, Troy had texted her to tell her that forensics would arrive by mid-morning and Amy was up and sitting at the farm table feeding Helena. The dimpled child was nearly a year old now—a lively bundle of joy and energy who liked nothing better than banging her spoon on the tray of her high chair.

Nothing better except for peek-a-boo. When she saw Mercy, she immediately dropped her spoon, hiding her big slate-blue eyes with her chubby little palms. Peek-a-boo was her new favorite game.

Mercy laughed and played along as she let Sunny and Elvis out the back door to do their morning business. "Oh no! Where did Helena go?" The baby squealed with delight and lowered her hands to reveal her sweet face. "There she is. There's our little Helena."

The game did not distract little Helena's mother.

"You've got that look," said Amy.

"I'm sure I don't know what you mean." Mercy helped herself to a cup of coffee. Since moving in with her, Amy had embraced her daily morning caffeine ritual: grind the medium-roast organic Vermont Coffee Company beans, brew a fresh pot of coffee, warm the milk, and fuel up to start the day off right.

"You know, like you've got a secret you're not ready to tell us yet." Amy studied her as she stirred Helena's oatmeal.

"No secrets." She showed Amy the postcard she'd found in Beth Kilgore's cold case files.

"I thought you were supposed to leave the files for forensics."

"I wore gloves. And I was careful to put everything back the way it was."

"If you say so." Amy studied the postcard. "I don't get it."

"I don't, either." Mercy sipped her coffee.

"What does it mean?" Amy teased a spoonful of oatmeal into Helena's mouth.

"I don't know."

"But you're going to find out."

"Yes. This was the case that haunted my Grandpa Red."

"And it's haunting *you* now."

"I want to get to the bottom of it." Mercy let Elvis and Sunny back in and they sat on their haunches, ears perked, waiting for their breakfast, which they knew came next. She measured a cup each of premium dry dog food into bowls. "I *need* to get to the bottom of it.

It may or may not have anything to do with what's happening right now, but either way I feel like I owe it to him. And to Patience." She sipped her coffee as the dogs devoured their kibble.

"You should eat something, too. Want some oatmeal?" Amy frowned as Helena spat out a mouthful. "Gross, baby."

Mercy smiled. "I don't think so. I'll get something on the way."

Amy pulled a baby wipe from the box on the table and wiped the goopy mess gently from her baby's face. "Where are you going?"

"I've got to go up to Lamoille County."

"What about forensics?"

"You can handle them. I need to check on some things."

Amy looked up at her. "Your mother's not going to like that."

"I'm a grown woman," said Mercy. "I don't have to ask permission. I don't have to do what my mother tells me to do."

Amy smiled. "I bet you never did what your mother told you to do."

"True enough." Mercy shook her head. "But you know Grace, even if I did do what she told me to do, it wouldn't be enough."

"Yeah." A frown creased her heart-shaped face. "What's up with that."

"Mothers."

"Mothers." Amy pursed her lips. "Don't worry," she said to her baby. "I'll never be that way with you." She kissed Helena's forehead.

Mercy believed it. Amy's mother was a nightmare who'd accused her own daughter of murder. Amy would die before she'd treat her baby like her mother had treated her. "You're a great mom. Helena is lucky to have you."

"I try." Amy twiddled the spoon, coaxing Helena to eat more of her breakfast.

Mercy got her pack and put on her down-filled parka with the fur-trimmed hood.

"You're going to need that coat," said Amy. "There's a big storm coming in today. More sleet and snow. Changing to ice after sundown. The roads will be bad."

"I've got the Jeep. And I'm leaving early, so I'll be up there and back here in no time."

"No, you don't." Amy stared at her. "The Jeep isn't here."

"I forgot." Mercy sighed. She'd obviously congratulated herself on escaping the premises without incident prematurely. "It's still at Patience's house."

"Brodie can drive you over there to get it. When he gets up."

"Let him sleep." Brodie habitually slept in like the teenager he was. "I'll call an Uber." She wondered how long that would take.

"You'll take the dogs with you." It was a statement, not a question.

"I'm taking Elvis with me. But I'd like to leave Sunny here with you."

Amy gave her an inquiring look.

"Going back there might traumatize her," Mercy explained. "Pitts is dying, and his sister doesn't like dogs." She told Amy about her unpleasant encounter with Eveline.

"She sounds like a terrible person." Amy stood up and lifted Helena out of the high chair, balancing her on one slender hip. "Sunny is a lovely dog."

"That she is."

"We'll be happy to take care of her, won't we, little girl?"

"Thanks."

"No problem. Are you sure you're up to this?" Amy looked Mercy over in that critical manner in which all young people viewed their elders. "I mean, you look a lot better, but still."

"I'm up to it. I feel much better. No worries." Mercy started to take her cell phone out of her pocket but stopped when Elvis barked and ran for the front door, Sunny on his heels.

Mercy followed the dogs and stepped outside onto the porch. It was cold and growing colder. No big snow yet, just flurries, but the occasional gust of wind blew frigid flakes into her face that even her hood could not block. She retrieved her gloves from her other coat pocket and put them on, brushing the snow off her cheeks as she watched Elvis and Sunny race out toward the driveway. Troy's truck plowed up the snowy drive.

Bad luck, she thought. She'd almost made it out without anyone slowing her down. She grabbed the snow shovel she always kept on a hook to the left of the door and swept the snow off the steps, hoping the game warden would just go away. Wishful thinking.

He pulled his truck up to the top of the drive and hopped out. Susie Bear placed her muzzle up against the passenger window of the back cab, a clear sign she'd like to join him.

Mercy ignored him, shoveling the walk now.

"I can help with that." Troy stood there, rooted to the ground, as the snow whirled around him.

"I got it."

"You could just wait until it dies down." Elvis and Sunny bounded up to him to say hello, and then bolted for his truck to see Susie Bear. The frustrated Newfie barked her greeting, and her displeasure at being unable to join her friends. "Unless you're going somewhere."

She ignored the question behind that statement. "I was just leaving." She hoped he'd take the hint and leave, too.

"Your Jeep's at Patience's house."

"I know that. I'm calling an Uber."

"Unnecessary. We're here to take you to pick up your Jeep. As promised."

"Oh. I forgot." Maybe she was more tired than she thought. She shook her head as if to clear it.

"Are you sure you're okay?"

"I'm fine."

"Where are you going?" He searched her face as if he'd find the answers printed there.

"I'm going to Lamoille County." There was no point in lying to him. She was a terrible liar, and even if she weren't, odds are he'd know. Like most law enforcement officers, he had a built-in BS detector.

"Why?"

"I found something that puzzles me. I want to figure it out."

"What did you find?"

"Remember how we said there was no connection between George Rucker and Beth Kilgore? Well, I think I've found one." She told him about the postcard.

"Interesting," he said. "And now you're going up there?"

"Yeah. I want to talk to Deputy Pitts again."

"We could go with you. The roads are supposed to be bad. You could use an escort."

She didn't need an escort. But it never hurt to have a game warden around. Game wardens were the kind of law enforcement officers who made folks feel safe, rather than threatened. Unless they were poachers. "Don't you have patrols?"

"I do. But this is related to Patience, and Patience is everyone's priority right now. Even Harrington knows that."

"Since when does Harrington want our help?"

Troy didn't answer that. He just whistled a tune she didn't quite recognize, gazing up at the sky.

"He sent you to spy on me."

"Keep your enemies close. . . ."

"And you *agreed*?" She couldn't believe he'd stoop to that. And for Harrington, of all people. She was going to kick him to the curb, starting now.

Troy held up his hands in mock surrender. "Don't go ballistic on me. This could work to your advantage."

"How?" Mercy folded her arms across her chest.

"Think about it. Left to his own devices, God knows what Harrington will do."

"True enough."

"You want to keep your family safe and figure out this cold case. I want to keep you and your family safe, and if that means helping you figure out the cold case, so be it."

"And Harrington?"

"We can handle Harrington."

As soon as she heard that, she knew she didn't have a choice. If she didn't go with him, he'd just follow her as ordered. Although to be fair, he'd probably follow her anyway. Like most good cops, when he was on a case he was like a dog with a bone. And right now, she was the bone. "Okay. Let me take Sunny back inside."

THEY DIDN'T TALK much on the way up to Lamoille County. The snow was falling faster and heavier now and the driving was treacherous. The farther north they went, the colder it got and the harder the snow came down. Visibility was poor.

Troy kept his eyes on the road. He was a good driver. Like all game wardens, he knew his way around vehicles—from cars and trucks and boats to snowmobiles and ATVs and Jet Skis. There were few machines he couldn't handle—even under the worst conditions.

Even so, Mercy couldn't relax. It wasn't the weather, it was the memory of Madeline. Troy's wife. Interrupting their dance. Susie Bear and Elvis had curled up in the back cab and gone right to sleep. She envied the dogs their ability to nap anywhere, anytime. Martinez could do that, too. He used to say that a good nap was a soldier's best friend, after a good gun and a good dog.

She was very aware of Troy. She closed her eyes and tried to meditate. She pictured a sandy beach on a tropical island, blue waves breaking on the shore, coming in and going out, coming in and going out, just like one of the shrinks her mother dragged her to after she came home from Afghanistan had advised her to do. But she didn't see a beautiful ocean of blue. All she saw were sharks.

"Are we ever going to talk about it?" Troy's voice startled her.

"What?"

"Are we ever going to talk about it," he repeated.

"No." The last thing she wanted to do was talk about it.

"We need to talk about it."

Maybe you need to talk about it, she thought, *but I don't.*

"Okay, I'll start," said Troy cheerfully. "My divorce will be final by summer."

"Congratulations," she said, cursing herself as soon as the words came out of her mouth.

Elvis and Susie Bear scrambled upright, their naps no doubt interrupted by the tone of her voice. Susie Bear settled her square head on the console, a black furry buffer. Elvis nudged her shoulder with his nose.

"No fighting in front of the kids," said Troy.

"We're not fighting."

"I think this may be our first fight." Troy grinned. "I'm sorry, honey."

"Shut up, Troy Warner."

"Could we just start over again?"

"What about Madeline?" Mercy knew his estranged wife was still in town, supposedly to help her mother through her recovery after knee-replacement surgery, but no one she knew believed that. Not even Troy.

"What about her?" Troy tightened his hands on the steering wheel. "It's over."

"It's never that simple."

"It is with me."

"It takes a long time to get over a relationship, no matter how it ends." *Even when it ends in death,* she thought, but did not say aloud.

Elvis nuzzled her neck with his muzzle. Trying to calm her down. Susie Bear just *whomped* her tail, her upper body solidly positioned right in the middle between them. The furry peacemaker showed no sign of moving.

"You're talking about you and Sergeant Martinez." Troy's voice softened. "Look, I know you're grieving for him. And I appreciate that. But this thing with me and Madeline is not the same. Our relationship has been over for years. The divorce is just a piece of paper acknowledging that."

"Tell that to your Madeline."

"She has no choice."

"Right." Mercy wondered how much it was costing Troy to rid himself of Madeline. Pride alone would provoke the woman once known as the most beautiful girl in Northshire into making him pay handsomely for the privilege of divorcing her. Even if she had left him first. "Maybe we're just not good at relationships."

"You were good with Martinez."

"I believed that once upon a time." She stared out the window at the snow brightening the dark trunks of the maple trees and the green boughs of the pines. "Looking back, I think Martinez was the one who was good at relationships. Because he was good, I was good."

"You've always been good."

"It wasn't me," Mercy insisted. "I didn't get that gene."

"What gene?"

"The good marriage gene. My parents got it, and Patience and Red got it, and my brother Nick and his wife, Paige, got it, but I didn't get it. You didn't get it, either."

"I don't think it works that way."

"Your marriage was a disaster." Mercy regretted the words as soon as they were out of her mouth.

"Ouch," he said.

"Sorry," she said, avoiding those warm brown eyes. "I told you I didn't want to talk about it."

"That was not an entirely accurate statement," he said. "At the beginning, our marriage was good. We were good. But we wanted different things out of life."

"You grew apart." Again, Mercy failed to keep the sarcasm out of her voice. Elvis licked her ear, as if to say, *Give the guy a break.*

"She ran off with another man," Troy said evenly. "So yeah, I guess you could say we grew apart."

"But she's back."

"Not for long." Troy paused. "There's a condo in Boca with her name on it."

So that was what the divorce was costing him, thought Mercy. She wondered what condos in Boca Raton were selling for these days. *Ouch* indeed.

"You know what the captain says is the secret to a happy marriage?"

"Thrasher doesn't count." Mercy knew that Thrasher had been happily married for twenty-five years until his wife, Carol, died of cancer a couple of years ago. He still mourned her. Every woman in southern Vermont was waiting for him to start dating again. "He got the marriage gene."

"It takes two," said Troy. "That's what the captain says. It takes *two.*"

Mercy looked out the window and was relieved to see the sign to Peace Junction. "It's the next exit."

"Okay."

She heard the relief in his voice, and she smiled. He didn't want to talk about relationships, either. Not really. Talking about relationships was tiresome. She'd dated a guy before Martinez who was always asking her about her feelings and telling her about his feelings in the name of "communication." It was like being stuck in a loop on the *Dr. Phil* show. She broke up with him out of sheer emotional exhaustion, and when he asked her why, she told him that she never wanted to talk about her feelings ever again. And she didn't. Not until Martinez, who convinced her that life was short and unpredictable, and so you'd better tell people how you feel while you could. And then he died and she never wanted to feel anything again, much less talk about it.

"Thank you for driving, Troy," she said formally.

"No problem."

She directed him through the picturesque village, which sat at the junction of the Gihon and Lamoille rivers in the shadow of Sterling Mountain. They passed the antique stores and the eateries, the community college and the art center, the converted mill buildings and the old covered bridge. They came out on the other side of town and drove on through the outskirts to the country road that led to Pitts' farmhouse.

"This is the one," she said.

Troy parked the truck in Pitts' driveway, which had been recently plowed. Even so, the snow was piling up again.

"I'm not sure how well we'll be received," she warned. "I don't think Pitts' sister likes me very much."

"Maybe she'll like me better."

"Maybe." Mercy grinned. "We won't be long, so let's leave the dogs in the truck. Eveline is not a big fan of canines."

"Never trust anyone who doesn't like dogs," Troy said solemnly.

"Agreed."

They stomped through the snow to the front door. Mercy rang the bell. A shrill voice shouted, "Hold on." A shuffling and then the door opened.

Eveline stood before them, dressed in her usual ill-fitting yoga attire. She looked at Mercy with disdain. "You again." She slammed the door shut.

Mercy rang the bell again. And again. And again.

Finally Eveline opened the door again. Troy stepped forward. "Game Warden Troy Warner. We're here to speak to August Pitts."

"You're too late." She glared at Mercy.

"What do you mean?"

"What are you doing here?" Eveline crossed her arms across her chest, straining the seams of her top. "You're not welcome here. You stole his dog." She turned to Troy. "This woman stole a dying man's dog. Arrest her."

"I did not steal his dog. He asked me to take his dog."

"That's ridiculous. Why would he do that. He knew that dog would be perfectly fine with me."

"Maybe he wanted to keep her closer to home."

Eveline gave her a blank look.

"Sunny is a Vermont dog."

"Look at this weather." Eveline raised her hands as if entreating the heavens to stop the snow. "Nobody in their right mind stays here in the winter. Even dogs would rather be in North Carolina this time of year."

"I don't know about that," said Mercy.

Troy nudged her gently with his elbow. Reminding her to get back on track. She hated to admit it but he was right. "Eveline," she said gently, "what happened to your brother?"

Eveline sniffed. "He died late last night."

"I'm so sorry," said Mercy.

"My condolences," said Troy.

Eveline ignored the game warden, her sharp eyes filling with tears as she stared Mercy down. "You people got him all worked up. You killed him."

"What people?"

"You," she said, "and that other guy."

Mercy leaned toward Eveline. "What other guy?"

Troy moved between her and Pitts' sister. "Could we come inside? As you say, it's wicked cold out here. And we'd like talk to you a little more about the man who came to visit your brother before he died." He smiled at her sympathetically. Troy had a good smile.

Eveline nodded. She gave a little wave of her hand and they traipsed after her into the living room where Mercy had last seen her grandfather's deputy. The portable hospital bed had been stripped and the medical paraphernalia was packed neatly into boxes on the old brown recliner.

"What was this visitor's name," asked Troy.

"I can't recall. I'm not sure he even told me his full name. August called him King. Weird, huh?"

"What did he look like?"

Eveline patted the uncased pillow on the bed absently. "Middle aged. Around late forties maybe. I think his hair was gray, but he was wearing a baseball cap so I'm not sure."

"Right."

"Anyway, this guy really upset August."

"What did they talk about?" asked Mercy.

"I don't know. I wasn't paying much attention," she said. "I was busy in the back of the house doing laundry."

"When was this?" Troy pulled a notebook out of his jacket pocket and started taking notes.

"Last night, around seven thirty P.M. I told him it was a little late for August, with his being so poorly and all, but he didn't listen. Bullied his way in here." Eveline sank onto the bare hospital bed. She ran her hand along the edge of the mattress. "August was sleeping. He'd had a rough couple of days, what with you coming and stealing his dog, and I was worried he wasn't going to make it through the night. You know the doctors didn't give him much time. You saw that for yourself."

"Yes," said Mercy softly.

"My brother took a turn for the worse in the late afternoon. I didn't want to let the guy in, but he wouldn't take no for an answer. So I told him he could only have a few minutes. Whether August woke up or not."

Mercy remembered how Deputy Pitts had dozed off and on during her short visit. "How long did he stay?"

"Not long. Maybe twenty minutes, half an hour at the most. But after he left, August was very agitated. Off his head, really."

"Did he say anything?" asked Troy.

"Nothing that made any sense."

"Try to remember," said Mercy. "It could be important."

"He kept saying something about Elvis Presley and Marilyn Monroe and lame men and limping. I don't know what he meant."

Mercy thought about it. "If you live with a lame man, you will learn to limp."

"Something like that, yeah."

Mercy nodded. "Plutarch."

"What does it mean?"

"I'm not sure," Mercy said.

"What happened after he left?" asked Troy.

"I heated us up some supper. Beef stew in a can."

Poor Deputy Pitts, thought Mercy. *What a terrible last meal.*

She looked over at Troy and could see from his face that he was thinking the same thing.

"When I took August his bowl, I saw he'd passed over." Eveline stared at the pillow, as if her brother were still there.

"And this was how long after the visitor left?"

"Maybe an hour, maybe less." Eveline looked from Mercy to Troy. "What are you thinking?"

"What did the doctor say?" asked Mercy.

"He said it was to be expected."

"I suppose it could be a coincidence, his dying right after this mysterious visitor pays him a visit, an encounter that clearly agitates him." Mercy heard the sarcasm in her voice and tried to soften it. "What do you think, Eveline?"

"I think he was getting tired." Eveline sighed. "That's when they go, you know. When they get tired of fighting to stay alive. They just give in to death."

The three of them fell into silence for a moment.

"Where's the body right now?" asked Troy finally.

"At the crematorium."

"What? You're having him cremated before the funeral?" Mercy asked. *Uh-oh,* Mercy thought. *No body, no autopsy, no evidence.*

"No funeral. We're going to have a memorial service instead. Come spring. August loved the spring."

"Eveline, we think that your brother might have been the victim of foul play." Troy explained that with George Rucker out of jail, her brother's life could have been at risk. "We'd at least like to rule it out."

"You think that King guy killed him?"

"We think it's possible," said Mercy.

"We'd like to do an autopsy. But we can't do it without a body."

"I'll call the crematorium." Eveline stood up. "Winter makes people do crazy things up here. I can't wait to get back to North Carolina."

CHAPTER SIXTEEN

ARRINGTON ISN'T GOING TO LIKE THIS," said MERCY as they left the farmhouse. "You could get reprimanded big time."

"He'll like it less if we let them cremate evidence of a murder."

"What will you do?"

"I'll let Thrasher handle it." They got into the truck and Troy contacted the captain to tell him what was going on. "We're good. The captain is on it. Where to next?"

"The library," she said. "That's the one place Beth Kilgore is known to have frequented on a regular basis. And that's where she was last seen before she disappeared."

One of the things Mercy loved best about her home state was its libraries. Vermont had more public libraries per capita than any other state in the union. The Peace Junction Free Public Library was one of the oldest libraries in the state, endowed by a local merchant in the mid-1800s. Housed in a former general store, the lovely nineteenth-century white clapboard building stood on the town common between the old Town Hall and the Peace Junction Historical Society.

The library had just opened for the day, but there were already several patrons roaming the stacks and using the computers. Mercy and Troy headed for the information desk, anchored by a very young woman with black semi-rimless glasses and dark brown hair braided into a long plait that hung over her left shoulder and fell down across her heart to her waist. Mercy wondered how anyone dealt with hair that long. She could hardly manage her shoulder-length mane and was tempted to cut it off every other day. But the shorter it was, the curlier it was—and that presented its own set of problems. So she kept it just long enough to pull easily into a ponytail.

She let Troy take the lead, since he was the one in uniform. American librarians were resolutely protective of their readers' First Amendment rights, and the ones here in Vermont were no exception. Like Mrs. Horgan, the Northshire librarian who'd befriended Mercy as a girl and encouraged her interest in Shakespeare's work (even the tragedies that her mother, Grace, would not have deemed appropriate for a ten-year-old). Mrs. Horgan had been charged with obstruction when she tried to stop the arrest of a library patron who dared to ask challenging questions of the guest speaker at a public book event. The charges were later dropped—and Mrs. Horgan became an even more mythical figure for Mercy and her fellow Northshire book-worms.

Troy introduced her and himself to the young woman, who in turn introduced herself as Kelsey Vo, Head Librarian. Ms. Vo looked barely old enough to vote. Mercy knew that didn't mean anything; she'd served with a lot of young recruits who had guts to spare.

"We're working on a cold case," said Troy. "The disappearance of a woman named Beth Kilgore in 2000. She was last seen here at this library."

"I'm afraid I wasn't here at that time." Kelsey smiled at Troy.

Of course not, thought Mercy. You were just a kid back then, like us, only you were still in diapers.

"Right," said Troy.

"Do you have any records from that era?" asked Mercy. "Anything that might help us understand our missing woman's frame of mind?"

"If you're talking about accessing a library user's borrowing re-cords, you'd need a warrant for that." Kelsey fingered the thick braid at her breast and then tossed it behind her back. "Even if you had a warrant, odds are those records are gone. We purge our user data on a regular basis."

"Understood." Mercy smiled at the young librarian. Mrs. Horgan used to say that all librarians were subversive by nature, and Kelsey Vo was no exception. The First Amendment rights of Vermont readers were safe here at the Peace Junction Free Public Library. She couldn't help but be glad about that. Mrs. Horgan would approve. "Is there anyone you can think of who was here at that time who might remember Beth Kilgore?"

Kelsey started to speak, and then hesitated.

"Beth Kilgore's family has been waiting a long time for answers," said Troy.

That seemed to sway her. "There is Louise Minnette. She was the head librarian here for many years. She's mostly retired now, but she still helps out from time to time. She's organizing books for our quarterly book and bake sale right now."

"That would be great. Thanks."

Kelsey pointed down the length of the library. "You'll find her in the back room, at the very end of the building." She pulled her braid back around her neck and held it like a rope against her chest. "Good luck."

"Do you think she'll remember her?" whispered Troy as they headed to the back room.

"Mrs. Horgan would remember."

"True." Troy smiled. "She knew everyone who ever came into the Northshire library, and she always remembered what they liked to read."

"Exactly. If Louise Minnette is anything like Mrs. Horgan, she'll remember Beth Kilgore."

They came to an antique oak door with frosted glass panes and a small brass plaque that read BACK ROOM.

"This must be the place." Troy opened the old door and they stepped into a wonderland of books. Towering heaps of hardcovers, trade paperbacks, and mass-market titles crowded the floor like giant Jenga puzzles. In the middle of these looming columns of literature sat a small elderly woman in black at a massive antique oak pedestal desk whose wooden pulls were carved in the shape of a lion's face. She looked rather fierce herself, with her cloud of white hair and the sharp brown eyes of a mature red-tailed hawk. Pen in hand, she looked up from the big ledger before her, the only thing on the broad expanse of leather desktop. She fixed a no-nonsense gaze on them.

"May I help you?" she asked, in the plummy, perfectly enunciated Yankee manner that served as a warning that she did not suffer fools gladly.

Mercy smiled. She figured they were in good hands with Louise Minnette. They introduced themselves and explained why they were there to see her.

"Beth Kilgore. Of course I remember her. She was an avid reader," Louise said approvingly, paying her the highest compliment a librarian can bestow. "I'm not sure what more I can tell you. Ask me what you will, but I do not promise to answer to your satisfaction."

"Fair enough," said Troy.

She waved at the books surrounding them. "I'd offer you a seat, but as you can see, I'm surrounded here." She surveyed the room, then slapped the ledger closed and swept it onto her lap. "You'll just have to perch on the edges of this big old thing."

"It's a beautiful piece," said Mercy.

"Scottish. Nineteenth century." She paused. "I thought you young people didn't like brown furniture. Isn't that what you call it these days?"

"Not me," said Mercy.

"Not me, either," said Troy.

"How very ingratiating of you," said Louise, pursing her lips.

Mercy shook her head. "We're not saying that just to please you. We value our Vermont history. Troy here lives in an old fire tower."

Louise tapped her pen on the desk, as if she were applauding the tower. "How fascinating. And you?"

"I live in a hunting cabin, circa 1920."

"Filled with brown furniture, no doubt." Louise put her pen down on top of the ledger in her lap and patted the surface of the desk. "Go ahead and sit down. It's as solid as granite."

Troy took up one corner of the immense desk and Mercy the other.

"I remember when Beth Kilgore left town. They said she and her husband went to California." Louise shook her head, and the white cloud shimmered around her face. "I never understood the appeal of Los Angeles. All those people crowded together on beaches and highways and at open-air malls. All that relentless sunshine. When do they read?"

"Not your kind of place."

"Heavens no. I went there once, for my cousin Donald's wedding. I couldn't wait to get back to Vermont."

"Do you think L.A. was Beth Kilgore's kind of place?"

"I wouldn't have thought so. But Beth was a very private person, and if she did have such plans to go there, she certainly did not share them with me."

"My grandfather could find no evidence that they'd gone out West. They both seemed to disappear without a trace."

"Your grandfather?"

"He was the sheriff at that time."

Louise smiled. "Of course. That red hair. You're an O'Sullivan."

"Yes. I'm Grace O'Sullivan's daughter."

"And Patience Fleury O'Sullivan is your grandmother."

Mercy nodded.

"A splendid woman. I was so sorry to see her leave after her husband died. But I could understand why she would want to start fresh somewhere else."

Mercy wondered if that were a reference to her grandfather's affair or his murder or both.

"How is she?" asked Louise.

Mercy told her about Patience's career as a veterinarian and the Sterling Animal Hospital. "She's well, but she is also part of the reason we're here."

"How so?"

"Someone left a pipe bomb on Patience's porch," said Troy.

Louise looked from Troy to Mercy, the question she seemed reluctant to ask hanging in the air between them.

"She's okay," said Mercy. "This time."

"She's still in danger."

"You are referring to George Rucker's escape from prison."

Troy nodded.

"I read about that. Not the sort of boy one would think could end up in prison, much less escape it. He was a dreamer, George. He read a lot of fantasy as a boy. C.S. Lewis, Tolkien, Terry Brooks." Her dark eyes softened for a moment, then sharpened again as she regarded Mercy. "What does this have to do with Beth Kilgore?"

"We're not sure. Maybe nothing. But she and her husband left for California that same summer George's wife left him and he killed my grandfather. And now George Rucker has escaped and August Pitts has asked me to look into Beth Kilgore's disappearance. The timing all seems, well, odd if nothing else."

"I understand." Louise folded her hands over the pen on the ledger in her lap. "How can I help?"

"Tell us what you can about Beth Kilgore."

"I'll talk and you sort." She pointed to the stacks to her right. "Go through those and sort them by genre: Romance, mystery, science fiction, etc."

"I'll do it," said Mercy. "Troy needs to take notes." She moved to the tallest of the stacks and carefully removed a small pile to sift.

"Ready when you are," said Troy, still sitting on the desk, pen and notebook at the ready.

"Yes," said Louise. "I knew Beth as a reader primarily, of course. I must have met her when she was around twelve. By that time she'd read all the books in the school library and was looking for more here. Slowly but surely, she made her way through most of the books in this library, as well."

"That's a lot of books," said Troy.

"I suspect she was a lonely child."

"Books were her friends." Mercy started a pile for romance and a pile for mystery.

"Yes." Louise smiled. "And her education and her entertainment and her escape." Her smile faded. "I don't think she had many friends. She kept herself to herself."

"She was shy?" asked Troy.

"I don't know if it was shyness or timidity or both." Louise sighed. "I suppose you know the story. Her mother took off when she was young and left her alone with her father, a wretched man completely unequipped to raise a young girl." The librarian frowned. "*Not* a reader."

"My grandfather arrested him more than once." Mercy added a new heap for cookbooks.

"A very difficult man." Louise nodded. "He kept her under his thumb, that was clear. She was such a bright girl. She should have gone to college."

"She got married instead," said Mercy.

"A very unfortunate turn of events."

"Out of the frying pan into the fire," said Troy.

"Indeed." Louise rested her elbows on the desk and leaned in. "That husband of hers was a bully. I would see the signs, you know, from time to time: a black eye here, a bruised arm there."

"The broken nose," said Mercy.

"Yes." Louise gave her a sharp look. "She was a pretty little thing, but at the rate that man was going she wouldn't be for very long."

"He abused her." Troy looked up from his notebook to confirm this.

"Yes, and he controlled her every move. She had to sneak into the library."

"What do you mean?"

"She would always stop here on her way home from food shopping. She always put the books she checked out in her recyclable grocery bags."

"To hide them from him." Mercy thought about that as she began a new pile for plays, several slim paperback volumes of Shakespeare among them. She tried to imagine having to hide books from your husband. Tried and failed.

"I believe so. Good thing he didn't read or he might have noticed she was always reading a different book." Louise watched Mercy as she dismantled another tower of books and started going through them. Most of the books she was sorting through now were mysteries and thrillers, modern bestsellers as well as Golden Age classics and noir.

"I worried about her," admitted Louise. "But she never said anything, and when I tried to talk to her about it, she changed the subject. You can't help people who aren't prepared to help themselves."

"She was too scared." Mercy had seen what fear did to people, and it was never pretty.

"I often wonder what happened to her," said Louise. "I can't imagine that she's any happier in California with that man than she was here."

"Fear follows you wherever you go," said Mercy.

"Yes." Louise put the ledger back on the desk. "Once it takes root in you, it's hard to get out. It simply grows back."

"People can conquer their fears," said Troy.

"They need help to do that," said Louise. "Support. I suppose I failed her there."

"You gave her the gift of stories," said Mercy. "Shakespeare helps me be brave."

"Of course he does," said Troy, with a smile.

"Beth read Shakespeare," said Louise. "She read everything there was to read—low-brow and high-brow, genre and literary, old and new. She tended to read in cycles—all romance and then all historical fiction and then Jane Austen and the Brontë sisters. And she ordered lots of books. We put in many special orders for her, many of which had to do with New England." Louise opened the ledger and picked up her pen. "That's another reason I couldn't believe she'd move to California. She loved being a Vermonter. She loved New England."

"What was Beth reading when she disappeared?" Mercy retrieved an empty cardboard box from the supply in the corner and dragged the first stack of sorted titles over to it.

"It was such a long time ago," said Louise. "I'm not sure I can re-member exact titles."

"Are there no borrowing records you can look up?" asked Troy.

"Not really." Louise sniffed. "We didn't go completely digital until 2005. And as I'm sure you already know we purge our user data on a regular basis."

"So Ms. Vo informed us," he said. "What system did you use prior to 2005?"

"We used the old card system. But a fire destroyed all those records."

Mercy knew that like any good cop Troy would be suspicious of any evidence destroyed by fire. As she would be, too. But librarians made no secret of the fact that they did not like to reveal the borrowing records of their patrons.

"We would have destroyed them ourselves sooner or later," said Louise.

"I'm ready to pack these up if you're ready to record them."

"Go ahead," said Louise.

Mercy rattled off the titles as she placed each book in the box. "*The Nine Tailors,* by Dorothy L. Sayers. *Killing Floor,* by Lee Child. *The Thin Man,* by Dashiell Hammett." She looked up at the librarian to make certain that she wasn't going too fast.

Louise dropped her pen and snapped her fingers. "That's it. I remember now. Beth was on a crime fiction kick. Noir especially. She was reading the classics mostly, but contemporary stories too. James M. Cain, Patricia Highsmith, that sort of thing."

"Pretty dark stuff," said Mercy.

"Yes," said Troy. "But then Beth was leading a pretty dark life."

Louise nodded. "Dorothy B. Hughes' *In a Lonely Place* comes to my mind. That may have been the last book she checked out, because I remember hoping that wherever she was, she was no longer in a lonely place."

"I'm sure she never felt lonely here in your library," Mercy said. "This was her haven. She had a friend in you."

"I was her friendly librarian. Not the same thing. But she may have had one real friend. Ruby Rucker."

Mercy and Troy exchanged looks. "Ruby Rucker?"

"I never figured her for a big reader," said Troy. "Not based on what we've learned about her so far."

"She wasn't. Sometimes she'd read the fashion and home décor magazines. Or check out travel books. I think she was bored to tears with our little village."

"So you knew her."

Louise laughed, a surprising titter that took both her and Troy by surprise. "Everyone in town knew Ruby Rucker. Or at least of her."

"Seems like a very *Odd Couple* kind of friendship."

"Indeed. But they shared an interest in film."

"Film?"

"Ruby mostly came to the library to check out movies. She liked action-adventure, romance, that sort of thing. Blockbusters. Beth preferred art films. I saw them together sometimes at the Two Rivers Theater," said Louise. "That's the independent theater here in town, on Main Street. They play second-run movies and art films."

"I'm surprised her husband let her go to the movies."

"I doubt he even knew. They were always matinées." Louise smiled. "Matinées are filled with people sneaking off from work and family to take in a show."

"You?"

"I like films, too, you know. Especially ones with George Clooney." Louise grinned at them. "Hubba hubba."

Mercy and Troy laughed.

"The theater shows old movies, classics, on Thursday afternoons. They serve wine and soda and popcorn with real butter. You should go sometime. It's all well and good to watch movies at home on a big-screen TV. But it's still not the same as the theater. A real theater."

"Do you remember which movies were playing when you saw Beth and Ruby?"

Louise shook her head. "I'm afraid not. But it must have been one of those Thursdays, because that's the only afternoon I could usually get away back then. And I love those old films. Now my time is more my own and I can go whenever I please."

"Did Beth ever talk to you about Ruby, or going to the movies?"

"Never." Louise sighed. "And I never mentioned seeing her there to her or Ruby or anyone else. It was Beth's one little rebellion, reading books and seeing films."

"Well, we know how subversive you librarians can be," said Mercy.

The librarian smiled. "Yes, we are subversive. Reading is subversive. What rebel there was inside Beth Kilgore was the reader in her."

Mercy finished up packing the books she'd sorted while Troy went out to the truck to check on the dogs. She thanked Louise Minnette, promising to return the next time she was in Lamoille County, and left, the librarian's last words ringing in her brain.

Reading is subversive.

CHAPTER SEVENTEEN

Troy sat in the truck with the dogs. He watched Mercy jog from the library entrance to his vehicle, appreciating the view. She was one of the few people he knew who looked good running.

"Time to eat," said Troy.

"I'm not hungry." Mercy slammed the door and put on her seat belt. "Let's go."

"You have to eat. Did you even have breakfast?"

At the word *breakfast* both Elvis and Susie Bear barked their approval.

"We've got a solid lead now. We know that Beth and Ruby were friends."

"Do you want to tell them we're not taking a break for breakfast? Because I'm not doing it."

Elvis leaned his muzzle in and pressed his cold nose against Mercy's pale neck. "Okay, okay."

"We passed a little place on Main Street that looked good. We can order take-out."

"Fine."

Wyetta's Café was deserted. It was around 10:30 A.M. now, that dead time between breakfast and lunch. It was a cute place with orange walls filled with brightly colored textile art, one long room with a lunch counter on one side with stools that twirled, a long row of booths on the other side, and a scattering of butcher block tables with yellow tulip chairs between. He could tell Mercy liked it. Especially the art.

They went up to the counter and sat down on the yellow vinyl stools. Mercy twirled her stool around a couple of times, and he did, too. Just for heck of it. She grinned at him, and in that moment, he saw the fourteen-year-old girl she was when he met her for the first time at the town pool one hot summer long ago.

A tall, striking woman appeared behind the counter. She had long dreads pulled away from her face in a wide headband and an orange uniform the same color as the walls. A yellow apron was slung around her hips. *Wyetta's Café* was embroidered in yellow over her breast pocket.

"Sit anywhere you want," she said. "As you can see, you got the place to yourselves."

"We just want to order take-out," said Mercy. "We can't stay long. We've got dogs in the car."

"Dogs." She looked at them as if she were not sure they could be trusted to care properly for a dog. "You're not from around here."

"No." Troy offered her his hand. "I'm Game Warden Troy Warner, and this is Mercy Carr."

"Wyetta Wright." She shook his hand with a grip worthy of Captain Thrasher and nodded at Mercy. "What kind of dogs?"

"Newfoundland retriever mix and a Belgian Malinois."

"Working dogs." She whistled, and a brown-and-white basset hound with ears that skimmed the floor shuffled out from behind the counter. "This is James Earl Jones. Earl for short."

Earl plodded over to Mercy. She leaned over and gave the droopy-eyed dog a scratch between his Dumbo ears.

"Are your dogs chill?" asked Wyetta.

"They'd love Earl," said Mercy, "if that's what you mean."

Wyetta put her hands on her hips. "And they must be well-trained."

"Yes, ma'am," said Troy.

She smiled. "Well, then, bring them on in."

"That's okay," he said. "We appreciate it, but—"

"I insist," she interrupted. "It's cold out there, even for your heavy-coated breeds. And then you can all sit and enjoy my fine cooking the way God intended."

"I'll get them." Mercy was out the door before he could say anything. So he just smiled back at Wyetta and rubbed Earl's long belly until she returned with Elvis and Susie Bear flanking her at her hips in perfect *heels*.

"That's a lot of dog," said Wyetta.

Earl rolled over and scuttled to his feet, standing as tall as he could on his short legs. Elvis and Susie Bear loomed over him, but he maintained his dignity, at least until the sniffing and snorting began as the three canines got to know each other.

"That's enough." Wyetta led them all over to a booth and handed them menus. Mercy pointed to the framed story quilt that hung above the booth. The fabric painting portrayed two African American women in church hats standing outside a classic white-steepled New England church surrounded by trees under a bright blue sky.

"I love this piece." Mercy waved her hand at the art on all the walls. "I love all these pieces."

"Thank you."

"You're the artist?"

"Yes." Wyetta gave a little bow. "I'll be right back with coffee."

"Thank you."

"She's an amazing talent," Mercy said to Troy as she slid into the booth. "Her work should be hanging in galleries."

Troy settled in across from her. Now he could face her directly, something he'd missed on the ride up. She picked up the menu and held it before her, obscuring her face again. But she couldn't do that the whole time. She'd find it harder to avoid his gaze, and he could gauge her reactions better.

Wyetta was back with coffee for them and water for the dogs. "So, what would you like?"

"Fried chicken and waffles," said Troy. "And a burger for Susie Bear."

"Breakfast and lunch." Mercy grinned. "Works for me. We'll have the same."

"You got it." Wyetta whistled for Earl and they both disappeared into the kitchen.

"Let's hear it," said Troy.

"What?"

"Whatever is going on in that supercharged brain of yours. You must have a theory by now." He leaned toward her conspiratorially. "You know, whatever you're thinking that you don't want me to tell Harrington."

Mercy sipped her coffee. "I'm not sure what to think. Grandpa Red must have suspected a connection between the two women. That's why the Vegas postcard was in Beth Kilgore's cold case files. And he was right. There was actually a link between Ruby and Beth. They were friends. Their friendship must mean something."

"It's hard to imagine two more different women, from what we know about them."

"They had some things in common. They were both lonely, unhappy people. Both stuck in situations neither liked."

"Ruby got out of hers."

"But Beth did not. As far as we know, anyway." Mercy leaned forward, her elbows on the table between them. A curly tangle of red hair fell into her face, and he resisted the urge to brush it away.

"People were always abandoning Beth," she went on. "First her mother abandoned her to her father. Then her father abandoned her to Thomas Kilgore. And finally Ruby abandoned her for Sin City."

"You can't blame Ruby Rucker for that," said Troy. "Beth Kilgore was a fearful person. I can't see her defying her husband. Any more than she defied her father."

"Maybe she changed."

"People don't change."

"Don't they?" She looked at him and he flushed.

"No." He should have seen that landmine coming. And stepped around it. "Not that much."

"I thought you were the optimist."

She was teasing him now. At least he hoped she was teasing. "I am. But not when it comes a person's character. How many people do you know who have truly changed?"

"For the better?"

"Yes, for the better. Changing for the worse is easy. We see people change for the worse all the time in law enforcement."

"You must know some alcoholics who stopped drinking for good," said Mercy, her blue eyes bright in her pale freckled face. "Like my cousin Ed."

"True enough." When they were teenagers, Ed's drinking had landed him in jail more than once. The second time he'd been driving under the influence, and he'd come within inches of killing a child on a bicycle. That sobered him up, and he'd been a model citizen ever since. "They usually have to hit rock bottom first."

"Maybe she hit rock bottom." Mercy leaned back and put her hands in her lap as Wyetta approached with their food. "Or maybe she finally saw things as they really were."

"Smells good," Troy told Wyetta, as she laid down two platters full of the best-looking fried chicken and waffles he'd ever seen.

"Wow," said Mercy.

"Enjoy." Wyetta placed two paper plates topped with open-faced burgers on the floor for the dogs. Both Elvis and Susie Bear sat there, waiting politely as they'd been trained to do.

"Impressive," she told them. "Go on and eat now." They chowed down and she waltzed away.

They ate in silence for a few moments. Mercy seemed totally focused on her food, but Troy was still mulling over her last remark. Sometimes she talked in riddles. "What did you mean exactly, when you said maybe Beth Kilgore finally saw things for what they really were?"

Mercy poured more Slopeside Syrup on her waffles. The woman could eat, that was for sure. How she stayed so slim, he didn't know. Must be a strong metabolism and all that hiking she did with Elvis.

"Martinez told me a story once about fear," she began.

Martinez again, thought Troy. He wondered if she'd ever talk about him the way she talked about her lost fiancé. If he were wasting his time hoping for something more than friendship to develop between them.

"There once was a man whose village was under attack from a neighboring tribe. He was captured by the enemy and locked in a cell overnight with a coiled snake whose venom was known to be lethal. He didn't dare budge an inch or the snake would strike and he'd die a terrible death. So he cowered in the corner of the cell, as far away from the snake as possible, paralyzed by fear. He waited in dread all night long, terrified of moving or sleeping or even breathing too hard. As the sun began to rise and the dark form of the snake began to take shape across the room, he congratulated himself for keeping so still that he survived the night. But as the rich light of dawn filled the cell, the snake was fully illuminated."

Troy could see where this was going. "Let me guess."

She smiled. "Go ahead."

"It wasn't a snake at all." He pointed at Mercy with a chicken leg. "It was just a rope or a cable or something snake-like."

"I could have told you that," said Wyetta, as she refilled their coffee cups.

Mercy laughed. "Okay, so it's a little predictable."

"It's lame." He grinned. He liked the idea that Martinez could tell a lame story. The sergeant was a hero, but he wasn't perfect. And yet Mercy still loved him. She would always love him. Troy wasn't perfect, either. Maybe someday she could love him, too.

"It's a little lame," Mercy conceded. "But the moral of the story is good. A lot of what we're afraid of is just rope—not snakes."

"But by all accounts, Thomas Kilgore was a snake," he said.

"I can confirm that," said Wyetta. "Not that you asked." She slapped a small stack of paper napkins on the table with one hand and held a coffeepot in the other.

They both looked up at her.

"Everyone needs more napkins when they eat my fried chicken."

"You knew Kilgore?" asked Mercy.

"Of course."

"So you've lived here a long time."

"I was born and raised here." She topped off their cups with hot coffee and set the pot on their table. "My people are originally from Mississippi. But my father settled here after Vietnam, said after surviving that jungle there was no way he was going back to the South. He wanted to live someplace clean and cool with lots of fresh water so he could go fishing whenever he wanted. Somewhere where there weren't too many people around. He had an Army buddy from Vermont, told him Vermont was heaven. So he moved here, met my mother at church, and married her. They opened the first soul food café in the county. Named it after their firstborn." She opened her arms and grinned. "That would be my own sweet self."

"And now it's your café."

"After Mom died, his heart just wasn't in it anymore. So I took over. He goes fishing, and I run the place."

"So you know this town and everybody in it," said Mercy.

He could see the wheels turning in her brain. Wyetta was going to get some grilling now.

"I do." Wyetta crossed her arms across her chest and leaned back on her heels. "May I ask what you're really doing here in Peace Junction? Not many people come up in the middle of a snowstorm to talk about a fool like Thomas Kilgore."

"We're here investigating a cold case," said Troy.

"Beth Kilgore."

"Yes," said Mercy. "Did you know her?"

"Sorrowful little thing. Married to your ordinary, run-of-the-mill bastard. Thomas Kilgore, who ruined everything he touched, sooner or later."

"You knew them both."

"As well as anyone else. She was a very private person, and he wasn't the kind of man anyone with any sense would want to get to know very well."

"What do you think happened to her?"

"If you all are going to keep on asking questions, I'm going to take a seat." Wyetta pulled one of the tulip chairs over to the edge of the booth and sat down, crossing her long legs. She was a good-looking woman, Troy thought. Smart and talented, too. The right kind of woman for Captain Thrasher. He wondered if she were involved with anyone. If she weren't, well, there was no point in even thinking about it. The captain would kill him for trying to fix him up with someone. Everyone else in Northshire was already trying.

"She and her husband took off for California. The one person who didn't believe that was her father, and he wasn't all that bright, if you get my meaning."

"My grandfather thought he might be right, and he was no fool."

"Sheriff Red O'Sullivan," explained Troy.

"Now there's a name I haven't heard in a long while." She smiled at Mercy. "He was a good man. Always looked out for me and my family." At their inquiring looks, she added, "He kept the rednecks at bay."

"That sounds about right." Mercy smiled back.

"And Sheriff Red didn't believe that Beth and Tom went out West." Wyetta paused. "Well, I hope he was wrong. I hope they moved out there to the Golden State and she went all California girl on him and dumped his ass."

"That would mean that she changed," said Mercy in a teasing voice. "And people don't change, according to our game warden here."

"People can't change, but they can grow." Wyetta looked at their plates, now empty except for tiny puddles of leftover syrup. "You finished here?"

"Sure."

She pushed her chair back and stood up.

Troy handed her his plate and Mercy's, too. "That may have been the best fried chicken I ever had."

"Don't ever let Patience hear you say that," said Mercy.

"Your grandmother," said Wyetta. "She's good people."

He could see that the mention of her grandmother was getting Mercy fired up again. "August Pitts gave me Beth Kilgore's case files and told me to find her."

"I heard that he passed last night." Wyetta set the dirty plates back down on the table.

"He knew he was dying. That's why he gave me the files."

"Just like the man. Leave someone else to deal with it."

"You didn't like him," Troy said.

"He wasn't a bad man, but then he wasn't much of a good man, either," Wyetta said. "Crooked as a three-dollar bill. May he rest in peace." She picked up the plates again. "How about some pecan pie?"

"I've never met a piece of pecan pie I didn't like," Troy said.

"À la mode?"

"Sure."

"That's the spirit." She grinned at Mercy. "You?"

"If you insist."

"I do. And it's on the house. In honor of Sheriff Red." Off she went with the dirty dishes to the kitchen.

Troy looked at Mercy. If anyone knew if her grandfather had an affair with Ruby, it seemed like Wyetta would. "Are you going to ask her about Ruby Rucker?"

"Of course." Mercy slipped out of the booth. "But first I'm going to check out the rest of the art." He watched as she moved around the restaurant, stopping before each piece to study it. When she stopped at the booth next to theirs, she said, "You have to see this one." He joined her in front of a twenty-four-inch by twenty-four-inch square quilted painting of a dark tunnel of trees that looked a lot like the Vermont woods. In the background on a hill beyond the forest was a small white building shining in the distance like a beacon. She leaned in. "See the people?"

He leaned in, too, looking more closely. There was a trail of shadowy figures tucked along a narrow path between the trees, barely visible in the gloom of the woods. "Who are they?"

"Slaves on their way to freedom," said Wyetta.

"It's so compelling. It reminds me of Faith Ringgold's work," said Mercy.

"Thank you," said Wyetta. "This piece is my tribute to her, and to my father and his Army buddy."

"The one from Vermont."

"That's right. His great-great-great grandfather was a Quaker. Very active in the anti-slavery movement. His farm was a stop on the Underground Railroad."

"Your work should really be in galleries."

Wyetta smiled. "I did the whole starving artist in Soho for a while after art school. But then Mom got sick and I came home. I wouldn't have lasted long in the big city regardless. I missed the woods, the mountains, the peace and quiet."

"I understand," said Mercy.

Troy understood, too. He didn't much like cities. Whenever he found himself in an urban environment, he had to fight the urge to flee to the nearest patch of green.

"One more question," asked Mercy as Wyetta served their pecan pie à la mode. "What about Ruby Rucker? Did you know her, too?"

"Ruby Rucker." Wyetta laughed. "Now she was a piece of work. Ran off on that hapless husband of hers not much more than a year after she married him. George Rucker wasn't man enough for Ruby."

"You liked her," said Mercy.

If Wyetta did like her, thought Troy, she was the first person they'd met who had.

"I did. Lots of folks around here didn't like her much, but I thought she was a hoot. She used to come in here all the time for lunch, nearly every workday. Big tipper."

"Great pie," he said. So good he figured he'd let Mercy ask the rest of the questions, so he'd have time for another piece.

"She worked?" asked Mercy.

"Sure. She was smart. Certainly smarter than George."

"What did she do?" asked Mercy between bites of pie.

"She worked for George, of course. The family business. Rucker Real Estate."

"What did she do for them?"

"She sold houses. That woman could sell ice in Alaska."

"We passed a Rucker-Smith business on the way here," said Troy. "Any relation?"

Wyetta nodded. "When Ruby went back to Vegas and George ended up in jail, that was the beginning of the end of the Vermont Ruckers. George's parents died of mortification, if you ask me. The business went to their distant relations. A second cousin once re-moved from New Hampshire named Mary Lou Rucker-Smith took over everything. Changed the name from Rucker Real Estate to Rucker-Smith Premiere Properties, but that doesn't fool anyone." Wyetta grinned. "You should go talk to her. She's the biggest gossip in town. If you want to know anything about Ruby, I'm sure she'll give you an earful."

CHAPTER EIGHTEEN

THE RUCKER-SMITH PREMIERE PROPERTIES OFFICES WERE located three blocks south of Wyetta's Café in a big old gingerbread Victorian pile painted in every shade of purple from pale lavender to eggplant. To Mercy, it looked more like a funeral home on steroids than a real estate office. But the sign out front was big and bold and the windows were full of pamphlets and brochures of local houses, so this was definitely the place.

At Wyetta's insistence, they'd left the two dogs in the café to sleep off their lunch with Earl. Apparently, Mary Lou Rucker-Smith was not very fond of animals, so much so that she boycotted the restaurant on account of the basset hound.

Mercy tramped up the stairs with Troy, and they stopped for a moment to stare at the ornate plum-colored front door with its stained-glass panel of a psychedelic peacock before venturing inside.

A tinkling bell announced their presence as they stepped into a huge entryway with an elegant staircase leading to the second of three floors. The house may have been all painted lady outside, but inside they'd taken down most of the walls, leaving big open spaces on either side of the foyer. The walls were all painted a pale sky blue with bright white baseboards and crown molding and hung with elaborately framed architectural drawings of fine houses from every era. The furniture was an eclectic mix of antiques and modern pieces.

A well-groomed woman in what Mercy's mother, Grace, would

have disdainfully called a St. John knockoff knit suit approached them. She wore lots of gold jewelry and her hair was an auburn helmet that had been sprayed into submission. She was attractive in that "let me find you the home of your dreams" real estate agent kind of way.

"Mary Lou Rucker-Smith," she said, holding out a perfectly manicured hand to shake, setting off a rippling of thin gold bracelets along her wrist. "May I interest you in a property here in Lamoille County?"

"I'm afraid not," said Mercy.

"Not this time," said Troy, introducing himself.

"So you're not a couple." She looked Troy up and down with renewed interest.

Mercy saved him. "We're colleagues. I'm Mercy Carr."

Mary Lou ignored her, focusing her laser-green eyes on the handsome game warden and favoring him with a seductive smile. "I'm always happy to help out law enforcement in any way I can. How can I be of service?"

She must be wearing colored contact lenses, thought Mercy. Nobody's eyes were really that color.

"We're here to talk about George Rucker," he said.

"George Rucker," she said. "I am sorry to inform you that he is no longer a resident of Lamoille County. He's a resident of Sneedville Farm, a maximum-security corrections facility in the middle of nowhere, Mississippi. But then you must know that, being an officer of the law." She curled her finger at him, red nails flashing, and sashayed out of the entryway to their right, her four-inch heels clicking on the well-polished parquet floors.

Troy shrugged at her and followed Mary Lou. Mercy sighed, knowing that they needed to interview this woman and yet dreading the hoops she'd make them jump through. She'd parse out information like dog trainers parsed out treats for dogs during training sessions. Troy would have it worse, unless Mary Lou was his type and he enjoyed the back-and-forth dance of reward and punishment to come. Surely he'd learned his lesson with Madeline; high-maintenance women like his wife and the Realtor were rarely worth the effort.

Mary Lou swirled around gracefully and leaned her narrow hips against the edge of her antique kidney-shaped writing desk. Hiking up her skirt just enough to tempt the game warden, should he be tempted. Mercy peeked at Troy out of the corner of her eye to see if it worked, but his eyes were on the woman's face, not her legs.

"I really should have changed the name of the business when I had the chance," Mary Lou said. "But the understanding was that we'd compromise. Of course, now that Uncle Edwin and Aunt Martha are gone, and George is incarcerated, I suppose there's nothing to stop me changing it." She smiled alluringly at Troy. "How does Mary Lou Smith Premiere Properties sound to you?"

"Didn't George object to your taking over the business?" asked Mercy.

"George Rucker was in no position to complain. He's lucky I took over. I've really turned the place around."

"What do you mean?"

Mary Lou drummed her long acrylic nails on the exquisite inlaid parquetry. Mercy imagined she could hear the desk screeching in protest. It was all she could do not to do so on its behalf. "George was a terrible businessperson. In the short time between Ruby leaving and his going to jail, he managed to make a lot of bad deals. Deals I inherited—and when the recession hit, I really had to scramble to keep the lights on."

"And now?" asked Troy.

"And now we're back on track."

"What happens when George comes home?"

Mary Lou laughed. "George killed a cop. He's not coming home anytime soon."

He frowned. "So you haven't heard."

"Heard what?"

"Rucker has escaped from prison."

Mary Lou stared at him. "I don't believe it." She looked from Troy to Mercy. "Seriously?"

"Seriously," said Mercy.

"It's possible he's on his way back here."

"Why would he do such a thing?" She straightened up from the desk and tucked her hands in the pockets of her suit as casually as a runway model. "The George Rucker I knew was barely capable of surviving jail, much less escaping it."

"Maybe so, but as it turns out he has survived *years* in prison, and now he has escaped."

Mary Lou removed her hands and pointed to the two upholstered Victorian balloon chairs that flanked her desk. "You may as well sit down. This calls for chocolate and coffee. Or maybe something stronger. I'll be right back."

Mercy and Troy exchanged a glance as the Realtor disappeared through a door at the back of the room.

"Why didn't the local authorities warn her about George?"

"I don't know," said Troy. "Something to check out."

"Maybe they did tell her, and she's lying about it."

"Why would she lie?"

"I don't know. But I don't trust her. I suspect she's a very good liar."

"I'll ask the captain to put out feelers."

The clatter of high heels signaled Mary Lou's return. She flitted in, carrying a silver tray set for coffee and placing the tray down on her desk. She handed a Queen Victoria bone china dessert plate heaped with chocolate macarons to Troy. "Have a cookie, Troy. May I call you Troy?"

"Yes, ma'am."

She raised an eyebrow at him, not sure whether to be insulted or flattered. Mercy choked back a laugh, taking a macaron and using it as cover.

"I'll pour." Mary Lou filled three Queen Victoria cups with strongly brewed coffee from the intricately engraved silver coffeepot and served Mercy and Troy with the aplomb of a geisha.

"Help yourself to milk and sugar." She settled herself in the tufted taupe armchair behind her kidney desk and sipped her coffee.

"There is a possibility that Rucker could be on his way here," said Troy.

"Why would he do that? There's nothing for him here." She placed her coffee cup on the desk and leaned back in her chair. "I imagine he's halfway to some country we don't have an extradition treaty with."

"Why do you say that? His home is here, his family business is here."

"And his share of the profits is deposited every quarter in his bank account by our firm's attorney. All aboveboard."

"So he's still a partner," said Mercy.

"A very silent partner," said Mary Lou with a smirk.

Mercy smiled at her little joke, but behind the Realtor's friendly if unnaturally green eyes was a very calculating mind. An ambitious woman who had no intention of giving George back his family business. Not that that should be possible, but if it were ever possible, Mary Lou Rucker-Smith would never allow that.

"So you're not worried about Rucker showing up here."

"Should I be?"

"We're not sure. But you should be aware of the possibility."

"Okay." She nibbled at a macaron. "So what can I tell you about George that you don't already know?"

"We'd like to know more about the circumstances that precipitated his fall from grace," said Mercy.

"You mean his wife."

Mercy nodded. "Ruby Rucker."

"How she talked that man into marrying her no one will ever know. He was a timid man, wouldn't say boo, could barely sell a house." Mary Lou popped the rest of the macaron into her mouth. Kept them waiting while she chewed and swallowed, her eyes on Troy the whole time. When she was finished, she grinned at him and went on. "George's parents were determined that he should take over the family business one day, so they sent him out to Las Vegas to this real estate convention at Caesars Palace, hoping that he would get inspired. All he did was get married."

"Do you know how he met her?"

Mary Lou shook her head, but not a hair moved. "Not at Caesars. That would have been a step up. Aunt Martha—George's mother— told me that he went to get a haircut at a barbershop off the strip somewhere called A Little Off the Top." She rolled her eyes. "Of course, it was a topless hair salon, but George didn't know that. He didn't even know there was such a thing." Mary Lou laughed out loud for the first time, a braying so surprising Mercy nearly jumped out of her seat.

"Can you imagine?" Mary Lou went on. "*A Little off the Top*? You know, that place was really just a front for other kinds of business." She put air quotes around the word *business*. "You know what people out there in the desert are like."

"So that's where George met Ruby."

"George went in there and Ruby cut his hair. She took a little off the top and decided she wanted to take it all."

"So Ruby was a hairdresser."

Mary Lou sniffed. "If you want to call it that. That's not what we call it here in Peace Junction. Anyway, poor George didn't know anything about women and she snookered him good. She gave him a haircut and God knows what else, and then she got him drunk and before you could say *'What happens in Vegas stays in Vegas'* George ends up at the Little Church of the West in an Elvis Presley costume marrying Marilyn Monroe. You should see the pictures. George looks practically unconscious, but he does look happy. I've got that picture somewhere."

"We'd love to see it," said Mercy.

Mary Lou looked to Troy for confirmation.

"That would be great," he said, and she sprang into action. "Have another cookie while I go look in the back room."

As soon as she was out of the room, Mercy slipped out of her chair and behind Mary Lou's desk. She opened the drawers and sifted through the usual clutter of pens and pencils, business cards, brochures, stationery, stamps, tape, paper clips, rubber bands. No daybook. No photos. She probably kept her calendar and her pictures on her smartphone, thought Mercy. More's the pity.

"What are you doing?" he whispered.

"Just looking."

"Stop snooping and get back to your seat before she comes back."

She'd just sat down when the Realtor reappeared with a dusty round beribboned hat box. "Here it is. I found these when I went through the attic a couple of years ago. I sent some to George, and just shelved the rest."

"You're in touch with George?"

"Not really. I mean, we mostly communicate through lawyers. Not that we have much to say to each other. I never really knew him. The occasional family reunion, weddings, funerals, that sort of thing. What I know about him is what Aunt Martha told me. After he went to jail, she confided in me. She needed someone to talk to. I felt sorry for her." Mary Lou removed the top of the box. "Go ahead, have a look."

The three of them began to sort through the photos. Most were childhood pictures of George, some with his parents, but the majority were simply George at every stage of his young life: George in his crib and his carriage, George learning to swim and skate and hit a baseball, George graduating from kindergarten and high school and college. He was their only child, and they obviously adored him. What could happen to a family.

"Here it is." Mary Lou held up a color photo of a confused-looking man in a white sparkly jumpsuit, black bouffant wig askew, hugging a curvy young woman in a platinum blond wig and white halter dress that left very little to the imagination. The young woman appeared attractive, but she was wearing such heavy makeup it was hard to know what she really looked like.

"What happened after the quickie wedding in Vegas?" asked Mercy.

"George brought her home, and his parents nearly disowned him. But she had a charm about her, I'll give her that. And she tried to fit in, at least at the beginning. She left her Sin City ways behind her and did all the things George Rucker's wife was expected to do. She sang in the choir at church. Joined the historical society. Worked here selling houses. And boy, could she sell a house."

"So she was good at it."

"Ruby was a born salesperson. Unlike poor George. When Uncle Edwin and Aunt Martha realized that she might be able to help their son figure out how to run the business successfully on his own, then they accepted her into the family. They thought that maybe with Ruby's help, George would man up and they'd be able to retire to

Florida sooner. So they put her to work in the office with George and she started learning the real estate business. She was good at it."

Mercy pulled out a photo of a young woman in front of a Cape Cod cottage holding a large SOLD sign. "Ruby?"

"Yes. You can see she toned down her Vegas look for one more in keeping with Vermont." Mary Lou smiled. "But not too tame. She'd wear one of those sexy outfits of hers, clever little pantsuits that were basically sewn on. Long sleeves to cover her tattoo. How many more she had—or where she had them—I'm sure I couldn't say." She winked at Troy. "Every man in town wanted Ruby Rucker to sell his house for him. Commercial real estate, too. All those leases ... she could talk men into doing anything. And she did. But she was nice to the women, too. Bowled them over with flattery and full-on charm. Soon she was listing and selling more property than anyone in the county."

"And how did George Rucker handle that?" he asked.

"He loved it." She pointed to another photo, this one of George and Ruby at the town common on what appeared to be the Fourth of July. They were in jeans and T-shirts and waving American flags. "She was good for him, at least at first, and she was really good for business. Rucker Real Estate became the hottest realty office in town. Anyone who was anyone did business with Ruby and George. Even the judge."

"What judge?"

"Judge McDermott. Married to the richest woman in the county. Between the two of them they owned a lot of property here and across Vermont. Ruby became their primary Realtor."

"You'd think Ruby would have liked her new life here, if she were so successful. What happened?"

"Word was she started fooling around. I suppose that was inevitable. There are few men on earth as boring as my cousin George."

Mercy could feel Troy glance her way. She asked the question, anyway, steeling herself for the answer. "With whom?"

"Anyone and everyone, at least that's what Aunt Martha said. Of course she was his mother, so she was biased in favor of her son. I personally can't imagine how he ever thought he could keep a woman like that happy in the bedroom." She pointed to another photo, this one of a sullen George in a suit and tie and a vamping Ruby in black leather pants and a red sweater in front of an old hunting lodge in the mountains.

"Just look at the poor man. He just didn't know what to do with her." She smiled at Troy, as if say, *I know you'd know what to do with me.* Mercy looked away before she laughed out loud.

"Not that it was all his fault," continued Mary Lou. "Ruby was a flatlander, big time. I think it amused her for a while, living in the mountains, playing the role of the wife of a local big shot, but not for long. Even the judge's parties couldn't keep her here."

"What do you mean?"

"The judge had houses all over Vermont. He'd send Ruby out to find out-of-the-way places he could buy and fix up for his parties." Once again Mary Lou made quotation marks with her fingers, her long red nails dramatizing the word *parties*.

"What kind of parties?" asked Troy.

"Wild parties." Mary Lou placed her elbows on the desk and leaned in toward Troy, revealing a cleavage worthy of a Victoria's Secret model. "I usually don't repeat gossip."

Mercy fought to keep her poker face but couldn't hold back a hiccup. Mary Lou glared at her, and then focused again on the game warden.

"But I suppose it wouldn't hurt just this once. To help you with your investigation."

"We would appreciate it, ma'am," said Troy.

Mercy marveled at how he managed to combine the authority of the law enforcement officer with the downhome appeal of the outdoorsman. He had often told her that he owed whatever people skills he had to Susie Bear's charisma, not his, but that was just false modesty. Troy was outplaying Mary Lou Rucker-Smith, and she didn't even know it. Susie Bear wasn't even in the building.

"I suppose since the old man is long gone, I can tell you what I've heard." Mary Lou straightened her spine, wiggled her chair back a bit, and crossed her legs high on her thighs, allowing one shoe to slip off her heel and dangle from her toes. "Rumor was that these parties were the kind where anything goes and the only women invited were the kind who could land a man in jail."

"Drugs? Prostitution? Money laundering?"

"All of the above." Mary Lou shrugged. "Bad boys and their toys."

"When did the judge die?"

"Oh, he didn't die. His wife found out about the parties and that was the end of that. He retired and they moved to Hilton Head. *Then* he died." Mary Lou paused. "His wife was the one with all the money, you know."

"What happened to the parties?"

"I'm sure I don't know." She examined her nails and her gold bangles jingled. "I can tell you that the judge's wife had me list all the properties they still owned up here." She beamed. "Sold them, too."

"Impressive," said Mercy. "When was this?"

"Before the recession hit," said Mary Lou. "Thank the Lord."

"So the parties went on after Ruby left town."

"Oh yes. She just bought and managed the properties for the judge. As far as I know, that was the extent of her involvement."

"And George?"

"George was too busy trying to keep Ruby happy. But that was always a lost cause." Mary Lou opened her arms as if to hug the world and then pulled back and placed her palms over her heart. "We love Vermont, and Vermont has its charms, but it can't compete with the temptations of a place like Las Vegas. Not for a woman like Ruby anyway."

"What do you know about the day she left?"

"Of course I wasn't there, but Aunt Martha told me it was like any other day. Ruby came into the office after filing some papers at the courthouse, and then went to lunch and never came back. Ruby often took long lunches so nobody noticed she was gone until closing time."

"Where was George?"

"George had lunch with his parents every day up at the Rucker Mansion on High Street. It's the home of the Peace Junction Historical Society now."

"You wouldn't happen to know what papers she filed that day," said Mercy.

Mary Lou frowned. "As it happens, I do know. They were the closing papers for a hunting camp down south. A terrible investment. Made worse by George, who bought it and some others from the judge."

"Why would he do that?"

"George wasn't too smart—and the judge was very smart. Or at least his wife was. He unloaded several white elephants on poor George. God knows what he promised him. George was desperate after Ruby left. Vulnerable to the likes of the judge." She frowned harder, and then seemed to think better of it. She smoothed the frown lines between her eyebrows with her manicured fingers. "Very bad for the business. It took me years to recoup the losses after the crash in 2008. And some I still haven't sold. Like that hunting lodge."

Mercy fished out the photo of George and Ruby in front of an old lodge. "This place?"

"That's it. What a dump."

"Down south where?" asked Troy.

"Down your way in the Green Mountains. Deep in the forest. Too remote for even the most avid hunters."

"Could you show us on a map?"

"Sure." Mary Lou turned to the bookshelf behind her desk and pulled down a roller map of Vermont. She pointed to a spot in the south.

"That's not too far from where Colby was killed," said Troy.

"Colby," repeated Mary Lou. "You mean the biologist who was murdered?"

"Yes. Did you know him?"

"Of course not," said Mary Lou. "But every murder hurts second home sales. And second home sales are what keeps us alive."

"Right."

"The sooner you catch the guy, the better. For all of us."

"We are on it," said Troy.

Mercy wondered if Mary Lou's self-interest truly knew no bounds.

"And George, too." Mary Lou folded her arms across her chest, showing her cleavage to best advantage once more. "After all those years in prison he must be a different man now. Tougher. Meaner. Dangerous. Should I be worried?" She turned those green eyes on Troy and Mercy swore she batted her false eyelashes.

"I don't think so. We really think he's looking for Ruby. But you should still be careful."

"He knows he won't find her here," said Mary Lou. "No one knows where she is. George hired a private detective to track her down after she took off, but the man never found her. Aunt Martha used to say he was throwing good money after bad."

"You wouldn't happen to have copies of that private investigator's reports, would you?" Troy drew his chair in closer to Mary Lou. Close enough for her to smell that heady combination of man, earth, and forest. If she swooned, Mercy wouldn't catch her.

"Of course." She floated over to a file cabinet, retrieved a file from the middle drawer, and returned as languidly as a bored courtesan. She handed Troy the file, and her fingers brushed his. *Score one for Mary Lou,* thought Mercy.

"Thank you," said Troy, placing the file across his knees.

"George could also be motivated by revenge," said Mercy. "That might bring him here."

Mary Lou rested her chin on her folded hands. "Aunt Martha said George blamed local law enforcement. He was convinced that they had something on Ruby and that's why she was leaving town."

"Not the adultery?"

"George didn't care about that. He would have forgiven her anything. Some folks said she was sleeping with the sheriff, but Aunt Martha never believed that for a minute. She said the sheriff was not that kind of man. She always felt bad about George shooting him."

Mercy felt her face flush.

"Now August Pitts was another story," said Mary Lou. "Aunt Martha thought that he was the more likely candidate. Not to speak ill of the dead but I can tell you from experience that he was a pig. May he rest in peace."

CHAPTER NINETEEN

ALL IT TOOK TO GET THE ADDRESS AND THE KEYS TO THE old hunting lodge from Mary Lou Rucker-Smith was Troy's cell phone number and the promise that he'd return the keys in person "very, very soon." She'd offered to show Troy the place herself, but she wasn't dressed for a trek through the woods and Mercy suspected she hardly ever was.

They picked up Elvis and Susie Bear from the café. Wyetta handed Mercy and Troy a boxed pecan pie "to share" and a couple of ham bones in a paper bag for the canines, and the dogs wagged their goodbyes to their new best friend Earl. They were only about five miles down the road when they heard the siren and saw the flashing lights behind them.

"That didn't take long," said Mercy.

"Nope." Troy slowed down and pulled over as far as he could onto the shoulder, which wasn't very far thanks to the walls of snow plowed along the sides of Route 15.

"Let me do the talking," he told her. They waited as the officer approached the vehicle. He was a big guy, well over six feet and built like a fullback.

The dogs sat up, alert, all eyes trained on the window where the deputy was now standing.

"Roll down your window, Warden Warner."

Troy obliged. "Deputy Purdie."

"You've been interrogating the good citizens of Peace Junction."

The deputy was wearing mirrored aviator sunglasses. The sun was bright on the snow but Mercy didn't think he wore them for the glare.

"No. Just asking a few questions."

"You're out of your jurisdiction." The way he said it made Elvis growl and Susie Bear thrust her big shaggy head and barrel chest up onto the console between the front seats.

"Down," said Mercy and Troy in unison, and the dogs fell back.

"Good call," said the deputy.

"We're following up on a few leads in connection with the explosion in Northshire. You can contact the Major Crime Unit for confirmation."

Mercy was surprised to hear him refer the deputy to the MCU and not the Vermont Fish and Wildlife Department.

"Heard about that. Glad everyone is okay." The deputy removed his sunglasses with a swagger.

Mercy bit her tongue to keep from laughing.

To Troy's credit, he did not react at all. "George Rucker escaped prison," he said evenly, "and may be a person of interest."

The deputy leaned over and crossed his arms against the edge of the truck's door on the driver's side. "Hard to believe Rucker is capable of that."

"Prison break or pipe bomb?"

"Either." The deputy straightened up again and leaned back on his heels, towering over them as they sat in the truck. This did not appear to faze the game warden.

"We have reason to believe that he may be on his way up here," said Troy. "He's expected to be armed and dangerous. And he may not be alone."

"We've got it covered." The deputy put his sunglasses back on.

"Then we'll be on our way." Troy gave the deputy a look that said, *don't try to stop us.*

The deputy tipped his hat to Mercy—his first acknowledgment of her at all—and stepped away from the Ford F-150. "Drive safe."

"WHAT WAS THAT all about?" asked Mercy as Troy pulled the truck back out onto Route 15 and headed toward Route 100, which led south to Interstate 89.

"Just the local boys strutting their stuff."

"Why did you tell him to call MCU?"

"The dumber staties think of Thrasher as nothing but the top fish cop. Purdie looks like he might be one of the dumber ones. But even the dumb and dumber are afraid of Harrington." Troy grinned.

"But if he does call the MCU, then what?"

"Then nothing. He won't call. And even if he did, and Harrington complains, I can blame you."

"You're enjoying this shell game with Harrington."

"You sound surprised."

"I guess I am. I thought you hated politics."

He looked over at her with those warm brown eyes. "I do recognize that I have to come out of the woods sometimes."

"Even though that's where you'd rather be."

He laughed. "Always."

"I hear you. Plenty of politics in the military, too." Mercy knew Troy had done a tour in Afghanistan himself. He never talked much about it. Neither did she. But the fact that they had both been there bonded them in a way only another soldier could understand.

"Probably worse for you as an MP," he said.

"Part of the job I loathed." Policing her fellow soldiers was often a thankless job, and politics sometimes influenced who got punished for what. Usually not in a good way.

"It's not so much that I hate it. Although I do." He smiled at her, and she felt that telltale tug in her gut. The one that told her that whether she liked it or not, she was facing an attraction that she may not be able to resist. She looked away from that smile to the winter wonderland beyond the windshield and tried to focus on what he was saying.

"I'm just no good at the politics thing," Troy was saying with typical self-deprecation. "I usually leave it to Thrasher."

"But not this time."

"He crossed a line when he told me to spy on you."

"I don't want you getting into trouble because of me."

"Sure you do. You don't mind a bit of trouble. Neither do I."

"Hallett says I can't help but get into trouble." Mercy sighed. "He says that's who I am."

"He's wrong."

"I wish I could believe that."

Troy reached over and placed his hand on her own. Even through his thick glove she could feel the heat of him. "There are two kinds of people in the world. People who run towards trouble, and people who run away from it. You run towards it. That makes you brave. Brave is who you are."

He squeezed her fingers and she squeezed back, letting his warmth sweep through her. She thought of her grandmother as a young girl holding her own hand under her pillow to dream of the boy named James. Silly.

Mercy reclaimed her hand and tucked it into her pocket. "Brave is who you are, too."

"And Elvis," said Troy.

"Yes, he is brave. But he has no choice." She stared at the snow-covered trees lining the narrow road. "It's true that I choose to run toward trouble. But Elvis doesn't have a choice. He goes because I go."

"You sound like Hallett now. Don't listen to that guy. He'll say or do anything to get what he wants."

Mercy didn't want to think about Hallett anymore. She changed the subject. "What do you want?"

"All I want to do is to solve Colby's murder and catch whoever planted that pipe bomb and broke into your house."

"Maybe we'll find some answers at the lodge."

"I believe in your hunches." He settled back into his seat with a smile, eyes on the road. The sun glinted on the snow, and he reached for the sport sunglasses that hung on his visor.

"You need some aviators. Like Deputy Purdie."

Troy laughed as he slipped on the specs. "I don't think so."

Mercy yawned. "Sorry." She didn't know if it was Wyetta's chicken and waffles and pecan pie à la mode or the noonday sun shining down as they wound their way through the cold beauty of her home state or just the cumulative effect of explosions, break-ins, and Mary Lou Rucker-Smith, but she suddenly felt exhausted. Too tired to move. Too tired to think.

"Take a nap," Troy said.

"Don't you want to talk through the interviews?"

"Not necessary. That hunting lodge is too close to where Colby was murdered for comfort. So we'll check it out. Now give that tired brain of yours a break." He switched on the radio to the Northshire NPR station and the mellow music of local folk duo Foamflower. As the strains of guitar and mandolin filled the truck, he reached back for his parka, which hung from the headrest of his seat. He pulled it off and handed it to Mercy. "Your pillow, ma'am."

"Thanks." Mercy bundled up the parka and placed it under her still sore head, curling up in her seat and using her own coat as a blanket. The last thing she heard before drifting off was Troy's soft tenor as he sang along to "Be the Clouds."

MERCY WOKE WITH a start, wild dreams of parties and white elephants and masked men still pinballing through her brain. Her head ached.

"Are you all right?" Troy flipped off the radio and looked at her with concern.

"I'm fine. Where are we?"

"Almost there. Well, at least almost to the point where we'll park the truck and meet Gil. He'll take us the rest of the way."

Mercy liked Gil. The park ranger knew the forest like the back of his hand. If anyone could find the old lodge, he could.

"Are you sure you're up to this?"

"I'm sure. Stop fussing."

Troy maneuvered his Ford F-150 into the parking lot at the trailhead. "We're here." They bundled up in their parkas and hats and gloves and slipped on their blaze orange and they all piled out of the truck.

They fastened the blaze orange hunter vests on Susie Bear and Elvis and clipped the leads onto their collars. Mercy shrugged on her backpack. Troy carried his pack and his gun and wore his duty belt as well.

Gil Guerrette was waiting for them. "It is a quick hike from here to the station. We can take snowmobiles from there. At least most of the way."

The hunting lodge was at the top of a ridge deep in the forest and accessible only by an old logging road built more than 150 years before. The road was now used primarily for ATVing half the year and snowmobiling the other half.

The ranger led the way down the trail through the woods. Troy followed with Susie Bear, and Mercy and Elvis took up the rear. Elvis never liked going last; he considered himself a leader, not a follower. He kept pulling on his leash, which was not like him, trying to barge ahead to join his canine pal. Usually he obeyed Mercy's *heel* commands, but then usually she left him off the lead on their hikes through the woods.

Susie Bear stopped in her tracks, waiting for Elvis to catch up. Troy laughed. "I say we let them go."

"Agreed," said Mercy.

They let the dogs off their leads and the Malinois and the Newfie retriever took off, stopping to say hello to Gil and then racing ahead again. Mercy knew they wouldn't wander too far ahead without them; the dogs would scout out the next section of the trail together and then circle back.

Troy dropped behind to join her. "That's more like it."

They tramped along in silence. It was mid-afternoon, and the sun was shining, illuminating the snowy path even as purple shadows began to gather under the pines. The forest was quiet this time of day; closer to dusk the deer and rabbits and possums would venture out in the open again to feed, accompanied by owls and bats and even bobcats and bears now that spring was in sight.

But right now even the squirrels were still. After about a quarter of a mile, they came across a small clearing that sat at the junction of the trail they were on and what looked like the old logging road Troy said would lead them up to the lodge. The ranger station was a simple wooden structure that reminded Mercy of a one-room schoolhouse without the bell. There were three snowmobiles flanking the building. Gil passed around the helmets and the keys. "Climb on and follow me."

Mercy mounted the smallest of the snow machines and put the shiny black helmet on over her blaze orange knit cap. She knew how to drive one of these beasts, but even so she always felt like she was astride a sixteen-hand horse ready to bolt at any moment. Gil started down the old logging road and waved for them to come along. She watched Troy speed after him, and she followed suit. The dogs trailed them as they'd been trained to do. Even Elvis would not challenge the noisy sleds.

It was cold—the temperature hovering around freezing—but she was warm in her parka and insulated gloves and boots. She loved the woods this time of year. Although she'd always prefer the slower pace of a hike, zooming along like this was exhilarating in its own way. And it was certainly faster.

The logging road veered uphill, and she thought about the loggers who'd clear-cut this forest all those years ago. It was dangerous work, for the workers, yes, but even more so for the woods, which nearly perished. But nature was resilient and once the clear-cutting subsided the trees grew back, only this time the hardwoods outnumbered the conifers, thanks to warmer soil. And Vermont, having come so close to losing her forests forever, now enjoyed an abundance of the splendid sugar maples whose bright foliage drew peepers from all over the world every autumn.

They rode for what seemed a very long time. The noise and the sheer physical effort to hold on as the snow machine chugged through the trees was wearing on Mercy; her whole body felt every rumble.

Finally Gil waved them to the side of the old logging road. They all pulled over and switched off their snowmobiles. Elvis greeted her as she dismounted, his curlicue tail held high. She removed her helmet and joined Troy and Gil.

"It is about one hundred yards through that copse of pines, I think," said Gil.

"You think?" Mercy rolled her eyes.

"Close enough," said Troy.

The trail, for lack of a better word, was not much more than a narrow slash through the snow-heavy trees. The dogs ran ahead.

"Why would anyone come up here for a party?" asked Mercy.

"That would depend on the party," said Gil.

"Remote may have been what they were after, if the Realtor's suspicions were correct," said Troy. "Although it's probably a lot easier to get here when there's no snow."

"It may have been more accessible twenty years ago."

They scrambled over a low old stone wall into a clearing where the snow cover was about a foot deep.

"This is probably filled with ferns as high as your derriere in the summer," said Gil.

The odd brown branch and twig poked up out of the white carpet burying any stone path that may have led up to the mountain lodge. The building itself was a hodgepodge of styles, with an 1800s-era granite rock foundation and massive chimney, dark shiplap siding, and a 1930s rustic-style porch addition with wide planked floors, log supports, and chicken-wire fencing. Once the hunting camp had been a beautiful place, but that had been many winters ago. Now the falling-down roof, broken windows, and general air of neglect lent the old lodge a haunted look worthy of a Stephen King novel.

"It doesn't look like anyone has been here in years," she said.

"Watch your step," warned Troy as she went up the stairs.

Mercy brushed the snow from the steps with her gloved hands, exposing the splintered planks below. She navigated around them, crossing to the front door. There was an ancient lockbox on the rusted handle, but since the panes were mostly all missing, she just reached in and opened the door, stepping inside to a pine-paneled room dominated by an enormous granite fireplace whose hearth ran the length of the room. Log furniture in various stages of disrepair littered the floor. Stuffed trophies stared down at her from every angle: the usual glass-eyed deer and moose, as well as fish on the fly, eagles in flight, and bears on the rampage. All coated in dust at least a decade thick.

"Nothing here but dirt," said Gil.

"Oh ye of little faith," said Mercy, and he grinned.

"Okay, *Merci,* we will look around."

They split up, making their way through the six rooms. Living room, kitchen, four bedrooms, and two bathrooms, all paneled in pine and furnished in classic hunting camp style with taxidermy being the one main decorative element.

As far as Mercy could tell, the only sign that anyone had been there this century was the pantry, which still held some canned goods—mostly stew and chili, corn and peas. She moved on to the kitchen cabinets and drawers, which revealed nothing but broken plates, a couple of rusted-out iron skillets, and a profusion of mouse droppings. She sneezed, and twisted away, spotting an old hand-drawn map tacked to the inside of one of the cabinet doors. The map showed the lodge, paths leading to a creek, a lake, a ski run, a fire tower, and a small bungalow.

She ripped the map from the cupboard and found Troy in the living room with Gil. "There's another building."

"There's nothing here to indicate anything went on here besides hunting and fishing trips," said Troy.

"There must be something," she said. "This place is our only link between Colby's murder and George Rucker."

"Maybe it is merely a coincidence," said Gil.

"Mercy doesn't believe in coincidences."

"Neither do you," she reminded him.

"Coincidences can be sexy." Gil chuckled. "We will check out the bungalow, *n'est-ce pas?*"

They all traipsed out of the lodge and south across the clearing to a tall stand of winterberry holly, the red berries bright as fresh blood against bare branches heavy with snow. At nearly eight feet high, the overgrown bushes nearly obscured the low-slung cabin behind them. What the map had labeled as BUNGALOW was more a glorified lean-to, with walls of logs and a time-worn weathered and warped tin roof. She tromped around the winterberry to get a close-up look at the building and spotted two sets of paw prints turning the corner of the bungalow.

"Where are the dogs?" Mercy looked at Troy, who'd joined her on the other side of the bushes. He shrugged. "They're around here somewhere."

She whistled for Elvis and the Belgian shepherd pranced through the snow toward her, stopping just short of her toes. Susie Bear romped in his wake, always happy to rumble through the white stuff. Both dogs sank down to their haunches, barked once, and raced off again.

"There seems to be a canine consensus," said Gil. "You two go on ahead, see what those dogs of yours are up to. I will check out the bungalow here."

He winked at Mercy and she ignored him. Gil was steadfast in his belief that she and Troy should be a couple; as a happily married man himself, the park ranger was always trying to marry off all the single people around him. Starting with her and Troy. And he was nothing if not obvious about it.

She and Troy huffed after Elvis and Susie Bear. They found the dogs behind the bungalow, rummaging through a clutter of junk half buried in snow: a couple of broken-down sawhorses, a disintegrating woodpile, scrap metal, an old axe and a couple of shovels, and several metal drums.

"Get out of there," ordered Mercy. She didn't want Elvis or Susie Bear slicing a paw on a dirty rusty nail and contracting tetanus.

Elvis picked his way cautiously through the rubbish. Susie Bear followed suit in a far less fastidious manner. The dogs sniffed around the barrels. Elvis sank into his classic Sphinx pose. Susie Bear spread out next to him, nose pointed towards the barrel in the middle, excited tail thumping away.

"They're alerting to the barrel."

"Why would they do that?"

"Weird, but they've never been wrong before."

"True enough."

"There's only one thing to do then. Open the barrel."

"What if Elvis is alerting to explosives?" Elvis's job in Afghanistan was to sniff out all manner of weaponry and explosive material— from det cord and gunpowder to IEDs and pipe bombs.

"Susie Bear is not trained to alert to those things. It must be something else."

Susie Bear alerted to people, not explosives.

"Elvis alerts to people, too. Dead and alive." Mercy was very proud of the way Elvis the bomb sniffer dog was adapting to civilian life, learning search-and-rescue as well as cadaver work.

He was way ahead of her in that regard; she was still figuring out how to best walk through the world now that she was no longer a soldier. "Let's take a closer look."

"Okay, but we err on the side of caution," said Troy.

"Right."

The fifty-five-gallon steel cylinders were about three feet high and two feet in diameter. They'd been there for years; the rust that had eaten away at the metal was proof of that.

"Any explosives that were in here would be ruined by now," said Mercy.

"Probably." Troy brushed the snow off the top of the barrel in the middle, the one in which the dogs had shown the most interest. There were cracks in the lid, and a sizable hole in the center. He fished his flashlight from his duty belt and snapped it on, shining the light into the opening.

"Look," he told Mercy. "See what you can see."

She leaned over and stared down into the cavity. She saw no electronic parts, no nails or wires or detonating cord. What she saw were bones. And what looked like the rubber sole of a shoe.

"It's not explosives." Mercy straightened up and faced Troy. "It's a body."

CHAPTER TWENTY

Troy and Mercy backed away from the barrel. They both pulled out their smartphones and started taking photos.

"Good job," Mercy said to the dogs.

"Come on," said Troy.

Elvis and Susie Bear followed them to the edge of the winterberry bushes, where Mercy pulled out a couple of peanut butter doggie biscuits to reward their discovery and Troy trumped those treats with two thick strips of beef jerky. Beef jerky being their very favorite treat of all time. Elvis also got his Kong to play with, a bonus that did not impress Susie Bear. She was all about the food.

"Stay," Mercy said, and together she and Troy went to find Gil. The door to the bungalow was hanging off its hinges. They stood in the frame and peered inside. The park ranger was in the far corner of the single garage-sized room, which looked like it had been inhabited by a succession of vagrants, all of whom had added another layer to the piles of litter that had been accumulating for years.

Gil looked up just as Troy called his name.

"What?" asked the park ranger.

"We've got a skeleton in a steel drum out there."

"Of course you do." Gil laughed. "I am stuck in here up to my eyeballs in *merde* and you are outside in the snow finding bodies in barrels."

"Did you find anything of interest?"

"I do not think so." Gil raised his gloved hands in a classic Gallic *meh*. "But in light of your discovery we will have to take a closer look."

Mercy stepped forward, and Troy put up his hand to stop her.

"Let's just wait for the forensics team," he said.

"Agreed." Gil smiled at Mercy. "*Dommage*. But you know the rules."

She did know. The three rules of crime scene investigation were: One, don't touch anything. Two, don't touch anything. Three, don't touch anything. At least that's what they always told the uniforms, and technically she was worse than a uniform, she was a civilian. She would have to settle for taking pictures until the crime scene techs got here.

Gil picked his way back across the multilayered clutter that covered the floor to join them near the door. "There is some evidence of recent activity here." He pointed to a listing picnic table under a window missing most of its panes on the far wall. There was a candle on one end of the table where a bit of the surface had been cleared. "It is relatively clean, compared to everything else."

"So someone has been here." Mercy snapped more photos.

"Many someones have been here," said Troy.

"I mean someone who might have something to do with Colby's murder."

"What about the body in the barrel?" asked Gil.

"It doesn't look like anyone has gone near that thing since whoever put it there put it there," said Troy.

"Show me."

They tramped outside and joined the dogs at the line of winterberry bushes.

"What exactly did you see inside?" Gil looked hard at the steel drum some ten feet away.

"Human bones. The sole of a shoe. Scraps of fabric."

"Decomposition was advanced."

Mercy nodded.

"Whose body do you think it is?" asked Gil.

"I don't know," she said.

evening. But for now the skies were gray and the temperature was dropping. Mercy shivered.

"It's getting colder. Let's go inside." Troy whistled for the dogs and they all tramped around to the front of the bungalow.

Their trips back and forth had pounded down the snow, leaving a muddle of boot prints and paw prints and reminding Mercy how completely snow, rain, wind, and sleet could destroy any evidence that may have been left behind. Not to mention the bugs, birds, squirrels, and other scavengers. The woods always reclaimed its own sooner or later. *How long will a man lie i' th' earth ere he rot?*

Mercy led the dogs to the left of the door and waved them down into a *sit* next to an old bench. Troy closed the sagging door behind them and braced it shut with his pack. She sank onto the bench and patted the space next to her. "Sit down."

Troy sat down on the bench and unzipped his parka. He pulled her toward him gently and wrapped one side of his coat around her. She leaned in against his chest, her head tucked under his long arm, her own arms around his waist. Elvis settled his handsome head on her feet and Susie Bear likewise plopped her massive head on Troy's feet.

He didn't say anything and neither did she. The wind howled around the little bungalow and Mercy closed her eyes. She breathed in the solid smell of him, all pine and earth and snow, and luxuriated in the heat he generated, fiery as a furnace. She was warm and comfortable and dangerously close to the man who kept showing up no matter how hard she tried to push him away. Maybe she should stop trying so hard.

MERCY HAD DOZED off again, cozy in Troy's coat cocoon, when she heard Elvis bark. That roused her, and she opened her eyes.

Gil stood before them, grinning, his backpack at his side.

She straightened up, pulling away from Troy. "You're back."

"Do pardon me for interrupting your little catnap," said Gil.

"That was fast." Troy removed his arm from around her waist and zipped up his coat.

"It'll take them about an hour to get here." Gil unhitched a portable trail stool from the back of his pack and set it up, taking a seat by Mercy and Troy on the bench, the dogs between them on the ground.

"Really? That soon?" said Mercy.

"You can thank Harrington for that."

"The pressure must be on," said Troy.

"The press is all over him. Harrington is pulling out all the stops to get these murders solved."

"Do they know about this one yet?" Mercy knew that bad news traveled fast—and murder was always bad news.

"There's no keeping a body in a barrel quiet for long." Gil petted a dog with each hand. "Harrington wants his forensics team here before the media. Dr. Darling and her techs are getting the star treatment. They've got police escort all the way to the woods, and the pick of the motor pool for traversing the old logging rail."

"What does that mean?" asked Mercy.

"Harrington's pride and joy. Second only to his helicopters." Troy grinned. "The Tucker Sno-Cats."

Sno-Cats were two-ton tracked vehicles that looked like enclosed tubs on tank treads. The truck-sized snow machines could navigate extreme terrain, including unpaved icy inclines.

"So he's coming after all," said Mercy.

"No," said Gil. "There's a big storm coming in and he won't risk getting stuck up here all night. Even in a Sno-Cat."

"With a storm coming they won't have much time. And the sun will be going down not too long after they arrive."

"And they'll need the Sno-Cats for the storm." Troy turned to Mercy. "We use them for grooming trails and rescue operations. The worse the storm, the greater the need."

While they waited, they went over everything they knew about the Colby murder, the pipe bombing, the break-in at Mercy's cabin, Beth and Thomas Kilgore, George and Ruby Rucker, and the body in the barrel.

And came up with nothing.

"I'm glad this is your problem," said Gil.

"It's Harrington's problem," said Troy.

"It's my problem." Mercy crossed her arms. "My family is at risk, and I don't exactly know why. It's all got to do with this mess somehow. And until I figure it out, my family is not going to be safe."

"Well, when you put it like that," said Gil, "then it's my problem, too."

"And mine," said Troy.

"Just as well," said Gil. "If *La Grande Merci* is stumped, imagine how confused Harrington must be. He'll never figure it out."

"But you will," said Troy.

Mercy hoped he was right. She had a terrible feeling they were running out of time.

They heard the Sno-Cat transporting the Crime Scene Search Team up the logging road long before Dr. Darling and her crime scene techs appeared at the bungalow. Mercy stood with Troy and Gil and the dogs to greet them as they trudged through the clearing loaded with gear, Captain Thrasher in the lead.

Harrington must be panicking, thought Mercy, if he convinced the captain to accompany the forensics team. Normally he kept the Fish and Wildlife folks as far away from his Major Crime Unit as he could, saving all the glory for himself and his team. Maybe he was sending Thrasher to keep an eye on Troy as he kept an eye on her. Devious even for the devious detective. Or maybe Thrasher had volunteered and Harrington was feeling so pressured he agreed. Harrington didn't think much of game wardens and didn't like them interfering in his crime scenes. Likewise Thrasher didn't think much of the detective—and even less of murderers on the loose in his woods. She looked at Troy, but if he were surprised by his superior's sudden appearance, he didn't let it show.

Thrasher nodded at her, and she nodded back. Dr. Darling greeted Mercy with a quick hug. The medical examiner was a small and scrappy woman whose good cheer never seemed to waver no matter how gruesome the crime.

"Over here beyond the winterberry." Gil pointed to the bushes and set off, and the group followed the ranger. Mercy kept Dr. Darling company as they headed for the crime scene proper.

"It's been awhile," said Dr. Darling. "But you must have missed me to go to such lengths to visit with me again."

"Always," said Mercy. "The body is in that barrel over there." She pointed to the side of the bungalow. "In all that junk."

"How did you find it?"

"The dogs found it. They led us right to it."

"Elvis and Susie Bear, the wonder dogs." At the sound of their names, the shepherd and the Newfie trotted up to the medical examiner for a good scratch, and she obliged. "You two are keeping me in corpses." She gave them each one last pat and straightened up. "Time to get to work."

Mercy called the dogs to her side and they settled at her feet.

The doctor retrieved her protective wear from her pack. She suited up, pulling on her white suit over her ski pants and jacket. She stretched plastic booties around her boots and snapped plastic gloves on over her regular gloves.

"What a pile of rubbish," she said cheerfully as she surveyed the crime scene. "But I've seen worse."

"So have I."

"Of course you have." She patted Mercy's arm. "Nothing about death is easy, my dear, whether it happens at war in Afghanistan or here at home in the mountains."

"But you're always so upbeat."

Dr. Darling smiled at her. "Force of habit."

They watched as the techs got to work, taking pictures of the crime scene and the steel drums from every angle.

"We took some photos, too," said Mercy, "when we realized that this was a crime scene."

"That's good," said Dr. Darling. "We're going to need all the help we can get with this one. If that body has been in that barrel for as long as it looks like it has from here, odds are, whatever evidence there may have been, in terms of footprints and fingerprints, it's all long gone. The evidence that matters is in that barrel. There's a storm coming in, so we need to collect as much evidence as quickly as we can, document as much as possible to establish chain of custody, and then get it all out of here before the blizzard hits."

"Right." Mercy looked up at the late afternoon sky, where billowing clouds were gathering in ominous nimbus formations that promised snow—and soon.

"How did you find this place way up here, anyway?" asked Dr. Darling. "What brought you to this neck of the woods, or should I even ask?"

"One thing led to another." She told Dr. Darling about their visit to Peace Junction as they watched the crime scene techs set up outside lights that lit up the scene like a stage set.

"So you think this might be Beth Kilgore."

"Maybe." The techs finished quickly with the lights and were now erecting a pop-up tent around the steel drums.

"You do have a gift for finding murder victims," she said to Mercy. "And for solving the crimes."

"I'm afraid I'm not very close to solving this one. Or the others."

"Which may or may not be related."

"Which may or may not be related," Mercy conceded. "I'm hoping you and your team can shed some light."

"Then we'd better get to it." Dr. Darling approached the tent. "We'll do our best. But this may be the toughest case you've brought us so far. It looks like this corpse has been here for a while. We'll see what's left of it and go from there." She disappeared inside, letting the door flap fall into place behind her.

CHAPTER TWENTY-ONE

W E NEED TO CATCH UP WITH THE CAPTAIN." TROY JOINED her, along with Thrasher and Gil, as she stood with the dogs while Dr. Darling and her team worked the crime scene.

"Sure."

"I've told him everything we've learned on this trip," said Troy. "But I wanted you to hear what's been going on at his end."

"There have been some developments," said the captain. "We've tracked down the guy who dropped off the kittens at your grandmother's house."

"How *is* my grandmother?"

"She's safe. Becker and Goodlove are with her at Lillian Jenkins' house."

Officer Becker was a junior Northshire police officer and Officer Goodlove was his rookie partner. They were trustworthy and loyal and inexperienced enough to make Mercy nervous.

"Thanks for that." At least her grandmother had someone watching over her. "How did you find the guy?"

"He came forward on his own when he heard about the bombing," said Thrasher. "He's just a kid. Eighteen-year-old student at Northshire Community College. Lives with a couple of roommates in one of those Victorian triples on Elm Street. He says they found the kittens under the porch, and the mother was long gone, so he dropped them off at Patience's house."

"How did he know about the rescue drop-off?" asked Gil.

"Everyone in town knows about it," said Mercy. "Patience sees to that."

"Did the kid see anything?"

"He said he didn't notice any cars on the road when he drove up, but that he wasn't really paying any attention. He parked at the bottom of the driveway on the side and walked up to the front door with the box of kittens. Rang the doorbell and left the way he came."

"And he saw nothing on the way back?" asked Mercy, stamping her feet to keep warm. It was growing colder now that dusk was approaching.

"No."

"I suppose it was always a long shot," said Troy.

"Not so fast." Captain Thrasher smiled. "He heard a snowmobile, and he reckons it was either an old model or a modified one, because it was very noisy."

"Noisy?"

"There are noise restrictions on snowmobiles," said Thrasher.

"For most snow machines, that's a noise level specification of not more than seventy-three decibels on the A scale at fifty feet," rattled off Troy.

"Nice recitation," said Mercy.

"I've given countless tickets to hot-doggers who tamper with their snowmobiles' exhaust systems so that they can scream down those paths. Thereby inciting the displeasure of their neighbors."

"So how does this help us?"

"We're tracking down the owners of antique models and those who've received tickets for noise."

"Don't forget the racers," said Gil. "They don't have to follow the same rules on the racetrack, and they like 'em loud."

"Good point," said Thrasher.

"How about George Rucker?"

The captain shook his head. "Thousands of tips coming, but all false sightings so far. But something may still turn up."

"The sooner, the better," said Mercy, thinking of her grandmother.

"He's out there somewhere," said Troy. "Sooner or later someone will see him and we'll get him."

"Any word on the forensics at the blast site?" asked Mercy.

"Not yet. Nothing traceable. Nothing at your cabin either. At least not yet."

"What about Colby?" asked Troy.

"Still trying to find that camera." Thrasher frowned. "Or anything else that might qualify as a real lead. All dead ends so far." The captain looked around the crime scene. "Although this may change everything."

"If the two deaths are related."

"Harrington would be very pleased if they were," said Thrasher.

"He could kill two birds with one stone," said Gil.

Thrasher cleared his throat. "Harrington is working as hard as I've ever seen him. He's committed to getting to the bottom of all this as soon as possible." The captain paused. "As is the governor."

"That's good news," said Mercy. The more the governor pressured Harrington for results, the better.

"The media are doing their part, too," said the captain. "Hounding Harrington. I think he's actually dreading the spotlight these days."

Mercy tried to picture the PR-hungry Harrington ducking the camera, and failed.

"Here comes Dr. Darling," said Gil.

The conversation came to a dead stop as they all watched the medical examiner make her way to the winterberry bushes. Mercy found herself holding her breath, and deliberately exhaled. She reminded herself to breathe, even as she hoped against hope that Beth Kilgore had not spent the last twenty years in that steel drum.

Dr. Darling removed the plastic gloves that covered her winter gloves and tucked them into a wristband of her crime scene coveralls. "We've moved as quickly as we can. We've bagged what we could and the rest will have to wait until we get back to the lab."

She looked up at the darkening sky. "With the storm coming in, the only thing to do is to get this evidence out before the weather takes a turn for the worse. We'll come back after the storm to make sure we haven't missed anything, not that there will be much to find. But we've done the best we can under the circumstances."

"What did you find?"

"We opened all the barrels. Only one body." Dr. Darling looked at Mercy. "The one you found."

"What was in the rest of them?" asked Gil.

"Mostly household and construction waste. Old cans of paint, motor oil, chemicals."

Mercy bit her tongue. All she cared about was the body, and whether or not it was Beth Kilgore.

"And the body?"

"Not much left of it. Mostly skeletal remains. Just bones, some hair, scraps of denim from the victim's jeans, and polyester fibers from what looks like a shirt. And a pair of boots—duck boots—that are in pretty good shape."

"Those rubber soles last forever," said Gil.

Dr. Darling nodded. "And even the high-grade leather uppers are more or less intact."

"That's what you get with L.L. Bean," said Gil. "When they say those boots last forever, they're not kidding."

"Which means our victim was killed how long ago?" asked Mercy.

"At least a decade. Maybe two."

That would mean this body could indeed be Beth Kilgore, thought Mercy. The timing worked. "Any indication how the victim died?"

"There's what looks to be a bullet hole in the skull. Low on the forehead, centered, right above the eyes. I'm guessing .38 caliber. But I'll have to take a closer look. I'll know more later."

"But you do believe that the victim was murdered."

"That's still a guess at this point. All I can say for sure right now is that he was pushed into that barrel headfirst, however he died."

Mercy stared at her. "He?"

"From the pelvic bone and the brow ridge, it looks like an adult male. And the duck boots were definitely men's boots. Around size eleven." Dr. Darling smiled at Mercy. "This is not your Beth Kilgore. This is a man."

CHAPTER TWENTY-TWO

MERCY DIDN'T KNOW WHAT TO THINK. PART OF HER WAS relieved that Beth Kilgore had not been shot and stuffed into that barrel. But another part of her was bewildered. If this were not Beth Kilgore, then who was it? And what, if anything, did it have to do with everything that had gone wrong for her family in the past forty-eight hours?

"Was there anything to identify the victim?" asked Thrasher, cutting right to the heart of the matter as he always seemed to do.

"No wallet, no ID," said Dr. Darling. "Nothing left of whatever was in his pockets."

"So whoever killed him didn't want anyone to know who he was."

"The only thing that we've found that might be traceable is a man's wedding ring. Plain gold band. Tarnished due to the other metals used in the ring, but not too badly. And it looks like there may be an inscription inside. I'll let you know when I've had a chance to clean it up a bit."

"That might help," said Troy, "depending on what the inscription is."

"Failing that," said Thrasher, "do you think you'll get enough DNA from what's left of him to make a clean identification if we can find a match?"

"I'm cautiously optimistic," said Dr. Darling. "Now we've got to get packed up and out of here, pronto."

The crime scene techs packed up their evidence and their gear and Mercy and Gil and Troy and the captain helped them carry it all to the Sno-Cats. By the time they were finished, it was dark and cold and the first flurries had begun. Mercy waved goodbye to the captain and Dr. Darling and her team as the noisy snow tanks took off with a roar, their bright headlights illuminating the old logging road stretching through the forest before them.

"Let's follow them at a distance," yelled Troy over the din.

She and Troy clipped waterproof red LED lights onto Elvis and Susie Bear's collars so they could keep track of them on the way back to the ranger station.

"Good to go," said Troy. "Stay with us."

Mercy, Gil, and Troy mounted the snowmobiles and took off, the dogs running along in their wake. The forest loomed all around them. Above them just a slim sliver of sky mirroring their path through the woods but hidden now in a swirl of snow. Mercy focused on the taillights of the snow machine in front of her, and the solid figure of Troy, its driver. As the snow fell like a veil between them, she found herself wishing that she could reach out and touch him.

THE MOOD IN Troy's Ford F-150 on the long ride home was restrained. Maybe it was the lingering echo of the snowmobiles' blare on the trail that silenced them. Or maybe it was the effort required to ignore the current that ran between them, charged with longing that seemed to intensify with every mile. Mercy didn't dare look at Troy; she didn't trust herself to hold back if he in any way acknowledged the electricity in the air.

Troy was quiet, too, his eyes on the road as they drove on as the snow whirled all around them. She wondered if he were keeping his distance and waiting for her to make the first move.

Or she could be reading him all wrong and he was simply preoccupied with thoughts of the investigation.

She tried to train her brain on the case, but she found her thinking clouded by the conundrum of variables and unknowns and suppositions. She let the flow of facts and figures, assertions and assumptions, detours and distractions wash over her. Stones skipping across a stream. Fog billowing over the sea. Starlings flocking through the sky.

It didn't help. She needed to get home and get organized. That always helped her think it through.

TROY DROPPED MERCY and Elvis off at her grandmother's house to pick up her Jeep. She didn't expect to find anyone at home, as Patience and Claude were staying at Lillian's house and the hospital was closed for the night and snow was still falling heavily. But there was a light on in the clinic, so Mercy and Elvis went in to investigate. Bea Garcia was there, coaxing recalcitrant felines into carriers. A tattoo of two red cherries on twin stems on the inside of her left wrist peeked out from the long sleeve of her blue silk jacquard blouse as she reached around one of the cat carriers to zip it up.

Bea didn't look like the kind of woman who'd have a tattoo of anything anywhere, much less one like that. Mercy had a roommate in college who was really into ink; she knew that cherry tattoos were favored by gamblers into Lady Luck, rockabilly fans into nostalgia, and women into symbols of innocence, sexuality, and fertility.

But cherry tattoos always reminded Mercy of women and friendship, like Helena and Hermia in *A Midsummer Night's Dream*. *So we grow together, Like to a double cherry, seeming parted, But yet an union in partition; Two lovely berries moulded on one stem.* . . . Mercy wondered what Bea's cherry tattoo meant to her.

"Interesting tattoo," she said.

"A youthful indiscretion," said Bea with a smile. "As I imagine most tattoos are."

"I don't know," said Mercy. "Seems like everyone's getting ink these days."

"You?"

"No," said Mercy. "I thought about it when I was in the Army, but I never got around to it." Martinez had a sugar skull tattooed on his left arm, which he said represented the thin line between life and death. She would trace the intricate lines of the death mask when they were in bed together. The image fascinated her. He'd gotten the tat when he was a teenager to honor his grandfather after he passed on to the other side. Martinez was a man of faith, and while she used to tease him about his religiosity, she was glad that he'd been a believer, and had died secure in the knowledge that he'd gone to his maker. When he was killed, she'd thought about getting one of her own to honor his death. She didn't do it, but from time to time she still dreamed about that tattoo, and Martinez's arms around her.

"Are you all right?" Bea stood there, balancing the cat carrier against her slender torso.

"Sorry, it's been a crazy couple of days."

"I understand," said Bea sympathetically. "Maybe you should go home."

"I'm fine," said Mercy for what felt like the hundredth time that day. "What are you doing here in this weather?"

"The Cat Ladies are full up. And Ed went home to his family to ride out the storm. So I'm taking your grandmother's cats and the kittens you found to stay with me."

"That's great. But that's a lot of cats. Are you sure you have enough room?"

"I've got a big old Greek Revival home," Bea said. "Early nineteenth century. Plenty of space."

"You live there by yourself?"

"I lost my husband six years ago."

"I'm sorry." *Everyone has lost someone,* thought Mercy. Everyone has secret sorrows casting shadows on their hearts and their minds and their souls.

"It is what it is." Bea shrugged. "I've been on my own since then. Well, except for the animals. I have two rescue black labs and a couple of rescue tabbies of my own, and I foster when your grandmother or the Cat Ladies call."

"Have you seen Patience today?"

Bea busied herself with the kittens, avoiding Mercy's gaze.

"You may as well tell me," said Mercy.

"She was here earlier, working," said Bea. "She didn't want you or Grace to know."

"I bet she didn't. What about Claude?"

"He didn't leave her side."

"And the police detail?"

Bea gave her a blank look.

"She's supposed to have twenty-four/seven police protection."

"I don't know anything about that."

"Okay." Mercy whistled for Elvis. "Let's get this place locked up and get you and the felines on the road."

"What are you going to do?"

"I'm going to go talk to my grandmother."

"You're upset."

"She needs to be more careful." Mercy punched the back of the padded office chair. "That pipe bomber is still out there."

"Of course."

Mercy helped load the carriers into the back of Bea's Subaru SUV.

Bea closed the hatch. "Look, I can see that you're worried. I didn't know she was supposed to stay at Lillian's house with a police guard. I didn't mean to enable any risky behavior on her part."

"Are you a shrink?" Mercy's mother, Grace, had dragged her to more than one therapist and she recognized the jargon. Or maybe Bea was in therapy herself. Which was all well and good; Mercy knew it worked for some people. As long as they kept her out of it.

"No. I'm a copy editor with a weakness for self-help books and nineteenth-century French novels."

Mercy laughed. "I have a weakness for dog training manuals and Shakespeare myself."

"Then you understand."

"Goodnight. Drive safe."

Bea waved goodbye as she got into her SUV, and Mercy waved back.

"Come on, Elvis," she said once Bea had driven away. "Let's go scold Patience."

LILLIAN JENKINS LIVED in a big white Colonial built on the two-hundred-acre farm that had been in her family since the mid-1700s. Her son Ethan and nine-year-old grandson Henry lived with her. Mercy was very fond of Henry, and when he answered the door with his dog, Robin, by his side, she and Elvis were glad to see them both. Henry was small for his age and liked numbers better than people and had a tendency to wander off when you weren't looking, but his service dog—a smart and loyal Great Pyrenees and Australian shepherd mix—made sure that he stayed out of trouble.

"Hi, Henry." She looked past him down the hall. "Why are you answering the door? Where are Officer Becker and Officer Goodlove?"

Henry ignored her and went straight for Elvis, oblivious to the cold billows of snow blowing into the house.

"Let's move this inside." She whistled and the shepherd untangled himself from Henry. She stepped into the foyer, closing the door and locking it behind her. Robin herded Henry down the hall toward the den.

Mercy and Elvis hurried after them into a large wood-paneled space with a game table and a big dark-red leather sofa. Lillian Jenkins and her son, Ethan, rose from the couch to greet them. For mother and son they couldn't have been more different; she was short and lively and outgoing and he was tall and serious and reserved. But together they were raising young Henry, whose mother had left and wasn't coming back.

"Mercy, how lovely to see you," said Lillian.

She didn't answer, surveilling the room and not seeing what she wanted to see. She felt her face redden with fear and panic and anger. "Where is my grandmother?"

CHAPTER TWENTY-THREE

L ILLIAN FROWNED. "I THOUGHT SHE WAS WITH YOU."

Mercy felt her heart sink. "And Claude?"

"Claude, too."

Ethan stepped forward. "Is there a problem?"

"They're not with me. I've been upstate all day. I just got back, and when I went to the animal hospital to get my Jeep, Bea Garcia told me that Patience and Claude had been at the clinic earlier but were here now." She pulled out her cell and texted both Patience and Claude:

Where r u? Call me NOW.

"I haven't seen them since late afternoon," said Lillian. "They did go into the clinic, and then they came back here for an early dinner. Afterward Patience said that they were going to talk to you."

Mercy glanced at her cell. She could see that the texts had been delivered, but not yet read. "They're not answering." She called her grandmother, knowing that she preferred calls to texts. "Straight to voice mail." She tried calling Claude. "Same thing."

"That's odd," said Lillian.

"She was supposed to stay here where Becker and Goodlove could keep an eye on her. Not to mention the blizzard out there," said Mercy. "Where did they go?"

"The officers were here," said Lillian. "They weren't happy when Patience said she was leaving."

"Patience told them they'd have to shoot her to keep her here," said Ethan.

"Of course she did." Mercy sighed. "So as far as you know they're at my cabin and Becker and Goodlove are with them."

"Correct," he said.

"I'm sure Patience won't do anything foolish," said Lillian.

"Well, that's one of us," said Mercy as she texted Amy to see if her grandmother was at the cabin. Maybe Patience and Claude had left their phones in the car.

"Do you know why she wanted to talk to me?"

"She said she remembered something that might be important," said Lillian.

"Did she say what it was?"

Lillian shook her head.

"Ethan?"

"No, I'm sorry."

Amy pinged back that Patience was not at the cabin.

"I've got to go."

"Is there anything we can do?" he asked.

She swiveled around again. "Stay here and if she comes back, keep her here. And let me know right away."

"Sure." Ethan walked her to the door. "Be careful."

Henry ran up to her, flapping his arms. He did that when he got excited or worried or scared.

"What's wrong?" Henry wasn't good at communicating but he was a genius who didn't miss much and often noticed what other people missed completely.

Elvis and Robin surrounded the boy, nudging his arms until he stopped stimming and started hugging them. He looked up at Mercy and said, "Ranger."

She smiled. If Henry liked you, he would call you by the character in his customized Dungeons & Dragons game that you most resembled. She was *Paladin* and Troy was *Ranger*. He was trying to tell her in his way that she should contact Troy to help them find Patience. "Don't worry, Henry. Contacting Troy is my very next move."

He nodded solemnly. She kissed his forehead, and he let her.

In the Jeep she texted Troy, to tell him that Patience and Claude were missing and to ask him where the hell Becker and Goodlove were.

"We're not waiting for an answer," she told Elvis. "Hold on."

And she drove much too fast through the swirl of snow over the slick roads all the way home.

Troy was glad to be back at the fire tower he called home. He was grateful that he could still call it home, since his soon-to-be-ex-wife Madeline had insisted that she was its rightful owner. Thank God for that condo in Boca.

He fed and watered Susie Bear. Belly full, the contented dog collapsed onto the couch for a nap while he stripped off his uniform, showered, and slipped into a long-sleeved T-shirt and a pair of sweatpants. It had been a long day, and he wanted nothing more than a ham sandwich and a Heady Topper and the hope that Mercy Carr was beginning to trust him again. The ham sandwich and the beer were the easy part, he thought, as he made the sandwich, poured the beer, and sat down on the other end of the sectional sofa to have his supper. The Mercy Carr part, not so much.

He'd left his phone downstairs, and so he went down to get it. He always plugged it in to charge upstairs in his sleeping quarters, since he was on call so much and needed to be available twenty-four/seven. That's when he saw the text from Mercy.

He texted back right away to tell her that he'd find out what he could and meet her at the cabin. He called Captain Thrasher, telling him about Patience and Claude gone missing and asking him where Officer Goodlove and Officer Becker had gone.

"I'm on my way to Mercy's," he told Thrasher.

"Let me track down Becker and Goodlove. I'll meet you there."

"This is not good."

"No," agreed the captain, and rang off.

Troy put on a fresh uniform and roused Susie Bear.

"Come on, girl."

She raised her big pumpkin head wearily as if to say, "Really?"

"We're going to see Mercy and Elvis."

That did it. The big dog lumbered to her feet with her signature elephantine grace. She wagged her long feathery tail.

"We've got to help find Patience." Troy grabbed his coat and his pack.

Susie Bear wagged her tail harder. There was no one she liked better than Patience, except maybe Troy, and nothing she liked better than finding people. For her, searching for Patience would be like the best game ever. The Newfie actually pranced out to the truck.

Troy hoped that Susie Bear's good vibes were prophetic. Because he had a very bad feeling about this.

BY THE TIME Troy and Susie Bear got to Mercy's cabin, the captain was already there, waiting on the porch for them before knocking on the door. This would allow the three of them—Troy, his dog, and his boss—to put up what the captain always called a united front, the better to comfort the family. The fact that Thrasher believed this situation called for a united front was the worst sort of red flag.

Mercy opened the door even before he and Susie Bear had gotten out of the truck. No surprise there, Elvis and Sunny alerted to all visitors long before they could ring the doorbell. But the captain did not enter the cabin. Instead, Mercy joined Thrasher on the porch, waiting for him and his dog. Now he wouldn't have time to ask the captain why they needed a united front to talk to her before they went inside.

The captain nodded at him and he huffed through deepening snow past the garden and up to the front door, the Newfie on his heels.

"Thanks for coming." She let them all in, and Elvis and Sunny greeted them enthusiastically, then ran off with Susie Bear into the living room. They followed them, Mercy leading the way. Troy couldn't tell from the captain's poker face what he was about to say, but he figured it wasn't good.

"Have a seat." Mercy waved them onto the larger of the two

leather couches in front of the flagstone fireplace, where her grandfather's hand-carved longbow hung in pride of place over the mantel.

Amy and Brodie were splayed out on the smaller one, and baby Helena was asleep in her play yard on the other side of the room. The kitten, Muse, was curled up in Amy's lap.

Troy loved this room. With its soaring ceiling and library wall of books and comfortable furniture, it was as pretty and smart and real as Mercy herself.

He sat down next to Thrasher, who'd settled himself in the exact center of the large sofa, legs apart, spine erect, dominating the space with his body language alone. Mercy sat cross-legged on the floor, Elvis and Susie Bear and Sunny surrounding her. The Buddha of Dogs, he thought.

But her expression was not serene. "What can you tell us?" She directed the question to the captain.

"We're working on it," said Thrasher, his voice rich with confidence. "We've got All Points Bulletins out on all of them."

"So you have, like, no idea where they are?" asked Amy.

"I don't get it," said Brodie. "I mean, Becker and Goodlove are cops."

Troy wondered how the captain would react to being challenged by teenagers. That couldn't happen very often.

"I understand your frustration. It's a very unusual situation." The captain rested his palms on his knees. "According to Harrington, Goodlove and Becker last checked in three hours ago. No one's heard from them since, but then they weren't due to check in again for a couple of hours. We've got everybody out looking for them. And Patience and Claude."

Troy knew that losing track of law enforcement officers was simply unacceptable. Sure, as a game warden he was often off the grid out in the wilderness, but this was different. These were local cops, in a police car, within the town limits. Losing track just didn't happen, unless something had gone very wrong.

"No sign of the vehicle?" asked Mercy.

"Not yet."

Troy could tell Mercy was worried by the way her cheeks reddened. "Don't worry, we'll find them."

"I do have some news," said Thrasher.

Mercy looked at him, her face bright with hope. It broke Troy's heart. "What?"

"Dr. Darling has been busy examining the remains and the other evidence. She took a look at that wedding ring, and we have a date."

"There was an inscription," she said.

"Yes." The captain smiled. "A wedding date engraved on the inner shank of the ring. June 13, 1999."

Mercy frowned. "That's right around the time that Beth and Thomas Kilgore could've gotten married. I've got a photo of their wedding somewhere." She went over to the farm table that separated the great room from the kitchen, where the forensics team had dumped the boxes. They'd come and gone while she and Troy were out, finding nothing, just as Mercy had predicted.

She pulled a cardboard box from one of the dining chairs. She deposited it next to the coffee table, and sank to the floor again, dragging all the files out and going through the photos while Troy and the rest of them watched.

"Here it is." She placed the faded picture on the table for them all to see. Two young people, a petite dark-haired girl looking sweet and virginal in an old-fashioned white lace dress. And a hulking guy with a scruffy beard and a dark look. He dwarfed his new wife.

Mercy snapped the photo over onto its other side. She pointed to the date on the back, written in a small, controlled hand. *Wedding Day: June 13, 1999.*

"It's the same date," said Amy.

"Random," said Brodie.

"I don't think so. What are the odds?"

"So our victim could be Thomas Kilgore." Troy looked at Mercy. "Not Beth Kilgore."

"We'll check to see if we have any fingerprints or DNA from Thomas Kilgore on file."

"You should. I know he's been arrested several times," said Mercy. "At least one time for assault. He broke his wife's nose."

"What a creep," said Brodie.

"We'll run his records," said Thrasher. "Dr. Darling says the body could have been in that barrel for twenty years, so it could conceivably be Thomas Kilgore. The timing fits—or at least it doesn't *not* fit."

"If it is Thomas Kilgore," said Troy, "then his wife could have killed him."

"That's a big if," said Mercy.

"Yes. A big if." Amy crossed her hands across her chest. The movement disturbed the kitty, and she leapt from her lap to Brodie's lap.

Troy smiled. It was sweet how Amy always aligned herself with Mercy. "Either way, we need to find Beth Kilgore."

"I can't believe that she would murder anyone," said Mercy.

"A battered wife gone too far," said the captain. "Pushed too hard, one too many times. Snaps. It wouldn't be the first time."

"What about Ruby Rucker? The crime scene was on a property that Ruby had listed. Maybe she killed him."

"No motive."

"That we know of."

"That we know of," conceded Troy. "Although Beth and Ruby were friends. Maybe that's how Beth knew about the place. Ruby may have taken her there."

"You're losing me," said Brodie.

"Who's Ruby Rucker?" asked Amy.

Mercy filled the others in on their trip to Peace Junction, where they'd met Louise Minnette at the library, and learned that Ruby Rucker and Beth Kilgore were friends and that Louise had seen them together at the theater. She told the story well, so well that Troy had nothing to add.

"So you're saying that both women disappeared that same summer," said Thrasher.

"Yes."

"What time period?"

"No one's really sure," said Mercy. "George reported Ruby missing right away. But no one knew exactly when Beth and Thomas Kilgore disappeared. They lived up there in Marvin, by the old asbestos mine."

"I didn't know that anyone still lived up there," said Thrasher.

"No one should."

"It's pretty isolated up there."

"Exactly. That's why nobody noticed they were missing. It wasn't until Beth's father, Clem Verdette, came back from his annual summer fishing trip to Canada that they were reported missing."

"More like a poaching trip," said Thrasher.

"Yeah," agreed Troy.

"Thomas Kilgore's family just assumed that he and Beth had moved to California," said Mercy. "They were about to get thrown out of their trailer, and Kilgore had been hitting up everyone he knew for money. The family figured that they just took off."

"So we have this window," said Thrasher, "in which Ruby and Thomas and Beth Kilgore disappeared."

"But Thomas Kilgore didn't disappear, he got murdered," said Amy.

"Epic," said Brodie.

"Ruby could have told Beth and Thomas about the lodge," said Troy. "Maybe they went to stay there, since they were getting thrown out of their trailer."

"It's possible," said Mercy.

But Troy could tell she didn't believe that scenario.

"Kilgore loses his temper," said Thrasher. "One thing leads to another, he ends up dead. Beth flees."

"I just can't see Beth as a murderer," said Mercy.

"Granted, what we've got here is mostly speculation," said Thrasher. "We'll see what other evidence we come across."

"What about the barrel?"

"There doesn't seem to be much more salvageable evidence at this point. No murder weapon except for the bullet and no gun. But we'll keep looking. I know they'll search the property again once the storm has passed, but there's a good chance we won't find the gun. That weapon could be long gone."

"At the bottom of a lake or a ravine somewhere," said Brodie, as if he disposed of murder weapons on a regular basis. The kid was such a goof, thought Troy. He knew Brodie drove Mercy crazy, but he got a real kick out of him.

"According to Mary Lou Rucker-Smith, George Rucker hired a private eye. Maybe if we can find Ruby, we can find Beth," said Mercy.

"Assuming, of course, that Dr. Darling can confirm what all this circumstantial evidence is telling us: that the victim is actually Thomas Kilgore." The captain always erred on the side of facts, rather than speculation. Troy admired that, but he had also come to value Mercy's gift for the educated guess.

"As much as I hate to admit it, I don't think there's much doubt that our victim is Kilgore," said Mercy. "Those dates are pretty conclusive, and all three of them went missing around the same time. It's just too much of a coincidence."

"It's all connected somehow," said Amy, warming to the idea now that Mercy had acknowledged it. "The question is, how."

"But you got no clue where Ruby Rucker or Beth Kilgore went." Brodie looked at them all as if they were mad to think they'd ever solve this case. "Am I right?"

"The answer's got to be in those files," said Mercy, "and I'm going to figure it out. But I have to find my grandmother first."

CHAPTER TWENTY-FOUR

Mercy just couldn't sit around and wait for local law enforcement to find Patience and Claude. She was going to have to do that herself. She just had to figure out where they were.

"We're on it," the captain assured Mercy as he pulled his ringing phone from his pocket. "The best thing you can do is stay here and go through those files."

Thrasher was half right, she thought.

He looked down at his cell. "It's Harrington. I'd better take it." He rose to his feet and strode toward the front door. Troy went with him, and Susie Bear shuffled to her feet and shambled after him.

Mercy watched them go, only to see Troy and Susie Bear return, escorting her parents into the growing gathering in the great room. This was the last thing she needed. "What are you doing here?"

"What do you mean, what am I doing here?" Her mother charged forward, a cat in Chanel on the attack.

Her father stepped between them. "We came to see about your grandmother."

"My mother is missing," said Grace in a tightly controlled voice, "and whether you like it or not, this is my family, and you are my daughter, and I have as much right to be here as you do. Maybe more."

Mercy bit back the uncharitable fact that this was actually *her* home, so her mother really didn't have as much right to be there as she did.

Her father knew what his daughter was thinking—he always seemed to know what she was thinking—and gave her one of his "give your mother a break" looks. He placed his arms around Grace's shoulders protectively. "We just want to know what's going on."

"I didn't want to worry you," said Mercy, sounding lame even to herself.

"You've been worrying me since you learned to walk," said Grace.

Brodie laughed, and her mother glared at him.

He held up his hands. "What?"

"I'm going to make us all some chili," said Amy, changing the subject.

"I'll help you," said Brodie, with a look that said he was happy to escape to the kitchen with Amy.

"How can you think of food at a time like this?" Grace looked from Amy and Brodie to Mercy, and she knew what her mother was leaving unasked: *You live with these people?*

"It's what Patience would do," explained Amy.

A small sob escaped from Grace. She folded in on herself, her former bravado forgotten. Her father helped her onto the sofa.

"That sounds great, Amy," said Mercy. "Thank you very much."

"Sure." Amy headed for the kitchen, Brodie on her heels.

"So what do we know?" asked her father.

This was the question he always asked when he was thinking through a case. When Mercy was a little girl and wanted to be just like him, he would humor her by talking about his cases, and sharing his thought process, in the hope that she'd take an interest in the law. While she didn't grow up to be an attorney, she did credit those early conversations with sharpening her critical thinking skills.

"We know that Patience and Claude are missing," said Mercy, perching on the arm of the sofa, close to her father. "And that the two police officers assigned to protect Patience have failed to check in."

"That doesn't sound good," said Grace, shaking off her husband and sitting up straight, smoothing her skirt. Readying herself for battle.

Mercy smiled. You couldn't keep her mother down for long.

"We'll find them," said Troy, settling across from them on the love seat, Susie Bear at his feet.

"Start at the beginning," said her father.

"I don't know where the beginning is," she said. "There is so much that doesn't make sense."

"Elaborate," said her mother.

"We've got the pipe bomber." Mercy pointed to the screen shot Brodie had captured for her and printed out and left on the coffee table. "We've got George Rucker escaping from prison, current whereabouts unknown."

"We've got a dead biologist named Colby in the woods," added Troy.

"And another dead man in a barrel not far from where Colby died," she said. "Been there some twenty years."

"Probably Thomas Kilgore."

"Kilgore?" asked Duncan.

"Thomas Kilgore," said Troy, "suspected of killing his wife and running off. Current whereabouts unknown."

"Not anymore. Dr. Darling has confirmed that the body in the barrel was Thomas Kilgore," said Thrasher, coming back into the living room. Much to the pleasure of Sunny, who shadowed him to the love seat and positioned herself between his knees as he sat down next to Troy. The golden retriever rested her silky head on the captain's thigh, as if she knew he was a widower who needed comfort. Maybe he did, even if he never showed it. The dog was a marvel.

Troy raised his eyebrows at Mercy. "We've got Beth Kilgore, the abused wife who went missing twenty years ago. Current whereabouts unknown."

"And Ruby Rucker," said Thrasher, "the adulterous wife who left her husband and ran off to Las Vegas around the same time."

"Current whereabouts unknown," Troy and Mercy said in unison.

"That's a lot of current whereabouts unknown," said Duncan.

"Ruby Rucker was trouble," said Grace. "What has she got to do with Patience gone missing?"

"I don't know. I'm not sure how what happened back then matters to what's happening now. Or even if it does."

"It must matter," said her father.

"Your father doesn't like coincidences, either," said Troy.

"No." Mercy smiled at him before going on. "Ruby and Beth were friends. Ruby may have confided in Beth, told her that she was planning to leave her husband. And encouraged her to come with her."

"So you think Beth Kilgore murdered her husband?" asked Duncan.

"Yes," said Thrasher.

Mercy's father looked at her.

"No."

The captain shrugged.

"Grandpa Red traced their last known movements. Beth Kilgore was last seen at the library, and Thomas Kilgore's truck was last seen heading south out of town."

"That's where the trail ends for both of them," said Troy.

"Although now we know that Thomas Kilgore ended up at the bottom of that barrel," said Thrasher.

"We have more than that on Ruby. She sent George a Dear John postcard from Las Vegas."

"Her hometown," said Grace.

"Yes."

"George hired a private eye to track her down," said Mercy. "Mary Lou Rucker-Smith gave us his files. All he had to link Ruby to Las Vegas was this postcard. It's definitely her handwriting. The private investigator corroborated that, but he never found any evidence of her in Las Vegas. He traced her as far as the bus station, where she parked her silver Audi sedan in the lot and left the keys under the seat. She bought a ticket for Las Vegas, got on the bus, and was never seen again."

"Las Vegas is a city of transients," said her father. "People come, people go."

"It's such a tacky town," said her mother. "There's no pride of place. They spend absurd amounts of money to build these outlandish casinos, and ten years later they blow them up and start all over again."

"The chili will be ready in about half an hour," announced Amy as she and Brodie joined them from the kitchen.

"I couldn't possibly eat a thing," said Grace.

"Thank you," Mercy said to Amy. She turned to Thrasher. "Did we ever track down Rocky Simko?"

"Mississippi law enforcement found a stolen car abandoned in a Walmart parking lot last night. Another car was reported missing from that same lot that same evening."

"Simko is a car thief," Mercy told her parents.

"Let me guess. They found that one, too."

"In Tennessee," said Thrasher.

"So Rucker and Simko could have made their way to Vermont one stolen car after another."

"I don't see how all this can help us find my mother," said Grace.

At that they all fell silent. Amy and Brodie sat down on the floor by the coffee table, their love seat now inhabited by Troy and Thrasher. Mercy closed her eyes and let her mind wander. She retraced her and Elvis's steps in her mind, from visiting Deputy Pitts to the bombing and finding the body in the barrel to going to Lillian's house to see Patience and realizing she was missing. She opened her eyes. "Where would they take her?"

"Everybody's looking for them," said Amy. "So they'd have to take Patience somewhere no one would see them."

Assuming she were still alive, thought Mercy. But she couldn't let herself go there.

"A hiding place," said Brodie. "We're looking for their hiding place."

"We're looking for Patience," said Grace.

"Brodie is right. They have to be keeping her somewhere."

"I've got to get back to the station." Thrasher rose to his feet. "Troy, keep me informed."

"Yes, sir."

Thrasher nodded to Grace and Duncan and left.

"This is getting us nowhere," said Grace.

"Let's go back to the Ruckers," said her father. "As far as we know, George Rucker is the only person who hates Patience enough to hurt her. So what do we know about him and his wife?"

"They were in real estate," said Grace.

"That's right. She was better at it than he was. Mary Lou Rucker-Smith, the woman who inherited George Rucker's real estate business, says that Ruby Rucker sold a lot of houses. The old hunting lodge where we found Thomas Kilgore was one of her listings."

"That's interesting," said Duncan.

"The murder happened on the property that Ruby Rucker bought for the judge, and that George Rucker later bought from the judge," she said.

"Not far from where Colby's body was found," added Troy.

"Another connection."

"We know that Ruby and Beth knew each other," said Troy. "Maybe Ruby showed Beth the lodge. Or maybe she went to one of the judge's parties there."

"I can't see Thomas Kilgore letting her go to one of those parties," said Mercy. "Although he might go himself."

"Would the judge let a man like him come to one of his soirées?" asked Grace.

"Maybe through the back door," said Mercy. "He was a compulsive gambler. Maybe we need to add illegal gambling to the mix of drugs, prostitution, and money laundering."

"Kilgore could have crossed the wrong guy at one of these parties," said Troy.

"And ended up dead," said her father.

"So it might not have been Beth Kilgore at all." Mercy just couldn't believe that the young woman whose happy place was the local library was a murderer.

"She's still missing," said Troy, "and that disappearance is looking more and more suspicious."

"George Rucker knew about the lodge, too."

"So he killed Thomas Kilgore? What motive would he have?"

"I'm not suggesting that. I'm thinking about George in the present now."

"Okay, I'll try to keep up."

Mercy laughed. "Very funny, Warden Warner."

"It's not always easy to know where your mind is going."

"Tell me about it," said her mother.

Mercy ignored Grace's comment and addressed Troy. "I don't always know where my mind is going, either. But back to George Rucker. He's escaped from prison and he needs a place to stay. If he is here, then where could he go?"

"You're thinking maybe he's hiding out at one of these white elephant properties," said Troy.

"It would make sense. Mary Lou told us that he was still part of the business, so he'd know which ones were still vacant."

"Hideouts," said Brodie, high-fiving Amy.

"We should find out which those are." Troy sighed. "*I* should find out which those are."

"She likes you a lot better than she likes me." Mercy waggled her brows at him.

"I'm on it." Troy waggled his eyebrows back. They both laughed, and Mercy found herself drawn to him again.

"Get a room, guys," said Brodie.

Amy giggled.

"Really," said Grace, giving Brodie a look that could kill even the bravest clockwork juggernaut.

"What?" Brodie looked to Amy for assistance.

"It's okay." Amy returned Grace's imperious stare dagger for dagger. "He didn't mean anything by it."

Mercy smiled, grateful to Amy for the distraction. She shifted away from Troy as she felt the flush rise up her neck to redden her cheeks. She turned her back to them all, examining the files again, her eyes coming to rest on the Las Vegas postcard, which continued to bother her, though she couldn't say why.

"I'll contact the Realtor for a list of those properties," said Troy, finally breaking the awkward silence that went on way too long as far as Mercy was concerned.

"Great," she said, without turning around.

Troy left the room, going outside to make his call.

"I think I'll make a pot of tea," said Amy. "For all of us."

"I'll help," said Mercy, grateful for the opportunity to escape. As she left the living area and moved beyond the farm table to the kitchen counter on the other side of the great room, out of the corner of her eye she saw her father take her mother's hand in his. She wondered what it would be like to have someone in your corner all the time even when you were wrong. Especially when you were wrong. Martinez always had her back, but she wasn't sure that was the same thing.

She filled the electric teakettle with water and switched it on while Amy gathered mugs and tea bags and milk and sugar on a tray. By the time the kettle boiled and she and Amy rejoined the group, placing the tray on the coffee table, Troy was back.

"She emailed me the list."

"That was fast," said Duncan.

"Mary Lou Rucker-Smith stands ready and willing to help law enforcement."

"I bet she does." Mercy handed him a cup of tea. "Is that a direct quote?"

"More or less." He handed her a piece of paper. "These are all the properties George Rucker bought from the judge during that time."

She scanned the columns of the spreadsheet. "There are only three on the list that remain unsold. The hunting lodge where they found Kilgore's body, a nineteenth-century Cape Cod off Old Buttonbush Road, and a 1940s ranch built by Emil Woznicki in Rutland County."

"Emil Woznicki," said Duncan. "He was a very successful business-man in the last century. He saw Hitler for the danger he was very early on, and went to make a fortune in munitions during the war. We were at law school with his grandson Avery Woznicki. Remember, darling?"

"Vaguely," said Grace.

Mercy wasn't surprised her father remembered. Duncan had amazing people skills; he never forgot a face or the name and story that went with that face.

"What are you thinking?" asked Troy.

"I'm thinking we start with the Cape Cod," Mercy told Troy. "Since it's closer."

"Do you think you'll find Patience there?" asked Brodie.

"I don't know," she said, sipping her tea. "I hope so."

"It's a long shot," said Troy.

"Do you have any better ideas?"

"Everyone in law enforcement is out looking for your grand-mother and Claude and Becker and Goodlove."

"But they don't have this list."

"No," he admitted.

"And even if they did, they'd ignore it," she said. "So Elvis and I will check it out. Sunny stays here."

"Sure," said Amy. "We'll watch her. And I'll keep the chili warm for you."

"We're going with you," said Troy, meaning him and Susie Bear.

"Thank you," Grace said to Troy.

It was the first time her mother had truly acknowledged Troy Warner since the Wild Game Supper. Grace was queen of the silent treatment; ending the silence meant he'd earned her forgiveness. And possibly more, if he kept on protecting Mercy like this. As swayed by loyalty as a feudal lord, her mother might come to see Troy's actions as proof of his sworn fealty to the O'Sullivan-Carr clan. That is, practically family.

Not that she needed her mother to approve of Troy, any more than she needed her to approve of Martinez.

But it might be nice, for a change.

SUMMER 2000

*B*eth was at the library at noon as planned. She'd ridden her old electric bicycle the seven miles into town and parked it in the back of the parking lot, just like Ruby had instructed.

"Good afternoon, Beth," said Mrs. Minnette.

The librarian was one of Beth's favorite people. Usually she'd go over to the desk and talk books with her, but not today. Beth didn't have the time, and she had no books to return. She shifted the big tote slung over her shoulder. It did not hold library books; it held her wallet, two changes of clothes, toiletries, a manila folder containing her birth certificate and her social security card, and the only pair of high heels she'd ever owned.

"Hi." She hoped Mrs. Minnette couldn't tell what was in her bag. She looked up at the old-school black-and-white clock on the wall behind the desk. Five minutes past. Where was Ruby? Why couldn't she be on time, just this once?

She moved over to the magazine section, close to the front door, pretending to peruse People and Redbook and InStyle, one eye on the entrance. A lame smoke screen, since she typically headed straight for the fiction shelves.

Ruby swept in, hooked her pointer finger at Beth, and swept back out again. Beth breathed in that musty library bouquet of grass and vanilla and mildew one last time.

She hurried past Mrs. Minnette, who raised her eyebrows at her. Beth smiled and waved and rushed out of the building before the woman she secretly thought of as the mother she'd never had could notice the tears filling her eyes. The only person in Lamoille County she would truly miss.

Ruby was waiting in her Audi at the back of the empty parking lot. "Your bike's in the trunk. Get in the back and lay down."

Beth placed her tote on the floor of the car and scrambled in, crouching down in the seat by a folded Red Sox stadium blanket.

"Cover yourself," ordered Ruby. "Just until we're out of the county."

Beth complied without complaint. She was terrified that Thomas would see her and follow her and kill her in her sleep. The same fear that had stalked her every day and night since she'd married Thomas. She wondered how long it would be and how far she would have to go before that fear went away.

CHAPTER TWENTY-FIVE

O LD BUTTONBUSH ROAD WAS THE OLD ROUTE TO BUTTON-bush Village that hardly anyone had used since they'd built the new county road fifteen years ago. The hamlet was located about twenty miles to nowhere from Northshire, and another ten miles to nowhere north of there was the gravel road that led to the nineteenth-century Cape Cod.

Mercy held on to her seat and the dogs huddled in the back cab as Troy steered the Ford F-150 onto the gravel road, slick with the ice and slush and snow the storm had left behind in its wake. It was a very bumpy ride that didn't seem to lead anywhere for several miles, winding through a series of snow-covered fallow fields in various stages of evolution, reverting to woodland or to marsh depending on the proximity to the many mostly frozen ponds that dotted the land-scape. The road was deeply rutted, and they bounced along.

"Someone's been out here, although how recently it's hard to say," he said. "We've had such variable weather, and the wind has drifted the snow so much that whatever tracks there are may have been compromised—unless maybe they've been here in the past couple of hours. We can take a closer look when we get to the house."

They passed one of the tallest stands of cattails Mercy had ever seen and came upon a small clearing upon which stood a falling-down weathered Cape Cod home that looked to be at least two hundred years old. A large barn that must have been built around the same time stood about a hundred yards east of the house. The barn was in slightly better form but still had seen better days.

"I can see why even the marvelous Mary Lou could not sell this place," she said.

"It's in pretty bad shape. Seems deserted."

"Maybe." Looks could be deceiving. In Afghanistan, abandoned buildings often harbored lethal secrets. Troy would know that, too, because he'd served over there.

"Yeah. Better take your weapon anyway."

Mercy had every intention of taking her Beretta. Troy parked at the end of the road, which abruptly gave way to an old stone wall that ran down past the house and beyond into the woods.

They got out of the truck, and the dogs leapt down to join them.

"Stay," she told Elvis, who was standing at attention, solid as a tank in the snow, leaning toward the house, desperate to breach the perimeter. Susie Bear sat at Troy's side, practically shimmying with excitement. Just waiting for the word.

Before they went to the house, Mercy and Troy searched the ground for areas of disturbance. The recent snowfall and steady winds had obscured any footprints that might have been left by people tramping back and forth to the house. There was an uneven and messy quality to the blanket of snow that indicated foot traffic, but again it was hard to say how long it had been since that foot traffic had occurred. The same was true of the ruts in the road. There were also long indentations in the snow that led from the house to the barn.

"Snowmobiles tracks," she said.

"Yep," said Troy. "Let's start with the house."

Mercy released Elvis with a wave of her hand, and he sprang toward the door of the Cape. Susie Bear jogged in place at Troy's hip, eager to follow her canine pal.

"Search," he told the Newfie, and off she romped after the shepherd.

Mercy and Troy marched after the dogs. By the time they got there, Elvis and Susie Bear were sniffing at the bottom of the door, tails wagging.

A good sign.

The ancient door was solid oak. Troy tried it, but it was locked. He looked at Mercy, and she shrugged.

"Who's going to care." She stood to the side and patted her thigh. Both dogs came to sit by her. Troy backed up a few feet, and kicked, driving the heel of his left boot into the door next to the lock. It splintered, and he kicked again.

This time the door gave way. Just as the first bullet struck the door jamb.

"Go," shouted Troy as he pushed her into the house and down onto the floor on her knees.

The dogs tumbled over them. She scrambled for her gun as Troy slammed the door shut. One, two, three more shots fired. Hits that shattered what was left of the door.

She found herself at the bottom of a steep staircase leading to the second floor. She crawled over to the right into the parlor. No furniture here for cover, just a filthy empty space long stripped of anything valuable. Many of the floorboards were torn up and the built-in hutches that framed the fireplace were in disarray, doors ripped off and drawers pulled out.

At least the narrow windows were set high in the walls, and Mercy was grateful for it.

"Are you all right?" yelled Troy from across the hall. He'd taken a left to her right and was hunched down in what Mercy believed was the dining room.

"Fine."

"I think the shooters are in the barn."

"Right." Mercy agreed that was where the bullets were coming from.

"Cover me."

"No way. You're not going out there alone."

"What do you propose we do?"

The roar of an engine answered the question for them. They clambered to their feet and ran for the door. A dark-gray Subaru charged down the dirt road. They both shot at the retreating vehicle as it swung wildly along before disappearing around a curve.

They were too late. The shooters were gone.

"Did you get the plates?"

"Covered in mud."

"Must be our guys then."

"Let's go after them." They whistled for the dogs but they didn't come.

"Where are they?"

They ran back into the house.

"Elvis!"

The shepherd barked and Mercy followed his howl, passing through the parlor and into the keeping room, the long room that ran the length of the back of the house. Troy was right behind her.

There they found Elvis and Susie Bear standing guard over Becker and Goodlove.

The two officers were bound and tied at their ankles and their wrists, their mouths gagged and taped.

"Go on after them," she said to Troy. "I'll handle things here."

He yelled for Susie Bear and they tore off for the front of the house.

Mercy untied Officer Alma Goodlove first. She was the junior officer, a pretty young woman with a moon-shaped face framed by dark curly hair, and blue eyes that gazed upon Mercy now with a mix of gratitude and shame. "Are you all right?"

"I'm fine. But Josh is hurt." Goodlove had tears in her eyes.

"Shot?"

She shook her head. "They hit him from behind. With a club of some kind."

Mercy and Goodlove crawled over to Becker. The young deputy was pale and clammy to the touch. His eyes were closed.

"You undo his feet and hands, I'll undo his mouth," she told Goodlove.

They untangled the unconscious Becker from his bindings. Mercy gently removed the gag from his mouth. She roused him gently, and he opened his eyes.

"Becker," she said.

"Mercy." He tried to sit up. "Where's Alma?"

"I'm right here."

Mercy moved away to let Goodlove take her place. She smoothed Becker's dark auburn hair from his forehead.

"What happened?"

"We were surveilling Patience O'Sullivan." Goodlove frowned at her. "I know she's your grandmother and all, but she was terrible. Really uncooperative."

"Alma," warned Becker.

"It's the truth, Josh, and you know it."

"Go on with your story."

"Right. Sorry." Goodlove paused. "Patience was on her way to see you at your cabin. She stopped by the animal clinic. She was just going to run in for a minute, she said."

"You should have gone in with her," said Mercy.

"I know," she said.

"This Subaru pulled into the parking lot," said Becker. "Just as Patience was coming out of the clinic."

"The driver rolled down his window and waved at her," said Goodlove, "and she went over to talk to him."

"The next thing we knew, the passenger up front got out, helped Patience into the front seat, slipped into the back seat with the third guy, and they took off." He gave Mercy a stricken look. "It all happened so fast."

"You didn't try to stop them? You didn't call for backup?"

"We thought she knew him," said Becker, his voice hoarse.

"She appeared to go voluntarily," added Goodlove. "There was no reason to think otherwise."

"You didn't think it was strange that she would go off like that after all that had happened to her." Mercy knew she wasn't making it easy on them.

"Like I said, she was not being cooperative," said Goodlove huffily. "We thought this was just more of the same."

"So you followed them."

"Here." Becker nodded, wincing. "The Subaru was parked down by the barn. There was a light on inside. We figured your grandmother was treating an animal there."

"We figured we'd just go check it out," said Goodlove. "We went down to the barn, identified ourselves, and knocked on the barn door."

"The passenger in the front seat opened the door, all friendly like, and invited us in." Becker was red with embarrassment now. "To see the calving, he said."

"That's when the other one came out of nowhere, and the short one bashed Josh over the head."

"They killed the lights and Josh went down and I went for my weapon, but not fast enough. The first guy slammed me to the floor and stomped on my gun hand. That's all I remember until I woke up in here with Josh."

"What about the third guy?"

Becker looked at Goodlove. "I never saw him. You?"

"No."

"Can you identify the two you did see?"

Goodlove shook her head. "The driver wore a baseball cap pulled down over his face."

"The guy in the front seat wore dark ski clothes and a hoodie. I don't know about the other one."

"Me either."

"But they were all men," said Goodlove.

Susie Bear burst into the room, and Troy followed her. "I lost them. But I got far enough out that I could call it in."

"They'll dump the Subaru," said Mercy.

"If they're smart," said Becker.

"They've been pretty smart so far," said Goodlove.

"We need to get Becker to the hospital," said Troy.

"What about Patience?"

"We don't know. We never saw her. We assume they took her with them."

"I thought they were gone for good," said Goodlove. "That they were never coming back and we would just die here."

"How did you know how to find us?"

"That's a long story," said Mercy.

"She figured it out, didn't she?" Becker asked Troy.

"She did. Where's your vehicle?"

"It's not out front?"

"No."

Becker groaned.

Mercy didn't blame him. She felt like groaning herself. These young cops did their best, but they'd let the bad guys snatch her grandmother and strike Becker in the head and steal their police car.

Not good. She wouldn't want to be the one to tell Harrington about that. She almost felt sorry for them. But until Patience was home safe and sound, Mercy would save her sympathy for her grandmother.

Mercy and Troy helped the officers to their feet and guided them outside to the Ford F-150. She whistled for Elvis but he sprinted for the barn instead of coming to the truck as instructed. Susie Bear lumbered after him, Troy on her heels.

"Elvis!" She ran after him and found the shepherd seated in his usual Sphinx pose at the bottom of the barn's wide double doors.

"We'd better go in," she told Troy. Together they unlatched the doors and opened them. There, inside of the broad old building, was Becker's police car. All its tires had been slashed.

"I guess we're all riding back together in the truck."

"I guess so." She pulled out some peanut butter doggie biscuits from her cargo pants pockets. "Good job, dogs. I thank you for your patience."

They all trudged back to the Ford F-150. Troy told Becker and Goodlove about the state of their vehicle.

"Great," said Becker.

"We are *so* suspended," said Goodlove.

"Maybe not." Mercy whistled for the dogs. "Search."

Elvis and Susie Bear circled the house and the barn a couple of times while Mercy and the others waited in the truck. The temperature was dropping and the wind was picking up. It was cold and growing colder.

"They aren't getting anywhere," said Troy.

"And we've got to get Josh to a hospital," said Goodlove.

"You should get checked out, too," said Mercy. "That hand doesn't look so good."

"I'm fine."

"We've got everyone looking out for that Subaru. Meanwhile, we may as well get you two to the hospital."

Every other car in Vermont was a Subaru. Still, Mercy knew Troy was right. "If there were anything else to find out here, the dogs would have found it by now."

"Forensics will be out here tomorrow," said Troy. "Maybe they'll find something."

Mercy sat in the back with Goodlove and the dogs, leaving the passenger seat to the injured Becker over his vehement objections.

"Just shut up," said Troy.

They dropped Becker and Goodlove off at the nearest hospital on the way home to Northshire. "Any chance Harrington will go easy on them?" From the front seat, she watched the two rookie cops limp into the emergency entrance. Elvis and Susie Bear were napping in the back cab.

"Not if his past reactions are any predictor," said Troy.

"Poor kids."

"Yeah. They just weren't ready for these guys, whoever they are."

"Let's hope my grandmother is better equipped to deal with them."

"There's one more house on the list. But the only way to get there is by snowmobile. So we'll have to go by the motor pool to pick up a trailer and a couple of sleds."

CHAPTER TWENTY-SIX

THEY PARKED THE TRUCK JUST INSIDE THE TURNOFF TO Old Mountain Road, which, like 80 percent of the roads in Vermont, was unpaved. They were in the wilds of Rutland County now, a rough and isolated part of the state, a slice of devil's land between upstate New York and Vermont. According to Mary Lou's directions, the Emil Woznicki house was tucked away at the end of a very long gravel driveway about a mile down Old Mountain Road. With the constant freezing and thawing and freezing and thawing that characterized March in Vermont, the road was a landmine of ice and melt, mud and snow. Even on snowmobiles, it was a rough ride.

The house, a low-slung mid-century ranch with a slanted roofline and lots of rectangular-shaped windows, sat in the curve of a crescent at the end of the gravel drive. The classic home wore a forlorn look after years of neglect.

"I'm thinking that if they are here, they've got her in the bunker," said Mercy.

"We should check the house first." He handed her a flashlight.

"If we do that and they're not there, and if they're in the bunker, then we could give ourselves away." She was set on hitting the bunker.

"If they're in the bunker, they won't know, will they?"

Troy had a point. Still she resisted. "It depends on how well equipped they are. There must be a way for them to see outside. Even back in the day, some of these places had hidden scopes and telephone lines.

By now they could have security cameras and God knows what else. We need to split up."

"I don't like it," he said.

The man could be stubborn sometimes. "We're both armed."

"I still don't like it."

"If Patience is here, Elvis will find her." She was eager to get on with it and confident that Elvis would lead them right to the bunker.

"Good point."

Troy may not trust *her* instincts, she thought, but he did trust those of these dogs. If there was anyone in the house or out in the bunker, the dogs would find them.

They both unclipped their dogs. Elvis stood next to her, ears perked and curlicue tail up, ready to work at her command. Susie Bear jigged up and down in front of Troy, in anticipation of her favorite word. Both dogs wore their red-lighted beacons on their collars.

"Search," he said to Susie Bear, and she scampered away toward the house, muzzle in the air, snuffling and snorting.

"Search," she said to Elvis. The handsome shepherd sniffed the air elegantly, and then raced past the house and around the back.

"So much for a consensus."

"Weird," he said.

It was weird, because usually the dogs were in sync. But Mercy knew they didn't have time to figure out why this was the exception. Patience could be here somewhere, fighting for her life.

"I'll follow my dog," she said. "You follow yours."

"Okay. But be careful." He gave her a stern look. "No heroics. Whistle if you need me. Or just fire your gun."

"Yes, sir." Mercy charged after Elvis at a fast jog. The snow was slushy and she slipped and slid and slued, catching herself more than once as she half ran, half tumbled down what was undoubtedly a wide expanse of lawn in the summertime. She could see Elvis, red light bobbing at his neck, at the bottom of the yard. Not too far from where the gathering of trees marked the edge of the forest.

She stumbled down to the shepherd, who sank down into his Sphinx pose at the foot of a thick rectangle of galvanized steel, recently swept free of snow. The entrance to the bunker, thought Mercy.

"Good boy." She leaned down and tugged hard at the handle, pulling the hatch open and revealing a steep flight of stairs. Pulling out her flashlight, she shined the light down the staircase.

But she didn't see anything. She wondered if she should go down or wait for Troy. Susie Bear had gone straight for the house, and there was no guarantee she'd lead Troy down here any time soon.

Mercy didn't want to get stuck down there in the bunker. As far as she knew there was only one way in and one way out. Always a dicey proposition.

Of course she knew her way around bunkers, but those were military bunkers, and they were bad enough. She couldn't imagine what these old Cold War bunkers built by crazy civilians would be like. But if there was any chance that Patience was down there, she had to go. She'd have to count on Elvis to stay up here above ground so Troy and Susie Bear could find the hatch if need be.

"Stay," she told Elvis.

But she was too late. The dog pushed past her and descended the steep steps too quickly for comfort. She had no choice but to follow him.

She made her way down the precipitous staircase, her flashlight pointed down to light her way. She tripped on one of the treads and reached for the walls with her palms to catch herself up and keep from plunging down the stairs. She dropped the flashlight, which skipped down the steel steps with a terrible clang. Elvis was out of sight, and she hoped that wherever he'd disappeared to, he was safe.

At the bottom of the stairs, she found herself in a long and narrow tunnel-shaped chamber that reminded her of a Quonset hut, only its curved walls and ceiling and floors were all made of concrete. The place was hemmed in shadow; a dim light shone at the far end of the room.

She retrieved her flashlight and swept the light around the perimeter. There was a picnic table in front of one wall; on the opposite wall stood a dismantled camp stove and an old refrigerator with its door propped open by a cement block. Farther down a series of twin-size bunkbeds ran alongside the right side. The mattresses had been shredded and their feathers littered the floor. Metal shelving lined the left side of the bunker; cans of food and plastic plates and bowls and utensils scattered haphazardly along the shelves. Someone had disturbed this frozen time capsule relatively recently, if the variations in dust were any indication.

Mercy did not see Elvis. She whistled for him, and he came bounding out of the gloom. He slid to a dead stop at her feet, cocked his head at her, and then ran off again. She followed him past the beds and the bookshelves to the very end of the bunker.

Elvis sat on his haunches before a metal door that was part of a three-foot by three-foot glorified locker, which she suspected housed the toilet. The door was secured with a standard padlock. She knocked on the door. "Anyone in there?"

She listened but heard nothing. "Are you sure about this?"

Elvis didn't answer. Just kept his nose pointed toward the door, unmoving in his posture and his conviction.

"Okay." She pulled her Swiss Army knife from her cargo pants pocket and pulled out its thinnest tool. The light was somewhat brighter down here at this end of the chamber but still too murky to pick a lock by. Lockpicking was an art she'd learned from Martinez, whose clever hands could pick locks, play the guitar, and field strip and reassemble a rifle blindfolded in less time than anyone else in the battalion. Teaching her to do the same was one way they amused themselves during the downtime between missions. She never did master the guitar, but her rifle breakdown and reassembly timing soon rivaled his own. And she could pick a lock efficiently as well, although rarely as quickly as he could.

In the civilian world, there wasn't much call for the blindfolded rifle business, but since leaving the military she'd been called upon to break into a surprising number of locked facilities. She stuck the flashlight under her chin and held it in place with her raised shoulder, spotlighting the padlock. She angled the thin tool into the lock mechanism. The flashlight slipped and she nudged it back into place and started again. She wiggled the tool to trip the mechanism, pulling the shackle out of the body of the lock. Snapping the tool back into the Swiss Army knife, she stowed the knife and the padlock back into her pants pocket. Martinez would be proud.

She opened the metal door.

"Patience!" There on the toilet slumped her grandmother, ankles and hands bound with yellow nylon rope, silver duct tape slapped across her mouth and around her head.

Elvis squeezed by Mercy, placing his front paws on Patience's knees and leaning forward, licking her face. Her grandmother opened her eyes and those baby blues shone with affection at the sight of Mercy and Elvis.

"This is going to hurt," Mercy warned. Elvis kept his head in Patience's lap while she unwound the duct tape from her grandmother's head as gently as possible. Then she used her knife to slice off the rope that bound her hands and feet.

"Are you all right?"

"I'm fine," said Patience. "But very, very glad to see you and this sweet boy here." She rubbed her hands together and then buried them in the Malinois's neck, scratching under the collar where dogs most appreciated it.

"Who did this to you?"

"I don't know. These guys in a Subaru pulled up in the parking lot and the driver waved me over, told me he had a calf in trouble. I told him I'd get my kit and meet him at his barn but when I walked around the car, the passenger from the front seat intercepted me. I felt this arm around me and this sickly-sweet-smelling cloth in my face, and then nothing. Chloroform, no doubt. The next thing I know I'm in this place. What is it?"

"It's a bunker. Behind a dilapidated 1950s ranch in the middle of nowhere in Rutland County."

"That makes no sense at all."

"I'll explain it later. Elvis, up." The shepherd backed away from Patience. "Where is Claude?"

"He's safe. I sent him home to Quebec."

"Well, that was premature." Mercy helped Patience to her feet.

"Don't I know it." Her grandmother clutched her hands.

"You're shaking." Mercy clucked her lips. "Go, Elvis."

"I'm fine. Just get me out of here."

The shepherd left the water closet, and Mercy followed him, half-carrying Patience.

"Do you think you can make it up those stairs?"

"Absolutely." Her grandmother looked around. "This place is creepy."

Mercy guided Patience down the room, but she kept stumbling.

"You're going to hurt yourself. Let me carry you."

"I can do it." But with her very next steps, Patience wobbled so badly that Mercy caught her just as she started crashing toward the concrete floor.

"Hold on." She leaned over and placed her hands on her knees. "Come on, we'll piggyback it."

"No way."

"Come on. We've got to get you out of here before whoever put you here comes back."

"Don't tell me you came here alone?"

"This from the woman who sent Claude home."

"I was wrong about that." Patience moved behind Mercy's back and wrapped her good arm and her legs around Mercy's waist and chest.

"You think?" She tucked her forearms under her grandmother's knees and straightened up. "Let's go."

"Put me down."

"Don't fuss, you'll just make it harder for me." Fortunately Patience was a trim woman, so Mercy could manage carrying her down the length of the bunker to the staircase. But carrying her up those steps would be a challenge. She stopped at the foot of the stairs for a breather.

"Go on up," she said to Elvis, and the shepherd sprinted up to the hatch and disappeared from view. Mercy began the slow and steady ascent, Patience leaning her head against her shoulder.

"You really are my favorite granddaughter," she whispered in Mercy's ear.

"I better be."

When they reached the top of the steps, Elvis was waiting for them, ears perked and curlicue tail at attention. Susie Bear's big pumpkin head appeared next to the shepherd's handsome face.

Troy was last to appear in the frame. "Let me help you."

She leaned out and over the hatch. She felt his strong arms embrace her grandmother and pull her to her feet.

Patience gave the game warden a sweet pat on the cheek. "Thank you." She stepped aside to greet the dogs, who were deliriously pleased to see her, licking and wagging and snorting and sniffing their favorite veterinarian. Not looking for treats but making sure she was all right. But she had treats in her fanny pack, as always.

"My pleasure." Troy extended his hand to Mercy, and she grasped it. He lifted her out of the bunker and onto the solid if snowy ground.

"Everyone okay?"

"I'm good," said Mercy.

Patience smiled. "I'm good, too. Now. I was beginning to get worried."

"Is the house clear?" asked Mercy.

"All clear. But ransacked, just like the others." He regarded her grandmother with concern. "Did you recognize the guys who kidnapped you?"

"No. The driver had a baseball cap pulled low onto his forehead. He had deep-set black eyes and he needed a shave. The other guy wore dark ski clothes and a hoodie."

"What about the guy in the back seat?"

"I never got a good look at him."

"Any of them from the security video?" he asked.

"I don't know."

"Do you think you'd recognize the passenger if you saw him again?"

"Maybe."

"I tried calling for backup but there's no signal out here," he said. "We don't know when these guys are coming back. We should leave now and take Patience back to the truck, where we can call for assistance and let Harrington's Major Crime Unit take over. They can track these guys down, and we can get you all home safe and sound."

The distant rumble of snowmobiles pierced the gloomy quiet of the deserted Woznicki homestead.

"We're out of time," Mercy said.

"We've got to get out of here. I'll take Patience." He scooped up

her grandmother into his arms with ease and strode for the snowmobiles, which they'd parked up by the edge of the driveway just short
of the crescent that fronted the house. Mercy and the dogs huffed
alongside him.

"I've got the bigger touring snowmobile," he said, "so Patience
rides with me. No arguments."

"Good call." Mercy had to admit that Troy was a far more skillful
sledder than she was, and certainly he was more experienced riding
the snow machines with heavy loads.

When they reached the snowmobiles, he put Patience down. He
climbed onto the larger of the sleds, and Mercy helped her grandmother
get on it behind Troy. Her cast made holding on to the rear handles a
challenge. "Forget those. Lean into him. Grip his waist with your knees
and hold on to his chest with your good arm as best you can."

"You can't hurt me," he said. "Don't worry."

He handed her a helmet and Mercy tugged it on over her grandmother's head. Troy slipped on his helmet and revved the engine. The
two of them roared off toward the truck, Susie Bear loping behind,
moving as powerfully along in the snow as a polar bear.

Elvis perked his triangular ears at her as if to say, *let's go already*. Mercy
swept her unruly curls off her forehead and clamped her helmet over
her hair before it could get away. Climbing onto her snowmobile, she
hurtled after Troy and her grandmother. Elvis raced with her, keeping
up easily.

She put on the speed to catch up to Troy. He was more comfortable going fast than she was on these monsters. She felt the enormous
power of the machine as she zoomed up to pull alongside Troy and
her grandmother.

The distant rumble of the other snowmobiles was not so distant
anymore.

"I'll head them off," she shouted above the din. "You get Patience
to the truck."

CHAPTER TWENTY-SEVEN

H OLD ON, PATIENCE," YELLED TROY.
They shot forward on the snowmobile, rocketing towards the truck. He hated leaving Mercy behind to serve as the diversion. But he knew that her first priority was her grandmother and she wouldn't have it any other way. The best thing he could do for Mercy was keep her grandmother safe.

Susie Bear galloped behind the snowmobile. When she wanted to, she could run nearly thirty miles an hour. Even so, the Newfie retriever was falling behind as Troy hit sixty miles an hour on the snow machine. His sled could go more than a hundred miles an hour, but he didn't want to risk losing Patience, who was hanging on for dear life. He looked in the rearview mirror, but he couldn't see anything but forest behind him. The whine of distant snowmobiles faded; the only snowmobile he could hear now was his own. He'd either outpaced the bad guys or Mercy had completely succeeded in sidetracking them, or both.

"Nearly there," he told Patience as his Ford F-150 came into sight. Patience didn't say anything, but he could feel her shivering against his back. As they plowed along, he could feel the solidity of the fiberglass cast protecting her broken wrist strike his torso with the precision of a metronome. He hoped the rough events of the past forty-eight hours hadn't worn her out too much. Like her granddaughter, she was tough, but she was also only human—something he wasn't sure either of them liked to admit.

Troy was never so glad to see his truck in his life. He slowed the sled down as they approached the vehicle, easing up on the throttle and slowing to a stop. He parked the machine right by the passenger side of the Ford F-150.

He helped Patience maneuver off the snowmobile and gently lifted her helmet from her silver-blond head. He yanked his own headgear off and dismounted. "Are you all right? You look a little shook up."

She stomped her feet in the snow and ran her hands through her hair. "If this game warden thing doesn't work out, you might consider a career as a snowmobile racer." She smiled at him. "Thank you for saving me."

"We're not there yet." He opened the truck door for her. "Let me help you up."

"We can't leave," said Patience.

He gripped her around her waist with both hands and lifted her onto the seat. "Buckle up."

She gripped his arms with the strong fingers of a seasoned veterinarian. "We can't leave without Mercy."

"We've got to get you out of here. That's what she wants."

"I'll be fine." She turned those bright blue eyes on him. "I'm a good shot."

Troy didn't doubt that for a minute. Seemed like everyone in Mercy's family was a good shot. Maybe even her mother.

Patience grinned. "I was married to a cop. I know you have a weapon to spare in here somewhere."

Susie Bear barged up to the truck, placing her big paws on Patience's lap, plumed tail wagging.

"Go help Mercy," she told Troy, scratching the Newfie mutt between the ears where she liked it most. "I've got Susie Bear to protect me. And that gun you're going to give me."

Troy sighed. He knew Patience would never take *no* for an answer. And he really didn't want to leave Mercy on her own. He knew she could take care of herself, and she had Elvis, but the guys she was up against were dangerous.

"Okay." He handed her his smartphone and his gun and pointed to the radio. "Call for backup. There's more ammo in the back if you need it. But try not to shoot anybody."

"Yes, sir."

He closed her door and then grabbed a rifle from the cab, leaving the door open for Susie Bear. She vaulted up into the back, and then pushed her considerable bulk over the console in the middle to take up her position as guard dog in the driver's seat.

"Good dog," he said to Susie Bear. "Stay."

"We will," said Patience. "Now go get our girl."

MERCY SPED AWAY, in the opposite direction of Troy's truck, toward the bunker. She knew Elvis would follow her. She steered the snow machine in a wide circle, passing right in front of the three guys on snowmobiles who were after them, two of them on one machine and one riding solo. The men who'd most likely snatched her grandmother and hog-tied Becker and Goodlove. They wore balaclavas under their helmets, looking more like aliens from a planet without snow than criminals on the run in wintry New England.

She wondered who they were. If George Rucker was one of them, who were the other two? Maybe Simko and another ex-con pal?

What did they hope to gain by kidnapping Patience? Revenge seemed like a far-fetched motive, after all these years. It was clear that, whoever they were, they were looking for something in all these houses, and usually that something was money. George had already killed her grandfather, killing Patience seemed like, well, overkill. She knew that revenge drove people mad—*Come, the croaking raven doth bellow for revenge*—but there must be more to it than that. Especially for the others, the ones who weren't George.

When they saw her coming, they took the bait and stormed through the snow after her. She bounced over a small rise and plunged down the slope, riding the machine like a runaway pony. This was faster than she'd ever gone before on a snowmobile. She could glance at the speedometer but she didn't dare.

Fast but not fast enough. The snowmobilers surged up to her, hemming her in between their speeding snow machines. She pumped the brake, slowing down her machine, and let her pursuers tear ahead.

These guys are real sledheads, she thought. She couldn't outrace them, so she'd have to outsmart them.

She headed for the woods. She spotted a trail to the right, and she gunned for it. The guys spun around in fierce sweeps of snow and barreled back toward her. She hit the trail first and scouted the route ahead. The trees grew thicker as she maneuvered the machine deeper into the woods. Stands of beech and birch gave way to dense knits of hemlock, cedar, and spruce. The sledding was more complicated here on this ungroomed trail and she was forced to slow down to avoid hanging branches and fallen logs and random boulders.

Mercy could hear the sleds storming behind her. The trail narrowed, barely room for two abreast now. No way for three. The good news was that they couldn't hem her in again. The bad news was they drove their sleds faster and more furiously.

Ahead she could see that the trail forked and as she approached the parting of ways she leaned toward the right, then steered to the left at the last minute. The guys directly behind her couldn't correct course fast enough and slammed into a snow-covered tangle of trunks, shrubs, and brambles.

But the other sledder made the turn. She could feel him gaining on her, but this side of the fork was tougher to navigate. Branches broad enough and low enough to knock her right off her sled stretched right across the path. She'd obviously taken the road less traveled by.

She was forced to slow down to avoid the low-slung limbs—as was her pursuer. But given his superior sledding skills he was bound to overtake her sooner rather than later.

A sliver of silver-white shone beyond the edge of forest, and Mercy knew they were headed for a body of water. Frozen water. A sudden movement to her left, and Elvis shot out of the trees and tackled her pursuer. He swerved wildly on his snow machine but held on. In the rearview mirror she saw Elvis land on his feet and keep on running, back off the trail and into the woods.

She knew the stubborn shepherd would try it again. Now that they were in the woods they couldn't go quite as fast, and Elvis could catch them up with all his shortcuts through the trees. Mercy could see a clearing ahead now, frozen marshland that fronted the lake beyond. As soon as she crossed the boundary between woods and wetland, she went full throttle, blazing over the open ground, the sledhead in swift pursuit. About fifty feet across the frozen marsh, she executed a wide turn, cutting the guy off. He revved his engine and aimed for the frozen lake that shimmered beyond the cattails.

Mercy smiled. Now the man in balaclava was the one on the run. She was the cat and he was the mouse.

She'd corner him at the cattails, where the frozen marsh became frozen lake. Traversing the lake this time of year was too dangerous, and she and Elvis would catch him as he tried to find another exit route.

The ice did not always hold during the Ides of March, that dangerous time marking the seasons of endings and beginnings, when what appeared thick as a block may be just a thin layer of ice ready to crack. Underneath its seemingly solid surface, she knew that the great pond seethed with life. Fish swam in restless circles, pushing their pale mouths against the cold barrier, tapping tapping tapping at the frozen veil between winter and spring, longing to leap up and out into warmer air come summer.

The man on the snowmobile did not stop at the edge of the frozen marsh. He flew out across the lake while she slowed to a stop just beyond the stand of cattails. Before her lay an icy expanse of white shadowed by perilous patches of gray and silver and blue.

For a moment she stood there in silence as she watched his snowmobile slip in and out of view as it ploughed through the snowy mists across the buried lake, away from her, away from capture, away from justice.

She had forgotten about Elvis. The shepherd charged across the frozen lake after the snowmobile. She yelled at him to stop, to come, to come back to her. *Now.*

But Elvis either didn't hear her or didn't care to hear her. The determined dog raced on, his howls echoing across the ice. She had to follow him on foot. Unzipping the storage compartment on the back of the seat, she reached in and grabbed a couple of ice picks and a tow rope, thankful to the game warden service, which took the Boy Scout motto "Be prepared" to a whole new level.

She set out across the ice, proceeding very carefully, one cautious step at a time. She didn't trust the lake or the ice or the spring. *Beware the Ides of March.*

Mercy hoped that Troy had contacted Thrasher and that backup was on the way. She tried to text him but the message did not go through. She whistled for Elvis and then yelled for him, and still he paid no attention. Whistling and yelling, whistling and yelling, whistling and yelling—but he ignored her. The stubborn shepherd was fixed on nailing the sledder no matter what she said.

She heard the ominous cracking before she saw it. She stared as the snow machine in the middle of the great pond skidded and the ice fragmented in crazy fractals all around and the path forward dissolved into water.

The man on the snowmobile leaned back, forcing the front end of the sled to rise in a desperate attempt to skip across the water like a stone. But the last-minute wheelie did not save him. The snow machine shuddered and plunged into the depths of the lake.

"Elvis!" she screamed again. This time the shepherd angled toward her, but he was too late. The ice fissured around him and he fell into the freezing water.

The hell with caution. Mercy ran lightly across the ice on foot as far as she dared. When she was within ten feet of the hole in the ice where Elvis had gone in, she lay down on the ice and stretched out to her full length, rolling like a log to the edge.

She peered into the murky water, but Elvis was nowhere to be seen. Neither was the snow machine or its racer.

The lake was too cold for anything but fish to tolerate, too deep for anyone to stand up, too dark to reveal the hidden secrets within its depths. Neither the man nor the dog could survive for long in that wet deep freeze. She didn't know where either of them was lost in that bitter body of water, or if she could find them in time.

She'd save the first one to surface. God help her, she hoped it was Elvis. What would Martinez do, she thought. He'd pray to St. Anthony, the patron saint of lost things.

"Okay, St. Anthony, do your thing," she whispered, and then she screamed Elvis's name once more.

Like the answer to her prayer—Martinez would say it *was* the answer to her prayer—the shepherd's black shiny nose broke the surface, followed by his dark muzzle and his eyes and his ears, until his entire head had emerged. Sodden and shivering, he paddled with his paws, flailing in the water.

Mercy scooted closer to the edge of the ice and reached for the dog, but he was too agitated.

"Stay," she warned.

Elvis did as he was told. He stopped moving and started to slip beneath the surface again. She grabbed his collar just as he went under. She jerked him up, holding his head above the water with one hand and wrapping the rope awkwardly around his chest with the other.

"Hold on, boy," she said. "Hold on."

CHAPTER TWENTY-EIGHT

THE DOG LOOKED AT HER WITH THOSE DARK BROWN EYES full of trust, and she prayed she was worthy of that trust. Her arms were damp with chill as the frigid water seeped under her sleeves and her gloves. It was so bitterly cold that she knew within minutes her hands would be too numb to function properly. She needed to move quickly.

One end of the rope held three carabiners, and she hooked all three of them to his collar. The other end held one carabiner, and she wrapped the rope around her waist and secured it with the remaining latch hook. "Okay, Elvis, now I'm going to pull you out."

Her arms ached as she grabbed him by his collar with both hands and rolled way from the edge of the water. The rope tightened around her torso and tugged the shepherd up onto the ice. As soon as his paws and belly felt solid ground, Elvis struggled to stand up.

"Down," she commanded.

Elvis collapsed onto the ice. He needed to stretch out over the ice as she had done, to distribute his body weight more evenly across the frozen surface. The better not to crack the ice again. But he simply lay there. Not moving. Not panting. Barely breathing.

"Elvis." She cuddled closer to him, hugged his chest, tried to feel his heartbeat. Nothing. His eyes were closed now. "Elvis."

She looked over at the dark pool in the ice where Elvis had gone under. The man and his snowmobile were still under there somewhere.

If backup didn't get here soon, the sledder and his sled might be gone for good.

The frozen lake didn't seem so frozen anymore. She had to get Elvis to shore, before she lost him forever. She didn't want to risk standing up. And she didn't think Elvis could stand up even if he wanted to. But she had to get him moving.

They were going to have to crawl back. The poor shepherd was shaking from the cold and crawling was no dog's favorite position but she needed to get him back to shore as quickly and safely as possible.

"Crawl," she said firmly.

Elvis opened his eyes. His pupils were dilated, which couldn't be good. He tried to move his legs, but he was too weak. He shuddered, and his limbs splayed across the ice.

"It's okay, boy."

She'd have to push him.

Pulling the dog in front of her, she steered him forward along the ice, crawling on her belly behind him. Seesawing across the frozen lake, nudging his limp body ahead, hitching along after him. "Hang in there, Elvis."

It probably only took ten minutes to scoot across the frozen lake with Elvis, but it seemed like a lifetime. When they finally reached the stand of cattails, signaling the beginning of the frozen marsh, she nearly cried in relief. She got up on her hands and knees and rose to her feet.

Elvis lifted his head. He seemed better now, or maybe that was just wishful thinking.

"Can you get up? Up?" Her arms and hands were aching with cold now and she wasn't sure if she could carry him. He pulled his legs under him, and staggered to a standing position, only to fall again. Not a good sign.

"It's okay." She squatted down to his level and gathered the freezing dog into her exhausted arms.

He weighed about sixty pounds, so she grunted as she picked the dog up and straightened her legs. He was so cold and so wet. Striding as quickly as she could, she huffed across the frozen marsh to the snowmobile. She put Elvis down and retrieved the thermal blanket from another one of the pockets on the seat and wrapped him up in it, holding him in her arms as she knelt beside him.

She heard the roar of another snow machine and looked up. When she recognized Troy's solid figure on the sled, she could feel the tears gathering the corner of her eyes.

"It's all right, boy." She rubbed his wet head with the top of the blanket. "Vermont Fish and Wildlife to the rescue."

Troy swung the snowmobile up to her and Elvis and jumped off.

"Are you alright?"

She nodded. "It's Elvis I'm worried about. He fell in and I got him out."

He retrieved another thermal blanket from a zippered pocket on his snow machine. "What about the perp?"

"Two snowmobiles, three perps. The one with two guys veered off-trail and crashed. Elvis charged after the solo rider who tried to escape over the lake. The ice was too thin. He didn't make it. He and his machine went down and they took Elvis in with them. I looked, but I didn't see him or his sled. Elvis finally surfaced, but he never did."

"You take Elvis back on the big snowmobile to the truck. Your grandmother is there."

"You were supposed to take care of her."

"She insisted I come after you. And it's a good thing I did." He took Elvis from her and wrapped him in the dry blanket. "Besides, I left Patience armed with a gun and Susie Bear."

"She's a very good shot." Mercy switched snowmobiles with Troy.

"So I've heard." He helped her onto the larger snowmobile and handed Elvis over to her. "Backup is on the way." He took off his parka and bound the shepherd to her with it.

"You'll freeze," she said.

"I'm not the one who's wet." He placed the helmet on her head. "And it's going to start snowing again any minute. Go."

Mercy hightailed it back to the truck, going as fast as she could without disturbing Elvis any more than she had to. She was terrified for him. He was still listless and lethargic, common symptoms of hypothermia. Snow was falling again now. She needed to get the shepherd out of the elements and into that warm Ford F-150.

The snowmobile purred along, the only sound in a forest silenced by snow. Fat wet flakes made it harder to see and even harder to steer, especially with a dog on her lap. Still, as she sped along, she stayed on the lookout for the sledders who'd crashed into the bramble. But there was no sign of them. The only other tracks she saw were hers and Troy's as far as she could tell.

Finally she caught sight of Troy's truck, a beacon of headlights and taillights in the blur of flurries. "Almost there, boy."

Patience opened the door and climbed out. Susie Bear followed. They waited as she drew the snow machine up alongside the vehicle.

"He fell through the ice," she told her grandmother. "I think he's hypothermic."

"Get in here, both of you." Patience helped Mercy load Elvis into the truck. Susie Bear sniffed and licked her cold, wet friend. "Backup is on the way. Where's Troy?"

"He went after the ones who got away." Mercy slipped into the front seat next to Elvis. Stripping off her wet gloves, she drew him up on her lap. The toasty cab felt warm and cozy as a tea shop after the frosty ordeal on the lake; she could only imagine what a welcome relief the heat was to Elvis, who still shivered in her arms.

Patience grabbed another thermal blanket from the back and handed it to Mercy. "Swap that out for that wet jacket. He needs heat. Lots of it."

As she bundled up the shepherd once again, she told Patience about the snowmobiler who went down into the water and the ones Troy was looking for, the ones who'd crashed their snowmobile into the bramble.

"Who were they?" Patience slipped into the driver's seat and dialed up the heater full blast.

"I'm not sure."

"Troy's going to need help. Go after him." She handed Mercy her own gloves.

"He can take care of himself." She was not leaving her grandmother or her dog.

"There are two of them," insisted Patience. "He needs Susie Bear and he needs you."

"I'm not leaving you and Elvis alone."

"I called for backup. They're on the way."

"That's what they always say. You know better than anyone it doesn't always work that way."

They stared each other down in a standoff of familial will. Patience won when the sound of sirens blared in the distance.

"Okay. But keep that gun at the ready."

"Troy told me not to shoot anybody."

"He didn't mean it." She transferred Elvis from her lap to Patience's lap and put on her grandmother's gloves. "I know you'll take good care of him." She got out of the truck and shut the passenger door. "Don't let him die."

"Go."

Mercy let Susie Bear out of the back cab. "Find Troy. Search."

The Newfie plowed off through the snow.

She climbed onto the snowmobile and followed Susie Bear into the silver blur of snow flurries. She couldn't see much, but the one thing she could see was the dog's shiny black coat against all that white. She knew that the snow couldn't keep Susie Bear down; snow was no deterrent to a Newfoundland.

The Newfie took a sharp right into the woods on an old trail just wide enough for the snow machine. She could only drive the snowmobile as fast as Susie Bear could run. Which was faster than seemed safe.

The trail forward grew narrower and narrower. The snow was still falling in a thick curtain and visibility was poor. No sign of Troy or the man he was pursuing. No sound of snow machines other than her own. Nothing to guide her but Susie Bear and her sensational nose. And blind faith.

The trees grew thicker here, crowding the slender path, tightening their grip until the path disappeared altogether, dissipating into a stand of hemlock. Susie Bear hustled into the trees. She was on the scent, tracking it as the crow flies, no consideration for snowmobiles and trails and humans who couldn't keep up. Susie Bear didn't need no stinkin' trail.

Mercy knew that once Susie Bear found Troy, she'd come back to lead her to him. At least she hoped that's what would happen. But she couldn't wait for that. She dismounted, grabbed her gun, and followed the dog's paw prints through the woods.

All was quiet. Nature seemed to stop in silent homage when a snowstorm descended on the forest. But there was no stopping the Newfie. Susie Bear was in a hurry, and the tracks reflected that: the prints were bigger and you could see where she'd slipped along the way.

Mercy trudged along as quickly as she could, careful not to trip on dead wood and rocks and tree roots buried under the snow. She wondered how far afield the men on the snowmobile had taken Troy, and what she'd find when Susie Bear led her wherever she was leading her. Maybe she should have stuck with the snowmobile, she'd be more help to Troy with wheels.

The tracks stopped at the edge of a partly frozen stream but indicated that Susie Bear had simply plunged across it without hesitation. It was fairly shallow and just wide enough that Mercy couldn't jump it. She crossed by way of the big flat rocks that lined the bed.

She spotted more of Susie Bear's prints on the other side of the stream, tailing the tracks to a small clearing. The purr of a snow machine alerted her and she hid behind a couple of trees, gun drawn. She peeked out and saw Troy pinned under his snowmobile. Susie Bear was trying push her big pumpkin head under the snow machine to get to her wounded friend.

Across from Troy was another snowmobile, this one crashed into a fallen log nearly obscured by a snowbank. One of the riders had been thrown clear. He appeared to be injured; his pants were torn and his arm hung limply at his side. He was crawling on his belly across the clearing toward Troy, a pistol in his good hand. The other rider was nowhere to be seen.

Mercy stepped out from behind the tree, rifle pointed right at him. Susie Bear backed out from under the snow machine and lifted her head in Mercy's direction. The man on the ground followed the dog's gaze and spotted her. He raised his gun.

And she fired. Shooting the gun right out of his hand. He was lucky, she'd been aiming higher but he'd moved just in time. He was still moving, edging toward his gun, which had spun a couple of feet to his left.

"Don't even think about it," she said. How he thought he'd manage to shoot with two bad wrists, even if he could retrieve the gun, she wasn't sure. "Stay," she told Susie Bear.

Rifle still trained on him, Mercy strode over toward the sledder, kicking his gun farther away. "If you move, I'll shoot you again."

The man closed his eyes in what she hoped was resignation, if not unconsciousness. She backed up, one eye still on the perp, until she could see Troy. His chest was pinned between a boulder and the snowmobile, so he couldn't move, but his arms were free and he had a clear view of the suspect.

"Where's the other guy?"

"He took off running," said Troy. "I doubt he's coming back."

"Are you okay?"

"Secure the suspect." His voice was firm, but she could hear the effort in it. She knew he carried handcuffs on his belt, but she couldn't get to them without hurting him.

"Hold on, backup's on the way." She shrugged her pack off her back and pulled some heavy-duty nylon cable zip ties from an outside pocket.

She put her rifle in Troy's hands.

"Got you covered," he said. But his voice was less firm this time. Susie Bear whimpered.

Mercy went back to the suspect. He was sprawled out on the ground, head to one side, eyes still closed. She sank down, kneeing him in the back, and grabbed his injured hands and cuffed them. He moaned and twitched, but that only exhausted him, and he fell silent again.

She pulled off his balaclava. Revealing an older, sadder, meaner-looking version of the man who'd killed her grandfather. George Rucker.

Mercy fought the urge to kick the man's face in, leaving him before she succumbed to that dark impulse. She went back to Troy. "We need to get this thing off you." She knew snowmobiles could weigh as much as six hundred pounds. Moving it might be dangerous for Troy. He could have broken ribs or even a punctured lung. No room for error.

Two uniforms crashed into the clearing.

She smiled at them. "Just in time."

As the EMTs carried Patience to the first ambulance, Mercy sat in Troy's truck with a terribly silent Elvis, rubbing his coat with a plaid woolen camp blanket. Patience had called Claude, who'd only gone as far as the nearest hotel. She asked him to drive the mobile veterinary unit to the Rutland County Medical Center, where they were taking them all to get checked out.

Susie Bear fretted from the back seat, whining her worries about Troy, Elvis, and Patience. Her grandmother would be fine, if her vehement insistence that she did not need to go to the hospital were any indication.

Mercy was more worried about Troy, whom they'd carried out of the woods on a stretcher after freeing him from the snowmobile. Troy was not happy about it; like Patience, he insisted he was okay. But his rescuers were as worried about broken ribs and punctured lungs as she was and didn't give him a choice. Susie Bear never left Troy's side, trotting alongside the EMTs, whining all the way, which only intensified Mercy's worries.

She'd tramped back to the snowmobile alone and driven back to the truck. Thrasher was there, along with two ambulances, one for Patience and Troy and the other for the suspect.

According to the captain, Rucker wasn't talking. He refused to name himself or his companions, nor did he ask after them. They'd have to find another way to establish their identities. There was a team tracking the other snowmobiler who'd gotten away, but he had a good head start, and so far he'd eluded them.

A dive team was tasked with looking for the man who went down with his snow machine into the lake. Since they had a location, they would give it a try, knowing that he had most likely drowned and that this would be a recovery operation, rather than a rescue. But this was dangerous work, and if the conditions were bad enough that the divers were at risk, they'd have to pull the operation until conditions improved. Sometimes that might not happen until spring.

Not that Mercy cared much at this point. She was only thinking about Troy and Patience and Elvis, hoping and praying their injuries weren't serious.

She kept on rubbing Elvis's cold back as she and Susie Bear watched as they carried Troy to join Patience in the first ambulance. The Newfoundland howled her displeasure, while the shepherd hung on, breathing but unconscious.

Mercy felt like howling, too. She and Susie Bear were desperate to help, but there was nothing they could do now, for Troy or for Patience or for Elvis.

Except wait.

CHAPTER TWENTY-NINE

A POLICE OFFICER NAMED WINSTON DROVE TROY'S TRUCK, racing Mercy and the dogs to the hospital after the ambulances, siren wailing. Still, it seemed like forever before he steered the Ford-150 into the Emergency entrance of the Rutland County Medical Center.

She pointed across the parking lot to the bright yellow oversized commercial van with STERLING MOBILE VETERINARY CLINIC emblazoned on the sides. This was the fully equipped mobile unit that allowed Patience to make house calls, treating big domesticated animals like horses, goats, sheep, and cows. As well as the occasional moose or bear, among other wildlife.

"Over there."

Winston pulled the truck up next to the van, jumped out, and came around to the passenger side to help Mercy and Elvis. She cradled the unresponsive shepherd in her arms.

"What about Susie Bear?" asked Winston.

"She'll stay with us. Come on, girl."

Susie Bear leapt from the truck and ran for Claude, who was waiting at the door of the van. Mercy thanked Winston, and hurried over to join them. She followed the veterinarian into the mobile unit, a bright and clean space lined with gleaming white and stainless steel medical fixtures and built-in cabinets. She could hear Susie Bear scrambling in behind her.

"On the table." He directed the Newfie to a mat in the corner while Mercy deposited Elvis on the examination table, which was covered in a large heating pad.

Claude wrapped thermal blankets around the shepherd and added more heating pads.

"Is he going to be all right?"

"He needs fluids," he said, not answering her question. "Let's get an IV in him. Hold his leg, please."

Mercy clasped Elvis's front right leg while the vet inserted an IV.

"This will help warm him from the inside out."

Elvis barely acknowledged the maneuver, which worried her all the more. Usually he was very alert during visits to the vet.

She scratched the sweet spot between the shepherd's ears as Claude retrieved an oxygen mask and placed it around the dog's muzzle. Elvis opened his eyes briefly. Still slightly dilated.

"Will he be all right?" she asked again.

"It's going to take time. We need to warm him up, keep him on the oxygen and the fluids."

She patted Elvis's back over the heating pads and blankets. His breathing seemed less labored now. His body more relaxed. Mercy nodded at Claude. He may not be Patience, but he was still a damn good veterinarian.

"I've got this," he said. "Go see your grandmother. Leave Susie Bear with us."

She hated to abandon Elvis, but one of them had to check on Patience. And Troy.

Elvis needed Claude more now than he needed her.

"I'll be back as soon as I can." Casting one long last look at her brave Malinois, completely sheathed in protective gear, only his dark eyes clearly visible, she said a silent prayer to St. Roch. The patron saint of dogs. One of Martinez's favorite saints. She hoped that wherever he was, Martinez was praying for Elvis, too.

Mercy spotted Thrasher in the lobby and cornered him immediately.

"How are they?"

"Patience is doing very well. Room 354."

"And Troy?"

"He'll be okay." The captain's handsome face was creased with worry or weariness or both. "No punctured lungs, but a couple of broken ribs. He's hurting, although he'd never admit it." He looked at her squarely. "I'm sure he would appreciate a visit. Room 367."

"Got it."

"How's Elvis?"

"I'm not sure. He's with Claude in the vet van."

"Susie Bear?"

"She's with them."

"Good." He dismissed her with a wave. "Get on up there."

Mercy excused herself and ran for the elevators.

HER FIRST STOP was her grandmother. Patience was sitting up, supported by her electric bed, her cast-encased arm elevated on a pillow, holding court. Surrounded by people and pink roses and bright *Get Well* balloons. Mercy's parents were there, as well as Lillian Jenkins and Bea Garcia.

"What are you all doing here?" She couldn't believe it. "Patience is supposed to be resting."

"We felt responsible for your grandmother's ordeal," said Lillian.

"We needed to see for ourselves that she was okay," said Bea.

"I keep telling everyone that I'm fine. And that it's nobody's fault."

"It's Becker and Goodlove's fault," said her mother, Grace, smoothing her perfectly creased Ralph Lauren trousers. Her idea of dressing down on the weekends. "You should consider legal action against the department."

"Nonsense." Patience patted the side of her bed. "Come and tell me about Elvis, Mercy."

She filled them in on the shepherd's condition.

"He's in good hands with Claude," Patience said. "Try not to worry."

"I'm sure he'll be fine." Lillian squeezed Mercy's shoulder. "He's a very strong character."

"That he is." Patience patted her hand. "Just like you. I was telling them everything that happened, and how strong you all were. Troy and Susie Bear, too. You should visit him."

"If you're sure you're all right . . ."

"You can report back to Claude that I couldn't be better."

"I'll do better than that. Smile." Mercy pulled out her cell and snapped a photo of Patience grinning at the camera.

"A picture is worth a thousand words," said Lillian approvingly.

"Go on," said her grandmother. "Go see your game warden."

Her mother caught her eye and waylaid her in the hallway. "Wesley Hallett came by."

"Already?"

"Captain Thrasher told us what he's trying to do. Unacceptable."

"The man must be glued to a police scanner."

Her mother frowned. "He'll try to use this against you. Evidence that your lifestyle puts Elvis in danger."

Mercy thought of Elvis, wet and cold and barely breathing. She leaned against the pale green wall and closed her eyes, willing the image out of her head. "Maybe he's right."

"You're the best that ever happened to that dog." Grace took Mercy's hands—still clammy with a cold she just couldn't shake—into her own warm ones. "We'll prove it."

"We?"

"Sometimes having lawyers in the family is a good thing."

Mercy opened her eyes and forced herself to smile. "And possession is nine-tenths of the law."

"Exactly." Her mother squeezed her fingers for a moment and then released them. "Say your thank-yous to Warden Warner, and then go take care of your dog. Don't let Hallett find him first."

Room 367.

The door was half open, and through it Mercy could see a pale-faced Troy flanked by a man and woman in their fifties. The man, an older, craggier version of Troy dressed in work boots and jeans. The woman, a taller and friendlier looking version of Grace, if she shopped at the Vermont Country Store instead of Newbury Street.

His parents. She'd come back another time. She didn't want to intrude, or maybe she was just being a coward. She eased back into the hallway, but not before the man caught her eye.

"Come on in," he yelled.

The woman smiled. Troy smiled, too, and that's when Mercy saw the mother's mark upon the son. He had his mother's smile—and it was a killer. The kind of smile that said *I see right through you, and I like you anyway.*

She waved her in, and Mercy had no choice but to comply. She couldn't be rude to the parents of the man who'd helped save her grandmother's life. And Elvis's life. And her own.

She resisted the urge to smooth her hair, but she put a smile on her face—not as brilliant as Troy's or his mother's, yet hopefully bright enough to hide her unease at having yet another Warner get under her skin—and pushed into the room.

"Harrison Warner." Troy's father stepped forward. "Harry." He squeezed his wife's shoulders. "And this is Lizzie."

"Lovely to meet you."

"We've heard so much about you," said Lizzie. With that smile.

Mercy ignored that. "How's the patient?"

"He'll be as good as new," said Lizzie. "If we can keep him down long enough to recover."

"I'm right here, people." Troy leaned forward, and then fell back with a wince.

"Keep that ice pack on." Lizzie bustled back to her son.

Mercy grinned as she watched Troy squirm under his mother's attentions.

"I'm fine, Mom."

Lizzie laughed. "Sure you are." She positioned the ice pack over the blue hospital gown along the right side of Troy's rib cage. "Hold that right there."

Troy did as he was told.

"Let's go get a cup of coffee, Harry." Lizzie took her husband by the arm.

"Sure." Harry winked at Mercy on his way out.

Mercy drew closer to the bed. "You look terrible."

And he did. He was ashen under his game warden's all-season tan. And she could see the tiny flinches of pain that flitted across his face every now and then.

"Thanks." He laughed, stiffened abruptly, and cursed. "Don't make me laugh."

"I'm sorry. Can't they get you something for that pain?"

He shrugged. "I hear Patience is doing well. How about Elvis?"

Troy was as good at avoiding questions he didn't want to answer as she was.

"He's had a rough time. He's with Claude and Susie Bear in the mobile clinic."

"The Nana Banana," he said, using her pet name for the big yellow van.

"That's right."

"Time for your meds." An attractive young nurse who obviously enjoyed having a handsome game warden to care for shooed Mercy away from Troy's bedside.

"This is Sophia," he said.

Sophia ignored Mercy, focusing all her attention on her good-looking patient. She handed him a tiny paper cup with two pills inside, and a large paper cup with water. "These will take the edge off the pain. And make you drowsy." The nurse frowned at Mercy. "Nap time."

Mercy wanted to talk to Troy on his own, discover what they'd found out about the suspects. And thank him for everything. And just be here with him for a minute. But not with Sophia the Super Nurse playing sentry. "I'd better get back to Elvis."

"You don't have to go just yet." Troy stifled a yawn and blanched.

"He needs his rest." Sophia glared at her.

"Agreed." Mercy reached over and squeezed his shoulder gently. "I need to go anyway. Hallett's been hanging around."

"Don't listen to him." Troy caught her fingers with his own as she pulled away. His hand curled around hers and she smiled in spite of herself. "He's wrong about Elvis. He's wrong about you." She wished she could believe him. But with Elvis so close to the brink, how could she?

"Time to take your blood pressure." The nurse waved her away from the bed.

Mercy untangled her fingers from Troy's.

"What about Hallett?" he asked her.

"My parents are on it."

"Outstanding." He smiled at Mercy as the nurse wrapped the monitor around his arm in a practiced but very proprietary way.

Too proprietary. After all, Troy did not belong to this interloper in scrubs. Troy belonged to her.

As soon as the thought popped into her head, Mercy rejected it outright. Troy was not hers, even if she wanted him to be.

Time to leave. "I'll be back when you're feeling better," she told Troy. "Rest easy."

He gave her a thumbs-up. Sophia the Super Nurse jerked the curtain around the bed, disappearing with Troy into her private world.

Mercy did not like Sophia the Super Nurse.

MERCY RELIEVED CLAUDE at the van, taking up his spot by Elvis so he could go visit Patience in the hospital. Susie Bear was snoring lightly on the mat in the corner. Didn't look like she'd moved an inch in her absence.

"Elvis's blood pressure is returning to normal," said Claude as he slipped off his white coat and slipped on his parka. "And he's breathing more easily. Let him sleep. The more rest, the better."

"So he's out of the woods?"

"Not completely." He smiled at her. "But he's getting there."

"Patience is doing well." She showed him the photo of her grandmother.

"She looks good," he said.

"I know you want to see for yourself. And I know she wants to see you. For what it's worth, she told me it was a mistake to send you packing."

"I knew she didn't really mean it." He changed the subject. "That soldier was here."

"Hallett?"

"He was asking about Elvis. I put him off. But he had a very determined look about him."

"Thanks for the warning." Hallett would be back, no question about that.

Claude gave her a quick hug. "I'll be right across the parking lot if you need me."

"Thank you."

Mercy watched Claude go, stroking the shepherd's soft belly. When the veterinarian disappeared into the hospital entrance, she leaned over and whispered into one of Elvis's triangular ears. "I'm here, boy. Hang in there."

She moved her palm up to the left side of his chest, behind his front leg, where she could feel the beating of his heart. Steady as a metronome. Stalwart as a good soldier. As true as her tears.

CHAPTER THIRTY

B Y THE NEXT MORNING, CLAUDE DECLARED ELVIS FIT TO leave the clinic—and up for a little celebratory Howl at Pizza Bob's, provided he went straight home to the cabin for a long nap afterward. The Malinois was still a little weak, and he was wearing a special bodysuit to stay warm, but he'd regained his composure, strutting along with her and Sunny down Main Street to meet Captain Thrasher and Troy and Susie Bear for lunch at Pizza Bob's. This was to be the golden retriever's first trip to the best pizza place in Northshire.

Pizza Bob smiled. "Another dog?"

Mercy laughed. "I sort of inherited her."

"She's a beauty." He petted the retriever first, and then Elvis. "What's with the fancy dress?"

"He caught a chill." She felt guilty just saying that out loud.

"Then let's get you inside away from the door." He ushered them around the reception area, pausing just long enough to envelop Mercy in a big bear hug. She breathed in the comforting scent of garlic and pepperoni. He presented Elvis and Sunny with breadsticks from his back pocket, and the dogs gobbled them down as he escorted them to their seats. Past the massive one-of-a-kind stone pizza oven that dominated the colorful Sixties-style restaurant and through the crowded dining room to the back, where the captain had commandeered a quiet booth.

Troy and Susie Bear were already there, Troy sitting across from Thrasher and the cheerful dog waiting patiently at the game warden's feet. Mercy stepped over Susie Bear and slipped into the booth next to Troy. The dogs exchanged a couple of sniffs and Elvis and Sunny settled in next to their canine pal. Elvis and Susie Bear knew the best was yet to come: two extra-large Howls—hand-tossed pies with pepperoni, sausage, bacon, meatballs, and ham—and fresh root beer on tap for the humans and a large bowl of water for them. But it would be a happy surprise for Sunny.

"The body in the lake was Rocky Simko," said the captain without preamble. "Rucker finally confirmed it."

"Guess who the guy who got away was," Troy said to her, a challenge in his eyes.

Mercy paused dramatically. "Ruby Rucker's son."

"Never bet against her," Troy told the captain.

"So I guess lunch is on me." Thrasher grinned as Pizza Bob put the tray holding two Long Trail Limbo IPAs and a glass of Big Barn Red on the table with one oversized hand and placed the dogs' water bowl down on the floor next to the dogs with the other. He slipped each of the canines another breadstick. "I'll be back with the pies shortly."

"What, no root beer?" asked Mercy.

"Technically we're off duty," said the captain.

"Right." She knew these guys worked all kinds of hours when they were on a case, on and off the clock.

Thrasher and Troy raised their beers to Mercy.

"To our own little Jessica Fletcher," said Troy, laughing.

The captain frowned.

"Just quoting the Cat Ladies."

"Very funny." Mercy clinked her wine glass against their beer bottles.

"I'm not sure I even want to know how you figured out that our runaway perp was Ruby Rucker's son," said the captain. "But tell us anyway."

"Just a guess."

"An educated guess," teased Troy.

Mercy sipped her wine, and thanked St. Vincent of Saragossa—patron saint of winemakers, according to Martinez—for red wine everywhere. "We knew from the private investigator's report that Ruby visited a Planned Parenthood clinic while she was in Albany. But she didn't have an abortion. So it stands to reason that she might have been pregnant and that she might have had a baby."

"That baby would have been George's son," said Troy.

"Most likely."

"Most likely?"

"Ruby had a number of affairs while she was married to George." Mercy sighed. "Any number of men could have been his father, including my own grandfather, if you believe the gossip."

Pizza Bob was back with the Howls. He placed the two pans on the table. "Enjoy!"

As soon the restaurateur walked away, Elvis and Susie Bear scrambled to their feet, sitting nicely back on their haunches and waiting politely to be served. Sunny followed suit. Only the synchronized wallop of their tails against the old pine floors and the glisten of saliva on their flews gave away their anticipation.

"You don't believe that." Thrasher served himself two slices of the pie and slipped each dog a generous slice as well.

When it came to dogs, thought Mercy, the captain was a pushover.

"No, I don't." Mercy removed one large piece of pizza, folded it lengthwise, and nibbled at the pointed end. "What else did Rucker say?"

"All he'll say is that his son had nothing to do with anything."

"I imagine everything is Rocky Simko's fault," said Mercy.

"Convenient, since he's dead." Troy helped himself to a couple of slices.

"Rucker's lawyering up." Thrasher retrieved a printout from his pocket and pushed it across the table. "But we found these in his wallet." The printout showed two photos. One of a tall skinny young man with strawberry-blond hair that stuck out in wild tufts and cowlicks, wearing a suit and tie in what was obviously a high school graduation picture. The back read: Arlo Martin, Class of 2018, Miami Latin High School. The other showed the same young man with an attractive woman in her early forties. A petite brunette with brown eyes, dressed in a bright pink jersey sundress that showed off her curves, smiling a smile that could sell a million houses. An older South Beach version of the Las Vegas blonde who'd taken George Rucker and Peace Junction by storm.

"That's Ruby Rucker all right."

Mercy smiled. "She hasn't changed much, apart from her hair color."

"She runs a successful decorating business in Little Havana."

"Of course she does," said Mercy. "When did Rucker find out about his son? I can't see Ruby telling him. Ever."

"Rucker said he got a letter from Arlo last year." Thrasher finished his first piece of pizza and wiped his hands elegantly on his napkin before starting in on his second piece. "After his stepfather died, he asked his mother who his real father was. She didn't want to tell him, but when he threatened to do a DNA test, she gave in and told him about Rucker. He took it upon himself to contact him."

"And now he's lost him just as he found him." She nibbled some more, but she just wasn't that hungry. Hard to eat when she knew she was missing something. "I can't help but feel a little sorry for Arlo. Unless he's the one who put that bomb on my grandmother's porch."

"Rucker's not saying," said Thrasher. "Although nothing we know about Rucker would lead us to believe he has a clue how to build a bomb."

"He could have picked up some pointers in prison." Troy flagged down Pizza Bob for another beer. "You need to eat, too, Mercy. Keep up your strength."

She noticed that Troy had already downed all his pizza and his beer. He must be feeling better, if he'd gotten his appetite back, she thought. Or he wasn't used to long lunches. Too much eating on the run. "Arlo could have learned how to build a bomb on the internet."

"A pipe bomb would be more Simko's style than Rucker's," said Thrasher. "But dead men don't talk. And as long as Rucker isn't talking, either, we've got more questions than answers."

"We've got to find Arlo Martin."

"Why is Arlo even here?" She peeled off a pepperoni and popped it in her mouth.

"To meet his father," said Troy.

"He could have just gone to visit him in prison." She tore off a piece of the crust. Pizza Bob made great crust. "Why go to all the trouble to escape from prison and travel to Vermont and raid all these properties?" She wiggled the crust at Troy and answered her own question. "Because Rucker is looking for something. Something he can give to Arlo."

"An inheritance," said Troy.

"That would explain why Simko came along. To share in the bounty," said Thrasher. "Whatever it is."

"Mary Lou said the judge's parties were all about drugs and prostitutes and gambling and money laundering," said Mercy.

"All cash businesses," Troy pointed out.

"The judge died unexpectedly," said Mercy. "Maybe some of that cash got lost in the shuffle."

"This is all speculation," said Thrasher.

"Where's Ruby in all this?" Ruby was the key to this puzzle, thought Mercy.

"We don't know," said Troy.

"We're trying to find her," said the captain. "We've asked local authorities down there to locate her."

Pizza Bob served them another round. "On me," he said, as he tried and failed to sneak the dogs another couple of breadsticks without their noticing.

"I saw that," she said. "We thank you. Dogs, too."

Pizza Bob shrugged away their thanks and went back to his other customers, the ones not talking about the missing and the murdered. Mercy wondered what it would be like to have a job like his. Where the only puzzle was how much cheese to order each week, not what happened to Ruby Rucker and Beth Kilgore.

"Why kidnap my grandmother?" She sipped the last of the wine in the first glass. She wasn't sure she needed—or wanted—the second. On the other hand, it was a shame to let a glass of Big Barn Red go unsipped.

"We thought Rucker blamed Patience for losing Ruby to Red, but maybe that's not it at all."

"It's not," she said.

"Maybe Rucker believed that Patience knew where the money was," said Troy.

"Local law enforcement must have been turning a blind eye to the judge's parties for a cut," said Thrasher. "Maybe he thought your grandfather was crooked."

"Or that he was sleeping with Ruby so he could find out more about where the judge was stashing the drugs and the cash," added Troy.

"And that your grandmother knew about it."

"But that's all wrong." She downed the last of the Big Barn Red. "Wyetta said that August Pitts was the crooked one."

"That's right," said Troy. "*Crooked as a three-dollar bill* were her exact words."

"Wyetta Wright? Best pecan pie in Vermont?"

"That's right." Troy told the captain about their visit to Wyetta's Café.

While the two men discussed the artist's many fine attributes, Mercy's attention wandered. She remembered the torn-up floorboards in the old bungalow. And the junk pile behind it where they'd found Kilgore's body in a barrel. The house where they'd found Becker and Goodlove in the keeping room. And the bunker where her grandmother had been locked in a bathroom. All good out-of-the-way places to host illicit parties and to hide whatever needed to be hid. Money, illegal substances, bodies.

"This is one crazy conundrum," she said.

"If anyone can figure it out, you can," said Troy.

"Most of the pieces are here," she told them. "Like you say, I should be able to figure it out. But I need to *see* it."

CHAPTER THIRTY-ONE

BACK AT THE CABIN, MERCY SETTLED ELVIS ONTO HIS SIDE of the couch for a long nap. Sunny abandoned the dog bed for the floor at the shepherd's feet, positioning her head on the sofa muzzle to muzzle with his. The golden seemed to understand that Elvis could use a little quiet canine company.

Mercy was ready to work. She went to her own hiding place, a small space in the back of the cabin. She'd painted the room the color of Buddhist monks' robes—saffron—and equipped it with tools meant to encourage her version of enlightenment: heavy bag and boxing gloves, yoga mat and bolster, and a tiny, intricately carved altar laden with candles and Buddhas and family photos. She'd added a large freestanding whiteboard recently, the better to think through the puzzles that kept popping up in her life, like it or not.

She wheeled the whiteboard into the great room. She did her best thinking here, under the soaring ceiling, surrounded by her books and her fireplace and her favorite sentient beings. Here in her own sunlit home, flooded with light from the tall windows that looked out onto the mountains, where Elvis was safe and sound and she could protect him. No more near-death experiences in the woods.

"You're making an incident board." Amy scooped up baby Helena in her arms to make way for Mercy and her board.

"Just like all those cop shows you binge watch," said Brodie, shaking his head. "Meta."

Mercy didn't watch much TV, but when she did it was mostly crime series: *Bosch, Vera,* and *Prime Suspect: Tennison* reruns. Brodie was more of a *Star Trek, Star Wars,* and *Game of Thrones* kind of guy.

"I have to. There are just so many pieces that don't fit." She positioned the whiteboard at the end of the farm table, facing Amy and Brodie. Amy put Helena in the high chair and snapped a bib on the toddler. She gave her a teething biscuit, pulling up a chair for herself. Brodie sat down next to her.

"Brodie and I are having leftover chili. Want some?"

"I'm good. Thanks to Pizza Bob."

Elvis and Sunny did not rise to the bait of Amy's chili as they normally would have done. They were both sleeping off all that pizza. Muse was curled up in the curve of Sunny's feathery tail, her new favorite place to doze.

While Amy served up chili for herself and Brodie, Mercy dragged all the files back to the farm table and gathered the materials she'd left on the coffee table. They'd been dusted for prints but nothing actionable had turned up from forensics yet. These things took time—too much time. And she didn't think there was anything to find anyway.

Mercy was prepared to figure it out herself. She posted all the pictures she had of the suspects: Beth and Thomas Kilgore on their wedding day, Ruby and George Rucker at the Little Chapel of the West, George Rucker and Rocky Simko's mugshots, Arlo Martin and his mother in Miami, Joey Colby in the woods, Deputy Pitts and her grandfather Sheriff Red in uniform, the masked man on her grandmother's front porch.

Next she added the crime scenes: Joey's camp, her grandmother's Victorian, the lodge, the barrel, the old Cape Cod, the 1950s house. Brodie brought her the Las Vegas postcard, the one that Ruby had written to George.

In black marker, Mercy wrote out a timeline with the dates of the murders and other key events.

"Cool," said Brodie, between bites of chili.

"I think you like investigative work," she told him.

"It's like a real-life escape room." Brodie and Amy had been on several escape room adventures, from Vermont to Boston.

"Brodie is good at solving the clues." Amy took a wet cloth and wiped down the mess Helena had made of the teething biscuit.

"Not as good as Amy," he said.

"We're both good."

"Great, then you can both help me." Mercy studied the board: The victims, the suspects, the dead, and the missing. The places where all these people, dead and alive and unaccounted for, had lived, congregated, passed through, never to be seen again.

"What are we looking for?" Amy took turns feeding herself and her baby, spooning chili first into her mouth with an adult-sized spoon in one hand and then into her daughter's with a baby spoon in the other hand.

"Something odd, something off, something that doesn't fit." They fell into a silence born of concentration and deliberation.

"Mercy, what do you think doesn't fit?" asked Amy finally.

"I'm not sure." She sighed. "But this postcard bothers me for some reason. It has from the beginning."

"Vegas is awesome." Brodie pointed to the postcard. "I was there a couple of years ago for the Consumer Electronics Show. It was a blast." He looked at Amy sheepishly. "That was before I met you."

"I know."

"You can tell this is an old postcard," he said. "The Hacienda isn't there anymore. It's the Mandalay Bay now. That's where we stayed."

Mercy stared at the image of the Las Vegas Strip on the postcard, with the Hacienda and the Luxor at one end and the Stratosphere at the other. What was it her mother had said about Las Vegas? *It's such a tacky town. There's no pride of place. They spend absurd amounts of money to build these outlandish casinos, and ten years later they blow them up and start all over again.*

"Wait a minute. What's wrong with this picture?" she asked her helpers, not really expecting an answer. She pulled her laptop across the table and opened it up, going online. Searching for the history of the brief happy life of the Hacienda Casino.

"What are you looking for?" asked Amy.

"Brodie, you are brilliant." Mercy grinned.

"Huh?"

"Listen to this." Mercy consulted her screen, where she'd pulled up several stories about various casinos on the strip. "Better yet, write these dates down on the board."

Brodie shuffled to his feet and took up the black marker as if it were a sword. "Ready."

"The Hacienda was imploded on December 31, 1996," said Mercy. "The Mandalay Bay did not open in its place until March 2, 1999." She looked up at Brodie, who was faithfully recording the names and dates as she rattled them off. "Good."

"I don't get it."

"Hold on," she said. "The Luxor next door opened its doors on October 15, 1993. The Stratosphere opened its doors on April 30, 1996." She could hear the squeak of the marker as Brodie documented her words.

"I still don't get it." He stepped back to examine his handiwork.

"I get it!" Amy clapped her hands, and her baby did the same.

Monkey see, monkey do, Mercy thought. "Then let's hear it."

"I want to get this right." Amy frowned, thinking. "The photo on this postcard would have to have been taken between April 30, 1996, and December 31, 1996."

She grinned. "Well done, Amy!"

"So what?' asked Brodie.

"It means that Ruby Rucker probably didn't buy it in Vegas in 2000 and mail it to George. She must have sent him an old postcard from 1996, one she had already."

"They could keep on selling the postcards even if they aren't accurate."

"Four years later?" Mercy shook her head. "I don't think so. Four years is an eternity in Las Vegas. Besides, the year 2000 was huge in Vegas. They had all sorts of special Millennium New Year merchandise."

"So there was only a short period time when this postcard could have could have been made, and it was obsolete almost as soon as it was produced," said Amy.

"You're right about Las Vegas." Brodie replaced the cap on the marker and tapped it on the postcard. "They don't do obsolete. They like everything shiny and new and neon. They would've put out new postcards."

"Ruby Rucker was a Las Vegas native," said Mercy. "She liked shiny and new and neon."

"Then why didn't she just buy a shiny new neon postcard when she got there and mail that one to her husband?" Amy smiled at Helena, who was still clapping her hands. "If she was into shiny new neon things."

"Exactly," Mercy said. "Why take that old postcard with her from Vermont when she could just buy a new one when she got to Vegas?"

"Unless she only wanted the guy to think she went to Vegas," said Brodie. "Maybe someone else sent the postcard for her."

"Good thinking," she said. "But the handwriting on the postcard is Ruby's. George hired a private investigator who confirmed that."

"Maybe he was bad at his job."

"Maybe. But the writing on the postcard matches the notes on the back of the old photos of Ruby and George that Mary Lou Rucker-Smith gave us."

Brodie squinted at the postmark on the postcard. "And the postmark *is* Las Vegas, August 5, 2000."

"Weird," said Amy.

"Indeed." Mercy scrutinized the white board one more time. "What if the handwriting is hers only because she needed the handwriting to be hers."

"To fool people?" asked Brodie.

"Yeah. Like she wanted George to believe that she went home to Vegas, but she really didn't," said Amy.

"Well, she didn't, at least not for long. She ended up in Miami," said Mercy.

"A long way from Las Vegas," said Brodie.

"But she could have sent a new postcard if all she wanted to do was throw George off her trail," she said. "Not go through all this premeditated subterfuge."

"That doesn't really prove anything. It could just be an old postcard." Brodie sat back down, handing the marker back to her.

"Sometimes a cigar is just a cigar," Mercy said.

"Whatever."

"I feel like we're just going in circles here." Mercy stood up. "I'm supposed to take Mr. Horgan his new kitten today. We'd better get going. Can I leave Elvis and Sunny here with you?"

"Sure," said Amy. "What about the whiteboard?"

"Let's leave it up for now. All these questions aren't going away."

"That's for sure," said Brodie.

"Leave her alone, Brodie. She needs to think. She'll figure it out."

Mercy hoped that Amy was right. She packed a basket full of essentials and treats for the little black kitty. Elvis unwound himself from the sofa and came over to help her, sticking his nose in the treat drawer and pulling out a package of the peanut butter doggie biscuits he and Sunny enjoyed so much.

She pretended not to see, grateful that the ailing shepherd appeared to be getting back to normal, letting him nab the bag of cookies and steal back to the sofa to share them with the golden unnoticed. Elvis tore open the sack, scattering the biscuits; he and Sunny gobbled them up in a matter of seconds and retreated to the couch once more.

Certainly his appetite was back in full force. That had to be a good sign. She threw on her coat, grabbed her pack, and picked up the basket.

"I'm off," she yelled to Amy.

Elvis and Sunny raised their heads.

"Stay," she told the dogs sternly, heading for the door.

Sunny obeyed, but Elvis ran after her.

"No." She pointed at the sofa. "Bed."

The Malinois didn't move.

"Elvis, you have to stay here. You're not well."

He tilted his triangular ears at her in rebuke.

"Seriously, you have to stay here. Stay."

Elvis stood his ground.

"I'm leaving and you're staying. End of story." She opened the door, basket on her hip, and before she could shut it behind her the shepherd slipped past her and raced for the Jeep.

He stood at attention by the passenger door barking furiously to be let in.

"You're getting yourself all worked up. It's not good for you."

Mercy sighed. "Okay, but I'm not opening this door until you calm down."

Elvis stopped mid-bark.

"Very funny," she told him. "Not."

When they got in the Jeep, Elvis curled up on the back seat and promptly went to sleep. Well, at least he could take his nap, as Claude advised.

The dog clearly didn't want to go anywhere without her. Even after nearly dying. How could she let Hallett have him, even if he were safer with him, if he really didn't want to go? Her mother would see to it that Elvis stayed with her if that's what she wanted; Grace was a fierce attorney who rarely lost a case. Hallett wouldn't know what hit him.

If that's what she wanted.

Too many questions to which she had no answers.

About the case, about Elvis, about her life.

CHAPTER THIRTY-TWO

MERCY STEERED HER JEEP THROUGH TOWN TO THE NORTH end of Maple Street. The address seemed familiar to her somehow. She knew this part of town; one of the girls she'd been to summer camp with as a teenager lived close by. But it had been years since she'd been up here.

This was one of Northshire's oldest and most beautiful streets, where large homes sat on wooded one-acre lots on a hill overlooking the village. Bea's elegant two-storied home dated back to the early nineteenth century. With its pedimented gables and open-entry porticos supported by Doric columns, the well-kept Greek Revival house was a standout even in a neighborhood celebrated for its classic residences.

Bea Garcia must spend a fortune keeping it up, thought Mercy. The Cat Ladies had told her that Bea was a woman of means, her late husband having left her a considerable fortune. Apparently, she'd been very generous to local charities, including the Cat House and other animal rescue organizations.

Mercy remembered after she rang the bell and the barking began that Bea had told her she'd adopted two Labrador retrievers. Elvis stood beside her, ears perked and curlicue tail aloft, ready to assess the newcomers and maybe make a couple of new friends. Maybe.

Bea Garcia opened the door, pretty in jeans and a coral silk sweater. She was holding a pair of lively black canines by their collars, one in each hand. She was losing the battle, as they were nearly as big as she was, and the sight of Elvis didn't help. "Please give me a minute."

She pulled the labs back and kicked the door shut. While they waited, Mercy looked around the front lawn, which would be breathtaking by mid-May if its many neatly groomed flower beds were any indication. She amused herself by picturing the garden in full bloom, awash with tulips and daffodils and hyacinth, pansies and petunias, primrose and snapdragons, azaleas and more. It was an act of active imagination, since right now the ground was bare of anything but dirty snow and gray slush and brown mud covering dead grass.

The front door opened again.

"I put the dogs in the backyard," said Bea. "Come on in." She stepped aside to welcome them into a light-filled rotunda.

Mercy stopped to admire the spectacular staircase that took center stage in the rotunda, rising up to a circular landing that graced the second floor. She looked up beyond the second floor to the ceiling of the domed rotunda. Sunlight poured through the dome, filling the entire space with light. "This is breathtaking."

"Thank you." Bea smiled. "I do love this house."

"I can see why." Mercy smiled back. "How's the kitten?"

"He's good. He's been neutered and vaccinated and groomed. He's ready for his forever home."

"I know Mr. Horgan will be thrilled to have him."

"Come on back to the kitchen with me."

"Sure." Mercy certainly wanted to see the rest of this house. She started to follow Bea through one of the doors at the back of the rotunda, but Elvis stayed put.

"Come on, boy."

The Belgian shepherd did not start toward her; instead he gracefully sank down into his classic Sphinx pose. Elvis was alerting to the bottom of the stairs.

"Weird." Mercy should have left him at home to recuperate. The shepherd was obviously not 100 percent yet. "Elvis, let's go. There's nothing there." She slapped the side of her thigh, twice, and reluctantly he joined her, his nose touching her hip. They met Bea in a state-of-the-art kitchen big enough and well-equipped enough to feed half the town. She was preparing the cat carrier for its new passenger.

"The kitty's in the library playing with my calico. They've become bosom buddies. You can fetch him if you'd like."

"Sure."

"Out through those columns to your left." Bea pointed to the other side of the large room, where a pair of columns stood at the opening of a book-lined space, and they headed into it. To Mercy, this room had it all: two overstuffed burgundy velveteen chairs flanked by good reading lights, floor to ceiling books, and a mahogany and brass bar cart well stocked with wine and whiskey.

She ran her finger along the spines of the books on the shelf nearest her, reading the titles as she went: *Double Indemnity, The Maltese Falcon, Strangers on a Train, Devil in a Blue Dress, In a Lonely Place, L.A. Confidential, Die a Little, Eight Million Ways to Die.*

Quite the collection of noir novels, Mercy thought. She pulled out what looked like a hardcover first edition of *The Maltese Falcon*, admired the dark regal bird on the yellow dust jacket, and flipped to the copyright page. Yep, first edition. She wondered how much it was worth, probably more than a year's pay for the soldier she used to be.

She replaced the Dashiell Hammett classic, right where it belonged, next to the Patricia Highsmith classic. *Strangers on a Train.*

"Do you like noir?" Bea appeared behind her, cat carrier in hand.

"Sure. But my real passion is Shakespeare."

Bea smiled. "You have good taste."

Mercy shrugged. "I found the crime fiction, but not the cats."

Bea pointed under one of the overstuffed chairs. "They're under here." She put the cat carrier down and knelt gracefully on the Aubusson rug and eased the kitten into her arms. She held it up to Mercy, who took the bright-eyed kitten and hugged it to her chest. He *was* cute.

Elvis sniffed the little guy and licked his ear. Mercy placed the kitten in the carrier and zipped up the opening. "Good to go."

Bea escorted them back through the rotunda to the front door. Again Elvis halted at the staircase and alerted to the bottom steps.

He really was not himself. Mercy cursed herself for bringing him with her before he was ready. The sooner she got him back home on his side of the couch, the better.

"Come on, Elvis."

Elvis didn't move a muscle. He didn't even bother to look up at her. He held perfectly still, wise as a pharaoh in his Sphinx pose. Ignoring her and her command.

"What's he doing?" asked Bea.

"He was a sniffer dog in the Army."

Bea laughed. "Well, there's no bomb here."

"That's what Patience would have said a week ago."

Bea looked at her with alarm. "You really don't think . . ."

"I don't know what to think. He's been through a lot."

But Elvis had been through a lot many times. That hadn't affected his abilities to find what mattered, whether it was an explosive device or a missing child or a dead body.

"*Always trust your dog*," Mercy muttered.

"What?" asked Bea.

But Mercy didn't answer the woman. She was challenging herself to do the right thing. But what was the right thing?

Whenever Elvis alerted to something and she followed up on it, he ended up in danger. Well, they both ended up in danger. He was supposed to be retired. But he didn't seem to know it.

And how could he? He went where she went. She didn't seem to know it, either.

She wasn't helping him ease into civilian life by putting him in these situations and then enabling him at every turn. She was going to have to stop that. She was a civilian now, and she needed to act like one. If only so Elvis could act like one, too.

As soon as she figured out what was up with these stairs. She examined the treads and the risers and the railing and ran her fingers along the lip of each step, starting at the bottom. There she felt the slight rise of a hinge. Mercy realized that the section of the stairs closest to the floor—the last three steps—must pull out. She unhitched the hinges and tugged.

Revealing an opening leading into a small underground room.

"Very clever of you to find it," said Bea.

"What is it?"

"It's a hiding place that dates back to the Underground Railroad. The original owner of the house, Horace Hopkins, was a prominent abolitionist."

"That's fascinating. I knew about these hidden rooms, but I've never seen one like this."

"From what I understand, it is unusual."

Elvis broke away from Mercy and leapt down into the hole.

"Elvis! Come back here!" She peered down into the hiding place, which appeared not much deeper than she was tall and no more than ten feet long and five feet wide. Not that she could see much as there was little light illuminating the space. "Elvis!"

"I'm afraid I've never been down there," said Bea. "I don't know what your dog may find."

"I can't see him." Mercy pulled out her cell and turned on the flashlight function. "I'm so sorry, but I think I'm going to have to go down after him. When he gets like this, there's no calling him back."

"Of course."

Bea watched her as she lowered herself down into the dark chamber, jumping the last few feet to the dirt floor beneath her. She shined her cell flashlight around the room. Which was more a tunneled-out cellar than a room. The old rock walls were dark with grime. At some point an attempt had been made to lay a rough planked floor, but the years had taken their toll. A rusted metal wine rack and some wooden crates stood against one wall, and an old gun cabinet nearly as tall as the room on the other. The latter held several rifles, all of which looked like they'd been there for years. Maybe they had.

"Good job," she told Elvis, who was sitting at the other end of the room in front of an old trunk half buried in the floor. He did not even acknowledge her compliment.

She stepped carefully over to the shepherd, who'd assumed his Sphinx pose and was alerting to the trunk. "What have you got there?"

Elvis looked up at her, his triangular ears perked. Waiting for his reward. She gave him a peanut butter treat from her pocket to nibble on while she checked out the trunk.

The trunk was made of faded gray metal and looked much like an old Army footlocker. She pried open the rusted hinges and tried to raise the lid but the trunk was locked.

"Really?" She tugged her Swiss Army knife out of her pocket and released the thin lockpicking tool. She was getting a lot of use out of it lately. Martinez would be pleased. The locks on metal trunks were typically easy to pick, and this one was no exception, rusty as it was. She slipped the tool back into place and returned the knife to her pocket.

"Open sesame," she said to Elvis, yanking the lid up and shining her cell flashlight on the trunk's interior.

Guns. Mostly pistols, with a couple of sawed off shotguns. "No wonder you alerted to this place. Weapons everywhere."

No ammunition that she could see. But there could be boxes of ammo under the pile of guns. She put on a pair of plastic gloves and carefully removed the weapons. There was no ammunition, there was nothing at all under the guns. But the depth of the trunk seemed too shallow.

A false bottom, she thought. She felt around the sides of the trunk's interior until she found the mechanism to release the secret space. She lifted the false bottom out and shone the light once again on the inside of the footlocker.

Money. Lots of it. Stacks and stacks of hundred-dollar bills. She wondered whose it was and how it came to be here. Although she supposed as the owner of the house it was Bea Garcia's now.

She put everything back the way it was before Elvis found it—the false bottom, the guns, the lid, the lock—and switched off the flashlight to save cell power. And rewarded him with another doggie biscuit. "Good job."

She crossed the small room, Elvis on her heels. She peered up into the opening at the bottom of the staircase, but she couldn't see anything. She called out for Bea, but she heard nothing.

"I guess we're on our own." The opening was too high up to make climbing out easy. She could always use the crates or the trunk for a leg up. She went back to the far corner where the crates were piled. They seemed sturdy enough.

Above her, Mercy heard a shuffling. Dogs barking. A woman screaming. Beside her, Elvis growled.

She twisted in the direction of the staircase just as Bea Garcia tumbled through the opening and landed hard on the dirt floor.

And the stairs slammed back into place.

Plunging them into total darkness.

They were trapped.

CHAPTER THIRTY-THREE

ERCY SWITCHED HER FLASHLIGHT BACK ON AND RAN over to Bea, helping her to her feet. "Are you okay?"

"I think so." The small woman wobbled a bit. She was very pale, and Mercy worried that she might fall again.

"The floor is very uneven. Hold on to me and we'll get you a seat." By the light of her cell she guided Bea to the crates in the corner. She grasped Bea's upper arm to hold her upright with one hand and overturned a crate with the other, creating a makeshift seat. "Sit here and catch your breath."

Elvis trotted over to Bea and placed his muzzle on her lap. Mercy tried to text Troy. No service. Not unusual down here. She turned her attention back to Bea. "Can you tell me what happened up there?"

Bea stroked the shepherd's ears. "Someone came up from behind me and hit me on the head. I fell down here. And then I heard the door slam."

"Who was it?"

"I have no idea."

"You didn't see them."

"No."

"Was there only one attacker?"

"I don't know. I was only aware of one. But there could have been more."

"Close your eyes. I'm going to shine this light on your head so I can see where you've been hurt." Mercy found the bloody spot on the left side of Bea's skull, and gently parted her brown hair to get a better look. "Okay, it doesn't look too bad, but head injuries can be tricky. We need to get you out of here as quickly as possible."

"How can we do that? They're still up there."

Mercy swept the light around the room. "Is there another way out of here?"

"There might be. They used to run tunnels from the underground rooms to the outside so they could move people and goods more discreetly."

"Goods?"

"A lot of these hiding places from the Underground Railroad were used by smugglers during Prohibition."

Mercy walked around the room, searching for any sign of another exit. Nothing stood out to her; the walls were all dirt and rock and rotting wood but she could see no evidence of a tunnel. The floor seemed relatively intact as well. There was only one place where you could camouflage the entrance to a tunnel.

The gun cabinet.

The old oak piece was about three feet wide and nearly eight feet tall. The bottom section was locked storage space fronted by two wood doors. For ammunition, she presumed.

The top section that held the old rifles had long ago lost its glass doors, but the guns seemed secure enough. She tried to pull the cabinet away from the wall, but it didn't budge. She removed the rifles carefully, checking for ammo. None of them was loaded. She set them aside, and then checked the back of the top section. "It's screwed into the rock wall."

"Why would anyone do that?"

"To keep people from moving it."

Mercy sighed and retrieved her Swiss Army knife once more.

"What are you doing?"

"Sit tight." She used the lockpicking tool to open the lower cabinet doors, revealing an empty space. No boxes of bullets, after all. She squatted down and pushed on the inside back panel of the bottom section. "Cardboard."

She pushed again and the cardboard panel gave way easily, revealing a large opening about three feet wide and two and a half feet high. She focused the beam of her flashlight into the opening, illuminating a tunnel running several yards into the unknown. "Bingo."

"What is it?"

"Our way out." Mercy knew that she needed to get Bea away from there, but she didn't like leaving the trunk with the guns and the money behind. Not that she had any other alternatives. She could only hope that she could get backup out here before whoever was in the house caught up with them—and the trunk.

They heard muffled voices and more shuffling above.

"I was going to check this tunnel out before we all went in there. But we may not have enough time for that. Do you think you can crawl through this?"

Bea stared up at the blocked entry of her staircase where the noise continued before answering. "That looks like our only option."

She helped Bea off the crate and over to the cabinet. "Go as far as you can on your hands and knees. If the tunnel narrows, you may have to drop down and crawl like a soldier on maneuvers."

Bea managed a wan smile. "I'm sure that means more to you than it does to me. But I will do my best."

"At least you're wearing jeans." She slapped her thigh and Elvis trotted over to her, ears perked. "We're going to let Elvis go first. He should be able to make his way without crawling, or at least be able to crouch his way through. You follow him."

Here she was, putting the dog in danger again. Maybe there *was* something wrong with her. She'd think about it later. After they got out of here. Pointing in the tunnel, she snapped her fingers. "Out."

Elvis dove into the tunnel without hesitation. Mercy helped Bea worm her way into the cabinet and through the opening and out into the tunnel. She handed the woman her cell phone. "Use the light so you can see where you're going. As soon as you get out, call 911."

"What are you going to do?"

"I'm going to make sure no one follows us." As Elvis and Bea proceeded down the passageway, Mercy got to work. She didn't have her gun, but at least she had her pack. Her Swiss Army knife. Her duct tape.

She crept into the tunnel opening backward, quickly brushing away their tracks as best she could in the dark. That would have to do. She pulled the cabinet doors shut. She couldn't lock them from the inside, so she simply duct taped them closed and hoped nobody noticed. On her hands and knees, she backed up, and replaced the cardboard panel, also securing it from the tunnel side with duct tape. She crawled on her hands and knees, pulling her pack along as she went, pushing herself backward toward what she hoped would be the light at the end of the tunnel.

It was slow going. As she suspected, the tunnel did narrow for a time, forcing her to drop onto her belly. She said a quick prayer of gratitude to whichever saint of Martinez's was the patron of push-ups and planks, a thank-you for her strong if increasingly fatigued forearms.

She had dirt in her hair and her mouth and everywhere else. If this tunnel went nowhere, they'd run out of oxygen and have to go back the way they came. But she didn't think that would happen. The tunnel was lined with rough planks and supported by wooden posts and was in better shape than it could have been. Which meant that someone had been using it. If not recently, in the not-so-long-ago past.

She couldn't see Bea or Elvis, but she could hear a faint scratching down the line, which grew louder as she continued to propel herself backward, cursing silently at the splinters scraping at her stomach whenever her Henley pulled up. Which was with every push.

The tunnel widened again, giving her more headroom. The gloom lightened, too, and she hoped that meant she was growing closer to Bea and her cell phone flashlight.

"Whoa."

Mercy felt her hiking boots hit something soft. "Bea?"

"Yes."

"Thank God." Mercy wriggled herself around so she was face up. Then she curled herself into a small ball, so she could turn around to face the other way, toward Bea and Elvis and the light.

"We're stuck," Bea said. "The exit is blocked." She directed the beam at Elvis, who was digging frantically at the ground above him. The way out was obstructed by dirt and rocks and roots.

"Good boy." Elvis paused in his digging to acknowledge Mercy's presence and went right back at it. She pulled her Swiss Army knife out and released the largest blade. "Sit back."

Bea did as she was told. She didn't look good. They needed to get her out of here, fast.

Mercy hacked away at the roots and dirt, stopping to wrench out the bigger rocks with her fingers. Elvis shoveled away, his sharp claws nature's digging machine. He was panting hard. *He shouldn't be exerting himself this much,* Mercy thought.

After what seemed an eternity, light broke through the debris. She and Elvis dug faster.

There was a thin layer of ice at the top, which Mercy just punched through with her fist. Her knuckles hurt, but she didn't care.

"Go on," she told Elvis, and the dog wriggled up and away into daylight. He shook the dirt from his coat, and then pivoted back to Mercy, his handsome head above her looking down at her.

"We're coming," she assured him.

"I don't think I can do this." Bea was having trouble breathing and her face was wet with perspiration despite the cold.

"We've got this. I'm going to lift you up by your hips. You grab Elvis, and he'll pull you out while I push from behind."

"Okay," Bea said, but she didn't sound okay.

Mercy squatted behind Bea, grasping her hips and shoving her upward toward the light. "I've got you. Now balance your belly against the ground."

"Down," she said to Elvis.

The shepherd lay down next to Bea.

"Grab his collar."

Bea reached up to the shepherd with her pale hands, the sleeves of her coral sweater slipping down around her forearms, revealing the tattoo of the two red cherries on the inside of her left wrist. "Got it."

"Good." Mercy stared at the tattoo. Lady Luck. The muse of gamblers. The goddess of fate. The personification of Las Vegas. She took a second to breathe. "Back, Elvis."

Elvis backed up, dragging Bea forward out of the tunnel as Mercy prodded her from behind.

When she was free and clear, she crawled back to the edge. "I'm out."

"Where are you?"

Bea looked around. "About a hundred yards from the house, in a wooded area to the left of the garage."

"Out of sight?"

"Yes, I think so. What about you? How will you get out?"

"I'll be fine." Mercy rose to a standing position. She was in a hole about four feet deep. "If you can get a signal, call 911."

She braced her feet against the opposite sides of the hole and jiggled her way up and out of the exit of the tunnel. She collapsed on the cold slushy ground, breathing heavily. Elvis licked her face, and she laughed softly.

"I called 911." Bea's face appeared above hers. "Are you all right?"

"I'm fine, Bea. Or should I call you Beth?"

SUMMER 2000

*T*hey'd been driving for a couple of hours, on back roads, in country Beth had never seen before. She'd lived in Vermont all her life, but she'd rarely left the county. And she never had learned to drive. Neither her father nor her husband would allow her that kind of freedom.

Ruby was a flatlander and yet she navigated the remote byways of these woodlands like she'd lived here all her life.

"How do you know where you're going?" Beth was still in the back seat of the Audi, but she was sitting up now, staring out the window at the endless forest that surrounded them, the only man-made element the ribbon of road stretching ahead.

"You can't sell listings you can't find." Ruby slowed down as they approached an old wooden bridge. "Look for a small sign with a red arrow that says PRIVATE. On the right."

Beth peered into the fully leafed woods, thick with thigh-high ferns and blackberry bushes and wildflowers as well as maples and birches and oaks. "There it is."

Too late. Ruby stomped on the brakes and the Audi screeched to a stop. She slammed the gearshift into reverse and backed up so they could see the sign, nearly hidden by a tangle of rambling rose. She steered the sedan onto the narrow dirt road by the sign, two rutted tracks with a strip of grass running through the middle.

"Almost there," Ruby said, as they bounced down the lane toward a large clearing where a once-handsome hunting lodge seemed to rise right out of the forest itself.

"What is this place?"

"Playground for the rich. Where they can get out of the city and pretend to be big game hunters."

"It looks abandoned."

"The owners moved to the South of France ten years ago. It's been sitting here unused ever since. No other family wanted it, so they've finally put it up for sale. I told them they need to clean up the place before we list it, but they don't want to spend the money. Rich people can be so cheap."

Ruby pulled the Audi up to the massive front porch that fronted the property.

"Bring in your stuff and we'll get started."

Beth followed her up the steps to the porch, to the carved oak front door. Ruby opened the lockbox, withdrew the house key, and let them into an imposing room with an enormous granite fireplace, several groupings of log furniture, and dozens of trophy heads and antlers adorning the walls. The dead animals looming over her gave Beth the creeps.

"Come on into the bathroom." Ruby led Beth down a long hallway graced with old-fashioned prints of bird dogs carrying dying pheasants, red-coated hunters riding with the hounds, foxes on the run.

The ladies' room—marked by a sign reading HUNTRESS—was a long room with stalls on one side, a long mirror and sinks on the other, and faded red-and-white toile wallpaper.

"First, your makeup lesson." Ruby pulled her shiny silver-and-gold metallic cosmetics bag out of her big Louis Vuitton purse. Beth didn't wear makeup, neither her father nor her husband approved of it, and she'd never developed the knack other girls had for enhancing their features with its deft application. She only used it to hide the bruises. Camouflage, not coquetry.

Ruby made up Beth, showing her how to darken her brows and eyelashes with mascara, sweeping her cheekbones and her eyelids with color, brightening her lips with a deep red gloss. By the time Ruth was finished, Beth barely recognized herself. She looked into the long bathroom mirror that ran the length of the ladies' room and watched as Ruby brushed her dark hair off her forehead and wrapped it up on top of her head, securing it with a scrunchie and bobby pins.

"The final touch." Ruby pulled out a blond wig and tugged it onto Beth's head. She straightened the hairpiece, tousling the shoulder-length bob until it fell into place as naturally as Ruby's own. Bombshell hair, thought Beth. She'd never had bombshell hair.

The two stood side by side. Before they had looked vaguely alike: about the same height, same shape, same round face, same dark eyes. Now they could have passed for sisters. Even twins, if you didn't look too closely.

The resemblance startled Beth. "Amazing." She shook her head, and the curtain of blond hair swung back and forth. "How is this possible?"

"The miracle of makeup." Ruby reached over and pulled Beth's shoulders back. "Stand tall, girl."

"I'm you."

"Almost," said Ruby. "I told you it would work. At least for as long as it takes to get us out of here. But get that nose fixed as soon as you can. For both our sakes." She loaded all the makeup into the cosmetics case and handed it to Beth. "All yours now. Use it well." She looked at her critically, and then smiled. "You're going to like being a blonde. We really do have more fun."

"What about you?"

"This was practice. So you know what to do when we get to Albany." Ruby pointed to the pack of wipes on the counter. "It's not showtime yet. Now take it all off and meet me outside."

Ruby left her alone in the bathroom. Alone with her brand new face and her brand new hair and her same old fear. It was one thing to be brave when Ruby was with her. She had enough courage for both of them. But what would happen after she got on that bus all by herself?

A flash of movement behind her. In the mirror she saw him. His face distorted by rage.

Thomas.

Nowhere to run. Her husband blocked the door. His pale blue eyes were bloodshot but his fingers were curled and clenched. Drunk enough that she might outrun him if she could get around him. Not so drunk he couldn't kill her if she couldn't.

"You look like a tramp." He grabbed at her, and she ducked. All he caught was hair. The wig slipped off, and Thomas stared at the blond mop in his thick hands, as if he weren't sure what it was. In that moment she wriggled away from him and darted through the door.

She heard a roar behind her and kept running, down the hallway and into the lobby of the lodge. Aware of all the deer and moose and bear staring down at her with their gleaming dead eyes.

An uneven pounding of steps behind her. Thomas lurching after her. Unsteady on his feet but steady with his fists.

She had to get out of here. Into the woods. He could never find her in the woods. It was always her best hiding place.

She tripped over a loose plank, stumbling to her knees. She caught herself with her arms, recovering her balance, hitching up her legs to sprint off again.

It was all the time her husband needed. Thomas rampaged above her. He tromped on her heel, hard, and kicked at her calf. She went down again. Banging her cheek on the floor. She crawled forward.

A pair of shiny black high heels shimmered in front of her.

She heard the crack! *of a gunshot. Followed by a long stammering wail. She looked up. There was Ruby, standing like a cop on TV, grasping a revolver in both hands, aiming straight ahead.*

Behind her.

Beth twisted around and saw her husband, his ruddy face marred by a hole right in the center of his high forehead.

Thomas pitched backward. Falling falling falling as if in slow motion. Thudding to the ground.

She stared at the sad hulk of him, willing him to move and praying that he did no such thing. Finally, she looked over at Ruby. "What have you done?"

"I did what needed to be done." She lowered the gun and nodded toward the body. "Now it's your turn."

CHAPTER THIRTY-FOUR

W HEN DID YOU KNOW?"

"I didn't. At least not for sure." Mercy took her cell phone from Bea, and texted Troy. The sooner he got here, the sooner she'd be able to figure all this out. Until then she had to keep Beth Kilgore safe.

They were standing about ten feet from the edge of the wood. Mercy could see Bea's house through the trees. "We're too close. The more space between us and them, whoever they are, the better. These woods lead to Old Church Road, right?"

"That's right."

"We used to hang out here when we were kids. If I remember correctly, it's about a quarter mile. Do you think you can make it?"

"Yes."

"Let's go." She texted Troy to tell him they were on the move.

Mercy was wearing her hiking boots, but Bea was only wearing ballet flats. The ground was half-frozen, a sludge of mud and ice and snow covering rock and root and dead wood. The petite brunette slipped and slid as she traipsed after Elvis. Mercy kept close behind her ready to catch her if she fell. When she fell.

The beech and birch and maple trees grew thicker here. Elvis navigated this dense terrain easily. You'd never know he'd been so sick just two days before.

Bea, not so much. Inevitably she tripped over a fallen limb. Mercy caught her—just—but not before she'd twisted her ankle.

Bea tried to put weight on her foot and winced. "I don't think I can walk."

Mercy eased the injured woman onto a squat boulder at the base of a large oak. Elvis stood at attention, sniffing the air, his nose pointing back toward the house.

"I'm so sorry," Bea said. "I've ruined everything."

"My fault," said Mercy. "We should have stayed put. Run for the Jeep."

"We would never have made it without their seeing us." Bea rubbed the side of her foot.

"Maybe. Maybe not. Let me take a look at that ankle."

"I'm fine. I just have to catch my breath."

"Hold on. Help is on the way."

As if to mark her words, sirens jangled from beyond the forest.

Mercy smiled. "Told you."

Another noise not so welcome brought Mercy to her feet. A crashing through the woods.

Elvis ran off in the direction opposite the noisy interloper. She didn't know why he did that, but she didn't call him back. The shepherd had his reasons and she needed to trust him. She grabbed a fallen branch from the forest floor, thick as a club, and took cover behind a small stand of spruce a few yards ahead of Bea. She raised her finger to her lips and Bea nodded her understanding.

They both kept very still as the swish and swoosh and snap of someone running through the woods in winter grew nearer and nearer. Mercy was worried that Bea would cry out, but she stayed quiet even as a woman in ski clothes stumbled into the clearing.

She was small and exhausted and as far as Mercy could see, unarmed. As she careened toward Bea, Mercy pushed the branch out across the ground and raised it high enough to trip her. The woman fell forward, and Mercy tackled her, clasping her wrists behind her back and pulling to her feet.

The woman cursed. "Let me go."

Bea stared at the woman on the ground.

Another crashing through the trees, this time from the other direction, and there was Elvis and Susie Bear. The woman on the ground screamed. Whether she was more afraid of the fierce shepherd or the enormous Newfie was unclear. Either way she didn't appear very fond of dogs.

Troy strode into their little patch of scrub, pushing a handcuffed young man with wild hair in front of him.

"Arlo!" said the woman on the ground.

"Mom."

"You haven't said anything, have you?"

Mercy helped the woman to her feet.

"Thank you," she said, then turned to her son. "Don't say another word. You are *so* grounded."

Arlo Martin hung his head. "How did you find me?"

"That's for me to know and you to find out."

Troy took in the scene before him and raised his eyebrows at Mercy. "What do we have here?"

She smiled at him. "Let me introduce you to Beth Kilgore and Ruby Rucker."

HALF AN HOUR later, Mercy and Troy were back at Bea's house with the dogs and Captain Thrasher, watching Harrington with the two women as he tried to sort out who was who and what was what.

"Ask Mercy," said Thrasher. "I'm sure she can tell you whatever you need to know."

Bea and Ruby stood together, each as silent as the past they had tried to outrun. Harrington—never known for his patience—finally addressed Mercy.

"What do you know about this?"

"Have you ever read *Strangers on a Train,* Detective?"

He looked at her blankly.

"It's a novel by Patricia Highsmith."

"I know what it is. But what does it have to do with this?"

Mercy smiled. "Let's go back to the beginning, shall we?" She looked at Bea and Ruby Rucker aka Isobel Martin. "Twenty years ago, two unhappy women meet at the town library. They discover a mutual love of film, and especially film noir. They both want to leave their husbands, one because her husband beats her, the other because her husband bores her. They devise a plan, inspired by *Strangers on a Train*."

"Where two men meet on a train and decide to murder each other's adversaries," interrupted Harrington. "Yes, I know. So Bea Kilgore and Ruby Rucker decide to do the same. Which is how Thomas Kilgore ends up dead in a barrel."

"No!" said Bea. "That's not how it happened."

"Lawyer," said Ruby.

"I think that was probably an accident," said Mercy. "They just wanted to get away, and not be found. So they traded identities." She paused, waving an arm in their direction. "Two women about the same size, brown eyes, fair skin, similar features. Ruby is a little curvier, but close enough. Easy enough to switch hair color. The only real difference would be the nose. Thomas Kilgore broke Beth's nose."

"Their noses look fine to me," said Harrington.

"I think you're looking at a very good nose job," said Mercy.

Ruby Rucker laughed.

"Remember, this was before 9/11," said Mercy. "Before Real IDs and TSA PreCheck. All they needed to do was trade Social Security cards and birth certificates and get new IDs when they settled in new places. And both remarried quickly and kept their new husbands' names. Elizabeth Ann Verdette Kilgore became Ruby 'Bea' Garcia and Ruby became Isobel Martin. Isobel being the Spanish for Elizabeth."

"Sounds pretty far-fetched to me," said Harrington.

A man of no imagination, thought Mercy. She'd have to spell it out for the detective. "They left town and went to the old lodge, one of Ruby's listings."

"The lodge where we found Thomas Kilgore," clarified Troy.

"I think he must have suspected something and followed them," said Mercy. "He confronted them, and he ended up dead. Given his history of violence, that's really no surprise."

"Sounds like murder to me," said Harrington.

"Or self-defense," said Mercy.

"So they put him in a barrel and leave?" asked Thrasher.

"Beth dyes her hair blond and Ruby dyes hers brown. Or maybe they wear wigs." Mercy looked at Ruby, who smiled at her coyly.

"And?" Harrington was nothing if not impatient.

"They drive to Albany, where Ruby goes to the Planned Parenthood to get an abortion, but she can't go through with it. She takes Beth to a tattoo parlor to get the same ink she has." Mercy looked at Ruby as she blinked back tears. "Check their wrists. You should find identical cherry tattoos. Lady Luck."

"Let's see 'em." Harrington nodded to Becker, who inspected their wrists.

"She's right," Becker said with a smile.

"They go to the bus station in Ruby's silver Audi and leave it in the parking lot. Beth, now posing as Ruby, boards the next Greyhound for Las Vegas. She mails that postcard, which Ruby has written beforehand."

"Clever," said Thrasher.

"Yes," said Mercy.

"And Ruby?"

"Ruby loved Las Vegas. But she couldn't go back there. Louise Minnette, the librarian, told us that she loved travel books. What's the next best thing to Vegas? Miami."

"That's quite a story," said Harrington, "but that's all in the past. What has it got to do with what's happening now?"

"Arlo Martin happened," said Thrasher.

"Ruby told him George Rucker was his father, and he contacted him. Rucker broke out of jail with his pal Simko's help and told Arlo Martin to meet him here to collect his inheritance."

"The money in the trunk Elvis and I found in Bea's hidden room."

"There's no trunk," said Harrington.

"It was there." Mercy glared at the detective.

"No trunk." Harrington crossed his arms, triumphant.

"What? You think I'm making this up?"

"I think you should write fiction." He hooked his thumb at Becker. "Book the ladies."

Hooked it again at Mercy. "Time for you to leave."

CHAPTER THIRTY-FIVE

Troy and Susie Bear dropped by the cabin to see Mercy and Elvis. He had something to tell her, and he knew she wasn't going to like it.

He parked the Ford F-150 at the top of the drive by her Jeep. Susie Bear jumped out and scampered off to find Elvis.

Mercy was leaning back in one of the old rocking chairs from her porch, her eyes closed and her red hair a curly cloud around her face. She'd pulled the chair out to the grass close to the flagpole, where the flag flew rain or shine or snow. No snow or rain today. Forty-five degrees and sunny, not a cloud in the sky. It wouldn't last long—the forecast called for freezing temperatures by sunset—but it did serve as a promise that spring was just around the corner.

He walked up the gravel path, which led from the driveway past the flag to the porch. The snow was melting, and patches of green peeped through the dead grass. Mercy didn't move when he approached her. Wrapped in a blanket, she was obviously enjoying the unseasonably warm weather. She may have been napping. Either way she looked beautiful.

Elvis and Susie Bear raced up from around the barn. They flanked Mercy, each laying a furry head on her lap. She smiled, eyes still closed, and petted the dogs. "Hello, Troy."

"Hi. Aren't you missing a dog?"

"Sunny is inside napping with little Helena. I think sometimes

Elvis wears her out," she said, eyes still closed, her face a pale moon dotted with freckles. "Shouldn't you be out on patrols?"

"Yeah." Troy couldn't wait to get back out in the woods where he belonged. "But I have some news."

Finally she opened her eyes. "What is that?"

"We got the results back from Deputy Pitts' autopsy."

"He was murdered."

"Yep. Want to tell me how you knew?"

"You wouldn't have come all the way out here to the cabin if it was natural causes."

He squatted down to talk to her, and the dogs moved in for their belly rubs. He didn't disappoint them. "Rucker insists they never killed him. Just went to talk to him about the money, which Pitts claimed to know nothing about. And Ruby was in Tampa at that home decor convention, just like she said she was, until law enforcement located her and she realized Arlo was gone."

"How did she trace him to Bea's house?"

Troy grinned. "His cell phone. She had a tracker on it."

Mercy laughed. "Poor Arlo."

He straightened up and the dogs ran off again. "Don't feel too badly for him. Ruby's lawyer got him out on bail and it wouldn't surprise me if they end up dismissing the charges altogether."

"Ruby turned out to be a very good mother, after all." She waved a pale hand at the other rocker on the porch. "Go get yourself a seat."

Troy retrieved the rocker as instructed. There was nothing he'd rather do than sit with Mercy and talk. Or not talk. Whatever she wanted.

For a moment they said nothing, just rolled back and forth in their rockers, in unison, like an old married couple. Like Patience and Red must have done, once upon a time.

"What about my grandmother?" she asked finally, breaking the silence.

"Rucker says the pipe bomb and the kidnapping were all Simko's idea. Simko believed your grandmother knew where the money was, and that he could scare her into telling them."

"He didn't know Patience."

"Rucker claims he'd never hurt a woman."

"I can believe that." She stared off into the distance, beyond the barn to the purple mountains beyond. "But what about Colby?"

"Wrong place, wrong time—if you believe Rucker. He told Harrington that they stayed at the lodge their first day in Vermont. Simko went off to gather firewood and got lost. Colby caught him on camera and he panicked. Snatched the camera, Colby tried to stop him, and Simko freaked out and killed him."

"I can believe that, too," said Mercy. "Simko was a Mississippi boy. Didn't know enough about winter in New England to keep from getting lost in the woods or riding a snowmobile into a thawing lake."

"He's not the first flatlander to die up here, and he won't be the last."

Neither of them said anything for a while. The only sounds the wind whistling around the trees and the dogs barking down by the barn.

Mercy stopped rocking. "What about the trunk?"

"I don't know. Simko is dead. Rucker's in jail. Arlo's with his mother. Looks like none of them took it. It's still missing."

"Maybe they didn't kill for it, either. Maybe Pitts' death has nothing to do with the Ruckers." She sat up abruptly, shaking off the blanket. "Field trip?"

Troy grinned. His patrols would have to wait. "Sure."

ON THE RIDE up to Peace Junction, the dogs napped in the back cab while Troy and Mercy talked about Joey Colby and the dwindling moose population, Beth Kilgore and Ruby Rucker, George and Arlo, and the power of storytelling.

"If it weren't for Patricia Highsmith writing *Strangers on a Train,* all this might never have happened," said Mercy, her face flush with excitement. He loved how worked up she got over literature.

"Beth would have stayed with Thomas," she went on. "Under his thumb."

"Until he killed her."

"Maybe."

"But Ruby still would have left George." Troy had learned the hard way that women like Ruby—and Madeline—needed more than Vermont could give them. More than he could give them.

"Yes. No doubt about that. She would have gone home to Las Vegas for good."

"Where George could have found her. And maybe kept her."

"Interesting theory." She looked over at him, and he could practically see the machinations burning up that sweet brain of hers.

"He was obsessed with her," she said. "And if she weren't worried about going to prison for killing Thomas Kilgore, she could have used the baby to get George to give her the good life in Las Vegas that she wanted."

"The perfect marriage of passion and greed."

"Go ahead," she told him. "Say it."

"Say what?" He loved teasing her.

"People don't change."

"But they can grow." He grinned at her.

"Smart ass," she said, laughing.

Troy wanted to spend the rest of his life making her laugh.

THERE WAS A Ford Explorer with a U-Haul trailer hitched to it in the driveway and a FOR SALE sign in the front yard at August Pitts' farmhouse now. One of Mary Lou Rucker-Smith's signs. He pointed at the sign. "So Eveline knows Mary Lou."

"Interesting," said Mercy. "Schemers, the two of them."

Troy parked on the street. They left the dogs in the truck—Mercy said she didn't trust the woman around dogs, and he didn't, either—and they went to talk to the deputy's grieving sister. He rang the bell several times before Eveline relented and answered the door.

"What do you want?"

"We'd like to talk to you about your brother's death," said Troy, using his "because I'm law enforcement and you're not" voice.

"Nothing to talk about," said Eveline, but she let them in anyway.

The house was nearly empty. Everything had been cleared out; all that was left in the living room was a ladderback chair, two cans of paint, several rolls of wallpaper, and assorted brushes. So much for the crime scene.

"I'm sorry to have to tell you that your brother did not die peacefully in his sleep." Troy explained the autopsy results to Eveline. "He was suffocated, by person or persons unknown."

"So that guy killed him. The one who came to visit August the night he died." Eveline crossed her arms across her large chest, stretching her tight yoga top to the breaking point. "I told you I didn't like the look of him."

"We don't think so," said Mercy. "He insists that he didn't kill the deputy."

"He's a liar."

"He had no motive."

"He's a liar," repeated Eveline.

"Maybe." Mercy looked around the stripped-down room, and her eyes came to rest on the painting and wallpapering tools neatly stacked in one corner. She rolled her eyes at Troy, and he knew she was thinking what he was thinking: Eveline had not wasted any time mourning her brother or any of his earthly possessions.

"What?" said Eveline. "You know you can't sell a house these days without staging it. Might as well get on with it."

That was Mary Lou Rucker-Smith talking, thought Troy.

"I thought you were going to keep it," said Mercy.

"Why would I freeze my ass off here when I could be back home in North Carolina?"

A rhetorical question, thought Troy.

"Your brother must have left you a nice little nest egg." Mercy smiled at the woman. One of her insincere smiles.

"That's none of your business."

"It speaks to motive."

Eveline narrowed her eyes at Mercy, and in that dark look Troy saw a glimpse of her true character. He was glad he was armed.

"August was dying. I was going to inherit everything anyway. Just a matter of time. I didn't have to kill him for it. All I had to was wait."

"Not if he changed his will."

Eveline glared at Mercy. "He didn't change his will."

"But he wanted to. He was going to leave it all to his son."

"August didn't have any children." Eveline edged toward the paint.

Troy wondered if she really planned on torpedoing them with a can of semi-gloss. He stepped forward. "Stay where you are."

"I'll do what I please. This is my house."

"Just barely," said Mercy.

Eveline lunged at her, fists raised. Troy stepped between them, grabbing her wrists.

"Let me go."

"Settle down."

"George came here that night to tell your brother that Ruby bore a son," said Mercy. "He showed him a picture of Arlo. All that strawberry-blond hair. Just like August had, back in the day, before old age and chemo. Told him he wanted the money for Arlo."

"That's ridiculous." Eveline tried to wrestle out of Troy's grip but failed.

"Is it?"

"You can't prove anything."

She was right, thought Troy. They couldn't prove anything. And he didn't have a warrant. And he was out of his jurisdiction. Not to mention Mercy was a civilian. He gave her a warning look.

"Not yet," Mercy said to Eveline.

"I'm going to let you go now. Behave." Troy released Pitts' sister.

Eveline rubbed her wrists. "Police brutality."

"He's a game warden."

"Whatever. You'll be hearing from my lawyer."

Troy ushered Mercy quickly out of the house. "Well, that went well."

"We knew she was too tough to cave," said Mercy. "But I was hoping to learn something that might help us."

The dogs jumped up and down on the back seat, pressing their black wet noses against the window glass.

"I think they need to go out," she said.

"It was a long ride. But I'd rather not let them out here."

"I think it's the perfect place to let them out." Mercy winked at him and flung open the back passenger door.

Elvis soared out of the truck and onto the lawn. Susie Bear followed, with an admittedly lumpier landing.

The dogs charged up the yard and around behind the house.

"I don't like it," Troy told Mercy as they waited for the shepherd and the Newfie to return.

"They'll be back," she said.

They stood together at the edge of the road, leaning against the hood of the truck, enjoying the sun, even if it was cooler up here in Lamoille County than it was down south in Northshire.

Just as Troy whistled to call Susie Bear back to him, she appeared at the side of the farmhouse. She scrambled past the U-Haul down the driveway to greet them. Troy slipped her a treat from his pocket.

Elvis blazed around from the back yard, headed straight for Mercy. But at the halfway mark he slid to a dead stop. Right at the trailer hitch between the Ford Explorer and the U-Haul. He sank into his standard alert position, the one Mercy called his Sphinx pose.

"What have we here?" Mercy elbowed Troy, a victorious look lighting up her pretty face.

"Get that dog out of here." Eveline stood on the porch of the deputy's house, a shotgun raised in her arms.

She was aiming right at Elvis.

CHAPTER THIRTY-SIX

S HOOT MY DOG AND YOU'RE A DEAD WOMAN." MERCY STARTED toward Eveline, but Troy held her back.

"Steady," he said. "Let me handle this. Susie Bear, stay."

Troy held his hands up. "Eveline, please put the gun down before someone gets hurt."

"You're trespassing."

A squeal of tires distracted Eveline, and she looked away. Troy took advantage of the distraction to pull his weapon. A Lamoille County Sheriff's Department SUV screeched to a stop behind his F-150. Eveline stared at it.

"Great," said Troy. "Just what we need."

"Lamoille County's finest."

"What's going on?" Deputy Purdie emerged from the SUV, hands on his holster.

"She pulled a shotgun on us," said Troy.

"She killed her brother."

"Sheriff Pitts?"

"Yes." Troy knew that to Purdie, Pitts was the sheriff, not Red's deputy. "You must know about the autopsy results."

"I heard. But that doesn't mean she killed him."

"We believe that he was going to change his will," said Troy. "Leave her out. That's motive."

"And she had means and opportunity," added Mercy, "there in the house with him all day and night."

"I didn't kill nobody," yelled Eveline. "And you can't prove any different."

"Elvis is alerting to her vehicle."

"Elvis?"

"The Malinois." Mercy pointed to Elvis on the ground by the U-Haul. "He's a police dog."

Troy frowned. That was not exactly true. Elvis was once a military working dog, but now he was as much a civilian as Mercy was. Not that either one of them ever acted like a civilian.

"Whatever," said Purdie, turning his attention to Eveline. "You need to drop your weapon, ma'am."

"No, sir." Eveline squared her shoulders. "These people are trespassing."

"Technically, we're not," said Mercy. "We're on a public roadway."

"Technically, this is a private road," said the deputy, softly enough so that Eveline couldn't hear him.

"Well, that dog is on my driveway. That's trespassing."

"Why would your dog alert to the vehicle?"

"Why does any law enforcement dog alert?" asked Mercy. "Evidence."

"Evidence of what?"

"Illegal activity."

Troy bit back a smile. Mercy was being just vague enough to convince Deputy Purdie that a search would be perfectly legal, because a police dog alerting to a vehicle constituted probable cause in the eyes of the law.

"You keep that dog away from my stuff." Eveline's voice rose to a screech. "I've never killed a dog before, but there's a first time for everything."

"Better call off your dog," Purdie told Mercy.

Mercy whistled for Elvis, but he didn't move.

"What's wrong with him?"

"I don't know. I guess he's waiting for me to go over and take a look." She whistled again. Elvis looked at her, triangular ears perked, but he did not come to her.

"That dog is a menace," said Eveline.

"I'll go get him," Mercy said.

"Don't you move," said Eveline, pumping her shotgun.

Troy stepped in front of Mercy, pistol raised.

"She's going to shoot Elvis," whispered Mercy. Troy could hear the desperation in her voice.

"Nobody's going to shoot anybody," said Deputy Purdie calmly. "Put down your weapon, Eveline. Let's talk this through."

"Nothing to talk about."

"Be smart. You're outnumbered and outgunned. And backup is on the way."

Troy wondered if that were true, or if that was Purdie's way of telling him that he was the backup.

"I'm covering you," he said quietly.

"Talk so I can hear you!" Eveline was growing increasingly agitated. Troy hoped Purdie knew what he was doing.

"You can hear me just fine." The deputy walked slowly toward the farmhouse. He held his pistol in the air. "I'm going to come a little closer so we don't have to yell at each other. Just take it easy."

Troy kept his weapon trained on Eveline. The woman was staring at Purdie, watching him walk toward her, her eyes focused on the deputy.

"You don't want to do this," said Purdie. "We can talk this through."

The wail of police sirens sounded in the distance, and Eveline looked past them all down toward the county road.

The deputy was nearly within reach of the woman now. "Just hand me the shotgun, Eveline."

Eveline's face crumpled and she collapsed against her front door. She lowered her shotgun. Purdie approached her, smooth as silk, talking softly to her. Troy could no longer hear what he was saying, but he admired the deputy's composure.

Purdie reached for the shotgun. And she gave it to him.

Troy lowered his weapon.

Two police cars swerved into sight, lights flaring and sirens blaring. Purdie handcuffed Eveline, who barely seemed to notice, seemingly transfixed by the cops swarming out of their vehicles in full SWAT gear, weapons all leveled straight at her.

TROY AND MERCY stood about ten feet away from the driveway, watching as Purdie and his team searched the U-Haul. Elvis and Susie Bear were at their feet, feasting on a surplus of treats, their reward for a job well done. Troy caught Mercy glancing down at Elvis several times, as if to reassure herself of his well-being. The shepherd had had a rough couple of days, but he seemed completely back to normal to Troy. But he didn't think that Mercy would agree with him.

The police officers had been slowly emptying out the trailer, spreading its contents out on lengths of plastic covering the driveway. Mostly odd bits of furniture, moving boxes, and garden tools.

"Just junk," said Purdie, emerging from the back of the U-Haul and surveying the remnants of August Pitts' life.

Mercy pointed to the trunk that the uniforms were carrying out of the trailer. "There you go."

"That old thing?" Purdie shook his head.

Elvis jumped up, abandoning the rawhide bone he'd been chewing. Mercy grabbed him by the collar just as he lunged forward.

"Whoa," said Purdie.

"That's the footlocker that went missing from Bea Garcia's house," said Mercy. "You'll find guns and lots of money in it."

"How did Eveline know it was there?" Troy asked her quietly.

Mercy pointed to the FOR SALE sign in the front yard. "Mary Lou is her Realtor. She must have told her about the judge and the parties and the money. Or she just bullied her brother into telling her about it. Either way, she knew enough to get the list of houses. Bea's house is on that list, one of the properties that Mary Lou managed to sell before the crash."

Purdie instructed the gloved officers to put the trunk down and open it.

"It's locked," said the taller of the two.

The deputy looked at Mercy. "You got a key?"

"No."

"Then how do you know what's in it?"

Troy grinned. "Why don't you let her show you?" He handed her a pair of gloves from his pocket.

They all watched as Mercy unpicked the lock and pulled up the lid.

"I see guns," said Purdie, waving at the officers to unload them from the trunk. "Where's the money?"

"Oh ye of little faith," she said.

"Not me," said Troy.

She removed the false bottom, revealing the many neat stacks of hundred-dollar bills.

Purdie whistled. "I'm a believer now."

MERCY WAS QUIET on the way home. She didn't say much, and Troy's efforts to engage her in conversation failed. Even the dogs were subdued, sensing her mood. Maybe he'd misread the signs that pointed to a growing closeness between them. Maybe she was just tired. He knew he should just leave it alone, leave her alone, and try again tomorrow.

Still, he couldn't help but ask how she was feeling before he dropped her off at the cabin.

He steered his truck up her driveway and pulled to a stop. "Are you all right?"

"I'm fine." She made no move to get out of the truck.

Troy waited for her to reveal herself. He knew she would eventually. Like waiting for wildlife in the woods.

"There's an old story about a struggling student who goes to the Buddha for advice," she said finally, not looking at him, her eyes straight ahead. "The student tells the Buddha that all of the various teachings he's been hearing at the monastery are confusing him. 'Can you just explain Buddhism in one line for me?' The Buddha does not hesitate, saying, 'Everything changes.'"

Troy thought about that for a moment. "Good one. Is that one of Martinez's stories?"

"No," she said. "It's one of mine."

She reached for the handle, gracing him with the smile of a sad Madonna. "Goodnight."

She did not ask him and Susie Bear in for a Heady Topper, as she usually would to celebrate their solving a crime together. She simply opened the door and got out, letting Elvis out of the cab. Susie Bear bounded after the shepherd before she could stop her.

"We'll walk you to the door." Troy hustled out of the Ford F-150 to join Mercy. The dogs were long gone, making their usual loop around the property: down to the barn and around the backyard and finally up to the flagpole in the front garden.

Mercy and Troy paused there as they always did to salute the flag, which flew day in and day out in honor of Martinez and their fallen brethren. She lowered her arm slowly and stood perfectly still, staring past the Stars and Stripes to something only she could see. He stood here, hands folded behind him, at ease. He'd stand there all night if that's what she needed.

Several minutes passed. It was late afternoon now, and the sun was sinking behind the cluster of cumulus clouds on the horizon. The dogs were still racing around, oblivious to the chill in the air.

"I keep seeing Eveline aiming that shotgun at Elvis," she said finally, not looking at him.

"Elvis is fine." He stepped behind her and gently placed his hands on her shoulders. "It's over."

"It's not over." She shook off his hands and spun around. "It's never over."

"It *is* over."

"For now." Her freckles stood out plainly against her pale skin. Her cheeks were splotched with patches of red from the growing cold.

"Now is all we've got." He reached up and brushed a curl from her forehead. "You're the yogi. I thought you knew that."

"I'm serious."

"So am I." He tugged on her parka and pulled her close to him. "Right now everything is good."

"Until the next time." Mercy leaned back, away from his embrace, until her spine aligned with the flagpole. "That's what Hallett said. Until the next time."

"That's life." He'd be lying if he said that it was over forever. Nothing was over forever. "Hallett knows that. He's just trying to guilt you into giving him Elvis."

"It's working." She blinked, lashes wet with tears.

"Don't give him the satisfaction." Troy fought the urge to kiss her tears away.

"There have been so many next times." Mercy raised her index finger. "One, the time Elvis got shot in the woods."

"That bullet just grazed him."

She held up another finger. "Two, the time they tied him up in the woods and left him to die of cold or starvation or worse."

"We found him. *You* found him."

A third finger went up. "Three, the time he nearly drowned in a frozen lake."

"You saved him."

"Claude saved him."

"You saved him."

"Not to mention his confrontations with armed robbers and arsonists and murderers and crazy rednecks with shotguns." Mercy held up both hands and wiggled all of her fingers.

"You forgot the poachers and kidnappers."

"Not funny."

"I'm not being funny." He caught her hands in his own. "Look, none of this is your fault."

"Sure it is," she said, but she didn't let go.

"Elvis is a bomb-sniffing military working dog trained to guard the good guys and attack the bad guys." At the sound of his name the handsome shepherd raced up to them, coming to a tight halt right at Mercy's side.

"He's retired."

"Could have fooled me. He even stands like a soldier. It's who he is."

Mercy ruffled the Malinois's triangular ears. "Who you are is not what you do."

"I'm not sure he'd agree with you there."

Susie Bear lumbered up to join them, squeezing between Troy and Mercy for a good petting. Elvis stood his ground, refusing to topple in the wake of the big black shaggy dog.

"You could be right. Or I could be right," she said, scratching the Newfie's broad chest. "Either way, Elvis can't tell us which life he'd choose. So I have to choose for him."

"Martinez left Elvis in your care. Not Hallett's." At Martinez's name, the shepherd perked his triangular ears. Or maybe it was Hallett's name that caught his attention. Troy wondered what the dog made of this conflict between his former handler and Mercy. He knew Elvis could feel the strain between them; no one was more sensitive to your emotions than your dog.

"Martinez thought we'd leave the war behind and move to Texas and he'd train dogs and I'd teach Shakespeare. That's what he chose for Elvis. Not this."

"He knew he was dying," Troy said softly. "He knew that future life would die with him. He still chose you to care for Elvis, not knowing what your future without him would bring."

Mercy wiped away the tears from her cheeks before Troy dared to do it himself. "Don't you ever feel guilty about the danger you put Susie Bear in?"

Troy thought about it. "Not really. Look at her. Her tail never stops wagging." To prove his point the Newfie thumped her tail wildly, feathering the snow and scattering the gravel.

"Patience calls her The Happiest Dog in the World." Mercy sighed. "Which begs the question, is she happy because she loves search-and-rescue? Or because she loves being with you?"

"Try not to overthink this. Maybe she's happy because she's not in that kill shelter waiting to die anymore. What does it matter as long as she's happy."

"If it were that simple all rescued dogs would be happy."

Troy thought that most of them were, but he could see that nothing he could say was going to make a difference. She was going to have to figure this out herself. For better or worse. "What are you going to do?"

"I don't know." She snapped her fingers and the shepherd jumped to his feet. "Goodnight."

Troy stood there with Susie Bear, watching as Mercy and Elvis disappeared inside the cabin. Susie Bear nudged his hip with her big pumpkin head and licked his hand. He scratched her head absently.

"Mercy's right," he told the Newfie. "Everything changes."

CHAPTER THIRTY-SEVEN

WESLEY HALLETT WAS STAYING AT THE SETH WARNER INN, a lovely bed-and-breakfast on the outskirts of town. The nineteenth-century Colonial was a favorite of hikers in the summer, skiers in the winter, and Troy Warner, too, no doubt, given the family connection. She wondered if Hallett knew the two Warners were related.

Intitially she was surprised that Hallett would choose the inn rather than a more modern hotel. But as she followed him into the General John Stark game room, she realized he might be more comfortable in this space celebrating military heroes like Seth Warner and John Stark, the New Hampshire warrior who'd served as a major general in the American Revolution and won the hearts of all Vermonters as the hero of the Battle of Bennington.

Hallett waved her into one of the two taupe velvet wingback chairs by the window and settled himself in the other. An antique chess table set to play a new game sat between them.

"What's up?"

"You can have Elvis."

Hallett stared at her. "Why the change of heart?"

"I'm no good for him." She filled him in on recent events.

"I'm glad to hear that your grandmother is all right." He balanced his elbows on the game table, careful not to disturb the chess pieces, and folded his hands as if he were praying. "That all of you are all right."

"Elvis could have died." She looked past him across the room to the portrait of a stern-looking General Stark that hung over the fireplace. A framed cross-stitch of his famous words, *Live free or die,* rested on the mantel under the general's picture. She'd believed that once, and she'd chosen to live her life accordingly. Today was proof that she still believed it. She may no longer be a soldier but she still chose to live her life accordingly, even as a so-called civilian. But she didn't have the right to make that choice for Elvis. She looked away from the general and met Hallett's eyes.

"You were right. He's earned his retirement."

Resting his chin on his intertwined fingers, Hallett smiled slightly. "It sounds like you did good. You *and* Elvis."

"We did." She sat up a little straighter. "*He* did. But like you said, he'll be safer with you."

Hallett gave her a sharp look that she knew was intended to unsettle her. A look that probably worked on some soldiers, who'd falter under that commanding gaze and spill their guts. She wasn't about to spill her guts; why she felt the way she felt was none of his business. But she would try to explain her decision, for Elvis's sake if not her own.

"Martinez used to tell a story about a young bishop on a fine horse who came to visit his village in Mexico," she began.

"Martinez was always full of stories." He laughed. "But I interrupted you. Go ahead." Mercy told the story as she had heard Martinez tell it more than once:

> This bishop was an arrogant and ambitious man from Mexico
> City. He challenged elderly Father Pedro, the local priest, to a
> contest. Father Pedro was known as the wisest and humblest man
> in the Mezquital Valley, and people came from miles around to
> tell him their confessions and to hear his sermons at Mass every
> Sunday. The bishop was not pleased with the old priest's growing
> popularity, which he saw as a threat to his growing power. This
> would be a duel of wits and wisdom worthy of King Solomon, the

bishop promised. Everyone came to the village square on Saturday morning to watch Father Pedro take on the bishop.

"Ask me anything," said the priest to the bishop. "Ask me forty questions, any questions you want, and I will address them all with one answer."

The bishop smiled, thinking it would be very easy for him to make a fool of this old man. The priest listened very politely to the bishop as he posed forty of the most complicated questions anyone had ever heard in the Mezquital Valley.

"Well," said the bishop, "what do you have to say?"

"I don't know anything," said Father Pedro.

Everyone started to laugh, and the bishop rode away on his fine horse, never to return.

Mercy looked at Hallett. "I don't know anything." She forced herself to smile. "I thought I did, but I was wrong."

"I can see that your mind is made up."

She rose to her feet. "You can pick him up tomorrow at the cabin."

"I must say I'm surprised. But thank you." Hallett stood up and offered her his hand.

She shook it gravely. "Ten o'clock."

That would give her and Elvis some time together before he left for Missouri. To walk through the woods. To play with her and his Kong. To nap on the couch.

She blinked away tears, tipped her fingers to General Stark on the wall, and left without saying goodbye.

Because there was nothing good about it.

CHAPTER THIRTY-EIGHT

THE WEATHER WAS PRACTICALLY BALMY AT FORTY DEGREES. The hardiest New Englanders would be out in shorts and T-shirts, cheering on the spring, but the chill of the past few frigid days seemed permanent to Mercy. She wore flannel-lined jeans, an oversized gray Army sweatshirt over a red Henley, and her last clean pair of Darn Tough socks, and still she shivered. Even inside the cabin, where she stared at the flames of the fire from her end of the long couch.

Elvis was on his side, enjoying his post-walk Kong, which she'd filled with peanut butter, the last in the succession of treats she'd bestowed on him. Sunny was across the room in Elvis's bed, which she'd claimed as her own, with her own peanut-butter-filled Kong.

Both dogs were enjoying all Elvis's favorite treats, a farewell feast. She knew she wouldn't be able to bear looking at them once he'd gone, and she wasn't packing them up for Hallett to give him later. Hallett could buy his own treats for Elvis. And he would; no doubt the Malinois would be showered with goodies in his new home. She'd get new ones—different ones—for Sunny.

Mercy had filled a duffel bag with the Belgian shepherd's toys and the teal quilt from his end of the sofa. She thought that they would help him transition more easily to his new living situation, and, selfishly, help him remember her through her scent, if only for a little while. She didn't want him to forget her completely, at least not right away.

She knew he'd never forgotten Martinez, and she hoped he never would. She had kept his memory alive for both of them—but who would do that now? She couldn't see Hallett talking to Elvis about Martinez the way she did. She hadn't seen him say anything much at all to the shepherd beyond the usual command and reward phrases. Maybe he just wasn't a big talker.

Or maybe it was more than that. He'd admitted that he was one of those soldiers who'd acted out his anger and grief and then hit rock bottom and crawled his way out. Now he channeled his emotions into his work with vets. She hoped he'd have enough emotional energy left to give Elvis the attention he deserved. Say what he might about the dangers the dog may have encountered during his time with her, he couldn't say that she hadn't given everything she'd had to Elvis. Martinez's Malinois had been her whole world.

It was only nine thirty in the morning but she was very tempted to pour herself a glass of Big Barn Red. She was jumping out of her skin. Only half an hour until she lost Elvis for good. She'd already tried yoga, so she defaulted to her old standby for stress. Shakespeare.

She unfurled herself from the couch and went to the wall of books that ran along one side of the great room. Her cousin Ed had custom-built the floor-to-ceiling shelves that held her cherished collection of books, many of which were Shakespeare or Shakespeare-related. She pulled out her beloved copy of the Oxford University Press's 1996 hardcover edition of *The Winter's Tale*. She sat back down on the sofa next to Elvis, and flipped to the speech by Cleomenes:

> Sir, you have done enough, and have perform'd
> A saint-like sorrow: no fault could you make,
> Which you have not redeem'd; indeed, paid down
> More penitence than done trespass: at the last,
> Do as the heavens have done, forget your evil;
> With them forgive yourself.

She'd never forgive herself for what was about to happen, or her part in what had led to it. She closed the book and placed it neatly on the coffee table before her. She gave Elvis a good scratch between the ears, and another along his belly. He nuzzled her for more and she laughed. She could do worse than spend her last minutes with him like this.

Too soon, it was time. Mercy pulled her duck boots on over her stockinged feet, wrapped a scarf around her neck, and grabbed the bag. She whistled for the dogs.

Elvis and Sunny followed her outside. The mountains were shrouded in fog, the forest murky in the mist. The snow was melting again. Perching on the edge of her grandfather's rocking chair, she watched as the canine pals scampered around the front garden, and then dashed down to the barn. She heard the truck start up her driveway, but she couldn't bring herself to look. She kept her eyes on Elvis.

The shepherd raced up the hill from the barn, the retriever on his heels. She heard the truck door slam but still she didn't look. Out of the corner of her eye she saw a huge blur of black fur bounce by her.

Susie Bear.

She spun around to find Troy walking through the arbor along the path that led past the flagpole and up to the porch.

"What are you doing here?"

"Hallett called me. Told me about Elvis." Troy placed a hand on her shoulder. "He thought you might need a friend here when he came by."

"That was presumptuous of him." She crossed her arms. "You don't have to stay."

"Where's Amy and the baby?"

"Amy's at the college. Helena's at day care."

"So you're alone."

"Yes."

Troy squeezed her shoulder. "I think we'll stay."

She nodded, not trusting herself to speak. This was the sort of unexpected kindness that could bring her to tears if she wasn't careful.

He stood back as the three dogs rushed up to her, tails wagging, falling all over each other to compete for hugs and head scratches. She pulled the scarf off her neck and tossed it onto the rocking chair. Squatting down, she let the dogs envelop her in wet kisses and damp fur. Their paws were dirty with snow and slush and mud, and now her jeans and her sweatshirt were, too. Not that she cared.

Elvis's triangular ears perked. Susie Bear and Sunny's long silky ears rose, too. The trio turned in unison as Hallett's truck roared up the drive. Elvis stood by Mercy, his curlicue tail held high, on the edge of a wag. Sunny wagged her tail unreservedly. Susie Bear barked. A friendly bark, but a bark just the same. Mercy knew exactly how the big shaggy girl felt.

Hallett got out of the truck, a bouquet of yellow tulips in his hand. He stopped to pet Sunny on his way, and she trailed him to the porch. Elvis greeted him with a nuzzle and lick, Susie Bear with a desultory sniff.

"Good morning," he said, handing Mercy the flowers. "I don't know if this is appropriate or not. But I wanted to bring something."

"Thanks." She placed the bouquet on the seat of the rocking chair by her scarf. Tulips had always been her favorite flowers, but she knew that from now on she'd always loathe the sight of them.

The dogs clamored around Hallett as he pulled doggie biscuits from his coat pocket and passed the treats around. They nibbled his fingers and he smiled.

Mercy fought the uncharitable urge to wipe that smile off his face. She picked up the duffel.

"I'll take Susie Bear and Sunny inside." Troy took the Newfie mutt and the golden retriever by their collars and guided them into the cabin, gently closing the door behind him.

She escorted Hallett down the porch steps and out to the flagpole, Elvis at her side.

"You know, he wasn't perfect," he said.

Mercy stared at him. "Who?"

"Martinez. He was a good soldier and a good guy but he wasn't perfect."

"Right." She wasn't about to stand here and let this guy talk trash about Martinez. Enough was enough. She held the duffel out to him. "This should be everything he needs."

"Okay." Hallett reached for the bag, his face solemn. Elvis stood between them, still as stone. They stood there, holding the duffel between them. The passing of the baton. The changing of the guard. The end of life as she knew it.

She released the bag and fell back. She tapped her chest with her palm. Elvis rose up on his back legs and placed his front paws on her chest. She wrapped her arms around the shepherd in a long hug. "Down," she said, and he dropped to the ground. She waved her hand toward Hallett. "Go."

"Come on, boy." He walked back down the garden path toward his truck. Elvis trotted after him, then hesitated, turning to look back at Mercy, and tipped his nose in the air.

"Go on," she said, more sternly this time.

The shepherd gave her another long look.

Hallett opened the door of his truck. "Come on, boy. Let's go for a ride."

Mercy smiled in spite of herself. *Ride* was one of Elvis's favorite words. She waved her hand toward Hallett's truck again.

Elvis sprinted the last couple of yards and then rocketed into the passenger seat.

"Good boy." Hallett shut the door after him. He walked around the truck to the driver's side. There he paused and raised his eyes to Mercy and the flag that flew above her. He saluted.

She saluted back.

He got into his truck, threw it in reverse, and backed expertly down the slushy driveway. She saw Elvis poke his nose out of the passenger window and heard him howl, just before the truck disappeared from sight.

She stood there for a moment, willing the truck back to her driveway. But that wouldn't happen. The reality hit her as hard as a punch to her solar plexus. She leaned back against the flagpole, her spine hugging the cold metal, and slowly, slowly, slowly slid down to the ground.

She sat there at the base of the flagpole, legs crossed and eyes closed. She tried to breathe. Susie Bear bound over to her, settling at her feet and placing her big pumpkin head in her lap. Sunny curled up at her side, her muzzle tucked into Mercy's left hip. Troy sank down to her right, his long legs stretched out in front of him.

"You'll get your uniform dirty," she said, curling the Newfie mutt's long silky hair around her fingers.

"I always get my uniform dirty," he said. "Occupational hazard."

"I failed him."

"You saved him."

"I failed Elvis and I failed Martinez," she repeated.

Troy didn't say anything this time. He took her free hand and wrapped his fingers gently through hers. She tightened her grip. Clenching his hand as hard as she could.

And she cried.

THEY SAT THERE in the slush at the base of the flagpole. Neither said anything. Her tears spent, Mercy laid her head on his shoulder. The dogs didn't move, content to stay as long as she and Troy stayed.

She closed her eyes again, trying to think happy thoughts about the dog she already missed so much it hurt. Falling into a daydream. Springtime. Hiking through the woods with Elvis. Sun dappling the pale green buds of the maples and sycamores and oaks. The shepherd running ahead on the trail, slipping out of view, then circling back to her when she called.

Elvis, she whispered.

There was a sudden shuffling all around her as she felt Sunny and Susie Bear scramble to their feet, startling her out of her reverie. She opened her eyes, and there he was.

Elvis. The smartest dog in the world, hurtling toward her. The Belgian shepherd skidded to a stop at her knees. She pulled him into her lap. Laughing. Crying. Hugging.

"Where did he come from?" She looked up at Troy.

"From the road. I saw him run up the hill, then cut across the lawn to you."

"I don't understand."

"Me either."

She heard the sound of a vehicle turning into the driveway and her heart sank. It was the red Toyota truck. Hallett's truck. "It was too good to be true."

"Let's see what he has to say."

They stood up and waited. The dogs lined up next to them, seated but alert.

Hallett got out of the truck. He strode toward them, carrying the duffel bag.

"What happened?"

He shrugged. "We only made it as far as Crossroads."

"What do you mean?"

"I stopped for gas a couple of miles down the road." He set the bag down on the ground. "As soon as I opened the door, Elvis pushed past me and jumped out of the truck and started running. Back to you."

Sunny trotted over to greet Hallett, leaning against him and lifting her pretty golden head as he petted her. Elvis wagged his tail at him, but he didn't move from Mercy's side. Susie Bear ignored him.

"Out on Route 7?" Mercy couldn't bear the thought of Elvis on that busy road.

"That's a major thoroughfare," said Troy. "He could have been hurt."

"I know that." Hallett ran his hand through his short hair. "I went after him on foot, but he was long gone. I figured he was on his way home, so I started back here in the truck. I found him, but when I pulled over, he refused to get in. I followed him the rest the way here, to make sure he got home safely." He smiled a crooked smile. "And he did."

"I'm so sorry." Mercy held Elvis's face in her hands. "What were you thinking?"

"He came back because he needs you," said Hallett.

"I don't think so." Mercy frowned. "He came back because I need him, and he knows it."

"Either way, you're his mission now." Hallett continued to stroke Sunny's silky coat. The golden retriever stood by him, knowing that he was the one who needed comforting now.

"What about my dangerous lifestyle?" Mercy couldn't dare hope that Elvis was truly home to stay. Surely Hallett wouldn't give up so easily. But she kept one hand on the shepherd's handsome head, just in case.

"Life is dangerous," said Troy. "No matter where you live it."

"True enough," said Hallett. "We have our troubles in Missouri, too."

"I don't know what to say," said Mercy.

"You know the bond you form with your fellow soldiers," said Hallett. "That's like the bond between dog handlers and their dogs. That's the bond Elvis and I have. The strongest of bonds, formed on the battlefield." He reached out and petted the shepherd's handsome head. Elvis licked his hand, even as he leaned against Mercy. "But maybe the bonds you form with the people who help you come home from the war are just as strong."

Mercy nodded. Her bond with Elvis was proof of that.

"Working with vets," Hallett went on, "I guess that shouldn't surprise me. As a vet myself."

Mercy held her breath, watching as he gave Elvis another good scratch between the ears and then removed his hand, letting it fall to his side.

Sunny nuzzled his fingers, and he smiled. "You're the one who helped Elvis come home from the war."

"He helped *me*."

"Two-way street." He looked at the shepherd, his stance poised but alert, his nose at her hip.

"Elvis just wants to be with you. You're his person now."

"Elvis has made his choice," said Troy. "Honor it."

She exhaled, realizing that Troy was right. She'd made the choice for Elvis, letting him go with Hallett, but Elvis had overturned her decision. No doubt about that. Hallett was honoring the shepherd's choice, and she should, too.

"Thank you," she told Hallett. "What will you do? What about the vets at your center?"

"We'll be fine."

"You need a dog."

He shook his head. She felt so badly for him. If it were any dog on earth but Elvis . . .

"Seems to me you've got your dog right here." Troy pointed to Sunny. "Sunny obviously likes you."

Mercy smiled at the golden retriever. "Troy's right. She's always thrilled to see you. And she's the most empathetic dog in the world. She'd be great with your veterans."

"She's a lovely girl," said Hallett. "But I thought you were just keeping her for a friend."

"She was Deputy Pitts' dog. He asked me to take her because he knew he was dying and he was afraid his sister would get rid of her."

"He was sure right about that," said Troy.

"I think she was meant to go with you," said Mercy. "I think Sunny is your dog."

"I appreciate what you're trying to do," he said. "I'll think about it." He gave Elvis one last salute. "Goodbye, boy."

"Take care." Mercy and Troy stood with Elvis and Susie Bear and watched Hallett walk back to his truck.

Sunny raised her muzzle at Mercy.

"Go on," she said. "You know you want to."

The golden retriever raced for the red Toyota, tearing around the bed of the truck to the driver's side. Hallett opened the door and she squeezed past him, jumping up into his seat.

They heard him laugh. Mercy waited, holding her breath once more. Hoping that he would see Sunny as the gift she was and take her with him.

The golden moved into the passenger seat and poked her nose out of the window as soon as Hallett rolled it down for her. Sunny barked, and Elvis and Susie Bear barked in return. A baying of goodbyes.

Mercy waved, and Hallett honked as he steered the truck down the driveway. He pulled out onto the main road and was gone.

Elvis was still here.

TEN DAYS LATER

CHAPTER THIRTY-NINE

MERCY CELEBRATED HER THIRTIETH BIRTHDAY BY TAKING a long hike through the Lye Brook Wilderness with Elvis. This was their happy place, the old bed of a logging railroad rising before them for two and a half miles up to the falls. She and the shepherd had spent countless hours here on this rocky trail in those lost days following their return from the wretchedness of Afghanistan. Marching off their sorrow and their rage and their remorse as a sort of penance and purification, achieving a kind of peace, if only temporarily.

Today was different. Today their hike was less of a hair shirt and more of a hallelujah. Celebrating the fact that they were still together, she and Elvis, still together to mourn their man and their mission and find their way forward in a world without Martinez and the military. They could do it, as long as they had each other. For the first time, Mercy truly believed she and Elvis would be okay.

It was cold and blustery but clear and sunny. The kind of day where she wore her long underwear under her flannel cargo pants, and a turtleneck and flannel shirt under her parka, her toughest Thinsulate gloves, and her insulated extreme-weather boots. A beautiful day, even if she could see the cloud of her breath before her as she huffed after the shepherd.

This was the part of the world she loved the most. And the part of the world she believed Elvis loved the most, too. She'd come so close to losing him. Turning thirty was bad enough but turning thirty without Elvis would have been unbearable. She was grateful to Elvis for choosing to come home and to Sunny for claiming Hallett as her own. Patience always said that the dogs were always the smartest people in the room, and Mercy would never doubt that again.

Hallett had emailed her pictures of Sunny hanging out with the vets at his center, already the belle of the ball and the best medicine for everyone in Springfield, Missouri.

She'd called him to thank him for the photos.

"Sunny is perfect," he told her. "Perfect for me and perfect for the center."

"She's the most compassionate dog I've ever known," said Mercy. And it was true. If Sunny were one of Brodie's beloved *Star Trek* characters, she'd be an empath.

"She knew we needed her, even if I did not," he said. "Sunny belongs with me and Elvis belongs with you."

"Always trust your dog," Mercy told him as she said goodbye and hung up.

Maybe someday she and Elvis would visit them in the Show Me State. For now they were content to be here at home in the Green Mountains of Vermont.

The bare beeches and birches and maples were dusted with new-fallen snow, and the forest floor was marked by the tracks of deer and squirrels and chipmunks, coyotes and bears and moose. Mercy stopped to snap pictures of the prints on the snow with her cell. Elvis raced ahead as he always did, disappearing into the trees. He would circle back from time to time to check on her. She spotted the telltale heart-shaped prints of a moose. She leaned over to take a closer look. Moose tracks, all right. But a little small for an adult moose, whose prints usually measured between five and seven inches.

She thought about Joey Colby, the wildlife biologist who died protecting the endangered moose of Vermont. Rucker was standing by his story that Simko killed Colby. The police found his camera among Simko's things, so maybe that was the truth. But they only had Rucker's word for it, and Simko was dead. So they might never know for sure.

She should follow this moose and try to capture it on film. In honor of the fallen scientist.

Mercy whistled for Elvis and he appeared moments later, sailing out from a small copse of aspen, a furry blur of fawn and black flying through the slim, stark tree trunks.

"Let's track this young moose." She squatted down by the tracks and pointed them out to Elvis.

The Malinois was not a hunting dog, but he always seemed to understand when the hunt was on, be it for a bomb or a lost child or a body in a barrel. She figured he would get the idea eventually. Meanwhile, Mercy could read the woods almost as well as Troy Warner and Gil Guerrette. She could track this moose.

She duck-walked alongside the prints, and Elvis trotted next to her. The moose tracks led down the trail for a while and then disappeared. She looked 90 degrees to one side of the last print, knowing that moose often circled back downwind of their trail, the better to watch out for the two-legged and four-legged predators that might be pursuing them.

Nothing.

She tried the other side, and there it was. Another set of prints.

"Quiet," she told Elvis, and together they crept silently after the prints, which led through a stand of balsam fir to a small clearing. She spotted a young moose there, nibbling on twigs. All legs and ears and triangular head.

She put her hand down on Elvis's neck, and he stood unmoving, still and silent, as she took as many photos of the moose as quickly as she could. She wasn't close enough to see if it were a male or female for sure, but from its light brown face she figured it might be female. The calf looked healthy, no bare patches in her coat from scratching away at a scourge of ticks. That was a blessing, as some moose were known to suffer more than a hundred thousand ticks at a time.

Mercy wished Colby were here to see her. She wondered if this could be his moose. It was unlikely, as the home range for moose usually topped out at twenty-five square miles.

But it was possible. Either way, she could only hope and pray that the calf made it through the next six weeks, the most dangerous time for moose, especially when the month of April was too warm and there was little snowfall and baby ticks fell off their moose-sucking mothers onto a welcoming ground bearing no snow. Only to jump onto the moose once again in bigger numbers. The Month of Death, some biologists called it.

The moose turned and looked at her, straight on. The calf didn't grunt or stomp her feet or lay back her ears—all signs that she may charge. The young moose just stared at her.

Mercy took advantage of that direct gaze to zoom in and take another couple of photographs.

The spell was broken when the moose noticed Elvis. The calf regarded the shepherd with alarm, moaning and stamping her feet.

Mercy quickly stepped behind a maple tree with a thick trunk, pulling Elvis with her. Out of sight, out of mind—or so she hoped.

It worked. The calf went back to nibbling on twigs. Ignoring them.

She and Elvis slowly backed out of the balsam fir stand and through the woods until they found the old trail. She pocketed her phone and set back down the trail. "Come on, boy."

Elvis hung back, turning back in the direction of the young moose.

"Don't worry, Elvis. We'll keep an eye on her."

As they hiked up to the falls, Mercy thought about the calf, whom she'd already christened Colby in her mind. She preferred to believe that it was Colby's moose, and that she would survive, and that Colby did not die in vain. She wasn't sure what she could do to help this baby—and all the moose babies—survive, if anything. But she would find out and do what she could.

Seeing Colby the Calf was a good omen. A sign of spring. Which was on its way, no matter how frigid the air might be today.

They climbed up onto one of the lookouts, a large rock across from the frozen-solid waterfalls. Slides of long icicles draped the outlines of the cliffside. These falls were among the tallest in the state, and people swarmed the trail to see them in the warmer months of the year. But these days she and Elvis had the falls all to themselves. At least until the water flowed freely again.

That was the glory of New England. The seasons here were so distinct and bright and vibrant each in their own way that you couldn't miss them. This reminder that spring always follows winter was never more evident than in Vermont. Soon the trees would bud and the trout lilies and trillium would bloom in the woods, and in her own garden forsythia would brighten the old stone wall and the crocuses would peek out of the snow, promising profusions of tulips and lilacs and roses to come.

"We've earned this spring," she told Elvis. "And we're going to enjoy it."

TWO HOURS LATER, Mercy and Elvis were exhilarated and tired and happy to be home. Amy and Brodie and the baby were out and about somewhere, so she and the shepherd and little Muse had the place to themselves. Mercy showered and changed her clothes while Elvis napped, the kitten curled up next to him. Since it was her birthday and her grandmother had promised her a chocolate *doberge* cake, she dressed up, donning black velvet jeans and one of the cashmere sweaters her mother had given her every Christmas without fail. She chose the soft yellow bell-sleeved tunic sweater, a nod to spring she couldn't resist, even as the temperature dropped to the teens.

She didn't look half bad for thirty, she thought, as she smoothed on moisturizer and lip gloss, a bit of blush and mascara. And she was well-dressed. At least for today.

They said that the older you get, the more like your mother you become. Maybe her dressing up in honor of her birthday was proof of that. She left her hair wild, if only to prove to herself that she hadn't completely morphed into her mother quite yet.

Today she and Elvis were going to try to deliver Mr. Horgan's kitten again. She repacked the basket, stuffing it with fancy cat food and kitty toys and a blue leather collar. She had a litter box and kitty litter in the Jeep already. Along with a birthday present for Henry, whose birthday was the day after hers.

Her birthday was March 13—313—a number Henry loved because it was a palindrome. Henry himself would turn ten years old tomorrow, on March 14—314—otherwise known as Pi Day, his favorite day of the year. She'd thought long and hard about what to get the little guy for his birthday and finally decided on a Tim Burton Batmobile Lego kit that set her back two hundred bucks. It took one grown-up Lego expert an entire weekend to build, so she figured it could at least keep Henry busy for a couple of hours. She and Elvis were going to deliver it to the little genius today, right after she dropped off the black kitten to Mr. Horgan.

"Come on, Elvis. We've got deliveries to make."

THEIR FIRST STOP was Bea Garcia's house. Mercy would never see this stately Greek Revival home without thinking of the many people who had passed through it over the past two hundred years. The many secrets this place had held: the slaves escaping on Underground Railroad, the judge's wild parties, the stacks of hundred-dollar bills. And Bea Garcia herself.

After her husband died, Bea left Arizona to come home to Vermont. Louise Minnette was right, she'd missed New England and thought she could come back twenty years later with a new name and a new nose, and no one would be the wiser. She remembered Ruby talking about this house—it had been one of her listings—and when she found that it was up for sale she couldn't resist making it her own. It had worked . . . almost.

The D.A. had refused to prosecute Bea or Ruby for Thomas Kilgore's death, infuriating Harrington but pleasing Mercy. There was no evidence to link either of them to the crime, and even if there were, they'd stick to their story of self-defense. And Mercy believed them.

Elvis stood quietly at her side, his handsome head at her hip. She rang the doorbell and waited but no one came. And no dogs barked.

"Bea said she'd be here," she told the shepherd.

She could hear movement inside the house. Bea opened the door. "Hi."

"Where are your dogs?"

"At the groomers." Bea stood there, a smile on her pretty face. "It's so good to see you. I don't how to thank you for all you've done. Laying my past to rest once and for all."

"You're the one taking in all the cats," said Mercy. "Just keep doing what you're doing. Be a friend to the Cat Ladies and to my grandmother, and to all the animals who need you. That's what you can do for me and Elvis."

Bea nodded. "I will."

The woman seemed to have forgotten why she and Elvis were here.

"And the kitten?"

"Of course." Bea laughed. "Sorry. Come on through. I've got him back in the den, ready for you and Mr. Horgan."

Elvis forged ahead of Bea, racing through the rotunda and out of view.

Mercy called for him but he did not reappear. "He's usually not like this. I don't know what's gotten into him." She wondered what the shepherd was up to. As far as she knew they'd discovered all the secrets this house had to keep. At least for now.

"He's fine," said Bea. "He seems to know where he's going."

She followed Bea through the rotunda, past the kitchen, to the back of the house where a new wing had been added onto the original footprint of the centuries-old house. The soaring space held an ultra-modern den; beyond that, a cavernous space stood shrouded in shadow. Was it a game room, a home theater, a ballroom? Anything was possible.

She tried to make out what was out there in the dark but the gloom was impenetrable.

She looked around for Elvis, but she couldn't see him, either.

A sudden blaze of light and the room came to life.

CHAPTER FORTY

S URPRISE!"
   Mercy stood there stunned, temporarily blinded by the specta-
cle before her. All she could see were balloons. Shiny yellow balloons
the color of her sweater. There must have been hundreds of them.

And daffodils. Pots and pots and pots of the sunny spring flowers
everywhere, the flower for the month of March, her birthday flower.

And, finally, people. The faces of all the people she knew and loved
and admired. All smiling and laughing and welcoming her into her
fourth decade on earth. Her parents, Patience and Claude, Amy and
Brodie and little Helena, Mr. Horgan, and more.

"Happy Birthday," said Bea.

"Happy Birthday," chorused everyone else.

"I don't know what to say." Mercy could feel her pale freckled skin
flush. Curse of the redhead. Seemed like she'd never outgrow that.

"The mind is the first thing to go," joked Brodie, who held Helena
on his hip.

Amy fake-punched him on the arm. "Thirty isn't *that* old."

"Happy Birthday, Mercy." Her mother, Grace, stepped up, a vision
of loveliness in a pale gold-and-white Chanel suit, flanked by her
father, Duncan, dapper as always in a dark gray three-piece suit, and
the always elegant Dan Feinberg, Mercy's neighbor and favorite billionaire.

"You look wonderful," said her father.

"She's wearing one of the sweaters we've given her," said Grace. "And it's the perfect color for this soirée. Serendipity." Her mother gave her a suspicious look. "Unless you somehow knew about the party."

"No way." Mercy laughed. "I couldn't be more surprised. Besides, when have you ever known me to color-coordinate my outfit with an event?"

Her mother smiled. "True enough. I'm glad we pulled it off."

"We?" Mercy frowned. "I assumed this was Patience's idea. You hate surprise parties."

"But *you* love them," said Grace.

Her mother had thrown her one surprise party in her life—a Sweet Sixteen retro extravaganza complete with a chocolate fondue fountain and a jukebox full of oldies. Mercy smiled at the memory. "I do."

"It wasn't easy with all these people," said her father.

"Everyone wanted to come," said Feinberg. "I thought we might have to have it at my place."

Feinberg's "place" was a thirty-thousand-square-foot mountain lodge on a massive estate called Nemeton high in the Green Mountains.

"But then Bea volunteered," said Grace. "You've certainly made a friend for life there."

"It's perfect, Mom."

Lillian Jenkins stepped up to wish her well, her son Ethan and his girlfriend Yolanda Yellowbird at her side. Hugs all around.

Henry wandered up in his Batman costume, tethered to his beautiful service dog, Robin, who was decked out as the eponymous junior caped crusader. "Palindrome."

"Thank you, Henry." Mercy knew that was the little boy's way of wishing her a happy birthday. "And Happy Birthday one day early to you. I've got your present in the back of the Jeep."

Henry unzipped the pack on his dog's harness, and retrieved a lavender book, tied up with a yellow ribbon. He handed it to her. It was a rare copy of *Old French Fairy Tales,* by Comtesse De Segur and illustrated by Virginia Frances Sterrett, a book they both loved.

"You're spoiling me." Mercy was very glad she'd sprung for that expensive Tim Burton Batman Lego kit.

Henry nodded and drifted away. But Mercy knew he wouldn't drift too far afield with Robin on watch.

"Thank you for coming, Daniel," she said to Feinberg.

"I wouldn't miss this rite of passage."

"You told Daniel I was turning thirty?" Mercy asked her mother.

"It's not like it's a secret," said her mother. "The whole town knows you're turning thirty."

"Don't look at me," said her father.

That was the bad news about living in a small town. Everybody knew everything about you. The good news was they loved a good party, no matter who threw it.

"There's the entertainment," said her mother, raising her chin in the direction of two musicians carrying guitars and mandolins. "We must go and help them get situated. You stay and mingle."

"Entertainment?" Mercy shook her head as her parents disappeared into the crowd of partygoers.

"Your mother went all out," said Feinberg.

"I don't understand. She doesn't even like me. I mean, I know she loves me, but . . ." She threw up her hands. "Mothers."

Feinberg smiled. "That reminds me of a story. A distraught woman went to see her rabbi. She was worried about her mother. 'My mother never visits, so I always have to go see her,' she told the rabbi. 'She rarely answers my letters or my phone calls. She's forgotten my birthday several years running. I don't know what to do about it.' The rabbi looked at the woman and said, 'Your mother doesn't like you.'"

Mercy laughed. "So I guess my mother likes me, after all. Well, except for my hair."

"Mothers can't help but be mothers." Patience appeared at the billionaire's elbow, Claude at her side. She leaned forward for a kiss.

Mercy happily obliged. "If you say so." She gave Claude a peck on the cheek as well.

"When you were a little girl, your mother spent hours fixing your hair for you."

"That's right, she did." She'd loved the feel of her mother's slender fingers playing with her hair. "French braids were my favorite."

Patience smiled. "Your mother was all thumbs at first, but she was determined to learn how to do those French braids prettily enough to please you."

"I don't remember that." She couldn't imagine Grace being all thumbs at anything. Poise was her mother's middle name.

"When you have a child, you always see her as a baby, a toddler, a teenager, no matter how old she gets, even as you acknowledge her as an adult," said Patience. "To your mother, you'll always be three days old and three years old and thirteen years old and thirty years old, all at once. And she'll always want to help you fix your hair."

"Thirty is too old for braids."

"Is it?"

Claude filled the awkward pause, much to Mercy's relief. "Aren't you going to tell her?"

"Tell me what?"

Her grandmother raised her left arm, still encased in its neon pink cast, and fluttered the fingers of her left hand at Mercy, flashing a dazzling diamond ring.

"Is that what I think it is?"

"It's an engagement ring."

"Really?" She looked from her grinning grandmother to the beaming Claude beside her.

"She asked *me* this time," he said.

"He said yes."

"Of course he did." Mercy gave them both a big hug. "I'm so happy for you both."

So the Fleury-O'Sullivan-Carr soulmate gene was alive and well, she thought. Good to know.

Patience leaned in and whispered in Mercy's ear. "I loved your grandfather, and he died too soon. But I think it's time I gave another man a chance."

"High time," she agreed.

"Go greet the rest of your guests," said Patience. "And don't miss that buffet, catered by Northshire Union Store."

"Shepherd's pie?" Northshire Union Store made the best mac and cheese and chicken pot pies, but the lamb shepherd's pie was her favorite.

"Of course."

"What about my *doberge* cake?"

"Oh, there will be cake," promised her grandmother. "And presents."

Mercy groaned, thinking of the inescapable "you're not getting better, you're getting older" gag gifts to come.

She made her way around the room, accepting all the birthday wishes and jokes about aging and the inevitability of death with as much grace as possible, trying not to think about the far better people whom she'd already outlived. It occurred to her that this black birthday party humor may be the civilian version of laughing in the face of death, and she smiled.

She wasn't altogether comfortable being the center of attention this way, but at least these were people she knew and loved. Apart from the entourage that appeared wherever Feinberg went, whether he liked it or not. Including local officials like the mayor, whom she spotted by the open bar.

Mercy made a beeline around the mayor and headed for Mr. Horgan, who sat in one of the many deeply cushioned burgundy couches that lined the perimeter of the space. He was talking to Louise Minnette, the librarian from Peace Junction. The black kitten was curled up on his lap, asleep.

"So I guess you two know each other."

"We've known each other for years," said Louise.

"Through Mrs. Horgan."

"Yes. A lovely woman, and a wonderful librarian."

"I see you've met your new kitten."

"A beautiful feline," said Louise approvingly.

"I've got a basket of kitty goodies in the Jeep," said Mercy. "I'll bring it in later. What will you call him?"

Mr. Horgan smiled. "His name is Shakespeare."

Mercy grinned. *"The cat will mew, and dog will have his day."*

"Precisely." The old man grinned back.

She regarded Louise, the only person here who'd known Bea Garcia back when she was Beth Kilgore. And now, decades later, she was in the woman's home. Had Louise recognized her? Or had she known all along?

"So you've met our hostess, Bea."

"Yes." Louise gave her that sharp hawk-eyed look.

"So cool of her to host this party for me."

"It's the perfect space for such an event," Louise said agreeably.

Mercy leaned in to whisper her inquiry. "You're never going to tell me, are you?"

Mr. Horgan coughed. "What are we talking about?"

"Reading is subversive," Louise reminded her.

Mr. Horgan smiled. "That's what my wife always used to say."

"And so are librarians," said Mercy. Whatever Louise Minnette knew about Beth Kilgore then or Bea Garcia now, she'd never tell.

The sound of acoustic guitars warming up interrupted their laughter.

"Foamflower," said Captain Thrasher, who joined their group along with Gil Guerrette and his wife, Françoise. The captain was in uniform—Mercy had never seen him in civvies—and Gil wore a beautifully tailored navy suit. But Françoise stole the show in a pale yellow shantung dress, high heels, and a fascinator fashioned from silk jonquils. She was easily the chicest woman in the room, out-dressing even Grace. Of course, as her mother no doubt would console herself, Françoise *was* French.

"Foamflower?"

"The musical duo," said Thrasher. "I think you must have Feinberg to thank for that."

Foamflower was one of Vermont's most talented folk acts, made up of two siblings from Northshire, a guitar-playing tenor named Tom and his baby sister Toni, a mandolin player with the voice of an angel.

"I've never seen them in person," said Mercy. "But I love their songs. Especially 'Be the Clouds.'"

"And how did Feinberg know that?" teased Gil.

Mercy flushed. She hadn't seen Troy or Susie Bear yet, but Gil's remark meant they must be here somewhere.

"Pay no attention to him," said Françoise. "He is always talking nonsense."

"This is not nonsense," said Gil. "This is the grand gesture. But the grandest is yet to come."

Françoise rolled her dark eyes and shrugged a perfectly Gallic shrug.

Mercy had no idea what Gil was talking about, and her confusion must have shown on her face.

"Have you not seen the gallery?" Gil waved an arm at the far end of the room, obscured by party guests and all those yellow balloons.

"Let me show you," said the captain, offering her his arm. He led her through the crowd beyond the buffet table and open bar, where elegant mobile gallery walls stood sentry to the enormous river rock fireplace that dominated the end wall. On these gallery walls were the brilliant colorful textile art pieces she'd last seen in Wyetta's Café.

And there was Wyetta herself, looking radiant in a curve-hugging tea-length swag dress the color of a good cabernet. The captain couldn't take his eyes off her.

Mercy smiled. *That's one for Troy,* she thought.

"Wyetta! This is amazing!"

"Happy Birthday!" Wyetta enveloped her in a big hug.

"How did this happen?"

The artist raised her arms to the heavens and twirled around. "You have some friends in high places, girl."

"Not by design," Mercy said, laughing.

"Maybe not. But you got your own PR department in that game warden of yours."

"He's not my game warden."

"Why not?" Wyetta raised her eyebrows. "What's wrong with you?"

Feinberg saved her, appearing at the artist's elbow. "So what do you think of our little art show?"

"It's wonderful."

"We knew that you're a fan of Wyetta's work, so we thought you might appreciate combining your party with an exhibition. We're doing a silent auction, and a portion of the proceeds will go to the animal rescue."

"That's genius. I'm thrilled. How did you know I loved her work?"

"Troy Warner told me. And I must thank you for introducing me to her work. I've commissioned a piece for Nemeton."

"That's great." She nodded toward the Foamflower duo, who were getting ready to play. "I understand I have you to thank for the musical entertainment."

Feinberg smiled. "What's a party without music?"

The musicians stood on a small stage at the head of the room, to the left of the fireplace. Her mother mounted the stage to join them, taking the microphone from the taller one.

"Thank you. Welcome." Grace smiled. "Thirty years ago today I gave birth to a seven-and-a-half-pound red-haired screamer who cried so loudly whenever I put her down that the nurse said to me, 'Lord have mercy on you and that noisy baby of yours.' And so her father and I decided to call her Mercy."

Everyone laughed. Mercy had heard the story many times before, but this may have been the first time she'd ever really thought it was funny. Maybe she was growing up, after all.

"You all know her as a soldier, a military policewoman, an animal lover, and a problem solver of the first order. But to Duncan and me, she's our Mercy. We love you. Happy Birthday."

Foamflower played "Happy Birthday" and everyone sang along while Patience and Claude brought out three large chocolate *doberge* cakes so ablaze with candles they probably constituted a fire hazard, making Mercy feel very happy and very old at the same time.

"Time for presents and cake and music," said her mother. "We're going roll up the carpet here by the band for dancing. Enjoy. And thank you very much for coming." She handed the microphone back to the mandolin player, and everyone cheered. Mercy, too.

Before she could wipe away the tears she felt gathering in the corners of her eyes, Elvis bounded up to her, Susie Bear on his heels. Mercy sank to her knees to receive her birthday kisses. The Belgian shepherd licked one cheek and the Newfie retriever the other, the latter adding a snort and a snuffle for good measure. She looked up and there was Troy. His parents, Harry and Lizzie, hovered behind him with big smiles so full of warmth and hope Mercy blushed.

He held out his hands and she let him pull her to her feet.

"Happy Birthday," he said.

She felt everyone's eyes on the two of them and released Troy's hands. Her mother waved her over to a table laden with gifts. She thanked his parents for coming and then excused herself. While Foamflower played folk songs, she opened her presents: a red-haired Batgirl action figure from Amy and Brodie, a first edition of *Strangers on the Train* from Bea Garcia, silver satin cargo pants and matching leather moto jacket from her parents, a forest green fedora from Gil and Françoise, a case of Big Barn Red wine from Captain Thrasher, a subscription to the Northshire Repertory Theater from Feinberg, and a gift certificate for a new snowmobile from Patience and Claude.

"You know you need one," said Patience. "Just learn to drive it more cautiously than your game warden."

She didn't even bother to correct her grandmother. She was running out of ways to say thank you with sufficient enthusiasm when Wyetta and Troy came up to her, carrying a large package wrapped in brown paper.

"We saved the best for last, if I do say so myself."

Everyone gathered around for this final offering. Troy held the gift while she tore off the brown paper in long sheets. Revealing one of Wyetta's one-of-a-kind quilted artworks. This piece framed the Green Mountains, a forest thick with trees in the background, the ground swept with snow, the midnight-blue sky strewn with stars. And, in the middle, a cabin, its windows lit from within, and Martinez's flag flying in the front yard, a red-haired figure and a handsome dog illuminated in the flagpole's spotlight.

It was her cabin: Mercy and Elvis and the Vermont woods they called home.

"It's called *Get You Home*," said Wyetta.

She smiled at the Shakespeare reference. *Get you home* was a phrase that appeared many times in the bard's plays. "Thank you. It's spectacular."

"I'm the artist," said Wyetta. "Not the giver. This is a present from Troy. He commissioned it for you."

She stared at Troy. "This is too much."

Foamflower started in on their own rendition of "Moonlight in Vermont."

"Let's dance," said Troy, holding out his hand to her.

She hesitated, feeling that telltale tug in her gut.

"We'll finish out the song this time," said Troy, his warm brown eyes serious with intent.

"I know we will." She took his hand and he led her out to the makeshift dance floor, an open space on the shining oak-planked floor by the band in front of the fireplace. The mellow melody of every Vermonter's favorite song filled the air. The strums of the guitar and the picking of the mandolin and the pure sweet serenade of the familiar lyrics eased Mercy into Troy's arms.

And they danced.

ACKNOWLEDGMENTS

Writing this book was both easier and harder than writing the first two books in this series. Easier, because in many ways the third time is the charm, and harder, because in many ways it isn't. But it was fun to write, at least as fun as anything was to do in 2020.

Writers need solitude to work, but during lockdown solitude takes on a whole new meaning. Time to write, but also time to brood and blunder and beat my head against the book as I wrote it. Luckily, I was quarantined with patient, compassionate, sentient beings, namely Michael, Mom and Dad, and our rescues: Newfoundland retriever mix Bear, Great Pyrenees and Australian cattle dog mix Bliss, Malinois mix Blondie (yes, just like Elvis!), and Ursula The Cat. My sons, Greg and Mikey, visited in-person when they could (safely), bringing wine and chocolate and love and laughter, and my daughter, Alexis, and granddaughters, Elektra, Calypso, and Demelza, brightened my spirits all the way from Switzerland via Skype.

That said, it takes a village to make a book, even if it was a virtual village this time around. Thanks to my fabulous agent and leader and friend, Gina Panettieri, whose generosity and wisdom exceed all expectation, and my talented Talcott Notch colleagues Saba Sulaiman, Dennis Schleicher, and (the one and only) Amy Collins. A special shout-out to my Career Authors pals Hank Phillippi Ryan, Brian Andrews, Jessica Strawser, and Dana Isaacson, as well as my fellow Stone Cold Writers Archer Mayor (and Margot Zalkind), Sarah

Stewart Taylor, and Julia Spencer-Fleming, all of whom humor me and enlighten me and inspire me in equal measure.

For some thirty years I've relied on my Scribe Tribe to keep me writing through good times and bad: Susan Reynolds, Meera Lester, John K. Waters, Indi Zeleny, Mardeene Mitchell, Barb Karg, and Colleen Sell. The same is true for our beloved crime-writing community, whose magnanimous members I am proud to call fellow authors and friends: Lee Child, Ann Cleeves, Jane Cleland, Deborah Crombie, Karen Dionne, Hannah Mary McKinnon, Hallie Ephron, Joe Finder, Lisa Gardner, Kellye Garrett, Elly Griffiths, Carolyn Haines, Edwin Hill, Kimberly Howe, Larry Kay, Jon Land, William Martin, Louise Penny, Spencer Quinn/Peter Abrahams, and Lori Rader-Day. And of course all of my clients, good writers and good people, one and all.

In a time when book events, conferences, and festivals were canceled more often than not, many adapted and went online, providing precious time with writers and readers and booksellers. My heartfelt thanks to indies everywhere, most especially Barbara Peters' Poisoned Pen, Forum Books, Gibson's Bookstore, and bookshop.org. More love to the Tucson Festival of Books, Michael Neff's New York Pitch Conference, ThrillerFest, Bouchercon, the Erma Bombeck Writers Workshop, the New Hampshire Writers Project, Mystery Writers of America, Sisters in Crime, the Dog Writers Association of America, and the New England Crime Bake.

And thank you, too, to the librarians and reviewers and bloggers and media personalities who help spread the word about books in general and my books in particular, most especially Katherine Bollenbach, Dru Ann Love, Kristopher Zgorski, Lesa Holstine, Sandy Kenyon, Sandra Beck, and Carolyn Hennesy. And most especially to Mark Combs: You are missed.

You may hear writers complain about their editors, but what you'll hear from me is nothing but praise. "Pit Bull Pete" Wolverton is a genius—seriously!—and he makes me a better writer and a better thinker with every book. Thanks to the entire Minotaur team at St. Martin's Press: Andy Martin, George Witte, Kelley Ragland, Hannah O'Grady, Allison Ziegler, Kayla Janas, Lily Cronig, Edwin

Chapman, Jonathan Bennett, Elizabeth Curione, and Julie Gutin. You're simply the best.

I also owe great thanks to those who shared their time and expertise with me: Dr. Jen Sula, Dr. Liz Kellett, and everyone at Blackwater Veterinary Services; Amy Knight and Susan Cable of White River Animal Rescue; all the volunteers at Mission K9 Rescue; Susan Warner, Director of Public Affairs for the Vermont Fish and Wildlife Department; Vermont State Game Warden Rob Sterling; Donna Larson Crockett, founding member and VP of the New England K9 Search and Rescue (nek9sar.org); Gardner "Bud" Browning and Scott Wood of the TSA; and Stasia Tretault, innkeeper at the Seth Warner Inn. Any mistakes are solely my own.

To Jerry Johnson and his splendid golden retriever, Baron, who inspired me to write a golden retriever into this story, I thank you. And thanks to Louise Minnette, who lent me her very name for this story. (And isn't it a great name?) Finally, I thank you, Dear Reader, for spending this time with Mercy and Elvis. I thank you, and Mercy and Elvis thank you. We are forever in your debt.